Pr
Witch Yo

'Fun, sweet and sexy'
SARAH HAWLEY, author of
A Witch's Guide to Fake-Dating a Demon

'Emma Jackson has a new fan! It has everything I
love in a romantasy. I absolutely adored it'
CARRIE ELKS, author of *Strictly Business*

'*Witch You Weren't Here* cast a spell on me from the
first page with its bewitching brew of angst, charm
and romance. A magical delight!'
M.A. KUZNIAR, author of *Midnight in Everwood*

'A magical rollercoaster which charm the charm the
hex out of the hardest of hearts'
JESSICA THORNE, author of *Mageborn*

'As effervescent as an Aperol Spritz, *Witch You
Weren't Here* is a light-hearted romp tempered by
the ever-present reminder that even with magic,
you can't make people fall in love with you'
LUNA MCNAMARA, author of *Psyche and Eros*

'As warm and gently soothing as a magicked cup of
tea - this is the perfect witchy comfort read'
LAURA WOOD, author of *Under Your Spell*

Emma Jackson has been a devoted bookworm and secret-story-scribbler since she was six years old. Her bestselling debut novel, *A Mistletoe Miracle*, was published in 2019 and a contender for the Joan Hessayon Award.

When she's not running around after her two daughters and trying to complete her current work-in-progress, Emma loves to read, bake, catch up on binge-watching TV programmes with her partner and plan lots of craft projects that will inevitably end up unfinished. Emma also hosts the SFFRomCast, a podcast dedicated to sharing the love for fantasy and sci-fi romance novels, with fellow writer, Jessica Haines.

You can sign up to Emma's monthly newsletter at www.esjackson.co.uk or follow her via social media https://linktr.ee/ESJackson

Witch You Weren't Here

EMMA JACKSON

ORION

First published in Great Britain in 2023 by Orion Books,
an imprint of The Orion Publishing Group Ltd
Carmelite House, 50 Victoria Embankment
London EC4Y 0DZ

An Hachette UK Company

1 3 5 7 9 10 8 6 4 2

A CIP catalogue record for this book is
available from the British Library.

ISBN (Mass Market Paperback) 978 1 3987 1796 1
ISBN (eBook) 978 1 3987 1795 4

Typeset by Born Group

Printed in Great Britain by Clays Ltd, Elcograf S.p.A.

MIX
Paper from
responsible sources
FSC® C104740

www.orionbooks.co.uk

For Jessica, a most excellent partner in crime.
The first steps of the plan are in motion. Narf.

Playlist

'Can't Hold Us' (feat Ray Dalton) – Macklemore, Ryan Lewis
'Sweet Talker' – Years & Years, Galantis
'Where Are You Now' – Lost Frequencies, Calum Scott
'Remember' – Becky Hill, David Guetta
'Thunderclouds' – LSD (Sia, Labrinth, Diplo)
'Remind Me' – Tom Grennan
'Open Up' – Matt Simons
'Ocean Eyes' – Billie Eilish
'Fly Away' – Tones and I
'Something to Someone' – Dermot Kennedy
'10:35' – Tiesto, Tate McRae
'Rescue Me' – OneRepublic
'Under Water' – AVEC
'Anti-Hero' – Taylor Swift
'Warmer' – Bea Miller
'Run' – Becky Hill, Galantis
'Fooling You' – Rachel Platten
'Flaws' – Bastille
'Still' – AVEC
'Somewhere Only We Know' – Lily Allen
'All of Me' – John Legend
'Bones' – Galantis (feat OneRepublic)

Prologue

Ashworth Hall, the village of Biddicote, Surrey

It is a truth universally acknowledged, that when a group of teenage witches are gathered, magical mischief soon follows.

Well, not *universally* acknowledged, since the existence of magic is a secret to the majority of the human race . . . but certainly throughout the witching community.

Which was why Kay Hendrix and her two friends, Tina and Jaz, were currently creeping down the corridor at Ashworth Hall, seeking escape from the annual May Day party.

Their families, along with many of the other local witches and non-magical residents of Biddicote, were out, either on the patio or freshly cut lawn, mingling. Staff were offering silver trays full of smoked salmon canapés, rolled up to look like roses, and bite-size vegetable tarts, and topping up their glasses with the dandelion wine, which Mrs Ashworth had made herself, infusing it with optimism and light-heartedness. That touch of magic helped to ensure the party had exactly the right vibe of renewal and positivity to suit the Beltane festival. It was why witches travelled miles to attend any of the festivities at Ashworth Hall – that and its famous legacy.

Ashworth Hall was over three hundred years old, built by legendary witches who layered protective spells over charms, over runes, as they founded the manor and much of the surrounding village. It was a unique community even within the witching world, and one of the only places in the UK where witches could mingle among non-magical neighbours and know that if they had a little slip-up with their magic, it would go unnoticed, dismissed or forgotten.

'No public displays of magic' was the second WWT (Worldwide Witches Tenet) and, in general, it wasn't too hard to obey, but having to repress your natural instincts every day would make any witch frustrated. Kay's gift had yet to emerge fully, despite puberty being painfully well established, but even with her remedial-level powers, she could appreciate how hard it would be, given that she went to an ordinary secondary school and had to make sure she wasn't tempted to access her magic around the other students.

But, honestly, who wanted to travel miles away to board at one of the few, tiny secret magical schools? She would have missed her family and her friends. And Biddicote offered enough of a sanctuary to her. Returning to the village after school was like taking off a pair of skinny jeans that she'd nearly outgrown.

The chatter of voices and strains of the string quartet out in the gardens faded further into the background as the teenage witches moved into the oldest part of the huge manor house, the shuffling of their feet absorbed by thick carpets and antique rugs displaying scenes almost like tapestries. Night skies and rituals and runes. Things that non-magical visitors would probably never even look at and notice were supernatural.

Kay was in the lead because her brother, Joe, had told her there was a side door in the East Wing which took you right to the edge of the woodland that made up part of the family estate. You had to go past Mr Ashworth's study, down a small stairwell, and it brought you into a vestibule with a wooden floor and bare brick walls. Even though Kay had never explored that part of the house – she'd only ever been there for seasonal celebrations, like Samhain, in the gardens or the ballroom – she knew exactly where she needed to go. Sometimes it was very handy that her older brother's particular gift as a magical influencer gave him the ability to explain things easily to people. Other times it just felt like he was the supernatural embodiment of a mansplainer.

A familiar zing of excitement and fear bubbled up in Kay's stomach, like a potion brewing in a crock-pot at the family healers. Would she get a gift within the influencer designation like Joe and end up taking after their dad, too? Or would she fall within the empath affinity, like their mum? Or maybe it would end up being something completely different, like an elemental gift. Whatever it was, she hoped it emerged soon.

She turned the next corner and walked straight into a statue of Cernunnos on a plinth, automatically reaching out and grabbing him by the antlers and another of his . . . protrusions to stop it from toppling off and smashing. She gave a little squeak of horror and hastily pulled her hands away, cheeks flaming, as Tina and Jaz burst into laughter behind her.

'Shh . . .' she tried her best to hush them around her own giggles. 'We're almost there.'

Jaz pressed her face into Tina's back, her shoulders heaving, and Tina clapped her hands over her mouth.

Kay plucked at the soft breeze bringing the sweet scent of blossom down the corridor, using her meagre level of magic to channel it towards her friends like her aunt had taught her, hoping it would work to cool them down and shock them out of their hysterics.

She could hear voices nearby.

As they wiped the tears of laughter from their eyes, she pressed her finger to her lips and tilted her head towards the door up ahead. It stood slightly ajar, allowing low male voices to carry out towards them. Were they about to get caught? It was most likely to be Mr Ashworth in his study, but who was he talking to? Maybe his son, Harry? Kay's belly turned over with that mixture of nerves and anticipation again, although it was for an entirely different reason.

Only one way to find out.

She crept closer.

'Kay,' Tina hissed behind her, tugging at the bow on the back of Kay's dress. It unravelled, allowing her to carry on down the hall. She crossed to the opposite wall so she was on the same side of the door, edging along as though she was in a James Bond film.

'You promise there'll be no more stories like the one that our media coven found?' a gruff male voice, bordering on elderly, asked.

'Not about Biddicote,' Adrian Ashworth's rich baritone rolled the three words out with the calm inevitability of the tide. Even without being in the same room or knowing what they were talking about, Kay felt the conviction of his words. She *believed* him. The Ashworths were a powerful line of influencers and Mr Ashworth's gift was the art of oral persuasion. A formidable ability.

'I'm looking into the breach,' he continued, 'and will shore up any charms that may have lapsed.'

4

'Perhaps something overgrew, or deteriorated?' The other man already sounded mollified.

'Perhaps. These things happen. Working with magic this established is a delicate business.'

'If it's becoming too painstaking or complicated a task, the Council will be happy to step in,' a third, younger voice joined the conversation. Not infused with magic but no less self-assured. 'With the concentration of witches here, failures are no small matter.'

There was a silence, then another tsunami of conviction sent goosebumps racing over Kay's shoulders: 'The Ashworth family is more than capable of maintaining its legacy.'

'Indeed, indeed,' the older man blustered. 'How about a drink?'

Kay's eyes widened. Mr Ashworth might have a bar in his study, but equally they might be planning to go back out to the party. She gestured quickly at Tina and Jaz to run for the stairwell. As they scurried past, Kay took one quick peek inside the study. She doubted Harry was in there but couldn't resist checking. Nothing was visible except the back of a man in a grey suit.

She followed her friends, wincing at the pounding of their feet down the short set of steps at the end of the corridor. Goddess, did they think they were auditioning for *Riverdance*? When she got there herself, she leapt from the top, using a brief levitation spell to stop herself from landing heavily. Since she'd only tried it with small objects before, she came down a lot quicker than she was expecting and barrelled into Tina and Jaz, sending them all tumbling into a rack of coats.

Giggles erupted again, so Kay untangled herself and leapt for the big door. It had an old iron latch, that she had to twist the metal hoop to lift. *Please be unlocked*. She yanked and the door swung open, allowing them all to escape outside. They looked at each other, then at the path leading into the woods and set off again.

'What was that all about?' Tina asked as they moved past the treeline into the shelter of the tall ash trees and pale-barked silver birches.

'I think they were from the Witches Council or something,' Kay said.

'Ugh, boring. But not what I meant.' Tina pulled a bottle of dandelion wine from inside the kangaroo pocket of her oversized sweatshirt. Her parents never made her wear dresses if she didn't want to. 'I meant you trying to eavesdrop and nearly getting us caught.'

Kay shrugged. 'All part of the fun.'

'All part of your obsession with sniffing out Harry Ashworth at every given opportunity,' Jaz accused, raising her eyebrows as though daring Kay to contradict her.

Was she obsessed with Harry Ashworth? Probably a bit. Had she been crushing on him for . . . ever? Pretty much. Had that crush reached terminal velocity over the last year, as he spent more and more time over at Kay's *actual* house, studying for his A levels with her brother? Yes, absolutely, because if she'd thought he was fascinating at a distance when she attended the seasonal parties at the Hall, getting to know him in person had blown her mind and fried her hormones simultaneously.

But she wasn't going to admit that. What she *was* going to do was poke her tongue out at her friend who knew her too well and coax the breeze again so the hawthorn bush Jaz was walking beside sprayed blossom up into her face.

'Is that all you've got,' Jaz teased as she shook petals out of her braids. 'You don't want to come at me with flowers, you know. I'll have to ask Tina to hold my beer.'

'Yeah, watch out, she's about to give you the worst bout of hay fever *ever*.' Tina snorted.

The sun was going down by the time they reached the small clearing and it was filled with green and golden light, pollen from the trees dancing above their heads like glitter in a snow globe. The mouth of the cave was only eight-foot square, heavy with encroaching foliage at this time of year, so it would have been easy to miss it. Exactly as any wandering non-magical people were supposed to. For witches, though, there was a tell-tale prickle of magic that tiptoed over their skin. Magic wasn't always detectable, nor did it always leave a mark, but the intensity of the energy that had been used there over the years made this place special. As special and important as Ashworth Hall.

This was where it had all started. Where Biddi – the namesake of Biddicote village – had once lived and practised. What was a colourful folkloric story to non-magical people, with an imaginary cave and a handful of places in Surrey it 'might' refer to, was witch history and Kay couldn't help being fascinated by it.

Even Tina and Jaz stopped joking for a few minutes as they all went up to the cave and peered inside. Beyond a couple of feet at the entrance, it was pitch black. There was no way of knowing how far it went back, if it went down, had twists and turns, or ended after a few long strides.

Jaz took out her phone and turned the flashlight on, trying to penetrate the darkness, but the beam was swallowed up.

'Cloaking spell?' Kay suggested.

'Probably. Do you think they're hiding something in there?' Tina bounced the big bottle of wine she'd stolen off the side of her thigh as she stared.

'Oooh, like what? Gold? Jewels?' Jaz switched off her phone.

'Maybe there are, like, really old runic signs and art on the walls depicting magical scenes or something?' Kay pushed at some of the ivy, leaning a little further in.

'Only you could act like that's more exciting than treasure,' Jaz scoffed. 'C'mon, let's get this wine open and get *our* party started.'

They took seats on the fallen logs outside the cave and then realised they didn't have a corkscrew and would have to figure out the best way of removing a cork from a bottle with magic. Tina was all for dispersing it, but since matter didn't ever truly vanish, Kay was worried that the particles would get into the wine and contaminate it. Jaz suggested an attraction spell, but none of them could conjure anything precise enough that didn't have the bottle and its contents straining towards their hands with it.

It was getting darker now and they competed at creating orbs of light after striking flint – catching the sparks in air bubbles and floating them above their heads until the oxygen inside the bubble ran out and the flame died – seeing who could make the biggest bubble and last the longest. Then Jaz picked bluebells, weaving them into a crown for Kay's hair as Tina pulled out her tarot cards and started doing a reading to tell her whether she was going to pass her GCSEs. It was only the seventh time Tina had done this in the last two weeks.

'Thank you,' Kay said as Jaz set the crown on her head and started threading her hair into a plait around the stems to hold it in place. 'Are we allowed to pick these, though? Aren't they endangered?'

'Are they? Huh. Well, luckily I can repair the damage.' Jaz dropped Kay's hair and went over to the patch where she'd picked the flowers. Grabbing a handful of grass, she rubbed it in between her hands, releasing the scent and sap, before murmuring a spell and pressing her hands into the soil.

Kay moved closer, watching quietly as petals began to bloom. Pale indigo blue unfurling slowly. 'That's so awesome.'

Jaz sent her a quick smile and looked back at the ground, her dark eyes alight with wonder and pride at what she was achieving with her elemental magic. Kay pressed her lips together, forcing down her desperation to have her *own* gift. It was like waiting for Christmas, but having no calendar available to see whether it was a whole year away or just a week.

'My magic is pretty awesome too, y'know,' Tina said conversationally, as she squinted at a card she'd pulled from the deck. 'I could make your ears smaller if you wanted. Or your nose.'

'Hey, what's wrong with my ears? *Or* my nose?' Kay stood up, putting her hand to it, as though it might have expanded suddenly like Pinocchio's when she wasn't looking.

Tina shook her head and held her hands up with a laugh. 'Nothing—'

'It's enormous,' a familiar voice said from the other side of the clearing. 'Honestly, Kay, you could hang washing from it.'

'Urgh, Joe,' she started to groan, as her brother stepped out. But just as she was about to pick some choice insults to fling back, Harry Ashworth came into view and all the air vanished from her lungs. Tall and lean, his crisp white polo shirt as bright as the coppery perfection of his tousled hair, he walked into the clearing alongside her brother. Joe could have turned green and sprouted feathers and she wouldn't have noticed.

'Ignore him – there is nothing wrong with your nose,' Harry said, in that husky voice that made her stomach flip.

9

She dropped her arms to her sides and twitched her nose, as if she could shake off all the attention it was getting. His mouth hitched up at the side like he was trying to repress a smile and her heart did a little flutter in her chest.

Fine, it wasn't a declaration that he found her stunningly beautiful, but Kay would definitely take it.

'He didn't say anything about your ears.' Joe held his hands up on either side of his head and flapped them like Dumbo.

Harry shook his head, his beautiful blue eyes still on hers, eyebrows quirking in a way that said: *I don't even have to say anything for you to know that's not true, right?* And she treasured that even more than the smile. It implied that they *knew* each other. Properly. Like they had an understanding of one another that went beyond having to say the obvious.

And maybe they did. Sometimes, they would have a late-night study snack in her kitchen, their voices hushed to avoid waking the rest of her family. Or they'd watch *Game of Thrones* together in the mornings in their pyjamas after he'd stayed over, before Joe was even up. Or he'd be there sketching while she was reading, and she'd get distracted, watching him experiment with how his gift to influence through artwork truly worked, while Joe obsessed in the background about the car he was saving up for.

OK, that wasn't exactly getting to know each other – that was more her being a bit stalkerish. Maybe she was just imagining it all, amplifying every small kindness into something more, like her brain was made entirely of dragon's eye stone, because, oh my Goddess, it was wishful thinking. Of all the wishes Kay had in the world, that was probably the biggest. That Harry Ashworth liked her as much as she liked him. That he wasn't only being nice to her because she was Joe's little sister. After all, Joe might tease and insult her, but he'd never let anyone else be rude to her.

'You know, tarot isn't actually magical unless you're a seer. Otherwise, they're just a deck of pretty playing cards,' Joe said, crossing his arms and looking down at Tina and the mix of major and minor arcana she had in front of her.

'You know, no one actually invited you.' Tina mirrored his crossed arms.

Kay didn't feel guilty about not applying the same sibling rules when it came to Tina arguing with Joe. She loved her brother, but it was almost always valid self-defence when he was being a pompous pain in the arse.

'Gutting.' He laughed. 'This is the lamest illicit party I've ever been to.'

'Feel free to leave. Don't let a tree topple on your head as you go.'

'No,' Kay blurted out. Her heart ricocheted around her chest and she sent a little look of pleading to Jaz. *Help me. Distract them from that desperate plea. But, also, don't let Harry leave.*

Jaz's eyes widened and she cleared her throat, dusting soil off her hands. 'Yeah, er, stay. The more, the merrier.'

'You are aware that this is actually Harry's land, it's not really for you to say whether he can stay or leave,' Joe pointed out.

Harry blushed, the pale skin beneath his freckles turning adorably pink. 'Joe, it's not like that—' he began to protest, but Tina interrupted.

'We weren't talking to *Harry*, obviously.'

'Quit flirting, you two, or I'll be forced to invent a new version of seven minutes in heaven. "Misbehave in the cave".' Jaz waved her hand through the air like she was envisioning a banner with the words written across it. Then she pointed her finger. 'And you two will be the first ones I send in.'

Joe rolled his eyes and Tina mimed gagging. Because the idea made Kay want to do the same, she grabbed the bottle from where they'd propped it against one of the logs and handed it to her brother. 'Why don't you make yourself useful. Know how to get a bottle of wine open without a corkscrew?'

'Sure we could figure it out.' He cocked his head to consider the bottle, never lacking for confidence, and Harry came over to examine it too.

Jaz set some music playing from her phone and the girls upended one of the logs and danced around it as though it was a maypole, only to the sound of Macklemore and Ryan Lewis's 'Can't Hold Us', and whenever it came to the chorus, they shot different colour sparks up from their fingers.

When Kay glanced out the corner of her eyes, it looked like the boys had frozen the liquid in the bottle and then decided to give it a bang of energy on the bottom. There was a loud pop and the cork sailed into the air, with them all cheering. They thawed the dandelion wine out again with a small handheld fire and then the bottle was passed around, with them all taking swigs of warm alcohol as they continued dancing.

'Go inside and wait for Harry,' Jaz whispered as she twirled Kay around.

'What?' Kay hadn't noticed the fact her friend had danced her over to the cave's entrance.

'I've got a plan. Trust me.' And before Kay could ask what exactly that meant, Jaz was pushing her through the ivy into the cave.

Kay's mouth went dry as the cool air washed additional tingles of magical awareness over her, unsure whether to be more nervous about the fact she was in a dark cave or that Jaz might be trying to launch 'misbehave in the cave' using her and Harry. She swallowed and turned on the spot, staying inside the curtain of ivy and out of the darkness, peeking out through the gaps between leaves to see what was happening.

Tina and Joe were sitting on one of the logs arguing again, backs to the cave, as Jaz refereed. She paused to say something to Harry and he nodded and . . .

And he was coming over.

Kay drew in a shaky breath and squeezed her eyes shut for a moment.

'Jaz said you wanted me to give you a tour?' Harry spoke from nearby and her eyes flew open. He was inside the entrance too, close enough to touch. 'That you wanted to see – and I quote – "boring historical shit".'

Kay winced. 'I don't want to pull you away from the party because of my geekiness.'

'I don't mind.' He put his hands in his pockets, his eyes lit with mischief. Or maybe it was affection? 'It takes all sorts.'

OK, definitely mischief; that lovely, gentle kind of teasing she never minded coming from him.

'What about the others?' Kay chewed her lip, not wanting to ask, but, also, not wanting to appear like she was trying to separate him from the herd and attack. 'D'you think they'd be interested?'

'Well, Jaz has Tina and your brother handcuffed with bark she grew from one of the logs and is refusing to let them go until they've resolved things. Reminds me of what my parents used to do to make me resolve conflicts with . . .' His brows knitted for a second. 'Other kids. Or maybe it was a teacher? Either way, I doubt they are getting off that log anytime soon.'

'I can't imagine you arguing with other kids.'

'Hey, I'm a redhead.' He gave his hair a quick ruffle and sent her another lopsided grin. 'You know what we're like, hot-tempered . . . mercurial.'

She laughed, shaking her head, because it was far from the truth, and he knew it.

His smile widened and then he turned, reaching up to grab a small piece of chalk from a little ledge she hadn't noticed. Then he stepped into the inky black. She made an involuntary squeak as he disappeared, but, seconds later, a warm light eased into the cave, diffusing from a torch further in and more lights in the distance she couldn't see clearly. He rubbed his thumb over the chalk in his hand and she saw the small rune he'd drawn on the wall. A simple arrowhead pointing left.

'Wow,' she breathed. Runes were old magic and they required a lot of energy and intention to get them to work, otherwise you were just drawing lines like any other person. Maybe it was his affinity for influential drawing which made him capable of invoking them despite being such a young witch.

'Don't be too impressed. I just drew over the marking Biddi worked into the wall. It's the equivalent of turning on a light switch. She did all the wiring.'

'You think that makes it less impressive?' Kay moved closer so she could see the groove in the wall. She wanted to touch it but didn't want to rub off the chalk. She was where Biddi had crafted a light and warmth spell, embellished it to anchor to objects. It always gave her a thrill to see the evidence of where someone had gone before.

'Definitely less impressive on my part. But there's no denying how powerful and clever Biddi was.' Their eyes caught as Kay looked up from the rune and Harry tilted his head towards the rest of the cave. 'It's safe. You can go ahead and explore.'

She couldn't help grinning as she walked deeper inside, Harry just behind her. If her gift emerging was going to be like Christmas Day finally arriving, this was surely her birthday.

At the end of the entrance passage, just past the old wooden torch, propped against the wall, there was a turn, which brought them into another chamber. In the centre, with a circle of stone seats surrounding it, was a small fire. Small shelves and cubbyholes were carved into the walls and there was a wide alcove that she imagined might have once had a bed in it.

'It's amazing, but it's just a home too,' she said, her voice breathy. 'Is there any evidence that people did come, asking for her to help them find lost things, like the legend says?'

'Nothing you can see here. But she kept a sort-of journal. It's part ledger, part diary really and she noted down all the things people living nearby would ask her to find, and the offering they brought for the service.'

'You're kidding me? You've got that at Ashworth Hall?' Kay spun around, her hand sliding over one of the shelves.

'No. I mean, I'm not kidding you.' He laughed, the light from the fire playing over his cheekbones. 'It's locked up in a physical *and* charmed safe. I wish I could show it to you, but that's one I really can't sneak out. Maybe one day.'

'When you're in charge?' she wiggled her eyebrows. He gave an awkward shrug and she sensed somehow she'd put her foot in it, so she changed the subject. A bit. 'Have you read it?'

'Oh, Goddess, no.' He sat down on one of the stone seats around the fire, any tension in his face disappearing. 'Normal history textbooks are hard enough for me, let alone ones with itty-bitty writing. And f's instead of s's,

15

or whatever it was they did back then. My parents have shown it to me, though.'

She came over to sit next to him. 'What do you remember most about it?'

'It's small.' He held out his hand and traced a rectangular shape from the heel of his palm to the furthest joint of his long fingers. 'About this big. The cover is brown leather hide, with runes tooled along the spine. As well as the squiggly writing, there are little drawings through it, like . . . like doodles really, illustrating her entries.'

'That's so cool.' She rested her chin on her fist. 'So . . . did she draw "the devil"?'

Harry's eyes crinkled at the edges as he laughed. 'What, great-great-granddad times nine?'

Kay laughed too, because how ridiculous would it be to think that Harry had anything demonic about him. Not that non-magical people – even in the village – had any idea that the Ashworth family was linked to the legend of Biddicote. For them, the story went that the devil himself had come to visit Biddi, disguised as a rich nobleman, leaving such a pile of jewels, she accepted the bargain before bothering to ask what he wanted. When he told her he had to find a woman who wielded unnatural powers, Biddi had to leave the cave and stand in the entrance, for that woman was her. And she was never seen after that.

Of course, the truth was, that although a rich man had come calling to her cave, it had been multiple times and he'd offered her nothing more than his love and a home up on the land overlooking the cave. She'd married him, taking his name and starting a family, and when the witch-hunters combed the country for people to persecute, the story that the devil had already taken that evil witch away had been extremely convenient. That, coupled with the protection of the Ashworths' magic, ended up inadvertently creating a safe haven.

'It's very handy that people never linked Biddi and the Ashworths,' Kay mused – wondering how they were able to keep locals from recognising her, or connecting the story to the truth, when it happened. Had that been why they had started laying the protective magic? Had they used the kind of magic Tina had – linked to the healing affinity – where you could change people's appearances? Kay desperately wanted to get into the library at Ashworth Hall and go through every old source record they had, then compare them to local non-magical records. She really *was* an utter geek.

'I guess I wouldn't be here if they had.' Harry picked up a dry leaf from the floor and twirled it by the stem before throwing it onto the small fire. 'The witch-hunters probably would have burned down the Hall.'

'Loads of witches wouldn't be here if that was the case. Probably me included.'

'That would be sad,' Harry said quietly, looking at her.

As they'd talked, Kay had forgotten to be nervous, finding herself comfortable with Harry in a way she wasn't with other boys she'd liked. It made the butterflies come surging back so much harder when he looked at her for a long moment and then reached out and softly touched the bluebells in her hair.

'Your hair looks really pretty. The flowers are a beautiful colour.'

'Thanks,' she managed, once she remembered how to breathe. 'Little bit immodest of you, though.'

'Of *me*?'

'Well, your eyes are almost the same shade as bluebells, aren't they?'

17

'You think so?' He raised his eyebrows, a strange expression crossing his face, but then his hand strayed from the flowers to twirl a lock of her dark hair around his finger. The nervous excitement buzzing inside Kay felt like it might explode at any minute. She tightened her arm around her midriff as though she could keep it under control that way. 'Are you OK?'

'Butterflies,' she admitted in a whisper.

'That can be a sign your gift is coming in. If that's where the centre of your magic is going to sit.' Those striking eyes of his lit up as though he was looking forward to it almost as much as her. And he was still touching her hair.

Still. Touching. Her. Hair.

She licked her lips. 'I don't think it's that.'

'No?'

She shook her head and the hair he'd caught around his finger came loose. His fingertips grazed her cheek instead as he took a deep breath and leaned towards her—

'Kay. Harry. Get your butts out here, someone's coming!'

Kay blinked as though she was coming out of a trance as Harry jerked away to look in the direction of the shouting.

Noooo. Had Harry been about to kiss her? Why was life so cruel?

They both scrambled up and headed outside before Jaz caused an avalanche with her yelling, Harry wiping the chalk rune off the wall as they left, so darkness fell inside the cave again.

Outside in the clearing, Jaz, Tina and Joe were all busy setting the log back to rights and hiding the bottle of wine. Kay wasn't even sure why Joe was hiding the wine since he was eighteen and it was legal for him to drink it.

Then, Mr Ashworth arrived. She glanced at Harry beside her, her pulse tip-tapping in her throat. He'd straightened his spine so she was reminded how much taller than her he really was and was checking his shirt was tucked in, as though he was about to undergo a military inspection.

'Harrison Ashworth. I did not expect to find you here.' Mr Ashworth didn't even need to raise his voice for them all to register how displeased he was. Angry would have gone too far. He was too controlled for angry, but his face was stark with disappointment. 'Back up to the Hall now, all of you. Find your parents, please. I expect you to tell them what you've been doing.' He paused, his stern, dark eyes sweeping around all of them and seeming to settle on her, stood close to Harry, before they narrowed. 'Go on ahead of us. The wisps will guide you.'

They started up the path. Tina and Jaz linked arms, huddling together, while Joe and Kay walked behind them and then, with a longer gap between them, the Ashworths finally followed. Their soft footfalls couldn't drown out the sound of Mr Ashworth's clipped tones. 'This cave is not an adolescent hangout. It's our family heritage and – even more than that – it's a place of power that must be kept hidden from non-magical people. What if someone had noticed the noise, or the spells I'm sure you were all playing at, and come to investigate—'

'Isn't it meant to be protected—'

'There are limits, and do not interrupt me.' Mr Ashworth took a breath and spoke more softly. 'I need you to show me you know how to behave in a way this family can rely on. There are guests – some from the Witches Council – and one day they'll all be your responsibility.'

Despite the gentle tone, Kay heard a touch of his power threading through the words. She slowed, glancing back with wide eyes. Adult influencers weren't meant to use their magic on minors to directly modify behaviour, only to help them. Maybe Harry's eighteenth birthday wasn't far away, but still—

'Kay.' She stifled a shriek as Joe grasped her arm. 'C'mon, stop eavesdropping. Give Harry a bit of dignity.'

She pulled her arm free of his but kept up as he walked faster, following the blue glowing lights that had been charmed to hover along the path once the sun set. They always winked out as soon as you looked at them directly, so it would be easy to think you imagined it, if you didn't know better.

Once they got back up to the gardens, they grimly wished each other luck and went to seek out their parents. Kay and Joe's mum, Tallulah, was sitting at a table on the patio by herself. As soon as they approached, she put her glass of wine down and tilted her head. 'What happened?'

Even if there hadn't been the risk of Mr Ashworth dropping them in it, there was still no chance they'd have been able to hide it from their mum. Kay dreaded to think what emotions were rolling off them for her to read. Guilt and nerves for definite, but Goddess knew what she was feeling, having come so close to kissing the boy of her dreams. Disappointment but, also, if she was honest, longing so fierce she wanted to crawl out of her own skin. If only teleportation was a real thing, achievable by magic, she would have zapped herself straight out of there and home to bed to hide under the covers.

Instead, between her and Joe, they offered a sanitised version of events, which their mother saw straight through.

Mr Ashworth and Harry had also arrived back in the garden, albeit talking to a crowd as far away as physically possible.

Tallulah looked over at them and grimaced. 'Look, kids, I know it's fun and natural to sneak off, but you do have to be careful. And respectful. Do you think you can exercise some of that common sense I know you both have next time?'

They nodded their heads sheepishly.

'Good. Now, for appearance's sake, we should probably leave. Mr Ashworth is . . . not pleased.'

Kay risked another glance in Harry's direction, chewing on her nail. Should she tell her mum about Mr Ashworth using his influence on Harry? Or was she making too big of a deal of it?

'I'm sure he'll get over it, darling,' her mum said, standing up to give her a brief hug. 'You know the mood I'm picking up on could be affected by any number of events that have happened this evening, not just you teenagers. The Ashworths have a lot of responsibility. With that kind of pressure, people's emotions can become extreme. I'll go find your dad and talk to him about leaving.'

They watched from the patio as their mum found their dad, Marvin, in a big, lively group by the water feature. Tallulah pulled him away to have a brief conversation and then started making her way back on her own. Kay and Joe exchanged a long look.

'He said to go ahead without him, he's been talking to a possible sponsor for the football team,' Tallulah announced as she rejoined them and picked up her handbag. 'Come on then, we'll do an Irish goodbye – your dad can do the thanking later.'

Kay wasn't exactly surprised. As an influential motivator, their dad loved social events, where he could engage people in conversations about what they were doing, in work or their personal life, and give them a boost towards meeting their goals – and sometimes his. He lived for this kind of thing. In contrast, being with large crowds was a strain on their mum as she was assailed by everyone's moods. Sometimes, she took a magic inhibitor, which a healer and alchemist had made up for her, but they were expensive, so she'd gone without one that evening, given that the party was usually flowing with good vibes. Kay could see the strain of it had worn her out by the time they'd walked back through the village to their cottage, and they all headed straight for their bedrooms.

Kay did her best to sleep with butterflies swarming around her tummy as she relived the moment Harry had touched her face and leaned towards her. Exam season was about to start, she knew he probably wouldn't come over to their house quite as much until he'd finished his A levels, and she had her own GCSEs to concentrate on, but once all that was done with . . . There would be the solstice celebration, of course, but . . . maybe she could even ask him out on a date?

When Kay opened her eyes the following morning, everything looked different. Harry had been right in his suspicions. The fluttering in her stomach hadn't solely been about her crush. Her gift had finally emerged.

And her world was about to fall apart.

Chapter One

Prague Congress Centre

820 miles and 47(+1) hours until the wedding

> *Mum: Aunty L says her teeth are aching like she's eaten nothing but hard toffee for a week. You need to leave Prague as soon as possible.*

Kay swore quietly as she read the message from her mother and tucked her mobile away before the glow disturbed the people sitting around her in the conference auditorium. Her boss, Mark, was only three rows behind her and had a pathological hatred of his staff getting distracted by their phones – even though their whole business was designing apps for people to download onto said phones.

She squinted up at the large presentation screen, but all her brain could compute was that the speaker had spent far too long fiddling with the transitions for the text animations and set the time at least a second too long for each. Some floated onto the screen, some span across, others faded in. It was, in fact, a pretty accurate visual representation of the thoughts her subconscious was now trying to push up to the surface.

A little jolt of electricity made Kay jump. Ilina, a fellow project manager from the German IT company Kay's UK employer was partnered with, was sitting next to her and had leaned in close enough to bump their shoulders. Ilina had always been one of the few people at work Kay looked forward to talking to, but they'd clicked as soon as they met in person at the conference. It was like they'd known each other eighteen years, rather than eighteen months. Realising they were both witches may have escalated the friendship between them, too.

'Hey,' Kay whispered, rubbing her shoulder theatrically. It hadn't really hurt, but there had been a leap in her chest, both of her own magic and of the anxiety that she was going to react without meaning to. She had no idea what her haywire magic was going to produce at the moment. It seemed capable of spells she'd not so much as learned, let alone tried to implement, and this conference had been one big stress-fest, with her terrified she was going to accidentally animate a cardboard cut-out on a stand, or start sneezing pink sparks.

'Sorry. Static. These seat covers must be nylon.' Ilina looked at her, all innocence, and Kay rolled her eyes, unable to suppress a smile.

'Yeah, sure.'

'Promise you won't report me for breaking WWT-One?' Ilina batted her eyelashes.

'As if I would even know where the Council stands on that kind of infraction at the moment. They probably changed their minds three times already today.' The first Worldwide Witching Tenet, 'Never use magic to do harm,' was always up for debate and led to constant making and breaking of smaller laws lobbied by the individual council in each country. And Kay had long since ceased paying close attention to current witch affairs, it made little difference to her life and the bureaucracy of it all frustrated her

24

because it never seemed to be centred around putting the majority of witches or non-magical people first.

Ilina gave the little cackle that always made Kay want to join in too.

'What was that for anyway?' Kay asked, her voice hushed even lower.

'You are squirming since you got your text message. Has something happened?'

'Not precisely. That storm is closer than the weather forecasters think.'

'You know someone with an affinity for the weather?' Ilina whispered back. 'How accurate?'

Kay glanced at the man to her right to see whether he was listening, but with the way his head was tilted back against the chair with his mouth open, she was pretty certain that he was asleep. And that he needed to have his tonsils removed. 'My aunt. She's as accurate as you ever can be with that, I guess.'

It wasn't an exact science, after all. It presented itself differently in everyone, even if you had the exact same gift. Aunt Lucille's was all about intensity and how it corresponded to the ailments in her body. If her teeth were aching that badly, the temperature was about to take a serious dive. And as for gale-force winds . . . well, you didn't want to be anywhere near her when that was happening, poor woman.

Thankfully, Lucille appeared to have kept that personal information to herself, but since the news had been warning people about a ridiculously severe storm front headed for Europe, with hurricane-level winds and torrential rain barrelling in off the Atlantic, Kay couldn't dismiss her mother's warning easily.

'Do you need to try to catch an earlier flight to be on the safe side?' Ilina asked.

Ideally, yes. Joe was getting married on Sunday and Kay was one of his fiancée, Sandy's, bridesmaids. There was also a rehearsal dinner tomorrow night, and her mother was already getting tense at the prospect of having to spend time around Kay's dad, her ex-husband. Kay needed to get home as soon as possible and mitigate any risk of getting delayed because of bad weather, but . . .

'I can't. I *have* to see Madam Hedvika this afternoon.' It was Kay's last chance to try to fix her magic before Joe's wedding. The mishaps were getting ridiculous and she was becoming increasingly concerned she was going to have a magical outburst in the middle of the ceremony. Her soon-to-be sister-in-law was not a witch and therefore over half of the guests were going to be non-magical.

Although *public* displays of magic were forbidden, witches didn't have to keep magic a complete secret from non-magical people. That wouldn't have been practical given the small numbers of witches. They were permitted to reveal their abilities to a long-term partner, so Sandy knew the truth – as did her parents – but that was it, and if Kay accidentally levitated a flower girl, it was going to take a lot of explaining and somewhat ruin the wedding. Especially if a mass cover-up operation by the Witches Council was needed, including the possibility of them wanting to nullify her powers . . .

She *needed* to make this appointment.

'You should just go. To be sure you will make it,' Ilina told her, and she wasn't wrong. The two different sides of Kay's life were battling to be seen as the priority, but again . . .

'I can't. Mark is behind us.'

She'd been trying to find the best time to speak to her boss about needing to skip this session, but he'd been tied up networking almost all weekend. Which he hated. Which made him even grumpier than usual. He wasn't an awful boss, but he was the type who would flay you alive if you tried to skip out of work early and thought his employees should have the gift of foresight, even though he was as unaware of the magical world as most people.

OK, so maybe he *was* a pretty awful boss.

'Tell him you have an emergency and need to go.'

'Hmm.' Kay didn't mind telling the odd white lie, but saying there was an emergency meant conjuring up a false-hood about something serious – and that always felt like tempting fate. Words held power.

It was becoming *kind of* an emergency, though.

Kay sneaked a quick glance behind her. Maybe she could email him from here and then indicate for him to check his phone? But, of course, he would object to that. And he hadn't even blinked in her direction. Short of waving her arms around and shouting 'yoo-hoo', she couldn't see how she was going to get him to tear his eyes away from the speaker and try to decipher her attempts at miming. His heavy grey brows were pulled right down over his eyes so they were resting on top of his glasses. Classic single-minded focus mode for him. Balls.

Kay turned back to Ilina. 'He won't even look my way when I'm staring right at him. I can't exactly zap him with electricity from here and blame it on the seats.'

Ilina gave a little snort. 'Maybe it's the hair. He probably doesn't recognise you.'

Last night, they'd been unable to shake a group of salesmen trying to chat them up in the bar and Kay had been worried she might manifest a hole in the floor for them to fall into, so they'd gone up to Ilina's room to chat and make use of the minibar. One too many tiny bottles of vodka had led to Ilina demonstrating her gift – which she protested was as useless as Kay's since it was basically a party trick or favour to be used among her witch friends and family.

But with a head full of beautiful indigo hair that she'd always wanted and the memory of their laughter as Kay geared herself up to look in the mirror, she begged to differ. Her *own* gift – seeing the emotional bonds between people – was useful for precisely nothing, other than telling people what they already knew or didn't want to hear. Oh, and to completely distract her with all the glowing colours floating from chest to chest. She'd been so lucky her cousin had the ability to infuse magic charms into objects and been able to make her glasses to filter it out.

'I doubt it's that. He saw me this morning at the team meeting. I had to say we'd gone out and bought the hair dye from the nearest pharmacy, then had an impromptu evening of pampering.'

As the speaker at the front of the auditorium took a deep breath and raised the clicker in his hand to move to the next slide, Kay crossed her fingers and wished – for the briefest of moments – that she had taken after her dad, the same way Joe had.

And then she remembered that being able to manipulate others was a moral sinkhole and contented herself with plain old hope.

Please let this finally be it. Please let the next slide on the PowerPoint presentation be the 'Any Questions' wrap up, signalling the end of the talk. There would only be two or three questions maximum from the audience if the other sessions at the conference were anything to go by and she could be out of here within fifteen minutes, if she was lucky.

The room dipped into blackness as the presentation transitioned between slides, exaggerating the heat of the hundred or so bodies and the smell of stale coffee . . .

Another page with three spaced-out topics.

She should have known. Luck had never exactly been on her side.

Kay didn't even bother to read the bullet points as she released a slow breath of frustration. She crossed her arms over her chest and tried to pay attention to the speaker again. Maybe the next one . . .

And then the presentation began to flick forward seemingly of its own accord, if the confusion and embarrassed laughter of the presenter was anything to go by.

'Oh, crap,' Kay muttered, grabbing the armrests of her chair tightly and sucking in her tummy, trying to contain the crackling flow of energy that was frying the poor man's computer and ruining his day. At least it wasn't visible.

Stop. It's OK. I'm not in a hurry, she recited to herself, trying to convince her magic to knock it off, but all that happened was a couple of light bulbs popped, causing a rising murmur of concern throughout the crowd.

Ilina nudged Kay firmly with her elbow – this time without the added burst of electricity. Clearly she didn't need any more energy to add to her overflow. 'Go.'

'*I can't.*'

'Yes, you can. And you need to. Now, before the fire alarm goes off or something. I will find your boss afterwards and tell him you got your period. You know men, he'll be so mortified, he won't even question you about it.'

'I wouldn't be so sure—'

'Fine, food poisoning then. You had a prawn sandwich at lunch, yes? If he had one too, he will not be surprised your stomach has rebelled. I think it was only the level of alcohol in my bloodstream that managed to kill off the bacteria.'

Kay chewed her lip, and then glanced around at the room where all the delegates were shifting and looking up at the lighting overhead suspiciously, while the presenter struggled to return to his place in his talk. 'Right, OK, yes, I'll do it. Thank you.'

'You're welcome. I hope she can help.'

'God, me too.'

'Let me know you made it safely onto your flight. *Auf Wiedersehen*.'

Kay squeezed Ilina's hand gently in lieu of kissing her on the cheek to say goodbye and inched her way out of their row. She slung her handbag over her shoulder, put her hand over her mouth as though nauseated and kept her eyes trained on the exit as she hurried towards it, hoping that if her boss had noticed her leave, she would look like someone who had an unpleasant date scheduled with the toilet.

Chapter Two

Old Town Square, Prague

819 miles and 46(+1) hours until the wedding

Madam Hedvika seemed to have taken the old adage of 'hiding in plain sight' to heart and literally themed her shop, Baba Yaga's, as a witch's shack – albeit one that was clean and attractive and sold souvenirs – playing off the regular witches' festival where effigies of witches were created and burned every year. Nice. Madam Hedvika obviously had a dark sense of humour and a flare for retail positioning.

Small children milled around inside, giggling at the cartoonishly ugly witch dolls made of corn husks. There was also all the typical 'witch' memorabilia to buy, from crystals and candles to little velvet-covered books claiming to hold love spells. The air was heavily scented with incense, which Kay might have dismissed as being part of the atmosphere, but she could detect the familiar notes of sage and rosemary beneath and there were at least two runes painted above the door. She doubted anyone ever shoplifted from this establishment.

As Kay approached the desk, the young woman at the till looked up at her with a smile. 'Kay?'

'Yes, that's me,' she answered.

'She's waiting through there for you,' the woman said in heavily accented English and pointed to a small doorway, covered with beads and wind chimes, which clacked as Kay pushed her way through.

Rather than the small room she was expecting, she came up against a wall and had to turn right to find a steep, narrow staircase. Kay sighed, looking at her wheelie suitcase, and decided to risk leaving it at the bottom of the stairs.

It wasn't that she'd overpacked for the three-day conference, but once she'd expressed an interest in going – somewhat more enthusiastically than would have been expected of her, so she could guarantee an opportunity to get to see Madam Hedvika – she'd been given the joyous task of ferrying across all the marketing material for their stand. Just for once, she wished any of the men in her office could have been chivalrous and offered to take the bulk of glossy brochures – which probably equated to the loss of a small Christmas tree farm – but no. It was equal opportunities in her office when it came to back strain and dislocated shoulders. Shame they didn't have the same attitude towards salaries.

She hurried up to the first floor and found a square sitting room with waxed wooden floors, a high ceiling and beautifully arched windows that looked out over the Old Town Square, the famous astronomical clock just within sight, the setting sun flashing off its gleaming dials.

A woman, around her mother's age, was sitting at a square worktable before one of the windows. A bunch of corn husks, thread and scissors was spread out before her.

'Kay,' she said without looking up from where she was organising the materials, sharing them out between her place at the table and the one opposite her. 'Come and take a seat. Would you like a drink?'

'Oh, no thank you.' She took the seat opposite Madam Hedvika and shrugged her coat off, letting it rest against the back of the chair. Her mouth was dry, but she doubted any liquid would help with that.

Madam Hedvika inclined her head in acknowledgement and carried on with her organising. She had a long plait draped over her shoulder, her hair a deep brown, streaked with grey.

Kay glanced out of the window again and linked her fingers tightly in her lap to avoid drumming them. She was here now. Seeking help for this crazy magic problem she was having. Even if she did have a flight to catch, she needed to be patient. Magic couldn't be rushed and Madam Hedvika's approach needed to be respected. She was the IT support of the witching community. Except there was only one like her in the whole of Europe and getting an appointment was as difficult as folding a fitted sheet neatly. (There were some things even magic couldn't help with.) All this . . . methodical approach might be vital to the ritual they needed to undertake.

'What I need you to do is copy how I'm making a corn husk doll,' the older woman explained once everything was organised to her liking, her grey eyes studying Kay's face calmly.

Kay restrained herself from lifting an eyebrow at the possibility she was being charged to help create stock for this woman's shop. Surely, that wasn't the case. *Benefit of the doubt, Kay, give it the benefit of the doubt.* It wasn't like she didn't know corn husk dolls were tied to magic. She used to make one each year at the Lughnasadh celebrations at Ashworth Hall . . . Her mind couldn't help wandering to the last year she'd done it, though. When the house had felt empty because a certain someone had been absent and she couldn't wait to leave.

33

'And as we work, I will ask you some questions about your magic and about your issues with it. Then, when it is finished, I'll take it and draw from it — hopefully — an answer as to what is going wrong and what you might be able to do to fix it.'

Kay nodded. 'Right. I'm not very crafty, though.'

'You don't need to be.' Madam Hedvika lifted some cotton batting and started to make a ball of it, the fluff moving pliantly between her skilled fingertips. 'Now, this is going to be the head. Tell me how you think of your magic when you access it.'

Kay licked her lips and picked up a bunch of the cottony stuff too, trying to compact it, but it kept fuzzing out of shape. 'Erm . . . I kind of visualise a well, inside me, where my energy is stored, and I dip down — like mentally — to pick out what I need to do a spell.'

Madam Hedvika's eyebrows pulled together slightly, so Kay immediately became paranoid that the way she accessed magic was not the same way as everyone else. She'd never really thought to ask. Her mother had described it to her in a similar way when Kay was little and trying to practise small incantations, and it had just kind of stuck.

The older witch picked up a piece of husk and wrapped it around the cotton batting, drawing it over, and then selecting a piece of thread to tie it in place. A bracelet on her wrist jingled faintly as she moved. 'And when it goes wrong, how does that happen? What do you feel?'

'I don't really feel anything until it's too late.' Kay fumbled to try to get the thread around the husk without letting go of all of it. 'It rushes out of me without warning. One minute I'm completely normal, and the next, a burst of magic has escaped and is causing havoc.'

Madam Hedvika nodded slowly. 'When did the problem become apparent?'

'Around . . . springtime, I guess. Although, I think it started before that. Smaller issues that I didn't take much notice of to begin with.'

'And how do you use your magic on a day-to-day basis?'

Kay licked her lips and tried her best to copy making the stick-like bundles which turned out to be arms, while also figuring out how to answer. She wasn't sure what was making her more frustrated, attempting to make the corn husk doll, or thinking about her magic. 'I have a job full-time in an office, so not much. Just small spells at home.' And even then, sometimes, when she was too tired, she didn't bother.

Madam Hedvika made a soft sound that Kay couldn't decipher and moved on to snipping the edges of one of the pieces of corn husk to help tear it into little strips.

It was actually quite therapeutic, but when it came to bundling them up and wrapping them around to make the bulk of the body, Kay's looked like it was trying to smuggle potatoes under its skirt. She was just about ready to throw the whole thing out the window, at the clock face which was taunting her as it counted down the minutes towards her flight. But Kay had to see this through.

'Now, wrap this large piece around the bottom and pin it in place. Then trim off the excess and stand it up. Take a deep breath and focus on it. Imagine it's you, using your gift.'

Kay stared at her doll, uneven pieces of corn husk poking out in odd places, completely lopsided, and the memory of her as sixteen-year-old came to her. How her gift had rushed in on her as she'd stumbled down the stairs at home, foggy-headed from having just woken up. Going into the kitchen where her family were all eating breakfast—

Whoosh. Her doll went up in flames.

Madam Hedvika let out an unfamiliar word that was probably swearing in Czech and leapt up from her chair. She grabbed a vase of flowers from her sideboard, yanked the flowers out and upended the water on Kay's corn doll, sending a flood across her worktable, soaking all the husks and dripping onto the floor.

'I am so sorry,' Kay whispered, looking at the wreckage and her smouldering doll.

Madam Hedvika opened her mouth and closed it a couple of times before she set the vase down. 'No need to apologise. It is why you're here after all.'

'Has this happened before then?'

'Er . . . no. Not precisely this.'

'So, you're not sure what this means?'

'Not yet.' She leaned across the table and picked up the soggy doll. 'But then I haven't done my part.' Madam Hedvika wrapped both her hands around the body of the doll lightly and closed her eyes.

Kay waited awkwardly, wanting to fix the mess that had been made of the table, but equally not wanting to disturb Madam Hedvika when she was concentrating.

After a minute, she opened her eyes, the little frown appearing between her eyebrows again. 'You have a blockage. You must see past it to find your centre again.'

Kay blinked a couple of times. 'What centre? The centre of my magic? Or, like, my centre as a person?'

Madam Hedvika tilted her head for a moment and studied Kay with infuriatingly opaque eyes. She passed Kay the charred doll and then held her hands out, palms down over the table. With a muttered spell and a gentle exhale, all the water rose and evaporated from the corn husks, thread, and puddles on the table.

She sat down opposite Kay once more and laced her fingers together. 'I think the best course of action is for you to stop using your magic entirely.'

'What? *Forever*?' Kay's stomach did a queasy flop at the thought. She wasn't the most active witch, and her feelings towards her gift were best left unsaid, but being told she couldn't ever use her magic was a little like someone insulting your sibling. You might find them irritating, but to have someone else hurt them was just wrong. An affront.

'No, no.' A small smile touched Madam Hedvika's lips. 'Just until you have had a chance to work out when *precisely* this blockage occurred and why. Once you've figured this out, you must take your doll, remove the pinned husk that is helping to shape her and repeat what you did here.'

Kay frowned and bit her lip on a number of retorts. First and foremost, the fact that she had come to Madam Hedvika to be told *why* she had this problem. That was the whole reason she was there – not to be instructed to go off and figure it all out by herself. If not practising magic and just thinking about when the problem started was going to fix her, then she'd already been doing *that*.

'I haven't really been doing magic for weeks,' she offered, working to keep her exasperation in check. 'I don't understand *how* I'm blocked, if the problem is that magic is happening when I don't want it to. That's more of a magical excess than a blockage, surely?'

Madam Hedvika raised an eyebrow. 'I can only tell you what my gift has shown to me. If you don't think it's right and choose to try other methods, that is, of course, up to you.'

Kay's cheeks flushed. 'No. I'm sorry. I'm just . . . very frustrated.'

'I understand.' The woman relented. 'Would you contact me once you have removed the pinned husk from your doll? To tell me what has happened? In fact, ideally, I would like you to come back here to do it. That way, if it hasn't worked, we can immediately try something else.'

'Sure, thank you.'

'You are welcome,' Madam Hedvika said with not a little hint of reprimand. Clearly, she felt Kay should be *very* grateful for her help and hadn't really shown it. Probably the fire hadn't helped in that respect.

The woman rose from the table, signifying the end of the meeting, and showed Kay to the door. She'd removed all the water from the table, but Kay's doll was still soaked and she tried to cradle it in a way that it wouldn't drip onto the floorboards.

'Good luck. And remember. You *must* clamp down on every single impulse you have to do magic. Yes?'

Kay nodded and thanked the woman again, though by the time she was at the bottom of the stairs, stuffing the soggy doll into a plastic bag within her tote and wheeling her suitcase out again, she had to wonder why. It felt like a colossal waste of time. Clamp down on her magic? Think about when it got blocked? Find her centre? It all sounded like impossibilities and riddles.

She sighed, stepping onto the busy Old Town Square, and pulling her phone out. The sky was darkening to a smoky purple above the ornate roof lines of the old buildings, splashes of bright orange sneaking between clouds, but, even if it wasn't particularly warm, it didn't look quite brooding enough for her to believe a hurricane was on the way. Aunt Lucille was rarely wrong, though. Kay needed to bury the magical time bomb ticking away inside her beneath several tonnes of metaphorical concrete so she could concentrate on making her flight. And not setting fire to anything else along the way.

There was a crowd accumulating in front of the astronomical clock as the minutes counted down to the hour, so she skirted around them, finding a spot on the corner that turned into the wider, open area of the square. She was pretty sure she needed to head north, to get to the A-Line Metro that would take her underneath the river; she just needed to reference some of the landmarks to get her bearings.

Diagonally across from her on the left was the statue of Jan Hus, greenish grey with age, people sitting on benches beside the fence surrounding its wide dais. Almost directly opposite her, the spires of the gothic cathedral stretched up, dwarfing the rest of the buildings but still not managing to dull their own individual shine. It was such an old place, so many different periods of architecture. There was the Storch House with its arresting fresco of a saint on a horse and its bay window overhanging the street below—

The clamour of bells rang out, some loud, some small chimes, and the crowd exclaimed in delight. Kay couldn't let herself get distracted. Maybe another time, it would be nice to visit, to get a guidebook and look up the history. But not now. She gave the map on her phone one last check, zipped it away and took the handle of her suitcase again. The weight of it made it feel a bit like trying to do a three-point turn in a monster truck. It teetered off the small kerb and she stepped down too, turning to straighten it, before she set off.

Only, as she tried to pivot back towards the main square, her leg didn't come with her. She tugged. Tugged again. The heel of her boot was caught in the small groove between two cobbles.

This was because she wished she could stay, wasn't it? Her magic had taken the opportunity to weld her heel into the ground. *Want to stay? Here's a perfect excuse,* it was saying. *You're welcome.*

Kay let go of her suitcase entirely, to pull at the spiked heel. Momentarily, she wished she could just blast it with a shot of telekinetic magic – or send a little magical lubrication its way – but no. *No* magic for her. Witch doctor's orders. In her current panic, she'd probably end up with an exploded suitcase, the street littered with marketing-brochure confetti while she was escorted to the nearest police station.

She glanced up, as though the solution might be found somewhere else, and saw the little skeleton figure on the closest corner of the clock, ringing its tiny golden bell. If that wasn't a cosmic message that time was a-ticking, she didn't know what was.

Right, push was coming to shove. She was going to have to take the boot off. On the plus side, at least she had other shoes in her suitcase, and if she had to snap the heel off her boot to free it, she could always mend it – or get it mended by someone who wasn't magically impaired.

Taking off her tote, so it didn't smack her in the head as she bent over to unzip the knee-high boot, she tucked it between her and her suitcase. Now the show on the clock was over, the crowd were dispersing and she had to keep her hands on both bags, apologising for getting in the way of people walking by, and simultaneously making sure no one stole her stuff. She'd just have to wait until the crowd had cleared.

Someone jostled her from the side and she wobbled, forced to crouch to avoid toppling over and breaking her ankle. Frustration bubbled up inside of her, her chest growing hot.

'Are you OK?'

Kay's heart did a strange tumble as she heard a man speaking from just behind her, the huskiness of his voice familiar. But – no. It couldn't be. She was in Prague. Not Biddicote. Or London. Or wherever he lived now.

And her luck couldn't be that bad. Could it?

'Can I help you?' A pair of white trainers, with a big rainbow Nike tick on the side that looked like it was dripping paint to the soles, came into view. And then he was crouching beside her and she was looking up, feeling like it was happening in slow motion. 'K-Kay? Is that really you?'

Yes, it was her. And apparently, it really was Harry Ashworth, too. Her luck *was* that bad.

'It's me,' she said, struggling to keep the defeat out of her voice.

He blinked. 'Wow. It *is* you. I didn't realise . . . your hair's blue, I mean . . .' He broke off and she ignored the tiny shiver that zoomed down her neck as his gaze followed the way her hair framed her face. He swallowed. 'It suits you.'

'Right. Thanks.' She frowned at him, hating that his compliments always sounded so genuine, even though she knew they weren't. She was also wondering why they were talking about her hair when they'd just bumped into each other in another country after not speaking to each other for years.

An awkward silence grew between them. He scratched his thumb against his temple for a second and cleared his throat. 'What's the problem, then?'

Where to start? She pushed her glasses up her nose, her mind first leaping to the strange idea that he was asking her what her problem was with *him*. As though he didn't know.

'Have you twisted your ankle? Are you feeling unwell?' he elaborated, tilting his head. He was still handsome in that unconventional way that made him even more infuriatingly gorgeous, but some of the softness had evaporated from around his cheekbones and jawline. Not from his mouth, though . . .

She must be unwell if she was letting herself appreciate Harry Ashworth's mouth. She looked away. 'My heel is stuck. In the cobbles.'

'Oh, right. May I?' He bent his head, giving her a perfect view of how shiny and soft the waves of his hair looked, as well as assaulting her nose with the smell of his shampoo, all stomach-tinglingly fresh.

'Sure,' she said between gritted teeth, even though she could think of any number of tortures she'd prefer to enjoy rather than Harry Ashworth examining the embarrassing situation she'd found herself in, even more closely. Especially in a way that meant him putting his head level with her butt.

She stood up abruptly, belatedly realising that it would give him a perfect view up her skirt if he decided to look. His fingers touched the back of her heel and as soon as she felt the tiniest magical push, she yanked her boot free – and would have toppled over again, if he hadn't quickly stood up and caught her elbow.

'Cheers,' she said, stepping back up onto the pavement as though the cobbles were lava.

'What brings you here, then?' he asked, glancing around the square, his head starting to turn towards Baba Yaga's.

'Work. Conference,' she blurted out. Getting his attention back on her. He was bound to know it was Madam Hedvika's shop. If he figured out she was having problems with her magic . . .

Well, it didn't really matter. It wasn't like he was friends with Joe anymore – that he had *ever* truly been friends with him – so her family wouldn't find out. Still, she'd prefer to keep her issues private.

'Ah. You do something clever in IT, don't you?'

'Clever' was rather overstating it, but Kay gave a robotic nod.

How did he know that? Maybe just through his parents listening to the small talk in the village – it was a tiny place. It was a surprise, nonetheless. What with Harry showing zero interest about whether she was alive or dead for the last ten years. Since the 'smiley-face' incident.

'Have you had a chance to do any sightseeing? The architecture is—'

'I have to go,' she interrupted with zero shame. She truly didn't have time to stop and make small talk. Definitely not with someone who was acting like they were going to sit and reminisce, or bond over shared interests, or whatever it was he was pretending would be totally normal between them.

'Oh, right. Sure.' He looked down at the cobbles which had very recently held her prisoner. When he met her gaze again, his eyebrows were drawn together in a way that shadowed his eyes. 'It was nice to see you.'

Every polite bone in her body was screaming at her to return the empty platitude. But she couldn't. With a quiet goodbye, she hurried away. And if she couldn't help glancing over her shoulder, it was just because she wanted to make sure he wasn't going in the same direction as her.

He wasn't. He was where she'd left him, his long, deep blue coat making him stand out among the tourists walking around him. He was facing Baba Yaga's again, rubbing a hand absently against his chest.

It didn't matter, Kay reminded herself. She'd left him behind. And she had a plane to catch.

Chapter Three

Prague Airport

810 miles and 44(+1) hours until the wedding

Delayed.

Kay had made it to the airport, only to find the departures board full of delays, including her flight to Heathrow. This did not bode well at all. It might only be a delay now, but what if the flights started getting cancelled?

The terminal was packed, with everyone either looking a little lost, staring up at the boards with concern, or charging off towards the customer service desks, which were already inundated with people.

Kay's knitted work dress clung to her in a number of unflattering places and her feet were cramping in the boots that had betrayed her in Old Town Square. All she really wanted to do was sit down and get a cup of tea, but she needed to know what was going on.

The queues for the desks were overlapping and winding around the terminal in a nonsensical way, like one of those 'find the right path' mazes in children's magazines. No doubt it was more organised than this usually, but no one had foreseen the bad weather picking up pace so much – apart from Aunt Lucille with her aching teeth, and probably a bunch of seers who weren't allowed to tell non-magical people anyway.

Apparently, there'd been a period in the eighties when some enterprising witches had decided to sell their talents to companies for extortionate amounts, giving those businesses a leg-up with financial forecasting, and influencing others to get unfairly beneficial agreements. Then had come the crash and the Witches Council had decided that it was unethical to participate. That it broke the 'do no harm' tenet. Now, witches were only allowed to use their gifts for a living secretly and if they ensured it brought about no undue attention. A healer could become a doctor, but not go performing full-blown miracles every single day. Not that healers could cure everything anyway.

Even if Kay's gift *was* useless, she was at least relieved her affinity wasn't something which had to be curtailed or was limited according to the tenets. It would have been more devastating to have all that potential and still not be able to save every sick child that came to the hospital. Like the moment in *The Imitation Game* when Benedict Cumberbatch realised, even though he'd cracked the code, they couldn't use the information or it would completely give them away. They couldn't save everybody once without the risk of losing the advantage and saving nobody going forwards. Soul-destroying.

Pushing Benedict Cumberbatch from her thoughts, she found the desk for her airline, wheeled her case over to join the end of the queue and perched herself on top of it to give her feet a rest for a minute and check her messages.

Mum: Are you on your plane yet?

Kay: We'll be leaving soon. Fancy anything from the duty-free while I'm here?

She was beginning to consider picking up a bottle of vodka herself. That might make the wait more bearable.

Mum: I don't know. Let me get back to you. I still haven't decided whether to take one of the pills for the rehearsal dinner tomorrow, or just leave it until the wedding? I might need you to drive my car for me if I do. What time are you arriving again?

Kay rolled her neck. This was not about her mother taking pills — it was about wanting to arrive with Kay and stay glued to her side when she was in the same building as her ex-husband. They might dampen her mother's ability, but they weren't going to make all the anxiety she was feeling about seeing Kay's dad disappear.

Kay: Probably mid-afternoon.

Mum: You could come straight here from the airport? I don't mind waiting up for you.

Kay rubbed her temple. It was like her mum thought Marvin was going to pop out of the rosebush at the bottom of the garden or something. Relationships really wrecked people.

A lifetime with a gift to read people's moods had left her mother a chronic people-pleaser, always trying to 'fix' bad feelings. When you coupled that with a husband who boosted people's motivation, it transpired to create a really unhealthy dynamic, encouraging Tallulah *even more* to try to make him happy all the time. And of course, ultimately, it had been a lost cause. With or without magic, you couldn't make people love you.

Although relationships with other witches might seem easier from the perspective of them understanding the supernatural world, both partners having gifts led to too many complications, in Kay's opinion. Especially if those gifts fell under the influencer, empath or seer designations. It all got too messy. Ripe for manipulation, over-sensitivity and second-guessing. Since she was in the empath camp, Kay thought it safest to only date non-magical people. It tended to keep things light – brief – and she'd managed to avoid getting hurt that way.

Kay: I have to pick up my clothes for the wedding first. I didn't bring them to Prague.

Mum: Oh, of course. Silly of me. Let me know when you're back home, OK?

Kay agreed that she would and debated sending a message to Joe about the level of their mother's anxiety, but held off. When she'd looked earlier, the WhatsApp chat for the wedding party had seventy-five new messages in it – partly to do with drinks before the rehearsal tomorrow and partly to do with cravats. He had enough he was juggling at the moment.

Standing up to wheel her suitcase forward a few paces, shuffling forward with the queue, a flash of blue caught her eye. Kay leaned around the couple in front of her, looking down the line, but whoever it had been wearing something the same colour as Harry's coat, they had disappeared. She was seeing Harry Ashworth everywhere and it was not helping her mood. Not least because she knew the initial leap in her stomach was excitement, before common sense took over.

And what *was* that coat all about, anyway? It was so long and dramatic – like he *wanted* to be pegged for a wizard or something. Maybe it was a male-ego thing? Joe had tried to get people to call him a sorcerer when they were little. Ha. Kay made a mental note to ask Sandy if he'd presented himself as a sorcerer rather than a witch, when he broke the magical news to her. It definitely would have appealed to her. Sandy tended to get excited about anything magical. It reminded Kay a little bit of how she used to be before the sparkle wore off and her gift had woken her up to the truth; magic was a paper aeroplane. It looked fun and easy, but it required engineering and, despite seeming harmless, the edges could still cut you.

An hour later, Kay had finally made it to the customer service desk. The woman there had explained that planes were grounded in the UK as winds of seventy-five miles an hour plus were expected for at least twelve hours. No flights were going in or out anymore. But she could transfer her to a flight to Paris that was leaving in the morning and – by that time – the storm should have passed and Kay would be able to get another flight into the UK or a ticket for the Eurostar.

Kay wasn't sure twelve hours for this storm sounded right at all, and even if the bad weather had moved on from the UK, where would it have moved on to? Surely it was heading east?

For want of any better options, though, she agreed to the transfer and thanked the woman. She'd been remarkably helpful and patient, considering the amount of grumpy travellers she was having to deal with. It made Kay wonder if maybe she was some kind of empath, but it was just as likely she was a non-magical person who was really good at her job. Kay left her with a thank you and the small box of chocolates she'd received as part of some swag at the conference.

The queue she walked away from was just as long as when it started, with more people arriving and finding their flights delayed. Gifting that box of chocolates felt like leaving someone a colander as a 'helpful tool' to empty a swimming pool. Everywhere she looked, there were people, and all the bars, eateries and shops were packed too. Finding somewhere to camp out for the night was going to be a challenge, but how much easier would it be to find accommodation in Prague now half the people at the airport were stuck?

Another flash of blue from inside one of the bars drew her eye. She swore, catching herself before she tried to find it again and instead spotted a small table tucked in the corner by the wooden barricade. Pushing past the throbbing in her feet, she raced over to claim it, dipping and dodging between people as fast as her suitcase would allow, and throwing herself onto the tall bar stool so it teetered onto its back legs and she had to grab the edge of the table to steady it.

She let out a breath of relief. An actual seat. Step one of the plan complete. Next, she needed some food and maybe a strong drink. Just the one. Something like that woman over there had. She was holding a large tumbler filled with bright orange liquid, a slice of orange on the side and a sprig of rosemary inside. Kay's mouth watered at the thought of all that refreshing citrus, she could almost feel the burn of vodka in her stomach now.

And then the drink was flying out of the woman's hand, speeding towards Kay like it was a bullet aimed at her face. All she had the time and brainpower to do was scream 'no' in her head. It arrested its motion mid-air, hovered for a second and smashed to the floor.

Heart pounding, Kay's cheeks flamed as the woman and her friends exclaimed over it – mostly swinging from joking about how she must have gestured and it slipped out of her hand, and apologising to the bartender who came over to sweep it up. Kay wanted to apologise too, but she couldn't. Obviously.

She put her elbows on the table and bracketed her face with her hands, trying to block out the scene she had created. It was so lucky no one had been hurt by the flying drink. How in the hell was she meant to *stop* using her magic, when she wasn't making a conscious choice to use it in the first place? And where was the so-called 'blockage' when her magic was shooting out of her like a geyser?

'Kay. Kay?' Outside Kay's little bubble of denial, a male voice was calling her. Getting closer. It wasn't husky and gentle, so her stomach decided it wasn't worth doing backflips, but when she dropped her hands to face the owner, she stifled a sigh. A young man of medium height and infinitely too much hair gel was grinning at her. 'Hey. It's me. Dean. You remember? From the conference bar last night?'

'Yeah.' How could she forget? 'Hi, Dean.'

He crossed his arms on the table, leaning towards her. 'Guess you're delayed too. We were probably meant to be on the same flight.' He pointed over his shoulder to a small booth closer to the bar that was spilling over with more of the sales team, suit jackets strewn everywhere in a fog of beer and aftershave. 'Why don't you come and join us?'

'Oh, that's OK thanks, I don't think I can see a spare seat.'

'Don't worry, we'll squeeze you in. I don't mind getting cosy.'

She was sure he wouldn't, given the explicit invitations he'd been issuing last night. His crew had come over to talk to them, and she and Ilina hadn't minded, but then Dean had gone from zero to a hundred with no encouragement, and they'd needed to beat a hasty retreat before Kay's magic reacted. 'No. Thanks. I've still got to sort out what I'm doing between now and my flight.'

'When's yours? Ours is in the morning now, so we figured we'd make the most of it. Managed to get a suite here. It was one of the last ones, but Paddy talked them into it . . .' He rolled his eyes with a grin. Obviously, that was classic Paddy. Bully for him.

None of them were witches as far as Kay could tell. It wasn't as easy to figure it out as one might have thought. You couldn't just go up and ask someone if you suspected – that might earn you a trip to a psychologist or a slap to the face if you were wrong. In some countries, witches used a little sign – Ilina had a rune pattern tattooed on her inner wrist – but British witches were far too old-fashioned and secretive for anything subtly inclusive like that.

'There's space in the suite for you too, if you need it.' Dean wiggled his eyebrows at her.

She struggled not to wrinkle her nose. Did he really think a woman on her own was going to feel comfortable going back to a hotel suite with four male strangers? 'Er, well, that's kind, but I'll let you know.'

He pulled out his phone. 'Give me your number and I'll text you mine.'

'Don't I have your card from last night?' she deflected.

'No. I don't think so . . .' he cocked his head, as though trying to remember.

'I'm sure I do—'

'Well, just to make certain you don't get stranded, why don't you give me yours.'

'I don't have any business cards on me.' She shrugged, all the while internally screaming, *please, someone, anyone, get him to take a hint.*

'Not your card, your number.' He rolled his eyes with a smile again. Clearly, she was being classic Kay now. 'I'll worry about you otherwise. It's going to be a nightmare finding somewhere to stay, you know. You don't want to end up sleeping on one of those plastic chairs, do you?'

Kay took a deep breath, preparing herself to tell him to push off in the politest way possible, when a voice spoke up from the other side of her. And this one *was* husky and gentle.

'This is a nice surprise, again.'

She turned to look at Harry, who was standing with his big coat undone, one side pushed back past his hip so he could put his hand in his trouser pockets, and a half-pint of Pilsner in the other hand which had barely an inch left at the bottom.

So. It probably had been him when she'd seen those flashes of blue earlier. One brief meeting in Old Town Square and her subconscious had dialled up her Harry-proximity-alert to obsessed teen sensitivity levels again.

She bit her lip, realising that how she responded here would determine whether she could shake off Dean – with his dubious protestations of worry about her – or not. She should have known better than to make that silent plea for help dealing with him, even in her head. Of *course* the person who would turn up would be the last one she would want to see. The last one she wanted to feel grateful towards.

Well, it was happening now, so the quicker she could get Dean to shove off, the quicker she could go back to ignoring Harry, too.

'Hey, Harry. Sorry I had to dash off so quickly earlier.' She forced a smile. 'Clearly it didn't get me very far.'

Harry's reddish-brown eyebrows drew together, making little lines appear in his faintly freckled skin, as his gaze lingered on her face for a moment, taking the time to study her.

She remembered this look. It could make you feel as though you were the most important person in the world to him at that particular moment. And then if he smiled . . . Kay's belly flipped over as her mind supplied the memory of how it could magnify all that intensity even further. Lopsided and wide and seemingly adorable. But this time it was just the corner of his mouth that ticked up, as though he couldn't quite muster the impetus. Which was fine. She didn't want to see his manipulatively lovely smile anyway.

'Have you got some time to catch up properly now?' he asked. 'Maybe grab something to eat? It's been a long time, and twice in one day seems like the universe trying to tell us something.'

She almost snorted at that. If the universe was trying to tell her anything, it was that she should never have come to Prague. She didn't know what god she had angered at the beginning of this year, but she had obviously done a thorough job.

'I thought you needed to sort out somewhere to stay?' Dean asked, wedging himself back into the conversation.

'Yes. I do.' She glanced over at him, but found her attention dragged – against her will – back to Harry, as though, if she didn't keep looking at him, she'd find that she'd been imagining it all.

'I have a place. It has a sofa bed. I'll take that and you can have the bedroom,' Harry immediately offered.

Of *course* he had a place. Sometimes they'd talked about the destinations they wanted to travel to and it looked like the job he'd walked into with his dad's company had given him that opportunity, with a generous enough salary to afford special-edition trainers and ostentatious coats. As well as being the head of one of the oldest witching families, Adrian Ashworth was the CEO for a very large marketing company. He had to find the money to keep Ashworth Hall running in its accustomed splendour somehow, and he'd had very clear plans for how Harry would play his part in upholding that.

She tapped a fingernail against the table. This had taken a turn she hadn't anticipated. Apparently she'd attempted to dodge the lava flow of a volcano by taking refuge in Satan's favourite torture chamber. 'Oh, that's—'

'Remember we've got that suite I offered,' Dean jumped in.

'I know, but—'

'And it's right here. Makes life a lot easier. Where's your place?' Dean asked Harry, the challenge in his tone unmistakable.

Kay blinked, wondering where all the men eager for her company had been when she was debating whether to take a date to Joe's wedding. Of course, what Dean was after was clearly *not* anything to do with being a potential wedding date, and as for Harry's motivation, who knew? Maybe he was just extending the Ashworth protection for a Biddicote witch? Because it definitely wasn't about genuinely wanting her company.

Harry put his pint down on the table and extended his hand across it. 'I'm sorry, so rude of me, butting in and interrupting your conversation. I'm Harry Ashworth, an old friend of Kay's.'

'Dean.' He shook Harry's hand briefly.

'Are you two . . .?' His gaze flitted quickly between Kay and Dean and back again.

'No, no. Oh God, no. Dean is an acquaintance from the work conference we've been on. We just bumped into each other. That's all.' She told herself that her eagerness to explain there was nothing going on between her and Dean was all so the salesman would finally realise his attentions weren't welcome. Subtlety obviously wasn't working. This man was thicker than Henry Cavill's thighs.

'I see.' Harry continued looking at Dean for a long moment, his jaw set, and Kay had a strange moment of seeing something in him she'd never seen before. Something hard and reminiscent of his father. It wasn't like she should be surprised. She'd known for a long time that his faux-humble, yet undeniably attractive, glory was the perfect sheep's clothing to hide the wolf inside. 'Kay? Would you like to stay with me?'

She didn't really want to spend any longer with Harry, but if she said no, Dean might take it as an indication she still wanted *him* around. And, despite everything, maybe it was a case of better-the-devil-you-know.

'Sounds like it would be perfect.' *To someone completely ignorant of our history* – as Dean was. 'I'll catch up with you another time, Dean. Have a safe journey home.'

Dean barely waited to hear her finish speaking, giving her a wave as he was turning away in a gesture that could be interpreted either as a goodbye or dismissal, depending on the way you chose to look at it. She was perfectly happy with either, other than the fact it left her with . . .

'He was persistent.' When she looked back, Harry was watching her, the deep blue of his eyes almost black in the dingy lighting of the bar, but she could still see an annoying twinkle in them – like triumph.

She glanced out at the travellers clogging the terminal, so she wasn't staring at him like his very presence had reawakened all her adolescent . . . yearnings. Ick. It made her cringe to think how desperate for every scrap of his attention she'd once been. Well, that wasn't who she was now.

'He's a salesman. They're like the influencers of the NM world, aren't they?' she commented coolly, keeping the reference to the non-magical world abbreviated in case they were overheard.

He raised his eyebrows and a quizzical smile touched his lips. 'Aren't . . . *online influencers* the influencers of the NM world?'

'Hmm, I don't think so. Online influencers gain a following by portraying an appealing lifestyle and then people listen to their opinion because they value it. Rightly or wrongly. Salespeople are about getting what *they* want from people and using their manipulative skills to achieve that end.'

'But most influencers' – he scanned the area around the table and leaned in closer, his voice lowering – 'magical ones – can't make anyone do what they don't want to do. It's suggestion. Closer to hypnosis.'

'It's *way* stronger than hypnosis. You can't always make people do it for *long*, necessarily, but you can definitely shove people in a different direction to the one they wanted to travel in.' She paused, her eyes narrowing, heart beating painfully against her ribs. 'Or if, like you say, they're predisposed to the feeling anyway, maybe they'll never shake it off.'

Awkward silence reigned again. Strange how even though she knew it was a point to her, she didn't feel like she'd won anything.

Harry's tongue poked out the corner of his mouth before swiping across his bottom lip. She did *not* allow herself to stare at it. He started riffling in his ridiculous coat, bringing out an enormous bag of pick 'n' mix sweets. How had he even fit that in there without a bulge? He'd probably Mary Poppins'ed his whole wardrobe into there.

He offered her the bag once he opened it.

'No thanks, I like my teeth with no fillings.' Even magic dentistry involved having someone up close and personal, poking about in your mouth, and not in the pleasant way.

'Comfort eating has numerous pitfalls,' he admitted with a small laugh, dipping his hand in to grab a sweet shaped like a banana, while simultaneously showing off his annoyingly neat, white teeth. 'Is there anyone else from your company you're travelling with?'

Ah, so, he was fishing to get rid of her now she'd shown she wasn't as enamoured with his presence as she'd first made out?

'Nope.' The two developers who'd flown out had left earlier in the week because they had a big project they were working on, and even though her boss had already planned to stay in Prague for the entire weekend, it wasn't like he was a viable person to call upon for assistance. He probably would have told her it was against company policy to share with colleagues. She would prefer to sleep on the runway than in the same room as that man anyway. 'Why?'

Harry swallowed the last mouthful of his sweet. 'Just in case they needed somewhere to stay, too. Shall we make a move, then?'

Huh. Maybe he wasn't trying to ditch her after all. It definitely had to be some Ashworth-code motivating him, then. It was bad enough she'd had to pretend to be happy to see him without knowing he was thinking of her as some kind of charity case.

'That's not necessary. I can find somewhere for myself.'

'But you said—'

'I was just trying to shake Dean off,' she admitted. 'I'll survive.'

He frowned. 'What if you can't find anywhere else? You can't sleep here, surrounded by all these strangers – and *Dean*.' He took the head of a gummy worm between his teeth and yanked it off with surprising aggression. 'It's not safe.'

She was about to argue back, because a) who was he trying to kid that he cared, and b) this was sounding like a very similar conversation she'd already had once this evening with a man who couldn't take a hint to go away. But then the woman whose glass she'd magically stolen and smashed caught her eye over Harry's shoulder. If Kay did get stuck at the airport all night, she *would* be surrounded by people. And security cameras. What if something else went wrong? It wouldn't be safe. Not for her, and not for other people.

If she went with him, it would at least minimise the risk. She could manage one night in the same room as Harry Ashworth if she really had to, couldn't she? And if something accidentally went flying at his head, he'd at least be able to use his own magic in self-defence.

'OK, fine,' she said. 'Let's go.'

Chapter Four

Heading back into the city in the back of a taxi with Harry sitting next to her was a disconcerting experience for Kay. He'd lived like a ghost in the haunted wreck of her brain for the last decade. Initially, more of a poltergeist, constantly banging around, sometimes making her lose sleep, other times just prompting a rage where she wished his entire presence could be exorcised. Over the years, he'd faded to one of those spectres caught out of the corner of her eye, walking up the stairs at the same time each night, yet still making her heart leap for a moment before she settled down and could ignore him again.

And now here he was, his body conspicuously solid. As a teenager, he'd been a collection of attractively long limbs, but now that height had filled out into an athletic build, still lean but firm too . . .

It had been a half an hour wait at the taxi rank. After they'd briefly confirmed they were both scheduled on the same flight to Paris early the next day, she'd kept her attention on her phone, letting her mum know that she wasn't going to be leaving Prague until the morning now.

Harry had occupied himself much the same way once he'd put the sweets away.

His quip about comfort eating brought his mother's gift to mind. Had she made him magical food when he was a child? Kay wasn't sure whether that would have counted as being against the rules about influencing a minor's behaviour. It felt like a grey area. If he'd had a tough day at school, a plate of milk and cookies from his mother would have *literally* changed his mood, and didn't mood dictate behaviour? It was also some dangerous Pavlov's Dog energy.

Not that Kay should care. *He* hadn't.

She glanced over at him. His head tipped against the window, the lights from the street lamps dancing over his face, causing a shadow in the hollow of his cheek and under his bottom lip, and illuminating his eyes momentarily. Either he was enraptured by the view, daydreaming of escape, or doing what she'd come to expect from him over the last decade – ignoring her.

She took a deep breath and forced her eyes away before she looked at his fingers. God, she'd been so obsessed with his fingers. How long and agile they were, and so controlled too – moving from quick sketches, barely discernible with the naked eye, to tiny, detailed strokes or strong, confident sweeps, with a pencil or pen.

The taxi pulled over and Harry sat up, turning to her as though he was waking. 'Ah, we're here.' He leaned forward and paid the cab driver, speaking some quick, pleasant-sounding words in Czech, and then proceeding to unfold himself, one long leg at a time, from the back seat onto the street.

Kay followed suit and found him removing her suitcase from the boot.

'Goddess around us, what is in this?' he grunted, setting it down with a thump on the pavement beside her.

'The skulls of my enemies,' she retorted. 'And shoes.'

He started wheeling her case away and she jogged a little to catch up, each impact making her sore feet throb, as though pointing out exactly where her weakness for lovely shoes had got her. 'You don't have to do that, I'm perfectly capable.'

'That's OK, I'm the one who knows the way and I can steamroller anyone who gets in our path.'

She snorted, tightening the belt on her coat against the frigid night air.

'So, what's the ratio?' he asked.

'Sorry?'

'I'm just curious as to what ratio of skulls to shoes was necessary for your conference. Or did you add to it during the trip?'

'Oh, I'm adding to my collection all the time.' She gave him a sharp smile, which she hoped communicated that she was very willing to add *his* if the opportunity presented itself. Skull or shoes. He could take his pick. His coat might be over the top, but those trainers with the painted rainbow ticks were exceptionally cool.

He gave a strange low laugh and then glanced over his shoulder at her. 'Why haven't you used a charm on it?' he asked, lightly. 'Too many skulls could cause you to sprain something.'

She pressed her lips together. There was no way she was going to tell him about her magic being on the fritz and therefore on lockdown too.

'It would take more energy than it's worth,' she said tightly and, to be fair, it was a solid excuse. An enchantment to alter gravity on something significantly heavy – without

61

it floating off – for more than a few moments, was hardly easy, everyday magic.

Well, it probably was for *him*. That was the irritating thing. While all witches had a special gift within their magical designation that allowed them easy access, other spells used up their energy, and even with the right words and rituals, it was a skill. A physical skill. They needed to exercise their magic, practise it regularly in order to keep it limber and strong. Even before her magic was having problems, Kay didn't exactly do that, and so everyday magic took marked concentration and could be draining. She was the wheezy, gaspy type of witch, whereas someone like Harry, who didn't even blink about using his magic in a public place like Old Town Square, was probably the equivalent of a triathlon champion.

He paused in front of a door inset between two shops and made a little shape with his mouth as though he was about to say something, but shook his head instead. 'Would you like—'

'No,' she cut him off quickly. 'I don't need you to do it for me.'

He frowned at her. 'That wasn't actually what I was going to say.'

'Oh.' She folded her arms over her chest. 'Go on then.'

'Would you like to go out to get something to eat once you've dropped your bag off? It would give us a chance to catch up.'

Catch up? A stab of pain flashed behind her eye. He was acting like they were old friends again. The only thing she was really interested in hearing from him was an apology, and he could have said that the moment he saw her, earlier in the day, or in the bar once Dean had gone, or during that silent taxi ride. But no, it was like he wanted to ignore what he'd done. Well, fine. He could ignore it, but she wasn't going to make nice while he did.

'No. I just want to get some sleep.'

He nodded slowly and drummed his fingers over the handle of her wheelie case before tapping in the code for the lockbox and retrieving the keys for her. 'It's on the first floor. Number two, on the left.'

She took the keys and ignored the traitorous tumble of disappointment in her chest that he was going out anyway. 'Half your body weight in pick and mix not satisfy your appetite?'

His mouth lifted at the corner, but he kept his eyes lowered. 'I guess not.'

'I'm going to book the Uber to get us to the airport in the morning. But if you get drunk and end up sleeping on a park bench, I'll have to leave without you,' she warned him.

'Goes without saying. I'll make sure I'm quiet when I come back in.'

She nodded and turned to the door, slotting the first key in the lock. When she turned back to get her case, he was already walking away, his hands burrowed into the pockets of his big ridiculous coat, the tails flapping behind him.

She grabbed the handle of her case and yanked to bump it up the steps, but instead of it weighing the same as a small tractor, it felt like it was empty, and the force she'd put behind it had her sprawling backwards and landing on her butt.

Bloody Harry. He'd gone and put the charm on it anyway. Just like that. A flick of his fingers. He hadn't even needed to mutter any words out loud. Show-off.

She levered herself up and carried it inside. There was one flight of steep stairs in the hallway, an automatic light flickering on. If her coccyx wasn't throbbing at that precise moment, she might have felt a tiny bit grateful for his unsolicited sharing of his superior magic – but it did hurt like a bastard, and he could have warned her.

The second key fit into the door on the left like he'd said, and she opened it up into a dark apartment. Other than the hum of refrigerator, it was blessedly quiet and warm. A faint whiff of Harry's aftershave lingered. The hallway was short, with a little kitchen off to the right and then it opened up into a small lounge with narrow windows and a room off to the side. The street lighting filtered in enough that she could walk through without switching on any lamps until she was in the bedroom.

He'd made the bed before he left in the morning and she stared at it, with its pale blue cover, hating that it was running through her mind about whether he'd slept in pyjamas or just his underwear – or nothing.

She squeezed her eyes shut and took a deep, slow breath. She didn't want to keep thinking about Harry – unavoidable as it might seem.

Shrugging her coat off, she booked the Uber and then dialled Ilina's number.

'Have you made it home yet?' she asked when Ilina answered.

'Not quite. Another fifteen minutes on this train, then I will be a short walk from my very own bed. Bliss. What about you? You don't sound like you're in an airport?'

'I'm not. I had to transfer my flight. I'm flying out in the morning now.'

'So where are you if you are not at the airport?'

'I bumped into an old acquaintance from Biddicote. He has a place in New Town and offered me a bed there.' Which was kind, regardless of his reasoning. Kay hadn't exactly been pleasant to him – understandably – and yet he was still giving up his bed to her, and taking the sofa bed, which probably wasn't anywhere near as comfortable. 'Anyway, how did my boss take the news?'

'Oh, him.' Kay could tell Ilina was rolling her eyes from the dryness of her tone. 'He said you need to fill out a sick form when you get back to the office.'

'What a dickhead. I barely left forty-five minutes early.'

'He is, indeed, a dickhead. But I noticed the subject change, which makes me suspicious. Let's go back to talking about the generous old friend who offered you a bed for the night. Layovers are the perfect hook-up opportunity. Is he hot?'

'Ilina, I'm exhausted and I just want to go home.'

'Also noted that you are avoiding the question of his hotness, but fair enough. If Dev Patel himself strode down this train and offered me a one-night stand, I might be inclined to say no.'

Kay laughed. 'Really? You'd say no to Dev Patel?'

'Well . . . maybe I couldn't pass up the opportunity, but it would not be the frenzy of passion we both deserve.' She sighed. 'What's the place like?'

Kay looked around her again. She would have thought an apartment of Harry's would've had a touch more colour, or artwork on the walls, but it was nice enough. 'It's small. Neat. Not in a dodgy neighbourhood so far as I can tell.' She sat down on the bed and did a little bounce on it to test the mattress. 'Bed feels comfy. It'll definitely—' She broke off as she noticed that the bed, which had looked totally normal initially, had rings – metal rings – set at each corner.

'What? Did you notice a dead rat somewhere?' Ilina asked.

'I'm going to put you on video calling now, is that OK?'

'Sure.'

Kay jumped up and flicked on the light switch and then turned the camera on her phone to face the bed. 'Tell me if I'm wrong, but aren't they for bondage ropes?' She zoomed in and, after a second, Ilina's gleeful cackle echoed out of the speaker of her phone.

'Yes. They do look like it to me. Oh, angle the camera up.'

Kay obeyed, scanning towards the small window and wardrobe, pausing when she found a big metal plate on the ceiling to the side of the bed, with more rings on it.

'And a sex swing,' Ilina hooted. Clearly, she didn't care too much about the people who overheard her on the train. 'Perhaps your friend is thinking of hook-up possibilities, too?'

A deep flush rushed across Kay's body and face. She turned her back on the bed and switched off the camera, putting the phone to her ear again. 'Not with me, he isn't.'

'Where is he now?'

'Out, getting something to eat.'

'I bet he is.'

'Ilina, stop it.' Kay half laughed, half groaned. It wasn't like she was kink-averse at all, it was the way it forced . . . scenarios with Harry involved directly into her brain – her overworked nervous system couldn't handle it.

'Seriously though, Kay. You trust this man, yes? You feel you are safe there, if he does suggest something and you say no?'

'Yes,' she answered, before she even really thought about it.

A loud announcement sounded in the background at the other end of the phone. 'Good. I have to go, *liebling*, but let me know tomorrow what is happening with you.'

Kay wished her a safe walk home and hung up. She turned to look at the bed again. Her coat was crumpled across it, looking far too much like a person with their arms flung out in welcome.

She wasn't just trying to appease Ilina when she said she was safe with Harry. She did truly believe that or she never would have come back here, but it didn't stop her from feeling all squirmy and uncomfortable now.

Had he entertained someone in here last night? In that bed. Maybe he had a partner who lived who lived in Prague. She'd assumed he was on a business trip, but he hadn't said either way, and she couldn't sleep in that bed now.

She pressed the backs of her cold fingers to her flaming cheeks. In fact, where could she even *sit* in the apartment? Perhaps it was the exhaustion kicking in, but her mind was busy arranging a slideshow of X-rated hypothetical images in her head. Harry tying a man to the bed, his long fingers deftly tightening ropes . . . rocking a woman back and forth in the swing, his narrow hips moving . . . bending a man over the back of the sofa in the living room . . . lifting a woman up and pressing her against the wall of the shower as water streamed down his face and chest . . .

Wow. It was like the Pandora's Box of all her repressed teenage hormones had been cracked open. Not that she'd have fantasised *those* kind of things when she was a teenager − when did her brain develop its own PornHub? Perhaps she needed to ease up on the spicy BookTok reading material.

Grabbing her coat, she went into the living room. There was no way she was even going to consider the sofa bed either. She took one of the brochures from inside her suitcase, putting it on the smallest, least clinch-inviting armchair, before she sat down on it. Then she plumped a cushion, thought better of it, and balled up her coat to rest her head against.

It was no great surprise that sleep didn't come easily. It wasn't exactly comfortable. Even so, Kay had dozed off before she heard the front door opening and snapped upright, swearing, and slapping a hand on the side of her neck as it refused to flex enough to let her straighten her head.

Harry strode into the lounge, and she didn't even question how he had let himself in without a key. He was pink-cheeked and windswept, probably both from drinking and from the cold. An eerie howl rattled at the windows now.

'What are you doing out here?' He paused halfway across the room, his great coat slipping down his shoulders before he threw it onto the sofa. She half expected it to jingle like it was full of treasure, but it made a soft slap and deflated. 'Why aren't you in bed?'

His husky voice uttering the word "bed" as he stood there, all elemental vitality and shadowy allure, had the images she'd been plagued with earlier whirling back to life. She stomped those ideas straight out, the same way she would an errant spark from a fire which had landed on the rug.

'I didn't fancy it much. You can take it. I'll sleep out here.' She massaged the muscles of her neck and tentatively stretched it in the opposite direction.

'You didn't fancy the big, comfy double bed?' Harry shoved back his hands back into his hair, rubbing it roughly and leaving it sticking up all over the place. 'Why not?'

'Because of all the . . .' She shook her head. *Don't blush, Kay, don't you dare blush.* 'Fixtures and fittings tailored to your . . . specific tastes.'

He did a slow blink and looked around the – admittedly innocuous – living room. 'I'm really not following. I've only had half a pint and that was hours ago. What are you talking about?'

Wow, he was really going to make her spell it out. Kay groaned and pushed herself up from her chair, the brochure crinkling as it stuck to her bottom. He did a double take at it, and she was forced to peel it away under his surveillance before she crossed to the threshold of the bedroom, flinging an arm out to indicate the entire space. 'It's pretty obvious what you use this place for.'

'Sleeping?' He followed her over. He was wearing a maroon jumper over a white shirt, and both smelt of aftershave and his warm skin. 'Is this a thing you can see with your gift? Because I'm really not getting it.'

She sighed and pointed to the circular hooks at the head and foot of the bed. 'These. To tie your partner up.' Then she gestured to the plate on the ceiling. 'And this. For the sex swing. I'm not an idiot, y'know.'

His mouth opened and shut a couple of times. 'Is that . . .' He tilted his head. 'Is that what those are for? I figured they were just industrial-style post-modernist bed knobs or something. And I didn't even notice *this*.' He moved beneath the metal plate for the swing and gazed up at it with the guileless curiosity she couldn't help remembering. Then, when he darted a look at her out of the corner of his eye and his mouth hitched up at the side, she recognised another one of his expressions. Teasing.

Only she'd always mistaken it for a joke they were sharing, when it was much more likely he'd been laughing *at* her, rather than *with* her.

Well, she wasn't some gullible sixteen-year-old anymore and he wasn't going to have fun at her expense.

She huffed and crossed her arms. 'So they were just here when you bought the flat, were they?'

'What?' The half-smile dropped and he frowned at her for a moment before going back to examining the plate. He stretched his arm up and looped one digit of his index finger through the hook and tugged on it. His jumper and shirt both rose with the motion, threatening to untuck from the waistband of his trousers. 'I don't own this apartment. Why would you think that?'

'You said you had a place.'

'Yeah, to stay in, not that I live in.' He gave a soft laugh, as though the idea was daft.

Kay bristled. 'Well, how should I know that?' *I don't know you anymore, I don't know if I ever knew you.* 'You *said* you had a place and then brought me here to it.'

He paused in his scientific exploration of the base plate for the sex swing, lowering his arm back down and putting his hands in his pockets. 'But you saw me get the key out of the lockbox.'

That was a good point. Not one she'd considered while her imagination rampaged off with him fan-cast in the starring role of a *365 Days* remake. The heat in her cheeks flared again. 'So? Maybe that's just what people do over here. Or maybe you rent it out as an Airbnb when you aren't using it.'

'Because I'd like to share my red-room with even more strangers?' He raised an eyebrow and his soft lips pressed together as he looked at her, his eyes narrowing slightly as though her furious blushing was giving something away.

A tense silence stretched out and it was only now that his laid-back attitude was receding to reveal a grim sort of resignation that she realised how her complaint might look to him. Like judgement of his sex life.

Shit. He was telling the truth. And she had let her careening emotions bulldoze her common sense.

She pinched the bridge of her nose, rubbing carefully underneath her glasses before settling them firmly back in place and looking him straight in his deep blue eyes. They had a guarded quality to them, but she held his gaze, maybe for the first time since they'd met in Prague, to be sure he believed what she said next.

'Look, I'm sorry for jumping to the wrong conclusion about this place being yours and then freaking out about the kinky shit. It was nothing to do with any assumptions or judgement about you personally, just the evidence.' She waved her hands at said evidence. 'I didn't think it through and my only excuse is that I'm exhausted, and I don't want to be in Prague *at all*, let alone snuggling up to go to sleep in someone else's soft-porn set.'

His gaze flickered across her face for a few more quiet seconds before he gave a little snort and scraped his teeth over his bottom lip, his shoulders lowering. 'I'd call you a prude, but clearly you know more about the exciting side of bed-sport than I do.'

Her face was practically melting off her at the intensity of her blush now. In a minute, she'd be able to add her own skull to her non-existent collection. She'd claimed not to be an idiot, but the leaps and bounds her imagination had taken had left her looking decidedly idiotic. 'Who the hell calls sex "bed-sport"?' she asked, like a crabby old woman.

He shrugged. 'Someone who doesn't recognise BDSM fixtures and fittings when they're right next to his head?'

She rolled her eyes and looked away, determined not to smile at the self-deprecating humour. It was all an act. She had to remember that. She was not going to let herself be charmed by him. This *should* be awkward. He shouldn't be able to joke and flatter his way out of the estrangement *he'd* instigated.

'Look, I understand it was unexpected, he continued. But the reality is, whenever you stay in a hotel or a holiday cottage or a caravan, the last occupants most likely had sex in it. That's why people go on holiday, isn't it? Or where they're having affairs.'

'Right. But that reality isn't usually slapping me in the face while I'm trying to get some sleep.' *Really, Kay? 'Slapping' you in the face? Great choice of words there.*

'So, as long as you can employ plausible deniability, it's all fine?'

'Yes. Maybe that's irrational, but—'

'It doesn't matter if it's irrational – it's making you uncomfortable.' Harry looked down at the covers, his fingers shifting restlessly through his hair. 'The bed seemed newly made when I arrived yesterday, and only I slept in it last night, but would it help to have fresh bedsheets?'

A tiny cold spot inside her chest thawed at his consideration of her feelings. Then she remembered that she'd been tricked into thinking he cared about her feelings before too. It had just made it hurt all the more when he'd trampled all over them. 'Yeah,' she said shortly. 'I can handle that though. It's late.'

She went out to grab her suitcase and coat, and when she returned to the room, she caught him chewing on his bottom lip and frowning at the bed.

Right. He'd be expecting her to use her magic to clean the sheets. It was a lot easier than changing them fully. Or it should be. In fact, he was probably wondering why she hadn't just done that in the first place, instead of freaking out about the very normal circumstance of people having sex in bedrooms. The suspicious boot was on the other foot now.

'I'll be fine now, thanks.' She looked pointedly at the door.

'Great.' He nodded hard, like he was trying to convince himself, and opened the wardrobe in the corner of the room, pulling out a small holdall that was at the bottom. 'I'll just go brush my teeth so I'm out of your hair for the rest of the night.'

She backed up, almost to the wall, giving him a wide berth as he passed her to use the small bathroom that adjoined the bedroom.

She unzipped her suitcase again, riffling slowly through for her pyjamas to give her an excuse for not getting on with magicking the bedsheets clean. To add insult to injury, she was now stuck sleeping in the bedsheets as they were, because if she sought out a fresh set, that would also make it obvious that she wasn't using her magic.

What was her life coming to? Trying her best to hide her magic in public, while simultaneously trying her best to hide the fact she couldn't do magic from other witches.

The buzz of his electric toothbrush ceased and she gathered all her own toiletries together, swapping places with him in the bathroom with a brief 'goodnight'. He was in a pair of loose pyjama bottoms and a T-shirt and it was only when she closed the door behind her that she realised the bag he'd taken from the wardrobe had already been in the apartment.

She knew he was capable of a lot, but turning it invisible and levitating all afternoon and evening was very unlikely. And unnecessary. Presumably, he'd been booked onto the same flight back to Heathrow as her. Why hadn't he taken it with him earlier at the airport? Maybe he'd been given a tip-off by his extensive magical network about the storm and hot-footed it over to the airport without bothering to pick it up? Being an Ashworth meant that hundreds of witches respected you and/or felt they owed you something in return for the protection of Biddicote. And all he'd had to do was be born into the right family.

She brushed her teeth and removed her glasses, so she could clean her make-up off, after she got changed. As she blinked between swipes of the cotton wool pad across her eyelids, she saw the shimmer starting at her abdomen, the glimmering rope of energy, coming into focus, and turned her back to the mirror, tipping her head up to the ceiling.

Nobody wanted to know how people truly felt about others. Not even her.

Kay had no idea what time it was when the noise woke her up, but she knew it was the darkest hour of the night. No street lights were even on outside.

She levered herself up in bed, disorientated. 'What? What?'

Not at home. Not at the hotel. Not at her mum's . . .

The gravelly voice from the other room, swearing, followed by the creak of springs, brought it all back. The tail-end of a dream that had featured Harry and restraints fading away. She didn't want to think about whether the restraints were because she was attaching him to a runaway horse, or to a bed . . .

More creaking and swearing.

'Oh God, what now?' she groaned.

'Kay? Are you awake?'

'Unfortunately.'

'I might need a bit of help.'

'With what?' she asked, even as she was stumbling out of bed and shoving her glasses onto her face. Technically, she didn't have to sleep with her glasses off – they'd been crafted by an alchemic witch, they wouldn't break – but it was more comfortable sleeping without the bits of plastic bending around her head.

'It's probably best for you to come in here and see.' He sounded oddly strained.

She pushed the folding door back and flicked the light on, blinking hard in the glare. And then again as she tried to figure out what was going on with the sofa bed.

Harry had pushed the coffee table out of the way to make room for it, but it wasn't the whole way out. Instead, it was making a shallow zigzag shape and Harry was balancing on the peak of it, bracing himself over the gap where it folded out from the base.

'Wh–what?'

'The sofa bed appears to have malfunctioned. And it's trying to eat me.'

Kay's stomach went cold. Was this her doing? She'd been dreaming about Harry – had her magic done this while she was *sleeping*? Had it ever done that before and she just hadn't noticed?

'Er . . . could you help me get free?' he carried on, breaking her from her panicked thoughts. He tugged his leg and the sofa bed made the creaking noise again. That explained that.

She moved to the other end of the sofa, where she could see his left leg was actually down in the void. 'Why don't you do your gravity-defying trick on it?' she asked. 'The one you put on my bag earlier.'

He frowned. 'Are you really annoyed because I put that charm on your suitcase? You'd prefer to lug it around and tear a ligament?'

'I'd have preferred you to listen to me when I said I didn't need your help with it. Not do it regardless so I fall on my butt when I go to move it.'

'Oh.' He looked down at the carpet. 'I'm sorry. I didn't mean for that to happen.'

A little bubble of anger in Kay's chest expanded. Not at him. It was at herself. She'd talked herself into a situation where she had to accept his apology. But it wasn't an apology for *that* she truly wanted. 'It's fine,' she managed to say. 'I don't think magic is the way to go with this either. Not without knowing what's gone wrong.'

He flopped his head back and grimaced. 'That's what I thought too. Maybe if you could just sit on the bed, your weight will force it down.'

She gave a short, involuntary laugh. 'Wow. I can't believe I *ever* thought you were charming.'

'What did I do now?' His eyes widened. 'You just said you aren't going to use magic and you do, undeniably, weigh *something* and that *something* is extra to what I weigh at the moment—'

'If you say "ergo" I'll leave you here for the next orgy participants to find.'

'Fine. You know what I meant, though. You don't have to take offence just for the sake of it.'

So, he was starting to get narky back with her now, was he? As though he didn't deserve everything she was dishing out – carnivorous couches and all.

'Fine.' She climbed onto the back of the sofa, rather than trying to hoist herself onto the raised edge of the bed, and braced her feet between his trapped leg and the one he was using to try to push the mattress down. 'Are we sure this is the best idea? How is your foot even stuck? If we force it, we might do damage.'

'I'll scream if I feel anything severing, believe me, I don't have a high pain threshold.'

'I remember,' she muttered.

'Then you should have realised I wouldn't be indulging in . . . flogging or such.'

'There are rumours that S and M and having your foot caught in a sofa are not the same kind of pain. Also, for all I knew, you were the dominant one. Dishing it out.'

'How did we get onto this subject again?' A bead of sweat had appeared at his hairline, and he shifted uncomfortably, the sofa making a groaning noise again.

'You brought it up.'

He gave a strained laugh. 'I think I'm trying to process the trauma of Joe's little sister knowing about this stuff.'

All her agitation grew a little bit more, affronted at being regulated in his past to the role of 'Joe's little sister' and then again at him dropping her brother's name as though they'd really been friends. But she bit back a retort because otherwise they might be stuck there all night, arguing. 'Right, on three, I'm going to push. One, two—'

She attempted to straighten her legs and push the sofa bed flat. Springs and mechanisms creaked, Harry's leg brushed beneath the back of her knees as something gave way a little and he jiggled it free. She jolted at the contact and pushed harder as though she could push *him* away and this time something gave way a lot. There was a snap and the sofa collapsed, first the fold-out part, making her land with her bottom in the gap and their legs tangled. And then the back fell away too, so she flopped with it.

Silence filled the apartment.

'Crap.' Harry breathed out from somewhere underneath her legs. 'Are you all right, Kay?'

'Yep. You?'

'Uh-huh. So, you definitely didn't use magic to do that?'

She paused. She was pretty sure she hadn't, but she had suddenly been filled with a desperation to get away from the physical contact with him. Not that she was going to tell him that. 'Nope.'

'I guess you never miss leg day at the gym. That was impressive. Even if it's going to cost me more than my fee to come out here to replace the damn thing.'

'If you're expecting me to apologise . . .' she began, pulling her legs free of him and executing a messy parachute roll off the wreckage of the sofa bed.

'Of course not. You freed me. You're my hero. Thank you.' He sat up and sent her a lopsided grin, pulling his foot in towards him and inspecting the damage. It did look a bit red, but there was no other damage as far as Kay could see around the rubbing of his long, agile fingers. She swallowed and averted her eyes. What was she, some desperate Victorian man getting all excited at a glimpse of ankle?

'Well, better get that two hours of sleep now.'

'Yes. Sorry. Night.'

'Goodnight.'

She walked back to the doorway of the bedroom and made the mistake of glancing over her shoulder at him. He'd jumped up onto his feet now and was attempting to flatten a space in the broken parts of the sofa. He pulled back the covers and revealed that the cushions had been punctured by springs.

It was highly unlikely the sofa bed had broken all by itself. She probably was a little – or totally – responsible, and she couldn't help the way the thought pricked at her conscience.

The words dragged up from the very soles of her feet. 'You can't sleep there now, can you.' She cleared her throat and crossed her arms over her chest. 'Come on. You can share the bed.'

He looked up. 'No. It'll be fine—'

'Harry. Just get in the damn bed before I change my mind, OK?'

She turned on her heel, climbed into the bed and kept herself as far over on the mattress as she could without falling out, ignoring the way her heart was pounding.

She didn't want this. She didn't. But as annoying a human being and witch as he was, she also couldn't leave him to be turned into Swiss cheese by a piece of furniture her misfit magic had trashed. Especially when he was only sleeping there because he'd given up the bed to her.

The light in the living room went out and she took her glasses off, putting them on the bedside cabinet and squeezing her eyes shut, as she heard him move quietly into the room. The bed dipped and he slid in on the other side.

She bit her lip hard, willing herself not to be so aware of him. When she'd braved the bed earlier, she had been reassured that what he'd told her was true, he'd been the only one to sleep in the sheets since they'd been put on the bed. The faintest hint of his sweetly spicy aftershave lingering on the cotton. But now he was actually in the bed, she could smell his skin beneath the cinnamon scent, along with his toothpaste, and the linen-fresh fabric softener his clothes had been washed in. Then there was the actual length of his body too, settling next to her. His head on the pillow beside hers. His legs stretching down past hers in the bed. And his heat. The bed had turned cold while she was out of it and it made the warmth radiating off him all the more obvious.

'Thank you,' he said again quietly, and it was too intimate now that they were in bed together. 'Goodnight, Kay.'

She made a non-committal noise, because there was no way this was going to be a 'good night'.

Chapter Five

The village of Biddicote, Surrey, England

Biddicote was uncannily pretty. The 'uncanny' bit being down to the fact that the large population of witches living there used their various special gifts to help them maintain the old buildings and keep their gardens flourishing. Whether it was Mr Ashworth ensuring the local authority awarded Grade II listed status to the quaint shops in the market square, or Jaz's mum making sure every flower bloomed (for a small fee, naturally – witches had to make a living too), it all helped to keep the village picture-postcard perfect.

At that moment, though, Kay couldn't have cared less whether the thatched Tudor cottages leaned at the most aesthetically pleasing angle beside the country lanes, their window boxes full of bright flowers, petals glistening from being freshly watered. It barely registered that the pond on the green reflected the clear blue skies, broken only by the ripples of the ducks, swimming towards the pristinely painted white bench where a mother and child waited with the offer of birdseed. She had much better things to bother her head with.

The weather was of slightly more interest, since the late

June temperature had allowed her to pair the bright pink Converse high tops she'd received for Christmas with her favourite summer dress. It swung about her legs, just over the knee, and had a bodice which made the most of the chest she was secretly hoping would develop a little more over the next few months, or years at least.

Even that barely mattered, though, because she was going to meet Harry. Going on a *date* with Harry.

The two months since she'd last seen him had been the longest of her life, and not just because of how much she'd missed seeing him. So much had happened in that time, and even though they'd texted each other frequently, him offering her words of support and consolation in the face of her parents' sudden divorce, it hadn't been the same as speaking to him in person.

Once both their exams were over, she'd finally screwed up her courage and sent him the text she'd been drafting in her mind ever since Beltane.

Kay: Would you'd like to go out sometime? Just me and you? I've missed you. We don't have to tell Joe if you think he'll be weird about it. He's still not really talking to me anyway.

After her initial burst of bravery, doubt had crept in. He'd always answered her really quickly before, but as time crept on and a week had passed, she'd worried that she'd read his feelings all wrong. Then, finally, he'd replied.

Harry: I've missed you too. Meet me at the cave on Saturday? 7 p.m.?

He'd missed her too! And he wanted to meet up! It was the best thing to happen to her in months. A patch of bright blue in a relentlessly grey sky. Just like his eyes.

Her stomach flipped at the thought of going down to the cave again, her mind straying to the memory she'd replayed over and over again. His fingers playing with her hair. Him leaning in towards her. She was so sure he was going to kiss her last time, and now they were going on an official date, how much more likely was it to happen? She wondered how his mouth would feel on hers. It looked so soft. Harry Ashworth's lips were the kind of pretty it was worth thinking about.

Slipping down the alleyway behind the old post office, she walked until she came to the stile which broke up the hedgerow. She climbed over nimbly enough, but almost lost her glasses as she jumped down onto the path. She wasn't used to wearing them yet and was doing her best not to worry about what Harry would think of them. She'd sent him a photo of her modelling them and he'd said she looked 'very chic', but maybe he was just being nice?

No. He liked her. He wouldn't have said yes to going on a date if he didn't.

The path wasn't as clear as the one down from Ashworth Hall. It wasn't meant to be, but she still managed to find it, the concentration of magic like a distant hum in the background. She took a couple of wrong turns, but when she got there, she wasn't late. Harry hadn't arrived yet.

She took a seat on the fallen log before the cave in the clearing. The dirt was soft under the soles of her shoes and had smudged them with an unfortunate brown colour. She dusted them off with her hand for a moment, seeing if it could be rectified with manual efforts, and when that didn't work, she took a deep breath, reached down to her centre of energy and muttered the words of the cleaning spell she'd seen her mother use a million times to deal with stains.

She gave a little gasp as her shoes were suddenly spotless. It felt a little like going to write with a fountain pen and accidentally pressing too hard, so the ink came out in a splat. Something about discovering your affinity allowed you to focus the magic more effectively, but it took a while to get used to using that power. Or so everyone said, anyway. After all that time waiting and dreaming of the day her gift would emerge, Kay wasn't entirely sure she *wanted* to get used to using it.

Still, for the moment, it was definitely useful to be clean. As long as she didn't wander around and get them messy again, Harry's first sight of her today would be a put-together one. Not like that time she'd been trying out face-packs with Tina and come out of her bedroom, bumping straight into him, with skin the colour of Shrek's.

Twenty minutes later, her butt was starting to hurt from the bark of the log.

She checked to see if he'd sent her a message to say he was running late.

Nothing.

After forty minutes, she double-checked to see if she'd got her wires crossed about which Saturday they were meant to meet.

Nope. Definitely this one.

At ten to eight, she was beginning to feel chilly and her heart had slipped down to sit with her feet in her very clean shoes.

She got up and walked around the clearing a little. Just in case. He might have got the time wrong, so she'd give him until eight. Harry's dyslexia sometimes meant he got a little muddled about arrangements or didn't manage his time particularly well. So, she gave him until 8 p.m., and then an extra ten minutes after that in case he was running late . . .

And then she had to face up to the fact that he wasn't coming.

Why wasn't he coming?

Walking back up to the village from the valley was harder work, each step tiring, her shoes dragging through the dirt and dust, the skirt of her summer dress too flimsy to keep her thighs warm as the wind picked up and she constantly had to pull it down.

She could have sent him a message to see where he was, but at that moment, she wasn't sure whether she wanted to know the answer. There was a chance he'd innocently forgotten, but there was also the possibility that he'd changed his mind.

As she went past the pub on the green, a cheer went up inside, drawing her attention through the leaded window. And there he was. Smiling. Punching the air in victory and hugging the other teens from the sixth form who were old enough to drink now.

He was watching some kind of match with them all. He wasn't even into sport, was he?

Either he'd completely forgotten about their date or he never intended to come and meet her *at all*.

Tears burned at the back of Kay's eyes and in her throat, but she wasn't going to cry. Especially not now, because somehow he must have felt her watching him and he was looking back through the window, straight at her, his arms hanging slack at his sides, his wide mouth downturned at the corners as some pretty girl from his class wrapped herself around him and planted a kiss on his perfectly freckly cheek.

He *had* known. He hadn't innocently forgotten, otherwise he'd be hurrying out now to apologise to her. Instead of staring at her with that grim expression.

He'd stood her up and been caught out.

She crossed her arms over her chest and glared back at him. It didn't take long for her humiliation to succumb to anger. She was about to storm in there and confront him about it, when suddenly, like tearing a wax strip off a shin bone, he turned and disappeared deeper into the pub.

Kay waited. Again. She couldn't help herself. Maybe he was going to come out and talk to her?. Like the decent person she'd thought he was.

Instead, her brother appeared. His face in that scowl he almost constantly had when he looked at her these days.

She turned away. She didn't need to deal with *that* on top of this.

'Hey, Kay. Wait.' Joe's voice was rough, like he was having to drag it out of himself to speak to her.

'What?' She stopped and looked back at him, arms still tight across her chest, fingers digging into the bare flesh of her goose-bumped upper arms.

'Harry asked me to give you this.' He stepped forward a couple of paces, coming down the smooth stone steps of the pub and waiting by the big tub full of roses, but moving no further, so she had to go over to him. In his hand, he had a folded napkin.

'When?' she croaked, reaching out and plucking it from Joe's fingers.

'"When" what?' Joe sighed and looked up at the sign for the pub rather than maintaining eye contact with her.

'When did he give *you* this, to give to *me*?' Perhaps this was a note to tell her he wanted to move their date, and Joe had just forgotten to give it to her. Or withheld it on purpose, just to hurt her the way he kept telling her she'd hurt the entire family when her gift came in.

'Just now,' Joe said, like she was an idiot. 'I'm going back in.'

It hadn't sounded like a lie and she had to face facts; if Harry had wanted to change the date or time of them meeting up, surely he would have texted her like a normal person?

Joe paused in the doorway. Sighed again and tromped back down the steps. 'Are you going to be OK?'

Kay bit her lip. 'Why wouldn't I be?'

'I don't know. It's not like I *wanted* to think about you having a crush on Harry, y'know, but I'm not blind.'

Kay's cheeks flushed. Had she been so obvious?

Joe shook his head. 'Look, why don't you come to Dad's with me later? Get away from the house?'

She took a deep breath, attempting to exchange one pain for another. 'Did he ask you to convince me to come?'

'No.'

'Then no. I don't want to see him, anyway.'

'Urgh, you're so stubborn, Kay. Suit yourself. I'll be back Monday.' And with that, he disappeared back inside the pub.

She looked down at the napkin. It had her name printed on it in beautiful black script, complete with curlicues. A twinge went through her chest – she could see the pen within Harry's agile fingers, the concentration on his face. He'd told her how his father had made him practise for hours every day in the lead-up to his GCSEs to improve his handwriting. It had paid off, she supposed.

She ran the rest of the way home. Went straight up the stairs of their small cottage, into her bedroom and threw herself down on the bed. Tears were already swimming in her eyes when she opened the napkin and read it:

Kay

I'm sorry I agreed to meet up with you when I knew I couldn't go through with it. I hope you make things up with Joe. He's being an idiot but he's hurting too. Good luck with your exam results. Sure you'll ace them.
Harry

The rush of pain she felt was so fast it burned up and blazed into anger instead. He'd drawn a smiley face underneath his name.

A. Smiley. Face.

On a napkin.

What the actual hell?

He hadn't even put any effort into it. She knew what a talented artist he was and yet he'd signed off with the kind of quick scribble a five-year-old could manage.

As she stared at it, mouth open, eyes blurry with tears, her breathing came faster. A bubble of hatred and pain grew and grew, like a balloon stretched thin, ready to burst. He was an awful person. Selfish and arrogant and stupid—

She gasped and dropped the napkin.

Harry had infused that smiley face with magic. That tiny image. Brimming with power to . . . make her hate him? She never would have thought he was stupid. Even if he didn't want to go out with her. Why would he do this to her? Influencing her – against the tenets – crossing a line even witches who were strangers didn't cross with each other. He might not want them to date, but she'd thought they were at least friends. You didn't treat friends like this, it was so . . . *violating.*

Why? Why would he do this?

87

Was it just so she would leave him alone? Had she been pestering him? It had been obvious to her friends, obvious to Joe, that she was infatuated with him. Had she been making things up in her head about how much they got along when really he was just wishing she'd stop trailing after him with goo-goo eyes?

Acid rose at the back of her throat.

And he must have known she would be able to tell he was trying to influence her. Even if that horrible little smiley face didn't work for longer than a couple of minutes, the point was made. He didn't want her to like him. He didn't want her anywhere near him.

She picked up the napkin again, a tear dropping on the bottom. It was such crude magic, clearly he hadn't had time to finesse it as he'd scribbled her a note in the pub, but it was still clever enough to tug at her natural response to feel hurt and pissed off at him.

She shoved it in the back of her diary and dumped it in the drawer of her bedside cabinet. Then she flopped onto the bed again, burying her head in her arms, forgetting about her new glasses and succeeding in bashing the bridge of her nose with them. Which was just too fitting really.

Why? Why had her affinity only shown itself just after Beltane? Having the ability to see the genuine feelings between people was no use to anyone – especially when it came after Harry had stopped visiting because he needed to concentrate on his exams. If it had happened just a week earlier, at least she would have known never to bother asking him out. The *one* thing it could have been useful for. She would have been disappointed, yes. But not embarrassed and rejected. Instead, she'd ended up with divorcing parents and utter humiliation.

There was a knock on her door and her mother's soft footsteps came towards her. Tallulah rarely came out of her own room since Kay's dad moved out. The intensity of Kay and Joe's anger at each other was too much for her on top of her broken heart.

Another thing for Kay to feel guilty about.

As if it wasn't enough that her ignorance about her own gift, her silly excitement, had meant she'd asked question after awkward, stupid question about the bonds she could see linking them all, until it became obvious that her dad no longer – if ever – loved their mum. She'd been so shocked, she hadn't even been able to hide the discovery. Joe was right, Kay had hurt them all.

'My darling girl,' Tallulah took her by the shoulders and folded Kay into her arms. 'What happened?'

'Ha-Harry,' was all Kay managed to splutter.

'Oh, sweetheart.' Her mum's arms tightened, her cheek resting upon her head, and Kay felt tears soaking into her head. 'Don't you worry, we'll get through this together. It's a privilege and a curse that being empaths make us feel this deeply. And so often for the wrong people. But we'll survive,' her mother managed to say between her own sobs.

The last piece of Kay's heart, battered from the collapse of her parents' marriage and the distance of her brother and her father, broke away. A Harry-shaped hole, that had once been filled with hope and the giddy high of a teenage crush and friendship, was now empty of anything but hatred for him and bitterness towards her own special brand of self-destructive magic.

If she never saw Harry Ashworth again, it would be too soon.

Chapter Six

New Town, Prague

818 miles and 35(+1) hours and 45 minutes until the wedding

The next time Kay blearily blinked her eyes open, it was to the sound of faint beeping and whistling wind. It had picked up in the night and every time there was a gust, it was joined by a splattering of rain against the windows. Not the kind of morning when you wanted to get out of bed. Especially when you'd had a stressful day, a late, interrupted night, and the bed was this toasty. She couldn't remember the last time she had felt so lethargic and snuggly in the morning.

She sneaked an arm out from underneath the covers to turn off her alarm, fumbling on the unfamiliar bedside table. It was still dark – which made sense since it was only 3.15 a.m. according to her phone – but it was a lesser darkness than before . . . When she'd had to rescue Harry from the sofa.

Suddenly, her eyes were a lot wider as the full reality of where she was, and with whom, came rushing back to her.

She dropped her phone back on the table and froze.

There was a very good reason she was so warm. Harry was lying right behind her, his body nearly flush with hers, the big spoon to her little spoon, so close she could tell each time he took a breath, the loose folds at the bottom of his T-shirt brushing against her waist, his hand resting on her hip. His soft exhales tickling the back of her neck.

Goosebumps spread from the top of her spine to her bruised coccyx.

She was still facing away from him, but she'd relaxed back from the edge in the night, curling into a foetal position, basically sticking her bum on his side of the bed. She wanted to turn to see whether his head was on her pillow or on his own but didn't dare move in case she woke him and he realised what had happened.

Or did he already know?

No. The quiet, evenness of his breathing was not fake. He was definitely still asleep and if he'd been taking advantage while she was sleeping to get close, surely he would have got a lot closer. The only two points at which they were fully touching were his hand, curled on her hip, and one of his knees kissing the back of her calf.

Don't think about kissing.

But she couldn't help it. Her teenage crush was spooning her. She'd spent so many nights imagining this. Daydreaming scenarios where they'd been watching a film in her room and both fallen asleep on her bed and she'd woken up in his arms, her head on his chest or face to face, so they blinked awake staring at each other and then moved those extra inches in the secret space of night-time, and let their lips touch.

A flush crawled from her cheeks to her chest. Embarrassment and desire.

But it was old desire. She didn't want this *now*. It was just going to make everything worse. Even more awkward than it already was.

Still. She couldn't seem to move. And just for a moment – with the tiredness tugging at her and the warmth of the bed holding her tight, the thrilling heat of Harry's palm burning her through the shorts of her pyjamas, his fingers relaxed but the tips of them pressing into her, like he was capturing her shape – she wanted to absorb it. For teenage Kay. The innocent, daydreamy Kay who had long since been pushed aside following the reality call of how people used each other.

For just a minute, she could allow herself to imagine how it might have been different, if Harry had actually been who she thought he was, and happily ever afters did come true—

Harry shifted behind her, he took a deeper breath and – before he woke up – she launched herself out of the bed, landing in a heap on the floor with a thump.

'What was that?' Harry sat up in the bed, scrubbing at his face. 'Kay?'

'I . . . er . . . I fell out of bed.' She grabbed for her glasses and pulled herself to her feet, jamming them onto her face and then straightening her clothes.

'Ouch. Are you all right? No damage done?'

No damage? Good question. How much had daydreaming damaged that barricade she'd raised against him?

He bent his knees beneath the covers and hooked his arms around them, squinting at her. God, his sleepy face was adorable. There was a crease in his cheek from the pillow, his mouth even more pouty and soft, bronze hair flopped forward over his brow with wisps and kinks. He looked more like his teenage self.

But he *wasn't*. It had been a silly indulgence and she hadn't even been able to steal a minute of the fantasy before it had been torn away and she'd ended up bruised.

Literally, according to the way her right knee was throbbing. She was adding to the collection.

'Kay?'

'No permanent damage. Just a strange bed.'

'In more ways than one, hey?' He chuckled, giving her a lopsided smile. 'Amazing. I managed to spend a night here by myself unharmed and in less than twenty-four hours we've had two bed-related accidents. What time is it?'

'Time to get up.' She picked up her phone, eager for a reason to look anywhere other than at Harry, and saw a message had come through from her brother in the night. 'We've got forty-five minutes until the Uber gets here. I'm going to jump in the shower.'

'I'll make some coffee.'

Kay grunted and grabbed her suitcase, virtually able to bounce it into the bathroom now it was so light. The sooner they got to the airport and went their separate ways, the better. Neither of them had volunteered their plans for when they landed in Paris, so she was working on an unspoken, mutual agreement that once they boarded their flight, this unwelcome interlude would be over.

The airport was still busy when they got there and queued up to check in their luggage. They'd barely spoken since the morning, swapping between bathroom and kitchen to get ready. He'd made her some toast, which she'd politely thanked him for because she was ravenous, having never gotten around to eating the night before for all the various irritating reasons (like salesmen interrupting her and cutting her own nose off to spite her face), and then they'd grabbed their bags and headed out to ride to the airport in the Uber.

The rain was coming down so heavily you could hardly see out through the windows, and it left a foreboding feeling in the pit of Kay's stomach. Harry was frowning at the lack of a view too and rubbing his thumb over the callus on his left middle finger repeatedly.

As they neared the check-in desk, she chewed her lip and turned to him. 'Look, can I give you some money for the apartment and the sofa and everything?'

He lifted his eyebrow at her. 'You don't need to do that.'

'I kind of do. I don't feel right letting you pay for it all.'

'Look, whether you were with me or not, it will either be expensed or paid off by my insurance, if I'm lucky.'

She would have retorted that influencers always seemed to be "lucky". Except, of course, he hadn't been particularly lucky in the last twenty-four hours at least. 'I'm not sure expenses or your travel insurance will cover the sofa bed.'

'Well, that wasn't your fault.'

Kay chewed her lip as they moved forward a step in the queue. She was pretty sure it was and even though there was no way she was going to admit that to him, she felt guilty. Especially because he was being so generous about it. She supposed it was easy to be generous about financial things when you were loaded.

She hated the idea that they'd come away from this with him thinking he'd done some kind of good deed for her, the charity case. She hadn't *needed* him last night. She could have *made* herself figure it out – instead of putting herself in a position where she now knew what it felt like to have him sleeping next to her. That kind of knowledge was detrimental to her sanity – she could feel it even now, her skin along her back and neck and hip all tight and hot like she had sunburn.

'I can afford it, you know,' she said shortly.

He blinked at her. 'I never said you couldn't.'

'So why won't you let me pay for it?'

94

'I don't even know that *I'll* have to pay for it yet.' He said it so dismissively, squinting up at the announcement boards, as though he had bigger things on his mind than contemplating his security deposit.

And then it clicked. Why *would* he be worried about it? 'Oh. I see. Stupid me. Of course.'

He frowned and looked back at her; his mouth pinched at the corners. 'What?'

'You're going to *persuade* them not to, aren't you?'

His eyes widened. 'No. That wouldn't be fair. And besides – my skills at persuasion don't work that way. You know how it . . .' he lowered his voice, 'manifests. What did you think I was planning to do? Draw them a diagram of what happened to make them feel guilty or something, so they didn't charge me? You don't think that would come across as a bit odd?'

She shrugged. 'Actually, I figured you'd just ask Daddy to speak to them and, poof, they'd let it go.'

Harry looked like he'd stopped breathing for a moment, his eyes burning into hers again, like he was trying to recognise her. 'You've got no idea,' he finally said in such a low voice, it was almost to himself.

The denial, to her face, was too much to take. He was still acting like he'd done nothing wrong. Like he hadn't used her brother, with his gift to disseminate information easily, to help Harry pass his A levels and then dropped him as soon as he no longer needed him. Like he hadn't led her on throughout that whole year of studying, of coming over to her house, and then influenced her when she became a nuisance and it was time for him to move on.

'I'm pretty sure I do, actually,' she said, tightly and when the person in front of them moved forward this time, she

95

let Harry step forward by himself. He glanced back at her over his shoulder, but she turned her face away.

They moved up to the check-in desk in silence and even though he waited for her after he'd put his bag up, when she was done, she walked straight past him, throwing a brief 'thanks for last night' at him before she hightailed it to the women's bathroom.

When enough time had passed that he should have given up and/or she'd given someone else the impression she had food poisoning, she sought out the pokiest-looking corner in the departure lounge and replied to her brother's message, asking what was happening with her delay. Their mum had obviously contacted him last night and mentioned it.

Kay: Sorry for not answering last night, but I'm about to board a flight now.

She knew Joe had a habit of getting up early – as a primary school teacher, his day in the classroom usually started at eight o'clock at least – but she wasn't expecting him to call straight back as soon as he read the message, after being up late last night.

'Hey. Is everything running on time again your end, then? Because the weather is terrible here.' He muffled a yawn, and she heard the sound of a kettle on in the background.

'As far as I can tell. It's stormy, but there are no delays,' she tried to reassure him. 'My flight is landing in Paris, and I'll catch the Eurostar from there. Plenty of time before the wedding rehearsal.'

'Great. Have you let Mum know?'

'Yeah. I did last night.'

'Right. Well. I guess it's seeing the weather here that has her freaking out then. She's been over to Aunty L's, and she's really worried about you getting stranded.'

Translation: Mum had been on the phone to him last night and given him an earful and he now wanted to make sure that Kay was keeping on top of managing their mother's anxiety. It was like an unwritten rule between them once they had made up after the divorce. It wasn't that Joe wouldn't be there for their mum if he needed to be, but he'd left for university and spent more time with their dad than Kay did, so she'd happened to be the one there. She was the default moral support, and how could she mind? She'd made her bed and she would lie in it.

'Look, don't you worry about it, OK? I'll keep her updated and let her know if anything changes. You just concentrate on the wedding, and I'll see you later.'

'Yeah, all right. Did you have to sleep at the airport last night?'

'Oh, no. I found somewhere. No issues.' Thankfully they weren't doing a video call because the memory of sharing a bed with Harry was making her face heat up like she'd fallen asleep on a sun lounger located on the equator.

'You sure? You sound weird.'

She forced a laugh. 'Just didn't get a lot of sleep.'

'I know that feeling.'

She almost asked if he was nervous but restrained herself. She didn't want to imply he was getting cold feet about marrying Sandy. He might think that she'd been using her gift to check out the bond between him and his fiancée and get paranoid that he actually had a *reason* to be nervous. There was no reason to think that her brother and Sandy weren't completely in love with each other. They acted that way.

And even if sometimes people did act like they felt one way when truly they didn't – it wasn't her business. It was an invasion of their privacy. In fact, even *with* people's consent, she wouldn't do it. Tina had badgered her for weeks the summer after she got her gift, desperate to know if the constant sniping between her and Joe was actually sexual frustration and . . . it turned out it wasn't. Joe really just didn't like Tina much. Needless to say, Tina was not best pleased hearing that, even when Kay had tried to sugar-coat it. She'd accused Kay of not wanting her friend and brother to get together because she'd fallen out with him and was bitter from what had happened with Harry. And that was the end of that friendship.

No, best to keep out of it entirely.

'Just a couple more days and then you'll be on your honeymoon, recovering from all the wedding hoopla. Plenty of lazy mornings in bed.'

Joe snorted. 'I don't intend to *sleep* during those lazy mornings in bed, though.'

'Ugh, Joe. Keep those kinds of comments to yourself please.'

He laughed and though she was smiling as they said goodbye, there was a strange feeling in her diaphragm, like her magic was trying to push up against her breastbone. Probably just heartburn from too much coffee.

She opened her tote bag to slip her phone back inside and found herself staring at her lumpy corn husk doll. With its scorch mark right across the chest.

Chapter Seven

German airspace

744 miles and 32(+1) hours and 40 minutes until the wedding

Kay was debating doing a cleansing ritual when they landed. She assumed if she'd been cursed, Madam Hedvika would have picked up on it, but all this bad luck was beginning to feel very hex-like.

Somehow, she'd been seated on the plane behind Dean and his sales team buddies. She'd slunk into her seat, crouching low and being as quiet as possible so he didn't hear her voice. But she'd also scored the chattiest couple of row-mates on the entire plane.

They *both* wanted to talk to her. One about her hair, the other about the weather *and* the flight *and* his hotel. It wasn't until twenty minutes after take-off that she'd realised they were actually married – but they'd allowed her to be seated in the middle of them, even though she offered to move to the aisle or the window. She might have been able to cope with that but then, once the seatbelt light turned off, Dean stood up and spotted her.

'Kay! You made it,' he said with a smirk, leaning on the headrest of the chairs in front.

'Uh-huh.' She forced a smile back, wishing her seat-mates

would interrupt *now*. Instead, the woman on her right was looking between them with a big smile.

'Where's your friend?' Dean asked.

Kay blinked and it took her a moment to realise he was asking about Harry. 'Oh. I don't know.' She shrugged, and when his grin grew, she could have kicked herself. Maybe she should have made more of her connection to Harry again, but without the prospect of being stuck in the airport with Dean, she was marginally less worried about him pestering her. Then the wife of the estranged couple piped up.

'Why don't I swap seats with you, young man? So you two can talk more easily?'

Kay wanted to zap her with static the way Ilina had done at the auditorium yesterday but clamped straight down on that thought. Unpredictable surges of electrical power were a massive no-no when you were thousands of feet up in the air.

'Oh, that would be great, thank you. I'm just going to use the facilities and then we can catch up properly.' He sent Kay a wink and she stifled a groan.

What had she done to this woman? Couldn't she read the desperation to escape an unwanted male on a fellow woman's face? Or maybe it was just a ploy to get even further away from her own husband, who was now examining the centrefold in his fishing magazine like it was a page-three model.

Dean disappeared down the aisle after pausing to tell his buddy what was happening, even though all he got was a grunt from the man, who seemed to be quietly dying in a haze of alcohol fumes with his earphones wedged in. The woman moved seats as soon as he was gone, making no comment to her salmon-ogling husband, but giving Kay another wink as she left her aisle seat open for Dean.

Was there enough time for Kay to pretend to fall asleep? She leaned out to spy on whether there was a queue for the bathrooms and saw Dean did have a couple of people to wait behind.

She also spotted a familiar indigo blue sleeve a couple of rows ahead of her, near where Dean was standing, and she was about to duck her head back in, when Harry got up to stand behind Dean.

What the ever-loving grimoire was going on now? Were they *chatting*?

It was hard to tell as Dean wasn't as tall as Harry, so she couldn't see as much of him. But then Harry bent his head to pull something out of one of his coat pockets and both men glanced her way. She was too seized up by suspicion to even bother pretending she wasn't watching them. Was Harry telling embarrassing stories about the braces she wore as a teenager? The time she'd tried to shave her legs and ended up looking like a scene from *Carrie*? The Shrek face-pack incident?

Except that would put Dean off. If Harry really wanted revenge after them parting ways so frostily, he'd be telling him that Kay had confessed she fancied Dean or something. Encouraging him with his pursuit.

It was a sketchbook and a pen. *No*. What was he up to? Harry leaned on his knee, sketching something quickly, and then tore it out of his book and handed it to Dean, who stared at it for a moment, before looking like he was going to be sick and tucking it in his back pocket.

The bare-faced cheek of that man, to tell her that he couldn't use his ability to influence through art to get out of the sofa bed debt, when she'd just witnessed him doing something *right there*. To a stranger. In the middle of a busy plane. As though it was perfectly ordinary to draw people pictures while you were waiting in the queue to use the bathroom.

She sat back, drumming her fingers on the armrest, waiting for Dean to return so she could find out what Harry had done to him. But instead of talking to Kay, or even acknowledging her at all, he went back to his row and addressed the woman who'd already swapped seats.

'I'm sorry, but could I have my seat back? I'm actually really tired. Heavy night. Going to have a nap.'

'Oh, well, you can nap there and chat with your young lady friend when you wake up,' the matchmaker-from-hell said.

'No,' Dean replied firmly. 'No.' He glanced over at Kay, and she was sure she actually saw him give a shiver of revulsion. '*No*. That won't be necessary at all.'

'But—'

'Look, I don't want to have to speak to a member of the crew about this, so if you wouldn't mind.' Finally, his polite facade slipped under the obvious horror of contemplating sitting beside Kay.

What the hell had Harry done?

'Well I never,' the woman muttered and heaved herself back up.

Kay jumped to her feet too and Dean leapt out of her way like she was brandishing a freshly filled nappy. Had Harry convinced him she had the plague or something?

She barely noticed the woman shuffling her way back into her seat as her eyes narrowed on Harry, who was just emerging from the toilet. Hurrying down the aisle, she caught him by the lapel of his coat and pushed him back inside the tiny cubicle, locking the door behind them.

'*What* did you do to him?' she hissed. She'd wanted privacy, but she hadn't thought about it being quite such close quarters, as she squeezed into the slender gap between the toilet and the door, blocking his exit.

'I'm sorry?'

'You know what I'm talking about.' She crossed her arms momentarily, before she caught hold of the edge of the sink as the plane dipped in a pocket of turbulence.

Harry swayed towards her, then regained his balance, his lips twisting to the side before he sighed. 'Look, I was just trying to make sure he wouldn't bother you again.'

'I *knew* you'd done something. How dare you? What if I need him to bother me? For work.'

'Then . . . I have severely misunderstood what your job is.'

'Ha ha. I just mean if I need to collaborate with his company or something.'

'Oh, well.' He licked his lip and his eyes darted around the tiny room. 'I'm sure you'll all be able to be professional about it. He'll be able to rise above the . . . feelings. Hopefully. And it'll wear off eventually anyway.'

'Rise. Above. What?' Her words came out like a shower of hail.

'A sort of feeling of, erm . . .'

'*Of . . .?*' Her nails dug into her palms as she glared at him.

He swallowed. 'Repulsion?'

'Repulsion. Towards me?'

He nodded.

'Oh my God, Harry.' She shook her head.

'I was trying to do you a favour.'

'That's not a *favour*. I don't need you swooping in, pretending to rescue me and coercing people. I'm not a damsel in distress, and even if I was, I wouldn't ask for *you* of all people to help me like *that*. Do you understand me?'

Another big dip of turbulence sent him across the cubicle towards her. He caught himself with a hand on the wall and one on the door, over her shoulders. He stayed there for a moment, staring down at her. She took a deep breath, his body so close, the smell of his spicy aftershave curling out towards her, fogging up her mind. His mouth virtually at eye level. Her heart rate accelerating.

'Loud and clear,' he said stonily.

She watched the shape of his mouth from mere inches away. Replayed it a couple of times in her mind before she realised what he'd actually said.

'Wh-what?' For a moment, she thought he was referring to her heart rate kicking up – loud and clear – because of his proximity.

'I understand you. Loud and clear. Last person on earth you'd ask for help. Me and my dirty, immoral magic, persuading someone to stop pestering a woman. Got it.'

'There are other ways, Harry.' She grit her teeth. 'It's high-handed and arrogant and unnecessary.'

'Well, that obviously comes naturally to me.' He pushed himself away and she missed it. It was like leaving the warmth of the house to step outside into a snowstorm and she hated herself for the yearning to have it back.

Hated him for making her feel that way.

'Of course it does. You're an influencer.'

'Ugh.' He drove a hand back into his hair and gripped it hard. 'I know I made a mistake before and I'm sorry about that, I am. But you're so prejudiced now. And such a hypocrite. You influence people constantly.'

Kay's mouth worked as she tried to think past the possibility he was referencing when he'd influenced her with the smiley face and that he was apologising for it. In an offhand, middle-of-a-different-conversation kind of way.

He'd followed it with a 'but' though. Even if it was an apology for the smiley face, it was a poor one. And what was he going on about; *her* influencing people?

'I beg your pardon. You know that's not my gift. You're talking rubbish.'

'It's not your main gift, but the influencer and empath magic has blended in you. Just your presence makes people more aware of their feelings for others.' He untangled his hand from his hair, leaving it standing up on end, and gestured as wildly as he could manage between them in the small space.

'What? No. No, it doesn't.'

He narrowed his eyes at her. 'You're kidding, right? Are you trying to tell me you never knew that?'

Instead of her cheeks flushing, for a nice change she could feel the blood draining from her face. 'Witches don't have more than one gift, you're talking rot.'

'That's what they used to tell us. They've done research on it now. Magical affinities are often multiple, across different designations. There's usually one dominant one but . . . You seriously haven't heard about that?'

No. She wouldn't have heard about it because she rarely talked about magic with her family. Rarely spent time with other witches apart from family visits and never consulted the witching news these days.

And as for her having an effect on everyone around her, making their feelings more obvious to them . . .

'How would you even know that?' she challenged. 'About me having another gift to make people more aware of their feelings?'

'I'm a person, in your vicinity, Kay. It's pretty obvious.' A touch of pink highlighted his sharp cheekbones and he shook his head vigorously like he could shake away whatever emotion it was she was making him more aware of. Probably how irritated he was with her, since he'd definitely been snappier today. That smarted. She was literally bringing out the worst in him. 'Why do you think people are always reacting so extremely towards you? Like Dean—'

'Oh, I see.' She poked him in the chest, pushing him over to the other side of the tiny toilet, so his back was bowed on the curved wall, inadvertently bringing his head down close to hers. 'This is just some way of blaming me for him pestering me, right? I've influenced him to not take a hint, is that it? I encouraged him subconsciously with my magic. The witches' equivalent of "what was she wearing?"'

'No! Of course not.' His exclamation made her glasses fog up for a second and she felt his weight against her finger press, then lighten as he shifted on his feet. 'How he behaves is still his choice. Why do you think I stepped in? He was out of order.'

'So your solution was to make him find me repellent? Is that your only solution to deal with someone's unwanted interest, make them hate the object of their affection?'

Harry swallowed, his gaze flickering down to look at her poking finger, but she didn't even pause. Just the idea that he thought it was fair to treat a teenage girl with a crush on a boy who'd acted like her friend for the best part of a year, in the same way as a grown man who wouldn't leave a very obviously reluctant woman alone was making her heartbeat pound in her ears.

'If I wanted a man I wasn't interested in to act like a dick towards me, I could have just told him to leave me alone. I was trying to be tactful. What you did was unnecessary and reckless. He looked like he was ready to

106

run screaming from me. That's dangerous. What if he gets completely paranoid and accuses me of something? Or panics and thinks he needs to defend himself from me—'

'All right. Yes. You're right. It was messy, clumsy magic. The best I could come up with in the moment but he'd . . .' he shook his head.

'He'd what?' She dropped her hand but didn't bother to move any further back.

'He asked me about us when I spoke to him. And said things. About you.'

'What things?'

'I don't want to repeat them.'

'Well, that's convenient.'

He finally looked at her again. 'Do you really think I'd lie about that?'

She didn't. That was the annoying thing. The thing that made her want to slap herself. Why couldn't her hormones get the message? She couldn't even accuse him of influencing her – at least not now – unless she counted the way the consuming blue of his eyes could still seem to reach down inside her and stir everything up into a flurry. She felt utterly empty and full of unbearable pressure at the same time.

The plane jolted up again and she fell forward, erasing the last tiny gap between them. The heat of him soaked through his shirt, the firmness of his chest sending waves of weakness through her body. Her stomach was careening all over the place and it was only partly to do with the turbulence.

She scrabbled back, trying to stand upright again, and he put a hand on her waist to steady her. She wanted him to tighten his grip. To pull her closer again. So she tried to take another step back, bashing her hip onto the sink.

Focus. She needed to focus. 'Whatever your excuses, you need to undo it.'

He tucked the hand he'd put on her waist into his pocket so violently, she swore she could hear the stitches tearing. 'I'll try.'

'Try *really* hard.'

'I *will*.'

She nodded. There. That was the end of the conversation. She turned towards the door to unlock it and jumped back as someone started banging on it from the other side.

'Sir? Madam? The seat-belt light is about to come on. You need to return to your seats.'

Kay's face immediately erupted into flame as she realised the flight attendant had seen them coming in there together. And was probably drawing their own conclusions. 'Oh my God,' she choked out.

Harry actually laughed behind her. 'Saying things like that won't help if you're worried about what they're assuming.'

'If you come out of there now, I won't report you, OK?' the voice offered.

Kay ripped the door open and flew out to see the flight attendant watching with an unamused expression. 'It's not what you think—'

'Honey, I've been doing this job for ten years, OK? The truth is, I'm really not bothered, but I do need you to return to your seats for safety reasons.'

Kay nodded and did a brisk walk of shame back to her seat, clutching the headrests as the plane dropped more frequently into pockets of turbulence. Far more than she'd ever experienced on other flights.

She ignored the disgusted look on Dean's face as she moved past his row. The wife had actually taken the seat in the middle now and was holding her husband's hand as he flinched every time the plane juddered. So maybe they weren't so estranged after all. Just in need of a little breather.

Or maybe when she'd been there sitting with them, she'd exacerbated all their niggling irritations with each other?

No. What Harry said couldn't be true. Witches didn't have more than one affinity. Did they? She supposed he could hardly make it up if it was widely known about in the witching community.

Kay buckled up, contemplating the fact that they were starting to hit the bad weather and they hadn't even been up in the air forty-five minutes. How much worse was it going to get? Infuriating as Harry Ashworth was, there were bigger things to worry about.

Like whether they would make it to Paris at all.

Chapter Eight

Kay wasn't sure there was anything more demoralising than watching a baggage carousel slowly empty of luggage, while all she had was her tote bag from the plane.

Except maybe watching a baggage carousel empty in an airport she wasn't meant to land in at all.

After another twenty minutes of tense compulsory seat-belt time, the plane bumping and dipping to increasingly worried noises from the passengers, the captain had announced they needed to land. It took another thirty minutes of turbulent flying before they'd touched down in Dusseldorf, wind and rain buffeting the plane. Then they'd had to wait on the tarmac for twenty minutes before they could even get off the plane. It was no wonder there had been a mishap with the luggage in all the changes.

Admittedly, she'd recognised several people from her flight who had *their* suitcases, but by this point she was kind of expecting a calamity with her name on it around every corner. And after almost an hour of genuinely being worried the plane wouldn't make it to safe ground, she was still too overcome with relief to worry about it. Now she needed to decide whether to try to deal with the lost-luggage situation, or the being-stranded-in-another-European-country situation, first.

Luggage initially, she determined, since there was probably a time limit on reporting it missing. She needed to deal with something. *Feel* like she could deal with something. Plus, the queues of confused and stressed travellers might have gone down a little by the time she was done. It was yesterday evening all over again. Except, this time, at least she wasn't going to bump into Dean. He'd be running screaming from her, because she highly doubted that Harry had managed to track the salesman down in the airport and reverse the effect of the sketch he'd done. However that worked.

Did he need to destroy it? He'd said it could fade naturally, but how long would that take? Did it depend on how susceptible the person he'd tried to influence was? How much they were willing to embrace the suggestion?

In the bar yesterday, she'd disagreed with Harry about influencer magic being like hypnosis, but she did know that suggestibility played its part. Her father mostly motivated people to do what they already wanted to do – whether that was in their best interests or not was still up for debate. Joe helped people understand things easily and it worked best with the children he taught because they wanted to learn. It always worked best with a willing audience.

She had been a willing audience. That smiley face couldn't have been that powerful. It had been tiny, dashed off quickly by an adolescent witch, it could barely have contained any magic. And yet it had impacted her like a wrecking ball through all her feelings for him. She'd been mad at him on the plane for treating her in the same way as Dean, but had she been as ready to hate Harry as Dean was to be so disgusted by her, just because she didn't want to have sex with him? Deep down, was her reaction to being rejected that petty?

If Harry hadn't gone about everything in such a thoughtless way, if he'd broken it to her gently, rather than letting her hope, would part of her still have hated him? It seemed unlikely, because she'd adored him. But she'd been angry at the time. Angry at her family, angry at the world, like a typical teenager.

And she'd been acting that way ever since Harry had shown up by the astronomical clock in Prague. Like he'd dialled back time and she was letting all her good, adult sense be blown apart by beguiling smiles, twinkly eyes, floofy hair and hurt feelings. She had a hierarchy of problems and he should be somewhere down the bottom. The top spot was currently taken by lost luggage.

Kay marched through the airport, heading for the baggage-claim information desk. Luckily, on all the blue signs around the airport, there was a handy translation into English, so she found it without too much hassle and got in line.

She considered texting her mum to update her, but until she knew what she was doing, there didn't seem much point. Were there going to be any flights at all taking off? The weather had been pretty atrocious out there. She flicked through reports on her phone as she waited and the endless warnings of red, red, amber, red, snow, high winds, fire, flood, the apocalypse, made her chest tight in a way that was very different to the pressure feeling she'd noticed at the airport in Prague – but no less concerning when it came to her magic. She was beginning to feel like a hand grenade with the pin pulled out.

Popping in her earphones, she put on some music and did her best to chill out until she got to the desk. The customer service person assisted her with filling out a form with the details of her missing bag and Kay reminded herself to be grateful she'd lost it on the way home rather than on the way out there.

Heading back into the main terminal and taking a look at the departures board made her forget the gratitude. Nothing was currently taking off from Dusseldorf. It looked like their plane had made it in by the skin of its teeth.

'Crap, crap, crap, crap,' she muttered to herself. What should she do? Queue up to speak to someone about when the next flights might be leaving? Start researching alternative means to get home? She chewed on her thumbnail and looked around her. The prospect of hanging around for hours in the crowded airport with a bunch of highly stressed people was not appealing – and when it came to her magic misfiring, it was downright worrying. For a moment, she even kind of wished she'd bump into Harry again, just for a familiar face. Regardless of the bad blood between them, he had been helping her – often in an annoying, high-handed kind of way, but the intention was there. It wouldn't be awful to feel like she had someone on her side.

But he wasn't the only person around here that she knew. Ilina lived in Germany. Maybe she'd be able to give her some advice about travelling?

Kay headed out of the main crowd towards the eateries and found her friend's number in the recent calls list.

'Hallo, Kay,' Ilina answered, her voice croaky with sleep. 'I know I said keep me up to date, but it is extremely early in the morning on a Saturday, so I am sure this is vitally important.'

'Well, I'm not back in London. I'm in Dusseldorf.'

'Ah. What happened?'

'Diversion because of the weather. And I have no clue if I can get any further. I was wondering if you could give me some advice? Tell me what the German news is saying? The queues here to speak to anyone are ridiculous.'

'Say no more. I'm very happy to do favours for you which mean I can stay in my pyjamas and scroll on my phone.'

'Thank you. That would be brilliant. Oh, just one more thing.' She caught Ilina before she hung up. 'This might seem like a crazy question – but do you have any other gifts?'

'Magical ones?'

'Yes.'

'No.' Ilina laughed like it was a silly notion, and Kay was just starting to feel reassured that Harry had been bullshitting her, when her friend carried on: 'I'm not from a very strong witching line. I did all those designation tests that were being circulated when that research paper came out, but, alas, no. I'm just stuck with magical hair dyeing. Why? Is this something to do with your visit to Madam Hedvika? Did she say you have an affinity you weren't aware of?'

'No. She didn't. I'll tell you more about that when I can speak privately,' she promised before saying goodbye.

How had that revelation about multiple affinities gone unmentioned between her and her family? She spoke to both her mum and her brother regularly – her dad sporadically – and she knew *they* all kept up to date with news from the witching community. Why didn't they say anything? Had she made magic a complete no-go zone around them?

How long ago had the news about this come out? If it was within the last year, it made more sense because most of their discussions tended to revolve around the wedding. And she'd probably been steering the conversations away from magic because of the problems she was having with it.

Stop, she instructed herself. She didn't need to be worrying about this on top of everything else. She had priorities. Getting out of Germany and back to England being the first. Keeping a firm hand on her magic being the second.

She'd barely had a moment to really think about why her magic might be blocked as Madam Hedvika had instructed her to. All she'd done was stop herself from using magic and that had mainly been trying to calm herself so she didn't have an unscheduled outburst. How many times had she actually been tempted to use her magic intentionally? Two or three?

This was getting her nowhere. She needed to find somewhere to set up and start figuring out how to get home, while she waited for Ilina to get back to her. Since the toast she'd eaten at silly-o-clock in the morning had evaporated from all the adrenaline, she headed to a coffee shop to grab something to eat, a very large latte and a seat.

She managed to find a small table near the counter and as she was getting organised, her mum started calling her. She'd probably expected to hear from her by now and Kay hesitated before answering. She liked to be calm whenever she spoke to her mother, even on the phone; though she knew her mum couldn't pick up on her emotions that way, it was an ingrained habit. And Kay was *not* feeling calm.

In the end, she still accepted the call, aware she'd given Joe the unspoken reassurance that she would do her best to keep a lid on their mother's anxiety. She spent ten minutes humming along while her mother worried out loud, trying not to let her own mind spiral out into hypothetical disasters, sipping her too-hot coffee and attempting to make sense of some of the web links Ilina was sending her.

The only useful thing her mother had to tell her was that the winds were still raging across Britain, with the added bonus of hail on occasion too, and Aunt Lucille said it wasn't going to be easing off anytime soon.

Just peachy.

Kay hung up and commenced chewing on her thumbnail again before the taste of nail polish had her grimacing.

Somehow, last night, it hadn't seemed quite so daunting to be alone in another country. Experiencing the wind and rain buffeting the plane made everything feel a bit more real this morning. The airport was hectic. The place where she was stranded entirely unknown. In Prague at least she'd had a passing knowledge of the city from staying there for the conference for a few days.

Almost like she'd been wanting to see a familiar face again and her magic had answered the call, she looked up and spotted Harry.

Be careful what you wished for, indeed.

He was on the other side of the barrier of the coffee shop tables, on the phone himself, his bag at his feet as he paced a perimeter around it, glancing up at the boards, his other hand pushing through his hair, knuckles white, and making a thorough mess of it. He looked even more stressed than *her*, which was saying a lot. And just to confirm it further, when he finished on the phone, he marched into the coffee shop, with his holdall hooked over his shoulder and purchased half a dozen pastries.

When he turned from the counter with his box, she found herself raising her hand to wave to him. It was a split-second decision. He might have marched straight out and never even noticed her, such seemed to be his focus on his travel issues and imminent pastry consumption.

And she *should* have let him go. Instead, here she was, half standing, waving her hand. It shocked him as much as it shocked her.

He blinked, before he manoeuvred his way through the tables.

'Hey, how are you doing after that flight? Bit nerve-wracking, wasn't it?' He gave her a brief smile which didn't even crinkle the corners of his eyes, let alone light them up.

'I'd say I'm happy to be on terra firma again, but we're a couple of countries too far to the east.'

He made a pained noise and put his holdall on the spare chair, freeing his hands so he could open up his box of pastries, staring at them intently. He was really, *really* stressed. Surely it wasn't that big of a deal for him to get home for Samhain? Why hadn't she noticed this yesterday?

She supposed she'd been trying her best not to notice anything about him if she could help it.

'I have an unsettling sense of déjà vu,' she said drily. 'Flights grounded. Stuck at the airport. You, about to comfort-eat your way to a coronary.'

'Ha.' The smile he gave to that showed a little bit more genuine amusement and she felt a disconcerting sense of achievement about it. Then he proceeded to pick up what looked like a pecan lattice, fold it in half and insert the entire thing into his mouth.

Kay's jaw dropped open, as he chewed and swallowed, shutting his eyes and uttering groans of pleasure. It shouldn't have been attractive, but the blissful look on his face, coupled with the attention it brought to his mouth, and the following swipes of his tongue along his lips which glistened with maple syrup, were practically pornographic.

He sighed, then finally opened his eyes and fastened them on her. 'I know, it's terrible for me, but sweet solstice, that does feel better. Here, go on, try it. Just blast your senses with something delicious and decadent.'

He gestured to her with the box, and she shook her head, but it was a gentle admonishment rather than a refusal and she still looked inside. There was an apple turnover, covered in crystallised sugar, golden and crisp, and frankly, after the kind of day – morning? – she'd already had, it did seem a lot more appealing than her granola. As she scooped it out, she caught another genuine smile on Harry's lips and couldn't keep the corners of her own mouth down.

'I'm not going to shove it in whole, though.'

'Of course not. Slow savouring is more your style, right?' Even as he finished asking the question, a blush touched his high cheekbones. What was he thinking about? Was it the same memory that had just popped into her mind? Them, sharing the last of an apple crumble, straight from the dish, leaning on their elbows to face each other across the island in her mother's kitchen? The way he'd shovelled in a massive scoopful to his mouth and then topped it with whipped cream straight from the can, making her laugh, while she'd taken teaspoonfuls, barely able to eat because of all the butterflies in her stomach.

Kay quickly averted her gaze, blinking the image away and sitting down to take a big bite of the pastry to avoid having to reply. There was a lot more cinnamon in it compared to the apple turnovers back home and, frankly, it was lovely. Cosy and warming her up inside.

She finished chewing her mouthful and put the pastry on the napkin next to her latte and usurped granola. Harry was still standing, watching her. 'Thank you, that is delicious.' She poked her tongue out of her mouth, checking for sugar. 'So, what's your plan?'

His gaze darted up to her eyes from her mouth and he scratched his nose. 'I'm afraid Dean disappeared off the plane too fast for me to catch him.'

'Oh, I didn't mean that. I was talking about your plan now we're not going to make it to Paris?'

All the humour disappeared from his face, and he folded the lid closed on the box and placed it on the table, shoving his hands in his pockets. 'Basically, whatever mode of transport will get me moving as quickly as possible towards England.'

Kay frowned – he truly did sound more desperate to get home than her. His family was all about tradition, hosting all the seasonal celebrations and spearheading the community, but surely they'd understand why he couldn't make it when there was a hurricane blocking all paths home?

Then again, she remembered the pressure his dad had always put on him. The days when he'd come over to their house, looking flattened and drained after debating his university choices once again or because they'd had a dinner with some representatives from the Witches Council. She supposed those pressures didn't vanish just because you were an adult and technically didn't have to listen anymore. Especially when you were an Ashworth.

'What about you?' he asked.

'I'm looking into my options.' That sounded so vague and pathetic, she found herself elaborating the last-resort offer Ilina had sent her in the latest one of her texts. 'I have a friend who lives in Berlin who I can go to stay with until the flights are taking off again, but it's not exactly around the corner.'

'No, it's not. And Berlin's in the opposite direction to home,' he said slowly, like he was unsure what he could and couldn't say, or why she was even entertaining this discussion with him. And, honestly, she wasn't sure herself, except that it seemed deliberately rude to ignore the fact they were both stranded, trying to get home to the same place.

As if reassured by the momentary lowering of her guard, he moved his holdall to the floor and settled on the chair beside her. A faint waft of his spicy aftershave reached her – enough to make her remember how the smell had made everything inside her go hazy when they'd been pressed together in the toilet of the aeroplane.

She cleared her throat. 'Very true. It's four and a half hours in the opposite direction by train, to be exact. But there's no hurricane there currently, and no handy sex-pad for me to stay in around here,' she pointed out ruefully and he gave a bark of laugher.

'So . . .' He paused, seemingly in the middle of something he was going to say. 'Hang on. Where's your suitcase?'

'Damned if I know.' She shrugged. 'It didn't make it off the plane. Or even onto it maybe? Either way, it's lost somewhere. I've filed a report.' She could have pointed out that his lightening spell probably hadn't helped it stay where it should, but he looked so concerned, she couldn't bring herself to do it.

'Oh crap.' Harry frowned. 'Was there anything special in there? Other than the skulls, of course.'

Kay laughed and Harry's smile grew at the sound. She bit her lip and shook her head. What was happening? She was letting herself get drawn into their old rhythm. She might not want to keep dragging out her past hurt and stropping off like a teenager, but she shouldn't let herself forget. She could talk to him amicably from her side of the wall, but it was nowhere near time to start removing bricks.

'I know someone,' he offered as she looked away to fiddle with a napkin. 'When we're back in England. If your case hasn't turned up by then. She could help.'

'She works at the airline?'

'Er, no. But she's very good at tracking things down. You remember my cousin, Becca?'

'Oh, right.' Kay nodded. 'I forgot that your family has a history of that kind of gift from Biddi. Before it got lost to influencers.'

'I wouldn't say it got lost to influencers. Many of us still have a touch of that gift too.'

Kay felt her eyebrows lift so high that her glasses shifted down her nose a little. 'Do you?'

'Yes, a bit.' He rubbed his hand over the short hair at the back of his head.

'It's your secondary affinity?' When he nodded, she lowered her voice and moved forward a little in her chair, unable to help herself being a little fascinated at him not only having another gift but it being proof of his genetic link to such a legendary witch. 'How does it manifest?'

'Kind of like a compass. I can't use it at will. It's not for objects. It's just there. Like an itch, irritating me until I listen to it.'

'But what is it telling you?'

'Where I need to be.' His eyes flicked up at her for a moment and then he sat back heavily in his chair.

She mulled the idea over in her head, letting her gaze rest on his long fingers curled, almost but not quite, into a fist on the edge of the table. It sounded like it leaned into foresight. If that were the case though . . .

She gave a little laugh. 'How did you get stuck on all these wrong flights, then?'

'Believe me, I've been asking myself the same question.' He shook his head and then he sighed. 'It's like anything with a seer designation, I think. No real explanation. You tend to piece it together after the fact. But . . .'

'But?'

'But, while I was looking at the departure boards and updates online, I was getting the feeling that maybe we should head to Amsterdam.'

Her spine tingled as she heard the word 'we' – although maybe he was just using the royal 'we'.

Him and his abundance of useful gifts.

'The reports say the weather isn't as bad there at the moment,' he continued. 'And it doesn't take long to reach. A couple of hours. Maybe by the time we get there, it would have passed from the south-east of England and France – we might be able to catch a flight from Amsterdam. Or a ferry? It just feels like there are more options open that way.'

'So, you want to try dog-legging it around the weather?' She drummed her fingers on the table and then paused, realising she'd unwittingly turned towards him, their knees almost touching.

'It's worth a go. If we're just going to wait out the storm, we might as well wait it out even closer to our destination, right?'

Kay crossed her legs, over and away from his. There was that 'we' again. 'Are you inviting me along with you?' she asked slowly, like she was easing out over the thinly frozen surface of a lake.

He shifted on his chair, pulling the tails of his bright blue coat free from beneath him. 'Well, yes. We're trying to get back to the same place, aren't we? Biddicote. And Joe's wedding.'

'*You've* been invited to the wedding?' she blurted out.

'Yeah,' he said, as though it was a given.

But how could it be when he and Harry weren't even friends? When he'd used her brother, just to help him study for his A levels? As soon as they'd taken them, he'd dropped Joe like a hexed porcelain doll. Did Joe not realise?

Or was it just one of those things where he had to be seen to invite the Ashworths? That had to be it. When she was growing up the Ashworths were always at weddings. She'd not thought anything of it, but it probably harked back to some "Lord of the Manor" custom and Harry was going to be the Ashworth representative at the Hendrix wedding, so his parents could host Samhain as usual.

She picked at a crystal of sugar on top of her pastry, not trusting herself to speak for a moment. The idea of him being there on her brother's special day had her foot twitching with the desire to stomp it, while telling him he had no right, but it wouldn't be wise to put his nose out of joint by picking another argument. He was offering to be her travelling companion, and while she knew it would be smart to keep an *emotional* distance from him, *physically*, if he had a magical leg-up pointing him in the right direction to get home, she'd be a fool to turn his offer down, wouldn't she? She needed to get back for Joe's wedding and if that meant throwing her lot in with Harry, so be it.

'So, you'll come with me?'

When she nodded, the relief on his face sent a tingle of confusion through her. He really was acting like he cared. Which didn't make any sense.

'It's still a gamble, though,' he caveated.

'I know.' There was always the possibility his gift was trying to take him somewhere other than Biddicote . . . 'But I have the wedding rehearsal dinner this evening. If this could help me make it − I can't say no. Luck hasn't exactly been on my side recently.' She gestured around her to indicate the absence of her luggage.

Harry nodded and then his eyes lit up. 'Oh, that gives me an idea.' He opened up his coat and pulled out a black fine-art pen, then beckoned with his right hand for hers.

'Give me your hand. Doesn't matter which.'

'What? Why?' She moved her hands into her lap. It wasn't that she had a particular objection to being drawn on, but a) she wanted to know why, and b) Harry's drawings were not ordinary drawings.

He leaned in even closer. Seriously, they may as well be sitting on the same chair, and the worst thing was, she didn't hate it. 'Have you heard of the community sign?' he asked in a low voice.

'The what?' she replied, mouth dry, trying not to throw herself off the chair like she had the bed that morning, in an act of self-preservation.

'I guess that's a no. In northern European countries, there's a tattoo a lot of people like us choose to get – to show they're part of the community and make it easier to help each other out with things, sensitive situations, et cetera.'

'Oh. Like the runes my friend Ilina has on her wrist.'

'If that's your friend who lives in Berlin, then yes, but that's just for Germans. This one is more general and inclusive.'

'That's a good idea.'

'Yes. It might be helpful for us to wear it for the rest of this journey in case we run into trouble. Worth a shot, isn't it?'

'I suppose so. Won't they be mad that we're not actual members of their community, though? The UK's separated itself from Europe and aren't the best at building bridges, are they?' She didn't need to keep up with witching news to know that.

Harry quirked his eyebrow, acknowledging the grim truth – non-magical and magical alike, the powers that be in the UK tended towards arrogance and twisting the rules, rather than joining the larger communities. 'I would hope they wouldn't hold it against us. And I can . . .' He paused and bit his lip.

'You can what?' She narrowed her eyes at him.

'Well, I could just infuse the image with a little push towards compassion.'

'Convenient.'

'It is. That's why it's called a "gift", Kay.' He pressed his lips together. 'Look, I know you don't like the principle of it. Especially from me. But it's such a small image, all it will really do is prompt a tiny amount of positivity, if that person is already inclined towards it. Is that such a bad thing?'

'If it's such a small amount, why bother?'

'Because . . . because I can, I guess. It's not going to hurt anyone.'

'That's what influencers always say, but it's trickier than that, isn't it? It removes people's own choice . . .' Kay broke off before they started down that path again.

Harry lowered his eyes to his pen and was quiet for a moment. She figured he was going to tell her to find her own way home, without him and his Biddicote magic compass. Why would he want her with him, constantly cramping his style by objecting to him influencing people to get a little extra luck and special treatment sent their way?

But then he just nodded. 'Fine. I'll do it without.'

She lifted her hand, and he took it in his, twisting it, so the side along her pinkie finger was turned to him. Her heart rate pattered fast at the feel of his cool fingers sneaking inside her palm, his thumb pressing gently against her knuckles.

But then he just held still.

'What are you waiting for?' she asked, sounding breathy

and hoping it came across as impatience.

His fingers twitched, seemingly involuntarily, around hers, the sensation of his hold tightening making a sudden wash of heat drop into her belly. He swallowed and took an exaggeratedly slow breath in, letting it out again with controlled steadiness, and his grip eased again. 'I just need to clear my thoughts and feelings. Have an empty mind if I'm to avoid putting anything into the picture.'

'Oh.' She nodded and tried to wait without fidgeting, while he took his time, looking like he was centring himself. She'd never really considered how difficult it would be for him *not* to use his gift. She'd assumed he just switched it on and off like a tap, but it wasn't like she could do that with hers, and there was no barrier he could put in between like she had with her glasses. It was either draw or not draw, she supposed. Or try to have an empty mind. Possibly not the easiest thing to do when he was feeling stressed.

That brought to mind her own current magical issues. She had always blocked being able to see her gift with her glasses, but surely that couldn't be the blockage Madam Hedvika was talking about? She'd told her about the glasses and plenty of witches used similar things to stop them from being distracted by their gifts constantly. No one had ever said that it would cause a problem.

And if Harry was right, there was nothing blocking the way she affected people's emotional awareness. Madam Hedvika couldn't have meant that kind of a block. It was too obvious.

Finally, after another minute, he put the pen to her skin and, with sure strokes, began to draw an intricate design, like a Celtic rune pattern, along the edge of her hand. The nib of the pen tickled, and he tightened his hold again when she flinched a little.

'No giggling, you'll jog me,' he murmured in a distracted

tone of voice, his breath caressing the sensitive skin on the inside of her wrist. Goosebumps rose along her arm. She couldn't help it. The feel of his hand, firmly wrapped around hers, the vision of his head bowed over, copper and bronze hair falling forward in a messy kink on his forehead and his eyelashes lowered, was like stepping into a teenage dream again. 'There, you're all done.'

Kay took a deep breath and turned her hand towards her, studying the pattern, all the while her heart skittered in her chest, fluttering like a trapped bird, because that wall she knew she needed to have between them was looking decidedly shaky.

Chapter Nine

They couldn't get a train leaving for Amsterdam until midday, which didn't make Kay optimistic about getting to the wedding rehearsal dinner that evening and felt like hours and hours to wait until they saw how ridiculously packed the station at the airport was. The journey to Dusseldorf central station was only about fifteen minutes but waiting in the queues was going to be tedious.

'Are you wearing comfortable shoes?' Harry asked her, as they stared down the ticket line. 'Fancy getting some fresh air and stretching your legs? It'd be nice to see a bit of Dusseldorf.'

'How far is it?' She wasn't worried about her feet. Despite all the marketing material she'd been lumbered with, she'd had the forethought to pack her purple flowery Doc Martens, and had put them on today to travel in. She couldn't help feeling a wave of sadness at the loss of her killer knee-high boots to the baggage claim system, though.

'About five miles.'

'That's a touch over a stroll across the city, isn't it?'

'For someone with your leg muscles, I would've thought it was a breeze.' He grinned and glanced down at her legs, possibly thinking about last night where she'd snapped the sofa bed in half, seemingly without the use of her magic.

His eyes lingered, moving up slowly, and Kay felt a betraying heat in her loins. At least she thought it was her loins.

He cleared his throat. 'Pretty boots.'

'Thanks.' She looked away and made her voice breezy. 'It might be nice to see something other than airports for a while, though. Do you think we'll make it?'

'If it gets tight, we can try to flag down a cab. I'm not sure I can face standing still for so long, if that makes sense? What if it takes longer waiting than to just get on with walking?'

She cocked her head, studying the queues again. Honestly, she doubted it. Everything was moving efficiently; it was just the sheer volume of people making the queues long. But she understood his desire to keep moving – at least to a certain point. Psychologically, it felt more productive. Perhaps he had that itch going in his chest too. Since she'd thrown her lot in with him, it made sense to pander to his whims just in case.

An issue that must crop up regularly if you were in a relationship with someone who had a seer designation. How would you know if they were genuinely convincing you to get Thai for the third date in a row because an accident was going to befall the Italian restaurant you wanted to go to, or just because they were leveraging their gift to get their own way? Trust, she supposed. Great big helpings of trust, that could backfire on you spectacularly.

Not dissimilar to the situation she was currently in, she reflected, as they made their way outside, and immediately realised this wasn't going to be a relaxing stroll through a picturesque city. Why she had imagined there was going to be blue skies and sunshine, when they had walked off a plane buffeted by high winds, she didn't know. Possibly her subconscious had been conjuring up rainbows too, as she and Harry walked hand in hand along cobbled streets.

You're losing your grip on reality, Kay.

She glanced at the fake tattoo he'd drawn on her hand and wondered if he had infused it with some kind of charm, even though he'd promised not to. Something that made her biddable and more prone to agreeing with him. But she couldn't feel anything emanating from it. Not that you could always tell. If it was mostly a push towards something people already wanted to feel, they might not even think to question it. Amplifying, subtly twisting, the things people genuinely felt was the easiest way to go undetected.

She flipped her collar up, buttoning it across her neck and burrowing her chin down into it — as though that would help her from being absolutely drenched by the time they reached the other train station.

'Are you sure this is a good idea?' she asked, watching people barely able to stand up straight against the driving rain as they waited for taxis.

'The weather is a tad more vigorous than I was expecting, admittedly.' Harry put his duffel bag down by her feet. 'Have you got an umbrella on you?'

Her eyebrows rose. 'I really don't think an umbrella would stand a chance against this wind.'

'Humour me for a minute.' He gave her his half-hitched smile, eyes warm with amusement, and she probably should have felt annoyance at the hint of smugness — or maybe even affection — in the expression.

'I can't, I don't have one.' She tucked the strap of her tote a little higher on her shoulder.

'Right. I'll be back in a sec.' And then he disappeared inside the airport.

She sighed, dribbling his bag out of the entranceway as she quickly sent another update text to her mum and a silent plea to whatever deity might take mercy on her that she wouldn't immediately receive a phone call about it.

When Harry returned five minutes later, he was brandishing a large golf umbrella. Kay rolled her eyes. He was still thinking this would work? 'Harry – the wind must be forty miles an hour. Unless you're planning on getting us there Mary Poppins style, I don't think that's going to help.'

'That's an idea, isn't it.' His eyes darted upwards, like he was picturing it happening in the sky. 'I wonder if there is anyone out there who could—'

'Not sure we've got time to find them even if there is,' she interrupted, when a familiar expression passed over his face. This one was different to the tuned-out look of concentration he got when he was sketching. It was the glazed, staring-into-an-imaginary-distance one, when he was coming up with his ideas or picturing the world a different way.

How could she have come to know him so well, all those years ago – and yet not have known him at all? Did falling in love with someone make you develop a photographic memory of that person—

Hold on. No. She'd never been *in love* with him. Just infatuated.

He blinked and focused on her face again. 'No. Of course not. Though it would be fun. We'll have to go for something a little more elementary.' And then he put the big umbrella up and stepped right up close to her. He shut his eyes for a moment, gripping the handle tight as the wind tried to carry it off, exactly as she predicted, and then his lips moved over a couple of phrases and Kay's ears popped as a hush descended.

The force on the umbrella disappeared, as did the cold wind and the splashes of rain which had been driving underneath it to soak her coat and jeans. She watched as droplets rolled away in front of her face as though there was now a windscreen around them, the circumference of the big umbrella.

'I'm not sure if it'll last the whole walk but . . .' he trailed off, looking at her face with a faint frown. 'What?'

Kay shook her head and chewed on her lip. Her initial response was to be irritated that he could summon up yet another handy spell – but didn't most witches do the same, if they could make sure it went undetected? Why was she truly taking so much offence at him being able to do a level of everyday magic which she couldn't? She didn't regret stifling her gift – because it was useless and distracting and suppressing it just now was, according to Madam Hedvika, necessary - but that wasn't his fault. And this was another example of him using it to help her out.

She'd been so angry with him, so bitter about the past, she could have hardly blamed him for not offering to share this shelter with her. She'd rejected his gift, chewed him out over influencing Dean . . . perhaps it was time that she called a truce. Internally. They were older now – adults – and stuck in this situation together. She didn't exactly have to trust him or accept it if he tried to use his influence over someone immorally – but she didn't have to bite his head off either.

'We should start walking and make the most of it then, right?' she said evenly.

He nodded slowly, and picked up his duffel bag, slinging it over his shoulder, and they started walking.

It was relatively quiet through the town, and Kay was sure that the comfortable bubble they found themselves in helped them make good time. The city was picturesque, but it felt like she was walking through a virtual reality game because she couldn't really hear its noises properly; the rain was hushed outside and the only real connection to it was the smell of the soaked pavement, which was undercut by the damp wool of Harry's big ridiculous coat, with notes of his aftershave, too.

They had to walk closely together to stay under the shelter of the umbrella and match their pace, which was a lot easier than she would have expected, given their different stride length. Harry was consulting the GPS on his phone to find their way and it was a reassuringly normal thing to do. At this stage, she wouldn't have been surprised to see him bespell a homing pigeon and chase it across the city.

They stopped at a bakery not far from the train station when they saw they had a good thirty minutes to spare, and Harry went in to grab some food. Despite the pastries he'd eaten earlier, he was still hungry. She expected the spell on the umbrella had used up a fair bit of his energy. Magic wasn't something witches had an infinite supply of.

She kept hold of the umbrella as he now had a sandwich as well as his phone out for directions and it meant he needed to duck his head down closer to hers. They turned a corner and found themselves facing a three-storey building, painted across the whole exterior as though it was see-through. An X-ray of rooms with people carrying out their everyday lives inside a bunch of different apartments. Without even discussing it, they both stopped and stared, taking in all the details as Harry polished off his sandwich.

'Would you ever want to paint something that big?' she asked, before she could help herself.

'No. I don't think I could. It would be too hard to do without bringing magic into it – and then I would probably shrivel up and die from expending too much into it,' he laughed, and then his laughter abruptly stopped, as though he'd heard the words back to himself and not found them funny. He swallowed. 'It's not like it needs magic anyway. I think NMs can wield as much power to move others emotionally, to create and influence and heal, it just hits the barrier of their physiology and science as they understand it. Some are capable of more, some less, depending on their innate skill and determination, just like how we differ within the application of our gifts.'

Kay let her eyes follow the lines of the huge mural, seeing the depictions of family and friends and loneliness laid out before her. 'There's something to that, I guess. What witches have is just an extension of gifts people already have.'

'Maybe some even push themselves that little bit extra and start accessing magic.'

She blinked and looked over at him in surprise. 'You think NMs can work to become witches?'

'I don't know. Maybe,' he repeated, with a smile.

'That's a surprising theory coming from an Ashworth.'

His smile turned rueful. 'I can see why you'd say that. People act like being from an old magical line is some kind of proof of pedigree but,' he shrugged, 'being one of them, I can confirm that you still have to work to understand and wield your magic just the same as everyone else. Why wouldn't it be possible for others to focus in a way that tapped into magical energy too?'

She raised an eyebrow, part of her immediately wanting to reject his humility, or the theory that it was some kind of meritocracy, with scepticism, because, of course, he didn't want to seem like he'd been born with a silver spoon in his mouth, but at the same time . . . if everyone expected you to perform and your legacy was staring you in the face every day, she supposed you would work hard to make the most of what you'd been given. His dad certainly wouldn't have allowed him to slack off. Which still meant being an Ashworth led to a high level of skill, but more because of circumstance than because of the gene pool. Nuture as well as narture.

'Wasn't it you who had the theory that there were lots of people back in history who were witches and didn't know it?' he said, drawing her thoughts back to the conversation. 'It could all be part of the same thing.'

It hadn't just been the intersection of non-magical history and witch history she'd been fascinated with – it had been the idea that some of the people celebrated as geniuses throughout history had been witches and hadn't known it. Or had hidden it. And he remembered her talking about it?

She shifted her grip on the handle of the umbrella when she thought of how she would randomly text him the name of some historic figure who'd cropped up in her schoolwork that she thought might fit the bill, and then when they next met up they'd debate it as a possibility.

'Maybe,' she said and the doubt that infused her tone wasn't really about her not believing it was possible, it was about her having rejected her plans to study history in favour of technology. She couldn't really answer him, because her theory was no more developed than it had been when she was a teenager.

Her plan had been to do a history degree, immerse herself in sources and evidence and root out the truth where she could – paint an accurate picture of the past that involved her ancestors. And instead, she'd chosen to spurn that for a job developing mobile phone apps.

Thinking about her job, and her irritating boss, she had to wonder if maybe she'd tried to convince herself that it was what she wanted because it was easier to ignore the magical side of herself that way and all the misery it had brought her. She hadn't stopped to think there might be a cost to that too.

She didn't really want to think about it now.

She nudged his arm. 'Come on, we'd better catch that train.'

'Just a sec, I want to take a photo.' He raised his camera, and she lifted the umbrella to help him get a full shot. As he lowered his phone, his thumb slipped over the button switching the camera to face them and she saw them framed on his screen for a moment. Her blue hair was practically the same shade as his coat as she leaned in closer to him than was warranted. He smiled, catching her eye, and hit the circle to take a photo.

'What did you do that for?'

'Maybe I wanted proof that we could be this close without you wanting to kill me.'

'The photo only proves we could be this close without me *trying* to kill you, it does not prove that the desire wasn't there,' she retorted, but there was no bite in her tone.

'Let a man delude himself for at least thirty seconds, would you.' He smirked and slipped his phone away.

They started walking again and she tried not to look at him and think about why he would even care. He was the one who had dumped her. As a friend. They hadn't even made it past that.

★

The German train felt wider than British ones – everything had a squared-off, right-angled feel to it and they managed to get two seats at a table. It was chilly with the air conditioning, especially after the gentle warmth of being under the umbrella bubble for the walk, and it gave the whole place the feeling of a clean, efficient office, reminding Kay of work again. Unfortunately.

On Tuesday, she was going to have to break it to her boss that all the expensive marketing materials were lost, and she doubted he'd react reasonably, despite it not being her fault. They had a networking event at the end of the week and the company would have to pay a premium to get the brochures made up in time – if it was possible at all.

But she had to relegate that to a substring of worries, as the one taking the top spot priority-wise was obviously making sure she was back in time for Joe's wedding. She could deal with work crap later.

After they'd been travelling north-west for at least half an hour, the sun broke through the clouds and the rain eased off. Perhaps they were on to something, going in this direction. Maybe they would manage to outrun the storm and circle back around it.

'*Regenbogen*,' the child sitting across the aisle from their table erupted loudly.

Kay looked up and saw Harry watching the boy with a smile. He caught her eye after a moment and pointed with one of the pencils he'd been sketching with.

'Rainbow,' he explained.

Kay leaned forward and spotted the wide arc in the distance through the train window, the colours standing out against the grey sky. 'You understand German, too?'

'Too?'

'I heard you speaking some Czech in Prague.'

'Oh.' He nodded and scratched the end of his pencil against the hair at his temple. 'I always try to learn some basics before I go to another country. Reading road names and signs can be a challenge sometimes, so it's easier to speak to someone.'

Kay was quiet for a moment. She hadn't forgotten about his dyslexia, but equally hadn't considered the ongoing complications it might add to his life. Especially in situations like this, where he might need to decipher other languages he was unprepared for as he got detoured across Europe. 'How many languages do you have a sample of, then?'

'Is that your way of finding out how well travelled I am?'

'I suppose I am curious. We did used to talk about the places we wanted to go . . .' she trailed off and his eyes flicked up from his sketchbook to catch hers. Yes, that's right. She'd gone there and mentioned the time they'd spent with each other as teenagers. He'd made reference to things he knew about her from before, but the relationship between them hadn't been referenced directly. The moments they'd shared. She could feel the mutual memories burning in her chest, like he'd scored that smiley face from his napkin note into the skin over her heart, and it was throbbing as she picked at it.

'We did,' he agreed slowly, like he was waiting for her to spring a trap. 'I haven't made it to South America yet, but I've been to a lot of European countries which were on my list. What about you?'

'Hardly any. I've been to New York at Christmastime, though.'

His eyes lit up and he folded his arms, leaning on the table towards her. 'What was that like?'

'Cold. Busy. Beautiful.'

He nodded, one side of his smile slowly lifting into place as his gaze scanned her face, as though he could read how much she'd enjoyed the trip there and was giving himself a moment to absorb it. The fine hairs rose on her arms, but she told herself it was just the over-enthusiastic air conditioning.

'Were you there for work?' he asked after what felt like an hour but was likely only three seconds.

'Oh, no. Graduation gift from my family. I don't do a lot of international travel for work. If fact, I only . . .' She caught herself before she admitted she'd only pushed to go on the Prague conference so she could get to see Madam Hedvika. That was still not something she wanted him knowing about. 'I only usually do UK events,' she switched it to, and then cleared her throat. 'Is all the travelling you do for work?'

'Generally.'

'I guess your dad's business must be thriving with all those foreign clients, then?'

'Oh, no.' He shook his head, the smile fading as he sat back. 'No. I don't work for my dad.'

'You don't? I thought that was always the plan? What do you do instead then?'

'I'm an illustrator. Mainly for children's picture books.'

Her mouth fell open. 'Oh. Wow. That's *really* different from marketing. What made you decide to do that?'

'It was just . . . what I found I enjoyed doing most when I was at university. When I'm doing that kind of artwork, everything flows. And, I don't know . . . the idea of bringing stories to life for kids, maybe help them discover a love for reading . . . it feels like a good use of what I can do.' He gave a one-shouldered shrug.

She refused to melt at that. Absolutely, point-blank, refused. 'How did your dad take it?'

Harry turned his head to squint out of the window. 'Honestly, not great. He felt that I'd missed the point that working for the business would have been a good use of my affinity too. The money goes towards the estate and the estate is there to help protect the community, which *is* important. Very important—' He broke off from what Kay suspected was a recitation of an argument with his dad. He swallowed and looked back at her. 'Joe hasn't been keeping you up to date?'

Kay stiffened. Did he really expect her to believe that he and Joe were still friends, when her brother *never* mentioned him? Not even in passing. Harry might have been invited to the wedding, but so was Minerva, their second cousin once removed, and they'd only met her a dozen times throughout their whole life. Some guests were an obligation. She didn't understand what he was playing at. 'With news about you? No. You never come up in conversation,' she said, pointedly.

'No. Of course. That makes sense.' He averted his eyes back to his sketchbook this time, his cheekbones flushed.

Kay pulled out the latest novel she was reading, pretending to get absorbed in the pages, when truly she was wishing it was a thriller rather than a romance. Although five minutes of peace from the constant roller-coaster of adjusting to being around Harry might help to soothe the ache in her chest, she didn't need to read any kissing scenes or swoony declarations of feelings.

Admitting there was a distance between them, that had widened and widened over time, made it impossible to avoid the fact that once there had been closeness too, which had been lost. The more he mentioned things from the past, the more she slipped into feeling comfortable with him, and enjoying their conversations, the more confused it made her.

She'd forced herself to believe that he'd only acted friendly with her that year because he'd needed to keep Joe on side to help him with his A levels. It made sense. Once they were done, he no longer had to pretend, and he could give her the shove she needed to stop mooning over him.

But he wasn't talking to her now like he thought of her as a nerdy irritation. And he needn't keep her on side. She was the one getting help from *him*. So, had she got it wrong? And if so, why had he pushed her away so hard? Or was it just that he'd changed? Had rose-tinted glasses on now? It was a problem she didn't have the capacity to try to figure out at the moment.

Flakes of snow began falling, but that didn't keep the little boy opposite them entertained for very long. He started to get remarkably fidgety and even though they were speaking in a different language, Kay recognised that frayed but subdued tone his mother was using to try to get him to calm down without hollering at him in public.

Harry shifted over onto the spare seat beside him next to the aisle so he was closer to them and used some of those German words he learned to get their attention. He showed the boy a flick book he'd made in the corner of his sketchbook. Kay couldn't see what he'd drawn but it enraptured the boy.

Then he pulled another smaller book out of his coat of many pockets, along with a pencil and gave it to the little boy. Harry and the mother exchanged some more words in German, and Harry scooted back across, the boy moved next to him and the mother moved over to sit next to Kay.

She gave her a smile and they both watched with interest – the mother openly, Kay covertly over the top of her book – as Harry started to show him how to draw what looked like a superhero, and then an assortment of animals.

Kay kept a sharp eye on him for a moment to see if Harry was going to use magic through his drawings to calm the boy down – modifying his behaviour – but she couldn't see any influence in them other than things that accentuated the picture. A sense of cheekiness in a monkey, the joy of a bird singing. The boy was captivated, and yet somehow still bouncing about, only occasionally settling to copy the shapes as best he could. Mostly, Harry appeared to be giving the mother a break from trying to entertain him.

She wondered if Harry used his influence in the illustrations for the children's books. Would that even work en masse and once it had been through a computer and printed out in production? Unlikely, as far as she understood magic (although perhaps she didn't understand it quite so well as she'd thought). Regardless, if it was only the initial artwork he could put his influence into, did that mean that he'd used an unfair advantage to move the commissioning editors when they were viewing his portfolio?

But he was a great artist – she knew that. And people wanted to be moved by art, didn't they? That was the point of it. If he could bring joy to children, help them enjoy the experience of reading or inspire them to be artistic themselves, was that so terrible? Joe using his gift in his teaching was acceptable, as long as it wasn't anything to do with behaviour, so why wouldn't Harry using his gift this way be?

And, sweet Goddess, she was tired of feeling self-righteous when it came to him. She supposed it was easy to judge how other people chose to use their gifts, when she'd been given an ability which she could block. Her day-to-day life wasn't complicated any further than her putting on a pair of glasses. Was she really that morally superior because she had chosen not to use her gift at all, rather than learn to balance it with who she was and make choices every day about what was best?

As one of the stops in the Netherlands was coming up, the mother of the boy started getting her things together to leave and accidentally knocked Kay's tote over, spilling some of the contents on the floor beneath the table.

'*Entschuldigung*,' she said, getting down on her knees in the aisle to gather the things that had escaped, as Kay rescued her bag. '*Es tut mir leid*.'

Even Kay could translate that. 'It's fine. Don't worry,' she said gently, taking her purse and hairbrush back with a smile.

Then the woman straightened, holding something pale and lumpy in her hand. She handed it slowly over, the bemusement plain on her face.

Kay reached for it, confused herself until she saw the scorch mark and realised it was her demented corn-husk doll. Heat rushed into her cheeks, and she forced a laugh. 'Souvenir,' she offered weakly and jammed the thing back in her bag.

The woman gave her a tentative smile and continued to organise their things so they could disembark at the next station. They left with profuse thanks to Harry, who looked like it had been as much a pleasure for him as it had been for them.

He glanced over at Kay briefly, gaze drifting to her tote bag, which was on the seat next to her, and looked like he wanted to say something, but she raised her book in front of her face again. There were too many mixed emotions swirling around inside her at the moment to face talking to him. Until she had to. And once they got off the train in Amsterdam, the conversaion would all be focused on journey logistics again, steering well clear of any awkward topics.

She stifled a sigh and glanced out of the window. The snow was growing heavier, the further north they went. So much flat land now, covered with pristine white blankets. Were they going to get stranded in Amsterdam next? She wasn't sure if there would be any other options to travel back if they were. And what would that mean? Them trying to find a hotel together?

She'd deal with that if it happened. For now, she was here, on the train with Harry, and part of her – the part that was considering he wasn't quite the evil villain she'd painted him as – kept trying to make her sink into the memory of last night when they had curled up together in a bed and she'd played make-believe on a future she'd once dreamed of.

Chapter Ten

Centraal Station, Amsterdam

331 miles and 24(+1) hours and 30 minutes until the wedding

Instead of heading straight outside once they got off the train at Centraal Station, they went deeper inside to where it backed onto the ferry docking. Harry went to each of the information desks there to figure out their travel options, while Kay bought them coffee and grabbed a couple of seats as people streamed past.

'Well, the bad news is, there are still no flights landing in the UK and no ferries directly from Amsterdam until tomorrow morning . . . and that's going to Newcastle.'

'Newcastle? Bloody hell. How long does the ferry take?' She handed him his coffee absently.

'Twelve hours.' He winced.

Her mouth fell open. That wouldn't work at all. 'I'll completely miss the wedding ceremony.' And barely make the reception, even if she raced the length of the country to arrive in the clothes she'd been wearing for two days at that point.

Her blood pressure sky-rocketed as she began lamenting the fact that she'd thrown in her lot with Harry and his itchy magic compass. Maybe they *should* have split up in

Dusseldorf. She could have gone to stay at Ilina's and just been patient.

A tingling started in her fingers, matching the beat of her frantic pulse, and she had to close her eyes and take a couple of deep breaths to calm herself. She supposed the only bright side was that if she *was* really going to miss the wedding, at least it would guarantee Joe a special day without her destroying it with her crazy magic. What if she accidentally set fire to Sandy's dress or something?

She jumped as Harry's hand lightly touched her wrist. Opening her eyes, she found him watching her, his brows slightly furrowed to cause a tiny crease between them. 'There's sort of good news too, though.'

'Yeah?'

'If we can get to the Hook of Holland, we can get a ferry to Harwich.'

'Where's Harwich? Is that closer to home than Newcastle?'

'Yes. It'll only take a few hours to get to Surrey from there. And the next one leaves at eleven, so we'll arrive first thing tomorrow morning.'

She nodded slowly. 'Nothing sooner?'

''Fraid not. I'm sorry. I know it means missing the rehearsal dinner, but it's the best option out of not very many options.' He gave her wrist a consoling squeeze, making her belly flop over, and then he dropped his hand.

'It's OK. The wedding is the most important bit,' she said, though she hated the thought of missing the dinner. Particularly when her mum and dad would be there, brooding, at opposite ends of the table. Mum would definitely be taking one of her magic mood-blocker pills. And drinking a lot of wine. Goddess, Kay hoped there wasn't a scene. Joe and Sandy didn't deserve that.

'So, I'll grab us tickets?'

'Let me come and pay for mine.'

'We'll divvy up the expenses once we get home. I'll try to figure out our best options for getting to the Hook as well. We'll need to be there for boarding at half past nine.'

'Is that far from here?'

'I don't think so. We should have plenty of time to get there.' He offered her a reassuring smile and disappeared off to queue again, while Kay braced herself and phoned her brother.

'Oh, crap,' Joe said, when she explained the ferry situation and broke the news about the dinner, already sounding a lot more harassed than he had first thing that morning. Was it only that morning? It felt like days ago at this point. 'I suppose it's not the end of the world. I'm not even quite sure why we *need* a rehearsal dinner . . . There's not a single flight? No, don't even bother to answer that. Of course you'd be flying back if you could, rather than taking a ferry. You're going to hang around in Amsterdam all day and most of the evening on your own, though? I don't like the sound of that.'

'It's fine,' she tried to reassure him. 'Well, I mean, not *fine*, obviously, because I was really hoping I'd be able to make it back, but it's not a problem to be stuck in Amsterdam for a little while. Then I'll be travelling to the Hook in time for the ferry.'

'Right. So, you'll only be wandering around Amsterdam, on your own, for *most* of the day and then taking a train or something at night. By yourself.' His tone made it clear that he didn't think that was a better scenario.

She chewed on her lip and decided that it wasn't fair to let him worry about that, on top of everything else. 'I'm not on my own.'

'No? You're with someone from work?'

'No.'

'Who then? Don't make friends with random people, Kay. That's not any safer.'

Kay let the patronising tone go because she knew he was extremely wound up about the wedding, she'd just broken some bad news to him, and despite all that, his main concern was her safety. 'It's not a stranger. I'm with Harry Ashworth.'

There was a moment of silence on the other end of the phone. 'Say again?'

'Harry Ashworth. You know. Who you went to school with?'

'Of course I know who Harry is. I'm just struggling with you two . . . bumping into each other? I mean, I assume this is a coincidence, unless there is something you're not telling me—'

'No,' she jumped in. 'Totally a coincidence. We were both in Prague and when the flight got delayed at the airport, we ran into each other, and since we're both heading in the same direction . . .'

'Well, sure. Makes sense. Especially if Harry's secondary affinity is helping him figure out which route to get you home.' Joe released a breath. 'Oh, that makes me feel much better.'

Kay went to respond and stopped, realising that Joe already knew about Harry's itchy magic compass. But that definitely wasn't something he'd known he had back when they were doing their A levels together. So Joe must have found out since. And Harry had known random facts about Kay's life . . . and been invited to the wedding. 'Are you . . . Joe, are you still in touch with Harry?'

Another pause. 'Yes?'

'Why are you saying that as though it's a question? I assumed you'd lost contact.'

'No. I just . . .'

'What?' *Spit it out*, she wanted to say, but restrained herself because he didn't deserve her blowing a gasket down the phone at him.

'We stayed in contact. We meet up quite regularly. As regularly as I manage to meet up with anyone these days.' He gave a beleaguered little huff, which she knew was more to do with the demands of his job than the demands of the wedding.

'You're friends still?'

'Well . . . yeah.'

'H-how? I thought he'd ditched you after your A levels?'

'No. Not at all.'

'But you literally never mention him.'

'OK . . . see, I just figured it would upset you. I know you took it hard when he . . .'

'Stood me up? Dropped me completely?' Her hand tightened on her phone at the memory of Joe handing her the napkin with Harry's scribbled message. Thinking of how he'd barely wanted to look at her at the time doubled the pain.

'Both. You know we weren't exactly talking back then and by the time we were, well, it was obvious that it would upset you.'

'Was it?'

'Yeah. Mum said never to mention the Ashworths even as a family.' He gave a soft laugh. 'You know how she is. She couldn't bear feeling how upset it made you.'

Kay's cheeks flushed. She *had* been upset, obviously, but her mother had made it sound like she was having a Bella Swan-esque breakdown. She knew her feelings must have been a lot for her mum to deal with, on top of her own, and she appreciated the protective sentiment, but she was capable of telling Joe if she didn't want to talk about something, she didn't need to be coddled. The reason she and Joe had fallen out so dramatically after the divorce was because they didn't shy away from being honest with each other. Or so she'd thought.

To prove the point to herself, she pushed her hair back from her face and spoke as neutrally as she could. 'If you thought I was so traumatised, why did you stay friends with him? Sisters before misters, no?'

Regardless of her easy tone, Joe sounded squirmy. 'Because . . . I knew what was going on with him at the time. And we were basically kids. He's not a bad person, Kay, he just screwed up. Maybe I screwed up a bit too, all right? We weren't on talking terms, but I still probably should have hauled him over the coals more about it than I did. Then, by the time you and I were cool again, it would've been weird to say: "Right, I've got a bone to pick with you now."'

'All right, I guess I can see that,' she said, all the more grudgingly because she knew he couldn't be using his gift on her to make her see his point of view. 'But weren't you annoyed at him on your own behalf. He *used* you.'

'How did you figure that one out?'

'Because you were always helping him with his work, leading up to his A levels. And then when they were done, he dropped you.'

Joe sighed. 'Kay, like I said, he *didn't* drop me. I tried to stay out of the house as much as I could that summer, then I went away to university. I kept in contact with him, but you weren't to know that, obviously. The thing with helping him with his A levels . . .' He cleared his throat.

'Look, I'm not proud of it, but his dad paid me to tutor him when he found out what my gift was. That's why Harry started coming around all the time, initially. I was saving up for that car, wasn't I? Harry and I had always been around each other through secondary school and got along OK, but we weren't what I would have called friends. But then when I started to tutor him, we got to know each other better and we were hanging out as much as working and I felt bad for taking the money, but Harry said not to worry because I *was* helping him and actually it meant he could come over and spend time with us, get some downtime too, without his dad constantly getting on his case . . .'

He trailed off and Kay sat down heavily on the cold metal bench.

'You think I'm awful for charging his dad to help him with his dyslexia, don't you?' Joe carried on, his voice pained. 'I do feel like a shit for it. Especially since it was the thing that made me realise I wanted to go into teaching and now when I see how hard it can be for kids, I can't believe I did it—'

'No,' she interrupted, like she was suddenly waking up, because there was no way she was ready to start thinking about the other implications of what he was saying just yet. 'No. That's not shitty, Joe. You get paid to teach now, don't you? It's fair enough. It's a great use of your gift.'

'That's what Harry always says.'

Of course he did. She felt like she'd put together some puzzle pieces years ago, figured it all out, and now she'd dusted the box off, it turned out the image didn't match. She'd forced pieces together that didn't belong. Finding out you were wrong about something was never a very comfortable feeling, but when you added the fact that it meant Kay was the *only* person Harry had decided he didn't want to continue a friendship with, it stung.

Joe had said he liked hanging out with both of them, so what had gone wrong? By trying to break out of the friend zone, had she freaked Harry out? It still didn't make his treatment of her respectful – he could have spoken to her, told her no thank you – but it not being the end of some underhand scheme to get what he wanted from Joe made it less of a character deficiency and more like one of those growing-pain moments, which everyone sometimes messes up. Goddess knew she'd messed up plenty. This news was having the simultaneous effect of making her think of him as less of a bastard, and herself as more of a reject.

Perfect.

She rubbed a hand hard over her sternum. 'Look, I'm sorry I dragged all this up now,' she said in a thick voice. 'I know you've got a million things to do, and I better call Mum.'

'Yeah,' Joe drew the word out slowly. 'Good luck with that.'

She gave a watery laugh. 'Thanks.'

They hung up and before she could chicken out of it – and also maybe because she didn't want the time to think too much – she immediately called her mother.

It sort of worked to snap her out of the stupor as she couldn't concentrate on her own misery when her mother's was so apparent. After they'd exhausted all the possibilities so her mum truly understood Kay was never going to make it to the dinner, they moved on to the strategy for her mum coping, with Kay encouraging her to enjoy it and not worry about her dad being there.

Even as she said these things, she wondered whether she was an enormous hypocrite because she had clearly let herself obsess over Harry and the emotional injuries she'd perceived he'd inflicted on her. Her parents had been married twenty years and there was no 'perceived' about it.

Not to mention what Kay had recently learned about herself and her extra 'gift'. Her presence would have brought all those feelings into stark relief, over and over again. Her mum hadn't stood a chance at ignoring how she felt and moving on from it with Kay around.

By the time she got off the phone, she was shaking, her eyes burning. Harry was walking over to her, and when he caught her eye, he accelerated his pace, taking her gently by the upper arms.

'What is it? Has something happened? Are you OK?'

What *had* happened? Good question. A wake-up call? A good hard slap around the face telling her she was *again* responsible for causing people around her additional pain? That she'd assumed a bunch of stuff about him and her brother, and now she was wondering how much she'd got wrong over the years.

'It . . . it just occurred to me that, not only did I cause my parents' divorce, my mum has never been able to get over it, because of me,' she admitted, because she had to admit something. And it wasn't going to be that she'd made a mistake about *him*. Something lay down that path, and she was far too anxious to follow it and find out what it was at the moment.

Harry's eyes darted over her face. 'Kay, the divorce wasn't your fault. Your parents' marriage was already dysfunctional. You just saw what your mum couldn't. Or even, what she could see, but couldn't face up to. As for never getting over the divorce, I don't understand?'

'Because I was always *there* exaggerating her feelings. I still am, always there, exaggerating her feelings. She turns to me for support and what I'm actually doing is making her painfully aware that she feels terrible. That she feels humiliated and hurt.'

'First off, no. You do not exaggerate people's emotions. They are just more aware of them around you. Secondly, you don't determine *what* the emotions are. They are what they are. Third, you don't even live with your mum. She's been living on her own for the majority of the last eight years if I've understood Joe correctly. And, finally, it's not your fault that it happens. It isn't something you can control. Just like I can't control the feeling about where I'm supposed to be or the eye thing. They're just there. Part of us.'

She stared up at him, the strength in his hands on her coat and the stern set of his jaw, accentuating the angle of it as a muscle popped. He was serious. And she knew he couldn't influence her this way – with a sheer force of his will – but it still seemed to filter through her as though it could.

It was a good point about her not having lived at home full time since she was eighteen or at all since she was twenty-one. She wasn't sure she could believe him necessarily about things not being her fault – because clearly the divorce wouldn't have happened if her gift hadn't revealed that her dad didn't love her mum anymore – but this secondary gift he said she had wasn't something she could feel happening or will in anyway so—

'Hang on. What eye thing?' She stared up into his eyes. Did they have something magical about them? Because she'd always felt like she was falling into them and if it was magic, then that might mean she was not as pathetically infatuated with him as she thought.

'My eyes change colour according to what the person looking at them wants to see. What's most aesthetically pleasing to them. It's an influencer thing to help . . .' he trailed off and cleared his throat, a blush touching his cheeks.

'To help make you attractive to them?' she concluded slowly.

He nodded and Kay watched his eyes like she was waiting to see something happen, like they would change colour in front of her like a mood ring, even though they'd always been the same to her. It made sense. That beautiful blue touched something within her soul. It was too perfect to be real.

'What colour are they really?'

Her own face heated up as the subject of finding him attractive was now firmly inserted into the small space between their bodies. Even though he'd said it was a general thing. It was to help *make* him attractive, not because you *found* him attractive already.

'It doesn't matter. But . . . not the colour of bluebells.' He gave a shrug and stepped back, shoving his hands in his pockets. She cringed internally, remembering when she'd made the comparison inside the cave. *Your eyes are like bluebells, your magic is so impressive, I'm going to follow you around Biddicote like a puppy unless you hit me on the nose with a rolled-up newspaper and send me away.*

An awkward silence stretched out, as though they were in their little bubble under the umbrella still and all the people passing them by were drops of rain separated from them by the magic.

'So. Feeling better?' Harry asked with a rueful smile as though he could tell he'd knocked her for another loop.

'Er . . . yes. Thank you.' She nodded, even though it wasn't true. They had other things to worry about.

'Right, so. I have the tickets, but all the car-rental places nearby don't have anything available until tomorrow at the earliest. There is one on the industrial estate outside of the city, but I actually have friends who live here, and I thought I might ask them if we could borrow theirs instead.'

Kay tightened the belt on her coat in lieu of pulling up her socks, because that's what she needed to do. 'You think they'd be OK with that? Would you be asking to drive it all the way back to England or leave it at the ferry port? Because we'll need to drive when we get to Harwich too, won't we?'

'I don't think they'll mind if we borrow it for the whole journey. They hardly ever use the car. And if we swing by there and they can't for some reason, we'll be halfway towards the industrial estate anyway.'

She nodded. Were his friends witches or non-magical? She should probably ask so she should probably ask, but, equally, she was beginning to feel a little exhausted by all the revelations about Harry and his life and his magic – not to mention how they seemed to spark revelations about her own – and she wasn't sure she could face mingling with his friends and rearranging more of the puzzle. Some space would really be good.

'Why don't you go sort that out and I'll do some sight-seeing, until you're ready with the car and it's time to go? I might go get myself some clean clothes as we're going to be stuck overnight again.'

Harry frowned and she knew he was entitled to look a little miffed about that. *You go sort everything out, and I'll go have a jolly.* It wasn't a good look, admittedly. But she felt like her emotions had been siphoned off into a cocktail maker, several scoopfuls of crushed ice and bitter lemon added, then given a violent shake.

'Come with me to Leon and Alex's,' Harry said, after a moment, in a tone that was half request and half persuasion.

'You'll freeze out in the snow and all this travelling is exhausting.'

'I could go to a museum, as well as the shops, and get some early dinner? By the time I've done all that, it'll probably be time to head off.'

'Maybe, but that's going to cost you and doesn't exactly give you rest time. We can figure something out with the clothes if that's bothering you. And they run a café; Leon is an amazing cook. We'll be comfortable there, honestly.'

Kay sighed. 'Why are you pushing this so much?'

'Because . . .' He dropped his gaze from hers, seemingly settling it on her tote bag for a moment. 'Because I'll be worried about you otherwise, Kay. Once it gets to the evening, there are some parts of Amsterdam that aren't great to walk around by yourself. The closer you get to the station in fact.'

It sounded so close to what Joe had been saying that it niggled painfully. Not because she minded people wanting her to be safe – but because it was *big-brotherly*. 'That's true of any city, Harry. I live in London.'

'Exactly. You know it.'

'I'm not a kid.'

'Believe me, I'm *aware*. But . . . what if you get lost? And we struggle to meet up on time? It just makes sense for us to stick together. I'll come with you if you really want to see the city that much. Forget borrowing the car, we'll get the rental.'

Now she was facing him tagging along with her anyway, there was really no point in objecting. She shook her head and grabbed her bag. 'No. It makes sense to go see your friends and ask for a favour. Let's do that. I'll come with you.'

'Great.' He gave her a big smile and picked up his duffel bag too, turning to lead the way.

They walked through the station again, the low ceilings and artificial lighting at the centre giving way to doors out onto a wide pedestrianised square, made all the brighter for the carpet of white hiding the pavement.

In contrast to the modern, clinical feeling inside the train station, Kay was shocked to turn and see it was housed in a grand old building of red brick, three or four storeys high and stretching out far past where she could see. There was a crest with lions looking down on the square and pointed dormers.

'Are we going to get a tram there?' she asked, cinching her collar together as snowflakes drifted down onto her hair. The tram stops were a lot more obvious than the ones in Prague had been and the rails were right there in front of them.

'Only if you really want to. Amsterdam isn't massive, and I could do with stretching my legs. Do you fancy seeing some of the city?'

'Sure.' Considering that she'd just been suggesting she go sightseeing without him, she could hardly say no. And besides which, as she looked out and saw the first canal, reflecting the warm colours of the buildings and the Victoria Hotel on the corner, the city stretched out before them, dusted white on its gabled roofs, she *did* want to walk through the streets and see what it was like.

Harry pulled out the umbrella but didn't put the spell on it again for some reason. Perhaps he needed to recoup after all the drawing with the little boy on the train. As they walked down the main thoroughfares, passing big shops, cars, bicycles and trams eased past them, forcing the snow into slushy grey piles at the edge of the pavement. Then they turned off onto some quieter streets, which only one or two cars ever drove through. The bridges over the

158

canals were gently curved affairs, barely noticeable until you were on top of their cobbles, looking down to see long canal boats gliding beneath their arches.

Kay nudged the handle of the umbrella and Harry obliged by tipping it back a little so she could look up properly, loving the way the buildings were narrow and tall, their roofs like milkmaids' hats, as they huddled either side of the roads. There were shiny black bollards to prevent cars driving through, capped with snowy hats, and places for bikes every couple of houses. Because there wasn't as much traffic, the snow was settling more and it crunched beneath her feet, making her toes numb. As they turned the corner, she slipped and skidded and Harry reached out to grab her arm, steadying her.

'Thanks,' she said and swallowed, trying to stop her heart from galloping up into her throat. Telling herself it was because she'd nearly landed on her butt – not because he'd pulled her close to him and his eyes looked bright and beautiful against the neutral backdrop of the brown town houses with the cream and white lintelled windows.

Those blue eyes. To make him more attractive to her. His magic must be as on the fritz as her own if it thought she needed any more convincing to find him attractive.

And that, right there, was what lay down the path she was too scared to travel.

Chapter Eleven

The alleyway was too narrow for even one car to pass down. They stopped before a single shopfront, with vibrant purple and yellow writing spelling out the word 'Abracadabra' over the window. Kay flicked a glance at Harry and wondered if she was about to walk into another place like Madam Hedvika's, set up to hide in plain sight. She still hadn't asked him whether his friends were witches or not. She'd barely said a word in fact, like her brain had grounded her tongue for its terrible behaviour of late and wasn't going to give it free rein again until it was very sure she wasn't going to say something stupid.

Now they were here, she no longer had an excuse to cling on to his arm and unwound it as they stepped inside. What she was not expecting, when they walked through the door, was to find out it was more of a coffee shop than a café. And not the latte, Frappuccino kind – although they obviously did serve beverages – but the kind Amsterdam was famous for. The aroma of nutty coffee was undercut with an earthy scent and the room hazy with smoke, even though it was only about half full.

'Harry . . .' she started.

'Don't worry, we're not going to be hanging out in this part . . .' He sent her a sly smile. 'Unless you want to?'

She wrinkled her nose. 'No. Thank you. Probably wouldn't be the best idea when we'll be going through customs in a few hours.'

'Good point.'

There was a huge man behind the counter, with shoulders the width of a doorway, long, wavy, dark-blond hair, a beard, and eyes a pale, icy blue. He did a double take as they grew closer to the bar and then slammed his hands down on the counter, leaning forward with a wide smile.

'*Snoepje!*' he boomed. 'Leon, Leon, Harry is *hier*!'

'*Hallo.*' Harry laughed and started to respond but was interrupted by someone else calling his name from the other end of the bar.

The man had just come into the coffee shop via another door, holding two plates with steaming toasties on them. Smaller in height and build than the Thor lookalike, with long locs pulled back into a ponytail and covered at the front of his head with a bright red bandana, he moved through the gap in the counter and started towards them. Then, he remembered himself, backtracked and slid the plates in front of a couple sitting at one of the small wooden tables. Once he was free of the food, he was bounding again towards Harry, grabbing him in a huge hug, and placing three smacking kisses, alternately, on his cheeks before leaning back.

'What the hell are you doing here?' he demanded, with a huge grin. 'You should have told us you were coming.'

'I was in Prague for a signing and the storm came in. It screwed up all the flights and we're trying to get home.'

At the mention of a 'we', Harry's friend looked over at Kay.

'Hello.' She gave a little wave.

'Hallo there,' he had a barely noticeable Dutch accent. 'Are you going to introduce me? Are you together-together, friends, or work colleagues?'

Well, here was a man who didn't beat around the bush with his questions.

'This is Kay. An old friend. We bumped into each other in Prague and teamed up, I suppose.' Harry looked over at her, his cheeks a little flushed. 'Kay, this is Leon—'

'Don't you dare call me an "old" friend.' Leon raised his eyebrow at Harry and moved around him to hold out his hand to Kay. She shook it and raised a tentative smile in the face of all this enthusiasm and familiarity.

'And Alex, his husband,' Harry continued, as Alex leaned down from his great height, offering her a hand the size of a pizza box.

'Nice to meet you, Kay. You are from England too, I take it?'

'That's right. Harry and I grew up in the same village.'

Leon gave a gasp. 'You're *that* Kay.'

'Leon . . .' Harry started, but Leon just gave what could only be described as a roguish smirk.

'Relax, H. That's great. It means you can both come through to the back.' His brown eyes twinkled as they studied her, and Kay's feeling of being all at sea only increased. He threw one arm around her shoulders and the other around Harry's waist and turned them towards Alex. 'Join us when Marje arrives for her shift?'

'As soon as I can,' his husband agreed.

'Perfect. Let's go through.' Leon continued to steer them.

'I've got a favour to ask actually,' Harry commented as they walked across the wooden floor towards the back.

'Sure, sure.'

162

'You don't even know what it is yet,' Harry said with a laugh.

'I know you'd never ask for anything unreasonable.' Leon shrugged as they came to the far end of the bar and a full-length tie-dyed curtain in shades of sunset red, orange and yellow. Beneath it was a pair of narrow wooden doors which looked like they had been crafted from pieces of driftwood but lacquered to a smooth-honeyed finish, with an all-seeing eye painted on each.

A faint tingle of magic touched Kay's skin, but nothing more, and Leon held the curtain back and ushered them through. There was a moment of coldness on the back of her neck, as though someone was watching her as she passed through, and she hesitated, but Harry was right behind her. The warmth of his body simultaneously reassured her and made her want to leap away in an act of self-preservation like that morning in bed.

At first, the other side just seemed like it was an even prettier extension of the coffee shop. There was a small stage in the back right-hand corner, carved wooden booths with embroidered cushions surrounding the tables, swaths of gauzy fabric hanging tepee-style over each, decorated with what looked like fairy lights but on closer inspection were glowing gems sewn into the weave of the delicate fabric.

That kind of enchantment could pass in the non-magical world, but of the two tables occupied, Kay noticed something openly magical happening at each. One group were playing a card game where the pack dealt itself according to raps on the top of the deck and a woman at the other was absently changing the colour of the petals on the flowering plant on the table as she talked to her friends.

Everyone in this room was either a witch or aware of the witching world. That was what Kay had felt as she'd come in through the doors – the all-seeing eye was infused with magic to dissuade non-magical people from trying to enter, and if that didn't work, there was a charm to repel them. It was a witches-only club.

Kay frowned and stuffed her hands in her pockets – wondering if Harry had felt the same coldness, the way she had – or if she'd noticed it more because of her magic going haywire.

Had she ignored her magic for so long she was beginning to lose it? Maybe all the mishaps were just the first symptom of it dying away completely? A soft ache of sadness closed up her throat. She knew she'd always thought of her gift as useless, but if she no longer had *any* magic, because she'd stopped using it voluntarily or because she was obligated to in order to protect others, would that mean she was no longer a witch?

'Right, let's get you some food,' Leon said, providing a blessed interruption to her fretting. 'More people will start arriving for dinner soon, but you can grab whatever table you like. Which calls to you?'

Kay looked at Leon. 'What's the difference? Are there charms on them or something?'

'So suspicious, Smurfette.'

'Smurfette had blonde hair, not blue,' Harry pointed out.

'Did she? Ah well, in answer to your question, Kay, yes, they are charmed, and whichever you pick helps to guide me when I'm cooking your meal.'

'Oh, you're an influencer too. With food.' She flicked a look at Harry, who chewed on his bottom lip in a way that made her think he was both nervous of how she was going to react . . . and ridiculously sexy. Blinking the lust away, she asked, in as neutral a tone as possible: 'What if I don't want influenced food?'

Leon frowned at her. '*Dropje*, I'm not trying to poison you.' He looked at Harry for a moment and they seemed to communicate something without speaking, which irritated her.

She took a deep breath, because getting irritated with the man you were hoping to borrow a car off, and who was offering to feed you in his beautiful and cosy restaurant, wasn't exactly a great move. Also, what if it was like Harry with his artwork and he had to try really hard *not* to infuse his food with his magic? Was she just being awkward for the sake of it?

'All right, all right.' She held up her hands and looked around the room, examining each of the vacant booths. They all seemed equally lovely, but, as she let her eyes wander, the one farthest away which had a stained-glass window inset into the wall, bathing the table softly in different coloured light, struck her as the one she most wanted to sit at. 'That one, please.'

Leon sent her a grin. 'OK then. That totally makes sense.'

Kay stifled another sigh. Why? Why did it make sense? She was getting kind of tired of the way most of the witches she was meeting this weekend seemed to understand something about her and her magic that she didn't understand herself.

But if she'd been learning anything about herself recently, it was that there really *was* a lot she didn't know, magical or otherwise. So, as they walked over, she tried again to leave her prickliness behind. Leon had been nothing but welcoming to her, and this was his business. He'd thought up a clever way to use his gift within the witching community; all the patrons would fully understand what they were getting when they came here, and it offered them a safe place to relax and freely use their magic which wasn't just the privacy of their own homes.

'What happens if someone wants the table where someone else is sitting?' she asked.

'Then they can choose to wait. Or their second choice is just as revealing.'

'And what if other people in the party want to sit somewhere else?'

'Generally, there is either a dominant member in need of something or a wavelength the group are on. I can tell the difference.'

'How?'

'Can't give away my secrets.' Leon tapped the side of his nose where a diamond stud glinted at her. 'That's what makes the place unique.'

She'd chosen the table, so did that mean she was the one whose needs were the most dominant or that she and Harry were on the same wavelength? She supposed the latter would make sense – they were both desperate to get home, worn out from the journey and trying to get along.

Leon settled them in the booth and left to grab drinks and menus. As Kay took off her coat, some of the tension immediately loosened from around her neck and shoulders. The cushions were softer than they looked, most likely because they had been fabricated with the magical equivalent of memory foam.

Harry was sitting opposite her, a lopsided smile tugging at his mouth as he tilted his face up to examine the stained-glass window. Kay's breath grew shallow as she tried to figure out why seeing the slope from the underside of his chin to his exposed throat gave her the same sensation as finding a rare piece of vintage jewellery; wanting to trace her fingers over it to learn every unique millimetre; wishing others could understand how precious it was without needing to touch it themselves, so she could keep it safe.

She blinked as he turned his head towards her, catching her staring. She tried to clear her throat and it came out like a little dry cough. 'Leon won't take offence at my questions, will he?' She chewed on the edge of her fingernail. 'I don't mean to sound so suspicious. Or judgemental.'

Harry raised his eyebrows. 'You don't mean to *sound* it, or don't mean to *be* it?'

A hot, uncomfortable emotion swirled in her chest, and she parted her lips, unsure how to answer that.

Harry shook his head. 'It's OK. Leon would much prefer to know if you have a problem with anything upfront. He's all for informed consent and he'll appreciate the way you want to examine things from all angles to make sure they're ethical.'

She blinked. 'Was that what I was doing?'

She might have been imagining it, but it seemed like his eyes warmed as they coasted briefly over her face. Or, it might have been a trick of his influencer eyes. 'Sure. It's your thing, Kay. You're Lawful Good. It's important to have people like you prompting regular healthy debates, making sure our powers don't get used for nefarious purposes.'

She couldn't tell whether he was teasing her or he meant it. Either way, the awkward burning sensation inside her eased. 'Was that a Dungeons and Dragons reference?'

'Yeah. You can blame Alex for getting me into all of that.'

'So, how long have you all been friends?'

'Well, I met Leon first, when we were both living in Edinburgh.'

'Oh, when was that?'

'I went to university there. We met in my second year.'

Kay's mouth fell open again. He'd gone to Edinburgh University? She'd thought he was going to go to the University of Arts in London. That had always been the plan. When had he changed his mind? Obviously before he decided he wanted to become an illustrator, as he'd said on the train that he'd decided that while studying for his degree. She bit down on the desire to ask a million follow-up questions that would lead to a conversation she wasn't ready to have yet. 'Leon was studying there too?'

'No. He's a couple of years older than me.'

She crossed her arms on the table, with a smirk. 'Is that why he's a bit sensitive about being called an "old" friend?'

Harry laughed. 'Probably. He was already through catering college and working at a restaurant I went to. I could tell there was magic in his food—'

'And when he said he wanted to give his compliments to the chef,' Leon appeared back at the table with their drinks, 'I walked out and saw this face.' He leaned over and tilted Harry's chin up at him, smiling down with affection. 'Who could resist? Had me cooking for him for three years.'

'You make it sound like I used you purely for your cooking skills.' Harry blushed and pulled his face away but gave Leon's hand a quick squeeze as he did so.

'Oh no, it was definitely a give-and-take relationship.' Leon winked at him and then pulled his notepad from his back pocket and took their orders. 'I'll go get that food cooking for you.'

Kay bit the inside of her cheek as she took the empty glass and bottle of chocolate milk Leon had brought out for her. She'd not ordered it, but it actually looked like the perfect thing she needed right at that moment, to wash away the taste of jealousy in her mouth.

Don't say it, don't say it—

'So, you and Leon were together?' she asked in a ridiculously high pitch, regardless of her better judgement or whatever passed for her self-respect these days. She poured the glossy brown liquid into the glass, watching it coat the sides and settle thickly at the bottom.

'Yes. Like he said, we were together three years. My first – only – long-term relationship, I suppose.'

Kay was nodding like a marionette. She was fine. Totally, totally not seething with envy that Leon could reach out and touch Harry's chin that way, with total confidence. Had been able to do so for years and years. 'Why – er – why didn't you say we were coming to see your ex, rather than your friend?' *Why didn't you warn me?*

'Because he *is* my friend. We've been friends for longer than we dated, so . . .' he shrugged. 'That's who he is now in my life.'

Kay took a sip of the chocolate milk. Sweet and creamy. The hit of comfort she needed at that moment. 'I guess that makes sense,' she managed when she realised he was watching her. He nodded slowly and his eyes caught hers, filled with some emotion she wasn't sure she understood. 'And I only thought it would have been good to mention that we were coming to ask a favour of your ex because it's a bit awkward,' she added.

'Why does his being my ex make it awkward?' Harry was studying her with the intensity of cat who had noticed a rustle in the bushes and was not going to miss the opportunity of an unsuspecting bird. She could tell a small smile was threatening his mouth, not because of his lips but because of the laughter lines deepening at the corners of his eyes.

'It's not. I mean. Not for *me*.' She rolled her eyes. 'But surely for Alex. It might have been nice to know you were dragging me along to a three's-a-crowd situation.' She raised an eyebrow to show she was mostly joking. 'I don't think you can even class me as a third wheel – I'm more like a deflated tyre that's been forgotten in the boot.'

'This kind of talk better not be premonitory of the next leg of our journey.'

'Goddess, you're right. Quick, give me the salt.'

He pushed it across the table towards her and she sprinkled a little in her hand, whispered some cleansing words and dabbed her tongue to it before she remembered she wasn't supposed to be doing any kind of magic whatsoever. Being in this restaurant, relaxing in a community of witches who didn't have to hide what they were, had made her forget herself. Kay tensed up, half expecting something awful to happen because she'd broken Madam Hedvika's instructions, but all she felt was the fizz of the spell erasing some of the negative energy she might've invoked.

Harry laughed and she cocked her head to one side. 'What?'

'I feel like maybe it's too little, too late. We should have cracked out the cleansing rituals in Prague.'

She laughed too. 'We would have died of kidney failure by now.'

He smiled back at her, his eyes scanning her face and landing on her mouth. Her heartbeat fluttered. She remembered that look. He'd looked at her like that when they were teenagers too. Like her laughter was fascinating. Or that's what she'd hoped it meant back then. Now, it was probably more a case that she'd not allowed herself to laugh much in his presence over the last twenty-four hours.

'Alex and I genuinely get along,' he said, when she looked away from him. 'There's no third- or fourth-wheel situation. I promise.'

She nodded quietly.

Hearing Harry talk about this grown-up relationship he'd had, and how they were all able to stay friends, which she could see with her own eyes was true – no magic gift necessary for that special insight – just threw into contrast how she'd been dealing with relationships in *her* adult life. Like a really depressing spot-the-difference. Avoiding serious relationships with witches and non-magical people alike because they were too complicated. Sure, she dated non-magical people, she'd even had a couple of boyfriends make it to the six-month mark, but she'd never considered committing enough to tell them about the witch stuff.

It was a little like that moment in films – the one Spielberg used in *Jaws* – where the camera went from doing this wide-focus shot, to narrowing right down on the man's face. All the hubbub and chaos on the beach, fading into the background to highlight this pinprick of horror-filled awareness.

'Are you OK?' Harry leaned towards her across the table and she realised she'd been having her '*Jaws*' moment right in front of him.

'Oh, yeah, sure.' She nodded again and sent him a smile. *Just having an epiphany about how I've been making myself an emotional cul-de-sac since I was sixteen.*

Leon appeared then with their food and her mouth automatically filled with saliva at the mind-blowing aroma wafting over to her.

'Enjoy. I'll leave you to eat, and then I have a favour to ask of *you*, H.'

'Of course. Anything.'

'Not a fan of your own advice, are you? You should know by now I *will* ask for unreasonable things.' Leon laughed and slid two deep white and blue striped dishes before them. They were heaped with a vegetable mash, slivers of beef and doused in a glossy tan gravy. It smelt like cosy afternoons in winter, windows steamed up and fire roaring as you snuggled up under a fleece, reading.

And it tasted even better. The mash wasn't completely smooth, so the textures of the onion and potato and carrot caught occasionally on her tongue before they melted away and the tender beef soaked in gravy added a rich umami flavour to it all.

There was silence as they ate, and Kay realised how much she'd needed the simple contentment of eating a lovingly prepared meal and being somewhere comfortable where she was welcomed. Conferences were such a rush, and it had all been buffet foods or working meals, with colleagues or clients, where you couldn't exactly relax. Then there was the travelling. The last time she'd felt even a smidgen this relaxed was on her impromptu spa evening with Ilina and that had been missing the nourishing, tasty food.

Was that the magic Leon had infused it with? Both she and Harry could probably do with the comfort of being at home after all the travelling. She supposed she'd have to wait and see once her body started properly digesting; at the moment, all she had was a tingle of magic on her tongue where it was beginning to enter her bloodstream.

Harry was already scraping the bottom of his dish. He licked the spoon and let out a groan of satisfaction and Kay felt a dangerous leap in her tummy. He caught her eye and then checked out how she was progressing with her own meal.

'He's good, isn't he?'

'*So* good.'

'To think, you wanted to wander the snowy streets and buy a random bagel somewhere.' He gave a faux-despairing sigh and a little shake of his head.

'I'm sure the bagel would have been adequate,' she said.

'You deserve better than adequate.'

Her hand trembled a little as she lowered her spoon. He was just bantering with her. To prove it to herself, she ignored the warmth his comment filled her with and continued the sallying instead. 'So, did you worry it was a little bit Freudian, you shacking up with someone with the same gift as your mother?'

'Kay, no,' Harry clapped his hands over his ears and shook his head, but he was laughing.

'Sorry,' she said, laughing too.

'You're not sorry,' he accused, dropping his hands.

'Well, it must have crossed your mind,' she protested. Why hadn't she done this earlier? She should have known that the best way to pretend she wasn't jealous of his history with Leon was – bizarrely – for her to tease him about it.

'OK, yes, it did. But obviously it wasn't what attracted me to him, because I'm not a character from a Greek tragedy. If anything—' he broke off, pressing his lips together and rubbing his finger over them.

'If anything . . .?'

'If anything . . . it was like jumping in the deep end. I had to learn to trust him, despite it. Leon proved to me that not everyone with the same gifts or affinities will use them in the same way. It's down to the person. Not the magic.'

Kay transferred her attention back to depositing the last of the delicious food into her mouth. As she chewed and swallowed slowly, she counted up the truths he was telling her. Even as an influencer himself, he'd had to learn to let his guard down around others of the same affinity. Maybe he hadn't been teasing her earlier when he'd said they needed people like her to question the ethics of magic.

Did his own parents lead him to feel that way? She'd seen his dad use his gift on Harry when he was underage, and now Harry was implying he hadn't been comfortable with the way his mother used her gift either.

'Did she use it on you a lot? Your mum?' she asked carefully.

Harry pushed a hand through his hair and tugged it a little. 'I think she meant well, but both my parents . . . they have such a responsibility. To Biddicote and all the witches that live there. They're used to employing their magic in a way that . . . They're looking at the big picture. For the greater good. And it didn't always . . . gel with what I felt I needed from them.'

'Like having their support for your career choice?' Kay shifted on her seat, hating the way that he was deliberating over his words. Hating the way his shoulders were hunched in.

He attempted a laugh, but she knew it wasn't genuine. His hand slipped to the back of his neck and squeezed. 'That sort of thing, I guess. They just wanted me to understand and were trying to prepare me for what was to come, I think. Like schmoozing with the Witches Council. It's not my favourite.'

'So they used their gifts to make you do it anyway?'

Harry exhaled slowly from his mouth. 'It's complicated.' He shook his head, all the humour of their banter having evaporated. 'Families, eh? D'you mind if we talk about something else?'

'Of course,' she murmured and then Leon came back over and saved her from dropping her face into her bowl and trying to drown herself in the leftover gravy for her unfailing ability to make things awkward again.

Harry shook off his mood almost immediately as Leon proceeded to ask him if he would complete a mural with runes that a local artist had left unfinished because he got a chance to exhibit at some fancy museum in Paris.

'That sounds a bit out of my area,' Harry objected. Rune magic was a complicated matter; the smallest deviations in design, intention or magical infusion caused big differences in their effects. They tapped into something ancient and drew a lot of energy.

'It's not. At all. They're not tricky runes. Very simple. He was the one that didn't really want to do it. It wasn't his thing and he's not done the greatest job with what little there is. I've had to cover it up because it's unsettling, left half-done.'

'What is it?' Harry asked.

'I actually spoke to you about it before, remember? It's a tree, over there by the stage.'

'Oh, yeah. Infused to do what again?'

'To encourage kindness. We have these poetry slams and guest musicians in sometimes and I just want to discourage hecklers. But the witch I had work on it – well, you'll understand when you look at it. Come over.'

When Kay stayed sitting, Leon made it clear he was inviting her too. He led them over to the stage and lifted a swathe of green velvet that had been tacked at door height on the right hand of the stage, where it would be visible to everyone. Beneath was the outline of a tree, in hyper-stylised lines of silver paint, limbs reaching out like fingers, curled subtly into rune shapes. Immediately, Kay felt a grip in her gut of shame.

Independent to the slow build-up she'd been experiencing over the last day, that was.

'Ugh,' Harry said and then coughed. 'Sorry – it was clearly going to be a beautiful tree; I'm not being critical of the art.'

'You can see my problem, though. It's in no way conditional to you borrowing the car by the way. But can you fix it, Harry? Please?'

Harry chewed on his bottom lip and then reached out, running his fingers over the paint. Kay found herself mesmerised by the way he used just his index and middle finger, such a light touch, skimming over it, while his eyes followed the line intently.

Artist-porn. Was that a thing? No sex, just watching a beautiful man with long fingers and lots of talent be all intense and precise.

She blinked and forced herself to look away, finding Leon watching her. He smirked a little but didn't say anything.

'Yes,' Harry said finally, dropping his hand, oblivious to the silent communication going on behind him. 'If you have paints. And some turps.'

'He left a bunch of stuff in the office. I'll go dig it out. Thank you. I wish you could have come out to do it in the first place. Your magic is always beautiful.'

'I'm sorry.' Harry rubbed the back of his neck, still talking to Leon. 'It's difficult at the moment.'

'Hush, hush. I know.' Leon took Harry by the head, bending it down so he could plant a kiss on his forehead before he went off to the office.

What was difficult for Harry at the moment? Kay wanted to know, the way Leon knew.

There was a blush on Harry's cheeks, but he was getting on with unbuttoning his cuffs and rolling up his sleeves. The rhythmic twist of his wrist as he folded back the material was hypnotic. 'This won't take long, I promise. About an hour.'

The truth was, she hadn't even thought about the time or the ferry or the journey. She'd just been thinking that she couldn't wait to see him at work on the mural.

And his forearms. She'd been thinking about those too. In detail. The lean, firm muscles, decorated with fair hair

176

and freckles. She wanted to trace them with her fingertip like she was mapping constellations on his skin.

Making some kind of noise at him, which she hoped passed for calm and collected, she retreated to their booth in the corner to finish her drink and watched as Harry set to work once Leon brought the paints out. He started by getting the turps and mixing it in a bowl with a tablespoon of salt and fresh sage which Leon supplied from the kitchen. Then he took a rag and carefully scuffed it over the outline of the top of the tree, while whispering a charm – probably something similar to the cleansing spell she'd used just before. The paint faded some but didn't get smeared or wiped away and then he started mixing his own paint.

With the comfortable seat, twinkly lights, warm, delicious food in her stomach and view of Harry, Kay was beginning to wish she could stay at Abracadabra's for far longer than a few hours. She didn't even need to worry about her magical mishaps so much – she was surrounded by witches. And when had the last one happened anyway?

Time slipped around her like a gentle river, tables filling up, Leon and another waitress bringing out food. Alex came in too at one point and Harry sat up on the edge of the stage, taking a break to have a drink and chat to him, their ease with each other obvious.

Kay hadn't even realised that she'd finished her drink until Leon slid a big cup of coffee in front of her. She thanked him, sitting up from the slouch she'd sunk into.

'Figured you could do with a cup of solace. Sounds like you've been having an exhausting journey and these seats will have you falling to sleep if you're not careful.'

'Is there an influence charm on them to make people want to stay?' she asked, lacing her hands around the warm mug.

Leon raised an eyebrow. 'Since that would be exploitative, I will choose to take that as a sign that you are enjoying your visit, rather than an accusation.'

'Could it be both?' she dared to say and was rewarded by Leon's laughter. Harry was right. Leon did appreciate candidness.

'It appears so. May I?'

'Sure. It's your place,' she pointed out with a laugh.

'I think customers would stop coming altogether, let alone want to stay, if I sat myself down beside them, uninvited.' He slid in opposite her, setting a thick earthen plate loaded with large cookies down. 'I'm enjoying your visit too,' he said, propping his elbow on the table and resting his chin on his knuckles. 'It's great to finally meet you. I've heard a lot about you.'

'Have you?' she tried to keep her voice light, even though the simple statement sent everything inside her up in a flurry.

'For sure. When we first got together, he'd always mention you. "Kay has this theory about Leonardo da Vinci." "Kay cracks up at this movie, even though it's terrible." That sort of thing.' Leon grinned at her.

'Oh. That's really . . . weird?' she blurted out. It *was* weird though. Unless . . . it kind of proved that Harry had liked her as a friend, but never had any romantic feelings towards her. Surely he wouldn't have chatted to his new boyfriend about her if he had?

'Is it? You were important to him.' Leon glanced at Kay as her heart betrayed her with a painfully hopeful flutter. 'It took his seer ability, sending him after *you*, to prise him away from Ashworth Hall.'

Kay took a sip of the frothy coffee, licking foam from her lips, to buy herself a moment. 'What? No. He was in

Prague doing a signing. It was just a coincidence that we bumped into each other.'

'Sure,' he snorted. 'Witches' lives are just full of "random coincidences". He's been asked to do *a lot* of signings over the last couple of years. He said no to all of them. Then the one he finally says yes to has him bumping into *you* when you're about to be stranded and need some help getting home.'

Leon was great, but he was obviously deluded. There was no way Harry's itchy magic compass had sent him all the way to the Czech capital, just to help her get back to Joe's wedding. She wasn't going to argue about it, though. 'Why has he been saying no? He loves travelling, doesn't he?'

Curiosity killed the cat, Kay. But she couldn't seem to help herself. Was it something about Leon or something he'd put in her food that was making her lose her brain to mouth filter?

'He hasn't told you about his dad?'

'What about his dad?' Had he been demanding things from him? Getting him involved with the business when Harry had his own career? Influencing him to stay at Ashworth Hall to represent the family?

'It's not really my place to say. I'm surprised you don't know, though.'

Kay's inner hedgehog quills flared. That wasn't *her* fault. And also . . . she hated the implication that Leon knew Harry better than she did. Even though it was inescapably true. They'd had a relationship. They were friends who shared the details of their lives with one another. 'We've not exactly been on talking terms for a long time.'

'I know.' Leon glanced over his shoulder at Harry, drumming his fingers on the table for a moment. 'I'm glad you've forgiven him.'

'I . . . I don't know that I have forgiven him yet,' she told Leon, an almost complete stranger, with a surprising amount of honesty.

'Why not?' Leon frowned at her, but she could tell it was more curiosity than censure.

She mentally smoothed her quills down. 'Because I still don't know why he did it.'

'Oh, OK.' He lifted his head from his hand, waving it in dismissal. 'That's an easy fix. You've got a tongue in your head, haven't you?'

She made a choked little laugh. He made it sound so simple.

The funny thing was, for a moment, it did seem pretty simple. Just ask Harry what happened.

But then a wave of fear crashed over her again as she imagined what he would say. Answers she probably didn't want to hear. But how would she ever move on if she didn't at least try to find out?

She took a deep breath. 'Are these for anyone in particular?' she asked, pointing to the plate of gooey cookies in front of Leon.

'Complimentary for everyone after their dinner,' he explained, sliding it over to her with a gentle magical push. 'Help yourself but—'

She'd already picked one up and taken a huge bite. The melt of the fudge chunks inside was heaven.

'Er, slow down a sec, there. I was about to tell you. They're space cookies.'

Kay was in the middle of swallowing and almost choked. The marijuana-laced food made it down her throat and settled heavily in her stomach. Another time bomb to add to her collection. 'That'll teach me for trying to self-soothe, won't it.' She placed the rest of it down on a napkin. 'It was only a bite, right? I should be fine.'

'Erm . . . yeah?' He winced in a way that wasn't exactly reassuring.

She shook her head. 'Don't worry about it. It's pretty standard for this trip, believe me.' Getting arrested at customs and excise was probably going to happen right on schedule. She started laughing, imagining them looking for her drugs stash and finding the battered corn husk doll. And once she started, she could hardly stop. There was no way it was anything to do with the cookie she'd only just eaten. The laughter was because, well, what else could she do at this point?

Across the room, Harry looked up from his painting, straight over to her, like her laughter had called to him. She took a deep breath and met his gaze.

Leon was right. It was time to get answers.

Chapter Twelve

'I'm just going to clean myself up in Leon and Alex's apartment,' Harry told her, coming back to the table a while later. Leon had needed to go back to work, so Kay had returned to watching Harry from a distance and she was feeling restless from the effect of that, alongside her sudden, urgent desire to Talk.

Harry wiped at the silvery flecks of paint on his hands and shirt with a crumpled rag and Kay noticed one on the corner of his chin. She stood up, just barely resisting the impulse to use her thumb to wipe it away. The sudden motion gave her a head rush and she caught the edge of the table to steady herself. Little magical tingles had been blooming on and off within her stomach and slowly spreading out, which she'd assumed were to do with Leon's magic, but the heaviness to her limbs and general softness around the edges of everything was more like what she remembered of the few times she'd smoked a joint back at university.

'Will you be OK here?' Harry asked her, his eyebrows pulling together.

'I wouldn't mind freshening up a bit myself before we start the next leg of the Odyssey,' she said, trying to style out the way she had almost launched herself across the table at him.

'Of course. Apparently, the snow is due to start coming down heavier through the evening, so I think we should leave sooner rather than later.' He reached for his bag and coat, but she got there first.

'I'll bring them. So you don't get paint on them.' She folded both their coats over her arm, tempted to give his a rattle, and then hooked their bags over her shoulder.

He blinked. 'Sure you're OK with all that?'

'Sure, I'm sure.' She patted the bags and then waddled out of the booth and followed him through a door at the back, and past the kitchens, where Leon waved to them. From there was another door, up a staircase to a beautiful apartment with high ceilings and wooden floors.

'The bathroom is through here.' Harry pointed to a door on the far side of the room. 'Do you want to use it first?'

'No. You go first. You're the one all' – she flicked her spare hand up and down at him – 'painty.'

He raised an eyebrow and went into the bathroom, clicking the light on and pulling the door shut, while Kay settled on the sofa, putting their coats and bags down. The seats were a gorgeous purple, with an embroidered deep red throw draped across the back. She ran her fingers over it as she heard the taps turning on.

Looking around the room, she saw little touches of Leon and Alex's life together and wondered if Harry and Leon had lived together too. In this other life he'd been living that was completely different to what she'd assumed. Paving his own way as an illustrator, maintaining his friendship with her brother, having grown-up relationships. What else didn't she know—

No. No more questions just bouncing around in her head.

She pushed herself up off the sofa and, before she'd even really thought it through, opened the door to the bathroom.

Harry straightened up from where he was at the sink, water running down his face and dripping off his hands. His gaze darted to the sides of her as though looking to see where the fire was. 'Kay, what are you doing in here?'

'Apparently, I like bursting in on you when you're in the bathroom.' She blinked at the droplets tracking down his neck, dampening the collar of his shirt.

'Does that mean I'm in trouble again?' he asked warily, as he shook his hands off and grabbed a towel, tilting his head as she pushed the door closed behind her.

'Harry. I need you to . . .' *Talk to me, tell me how you felt about me, tell me what went wrong* – all of these were great options. Instead, what came out of her mouth was: 'Kiss me.'

Whoa.

She clapped a palm over her mouth and then held out the index finger from her other hand, as though that could stall him from reacting. Weirdly, it did seem to work. He dropped the towel on the floor, but then stood frozen, staring at her, his eyes wide.

A wave of sensation, like pins and needles, rippled throughout her. It was strange but not unpleasant. She swallowed and lowered both her hands. 'That . . . that was not what I intended to say.'

He nodded slowly. Both of them were acting as though they were pointing guns at each other. 'What *did* you intend to say?'

'I . . .' She took a moment to refocus on the reason she'd come in the bathroom. 'I'd like to know why you

184

tried to influence me, in that note when you stood me up. And *why* you stood me up. I mean . . . I don't need you to explain that you didn't want to date. I get that, it's fine, you didn't want to. But you could have just said "no" when I asked you out. It would have been enough.'

Harry looked down for a moment at the towel he'd dropped. He bent his knees to pick it up and hung it on the rack carefully – all without looking at her. The bathroom was a lot bigger than the one on the plane, but Kay felt more exposed than if he'd walked in on *her* in the shower.

Raking both hands back through his hair, he finally fastened those blue eyes on her. 'No,' he said simply. 'No, it wouldn't have been enough.'

She flushed. 'I know I was a bit starry-eyed, but I wouldn't have chased after you. I would have understood. We could have still been friends. Unless . . . we weren't ever friends. You were just humouring me because you didn't want to upset Joe?'

'No . . .' He shook his head, stopping abruptly like he'd run into an invisible wall. 'I'm not sure we should be having this conversation now. I think Leon's food is working.'

'You know what he influenced it with?'

'Bravery. I think. Or honesty. I guess they often amount to the same thing.'

'Well, that makes sense. Because I'm not sure I would have opened myself up to sounding quite this pathetic without any encouragement,' she admitted and then gasped as though the words had been torn from her throat. 'OK, wow. That's some strong magic.'

'Right. Maybe we should talk about it later, when the influence has passed?'

'I don't know.' She crossed her arms. Her stomach was flipping and she could feel the influence pushing on her now.

Convincing her that it wasn't a good idea to leave it until later, because she'd chicken out. Damn, Leon was good at what he did. She might have resented it, but it *was* exactly what she needed, wasn't it? 'You don't seem to be having the same kind of trouble, keeping your own counsel.'

Harry wiped his hand down his face and gave a humourless laugh. 'I guess I'm not so inclined towards honesty or bravery as you are.'

'That's a shame. Because I think I deserve an answer.' Her chest ached as she pulled in a deep breath to say something she knew to be true, but wasn't necessarily easy to face. 'But if you can't bring yourself to tell me, even now, maybe that's everything I need to know.' She turned towards the door.

'Wait.' His footsteps approached swiftly, and he put his hand flat on the door over her shoulder, stopping her from opening it. 'You do deserve an answer.' His breath puffed, soft and warm against the back of her neck, sending goosebumps along her skin.

She turned back to face him, leaning against the door. He swallowed, and her eyes tracked the ripple down his throat, before heading back up to his mouth.

'I convinced myself I needed to leave Biddicote,' he continued, softly. 'I'd applied to Edinburgh, told my dad it was just as a back-up, in case London didn't accept me . . . but that was my escape plan.'

'Escape from what?' she whispered back, like she didn't want to speak too loudly in case she spooked him, when he was finally opening up.

'The pressure from my family that last year of sixth form. I didn't understand where it had come from, why it suddenly felt so stifling. Every move I made, my parents were there, judging me against the yardstick of the Ashworth family legacy, reminding me what I have to live up to . . .' He removed his hand from the door, straightening up but not moving back. Her chest was hot, the heat of his body sinking into her. 'I didn't know how much of what I felt was what they told me I *should* feel, or what was genuinely me. And then I started tutoring with Joe and I spent more and more time with you . . . and I kept telling myself it was just a crush, and that I'd get over it, but you were so clever, and funny, and passionate, and kind, and I knew – *I knew* – if you and I had started dating, or even if we'd just stayed friends, I would have wanted to take that university place in London so I could still see you. I would have come back home on the weekends, all the holidays . . .'

She flattened her hands against the cool, painted wood of the door behind her, trying to ground herself, because it was hard to believe what she was hearing. He'd had a crush. On *her*. He thought she was all those wonderful things?

Or had been.

But his parents had pushed him so hard he'd been that desperate to get away?

'If you'd explained it to me, I would have understood. I would have supported you to go to Edinburgh, I already knew the way your dad was always on your case—'

He shook his head. 'You're not hearing me. *I* couldn't have gone. Not all the while I thought you might want me . . . the way I wanted you.' His gaze flickered over her face before he met her eyes for a long, intense moment, rousing all her attraction into a fiery storm. She had to drag in a deep breath in order to be able to speak again, because she still needed to understand.

'So . . . that's why you made me hate you?'

He shut his eyes. 'Yes. It was so selfish. I know it was. I hurt you on purpose. It was mostly accidental – the influencing – it just poured out of me as I wrote the note, but I still made the choice to give it to you, knowing how it would make you feel. And part of me thought it would at least be better than hurting, even more than you already were because of what was going on with your family. You hating me is only what I deserve.' He let out a shaky breath, then opened his eyes but kept looking down, his coppery eyelashes fanning against the pale shadows beneath. 'I fucked up in so many ways and I'm sorry. So sorry.'

There it was. The answer. And the apology. In an abstract way she knew it was good to finally have it, but it was like she'd been digging for a treasure chest and though she'd found it, the actual gems were scattered around it, rather than inside, and they didn't look anything like she'd expected. They were the things she was more interested in at the moment.

'You did want me?' she breathed. 'Back then?'

He nodded and lifted his chin, his eyes hooded as he looked down at her. 'So much.'

There were a couple of small dark freckles, sitting at the edge of his lips where they met his skin. She touched her finger to one then followed the generous curve of his mouth, tingles racing down her hand and up her arm. Not magic tingles. Not space cookie tingles. These were Harry tingles.

She ran her tongue along her own lower lip and his breath shuddered out and over her skin.

He cupped her face, sliding his hands up, so his damp fingers caught in the strands of her hair and his fingertips rested, cool and gentle, against her scalp, sending shivers down her neck. He leaned in. 'Still do.'

Her heart had fought its way up to hammer at the base of her throat. Electricity crackled beneath her skin.

She was sixteen, in the cave again, the hope that she was finally going to get to kiss Harry Ashworth making her weak. She wasn't going to risk the chance being taken away from her this time.

She took him by the collar, lifted up onto her tiptoes and fitted her mouth against his.

His lips were as amazing as they had always looked, soft but firm, and she was already melting from the feel of them on hers, when he responded and everything became a dizzying rush of the world falling away, but her body sparking to life in an agony of awareness.

His mouth brushed over hers, again and again, gentle as waves lapping at a shore, approaching, and retreating, learning what made her breath hitch, teasing her by doing it again, drugging her with a slow rhythm, winding her desire tighter and tighter within her until she was desperate for more.

She ran her hands down his shirt, the feel of his lean, warm muscles beneath adding to the charge building within her. She clutched handfuls of the material, pulling him closer, and his fingers mirrored the motion, tightening in her hair, tipping her head back further. The glide of their mouths grew faster, greedier, as he guided her head from one angle to another, exploring so thoroughly, she could barely catch her breath. The confidence that this was *happening* and it was *good* sinking in. So good.

Her legs lost their strength, the bones and muscles dissolving. She had to come down off her tiptoes, making a dull thump against the door as she leaned back against it. Harry's body crowded closer and Kay slipped her hands around his waist, tugging his shirt free of his trousers until her palms could slide up his back, skin against skin.

A moan rumbled up from his throat and he grabbed her by the thighs, lifting her up, carrying her the couple of steps over to the bathroom counter and sitting her on the edge of it. She tugged him even nearer with her fingers hooked in his belt loops. A sound that was somehow both surprise and relief escaped her as he slotted into the space between her spread thighs, pressing against her where she was growing heavy with warmth and anticipation, where he was solid and thick.

He swore under his breath and his hand was at her jaw, thumb tracing her bottom lip, dipping inside just enough to make her gasp, to make her hungry for their next kiss. His hands dropped to the counter, bracketing her hips as he bent to find her mouth again with his. Their tongues met, slick and addictive. She wrapped her arms around his shoulders, trying to hold herself up, as everything liquefied inside her.

The kiss deepened, and he gripped her waist, jerking her closer to the edge of the counter. There was nothing but this and their bodies, fused from hip, to stomach, to chest, making heat bloom inside her, from her heart down to the pulse between her legs, which she rolled against him, seeking more friction.

A desperate noise escaped his throat and he broke away, pressing his temple to hers, as damp gusts of air fell from his mouth. She was breathing just as fast. He nuzzled her hair and his head nudged the arm on her glasses, shifting them to the side. She reacted automatically, releasing him, and leaning away so she could push them back into place.

He was straightening up too, space growing between them, and even now – even in the centre of this storm – she recognised that her fear of releasing her gift had managed to override every other pleasurable sensation flooding her body and mind. She should have just taken her glasses off and carried on kissing him.

But she couldn't do it. He might have told her how he felt, and she definitely had the evidence of his desire, but she didn't want to use her gift to see anything more. To know if that was all there was between them now. To know if there was something he hadn't mentioned. To see the extent of what she felt herself.

The effort of holding herself upright became too much and she fell back onto her elbows, her head hitting the mirror behind her.

'Shit, are you OK?' Harry's voice was rough, his body close again, but he was cradling her head gently and encouraging her to sit up. 'What happened?'

She slumped against his shoulder, her cheek crumpling his shirt, or his shirt crumpling her cheek, one of those. There was ringing in her ears. 'I'm great,' she slurred into the crook of his neck.

'You're really not. Did you hit your head really hard?'

'No. It's fine. Doesn't hurt at all.' She tried to rub her hand up his chest, but it flopped like a dead fish instead.

'Are you feeling ill? This can't be Leon's magic—'

'Not magic. Space. Space cookie. I might be stoned.'

'You ate a *space cookie*?' His laugh was weak, incredulous. His skin smelt amazing, she turned her nose into the crook of his neck and breathed in deeply. A wave of dizziness washed over her. 'Kay?'

'Oh. Yes? Just one bite. One *big* bite.' She put her hand on his other shoulder to try to push herself upright. 'Guess it's hitting me now.'

Harry was quiet for a moment, and she felt him taking a few deep breaths. He smoothed his hands down her back and then gripped her shoulders gently to help her sit up.

She squinted at him, her eyes already feeling heavy-lidded. His face was pale beneath his freckles, apart from

191

two reddened patches on his cheekbones, his kiss-swollen mouth downturned at the corners. 'Are you all right to stand?'

'Yeah . . . but . . .' She bit her lip and pushed her finger against his bottom lip, admittedly not with the same gentle caress she'd used before since her co-ordination was a little off and her arm weighed two tonnes. Weirdly, gravity had also disappeared. 'Why . . . don't you want to kiss me anymore?'

He swallowed and looked down. 'Kay, you're not yourself. I didn't realise. This isn't right. And you need to try to sober up as much as possible before we go get the car.'

A disappointed noise surfaced from her throat, but she nodded. Then brightened. 'Hey, we get to do a road trip. We always wanted to, didn't we?'

Harry answered with a brief smile. Then he half-carried her back into Leon and Alex's living room and laid her on the sofa. She probably could have done a lot of it on her own if she'd tried, but it was too nice having him so close, his arms all around her.

'Where you going?' She caught hold of his untucked shirt as he straightened up after pushing a pillow underneath her head. She tugged hard and he had to put his hands out either side of her to stop himself from toppling onto her. Boo hiss to his quick reflexes. His taste filled her mouth, and she wanted more of it. Goddess, she wanted to feel the weight of his body on top of hers so much, her mouth was watering.

'I have to . . .' He took a shaky breath and shook his head. 'I have to get us ready to leave.' He pushed himself up. 'I'll be back in a minute. Will you be OK without me?'

No, she wanted to say. *Stay*. But that was too reminiscent of how she'd felt as a teenager and she was a grown-up now, after all.

'Sure,' she said in what she planned to be a nonchalant voice, but it came out weirdly high-pitched, as she flopped her heavy arms back over her head.

Harry blinked, his gaze travelling up her, before he stood up straight, driving a hand into his hair. 'I'll be back in a minute,' he repeated and headed for the door.

The sofa was really comfortable, almost as comfortable as the booths downstairs, and she ran her hand over the throw, back and forth, feeling the silky threads, the bumps against her palm, the odd place where they were starting to fray. There was an art deco style lampshade above her, hovering like a spaceship. Such a gorgeous shade of blue. Like Harry's eyes.

But no. His eyes *weren't* blue apparently. Would she ever see the right colour, and if she did, would it be because of how she felt, or because of how *he* felt? What she needed was evidence, if he wasn't going to tell her.

She rolled onto her side, scrabbling for her tote, digging around for her phone. It wouldn't be odd to text Joe and ask him for a photo of Harry, would it . . .

'We need to leave as soon as possible. Is there anything you can make her?'

Harry was back, and Kay realised she'd shut her eyes and drifted off, her mind full of bright shapes, like the lampshade and the stained-glass window downstairs. She pried her eyelids up to see her head was level with the coffee table, one arm and one leg hanging off the sofa.

'Not really, H – my magic is emotive, rather than physiological. She has a drug in her system. You can't counteract that with good vibes. I mean, I could help if she's feeling paranoid?'

'Not that I've noticed,' Harry mumbled.

Kay wondered why he sounded so shifty about it. Maybe because the only real emotion she'd been showing him was that she was horny.

She giggled.

'Hey,' Leon crouched down by her head and she grinned at him. He raised an eyebrow. 'Someone is buzzing.'

'I don't think it's just because of the cookie,' Kay whispered. 'I kissed Harry. Shh.' She pressed her finger to her lips and giggled again.

Leon laughed and whispered back, 'Glad to see he hasn't lost his touch.'

'What about coffee or . . . orange juice?' Harry sounded like he was a million miles away. Kay forced herself up onto her elbow, saw he was actually just in the kitchen with Alex, and flopped onto her back again. 'Does that help or was it just an urban myth I heard back at uni?'

'It can help,' Alex said. 'Since she ingested it rather than smoked it. She might feel more stoned to begin with, but she'll digest it quicker.'

'That doesn't necessarily sound helpful.'

'Harry, it's OK, it'll pass. She'll be fine.' Leon's voice moved further away and Kay realised her eyes were shut again. They were too heavy to open, even though she wanted to see what was going on.

'I need to get her on a ferry. At the moment, she can't even stand up. If we miss that ferry . . .' his voice cracked and there was some movement in the room.

'I know. I know.' Leon's voice was soft and when Kay forced her sticky eyelids open, she saw Alex had one of his huge hands on Harry's shoulder, squeezing him with a comforting gesture. Why was he comforting Harry? Sure, he wanted to get them back for the wedding, but he wasn't going to get that upset about it, was he? Her own desperation must have been leaking off onto him.

At least her magic hadn't been leaking. A miracle, considering how she'd felt so full of . . . sparks. She couldn't help but give a hum of satisfaction.

'She really didn't eat that much. Are you sure she isn't just drunk on you?' Leon's voice was full of barely contained amusement.

'Stop it. I feel terrible. I didn't know she'd eaten anything. Goddess, why am I always such a disaster around her? Even when I *think* I'm doing the right thing, it turns out to be selfish and ends up hurting people—'

'Now *you* stop it. You said it yourself; you didn't know. And you stopped as soon as you realised.' There was a pause where Harry must have nodded because that was the truth. 'Did you talk beforehand?'

'A bit. Not about everything, we got distracted . . .'

'Are you going to make sure you pick up the conversation again . . .? Harry?'

'Yes. Yes. I will.'

He had more he needed to tell her? They hadn't covered everything? She guessed she didn't know what she didn't know. That was the problem there. At that moment, it was tricky to remember what they had covered. Enough for her to want to kiss him anyway. If she hadn't panicked about her stupid glasses, she could *still* be kissing him.

She pressed her glasses firmly onto the bridge of her nose, causing a pain across her sinuses. Stupid glasses. No. Stupid gift. 'Ouch.'

Harry came over to help her sit up, his hand sliding behind her back and supporting her. 'Are you OK?'

'Yeah.' She licked her lips. Where had all the moisture gone? 'Good, good. Fine and dandy.'

'Fine enough to walk to the car park where Leon's car is, or shall I just get it and drive down here?' Harry sounded sceptical and sat on the sofa next to her, his arm still behind her back, all strong and warm. It made her want to turn and crawl into his lap.

'I think, with the snow, and the roads around here, it would be safer if you walked to the car,' Alex said. 'The fresh air will probably help her too.'

'Think you're up to that?' Harry asked her, the lines between his eyebrows deep.

She reached out and smoothed them with the pad of her index finger. 'I will do my absolutely-tootly best.'

Harry smiled and caught her finger, giving it a brief squeeze.

'Right, let's get Operation Sober-Kay-Up on the go then.' Leon clapped his hands together.

The next twenty minutes were a flurry of Kay being bossed about in a way that she never would have tolerated normally. She was coaxed into the shower, to be blasted with cold water – by herself unfortunately. Once she was dressed, they filled her up with very strong coffee and very sharp juice, until her stomach was sloshing, tucked a couple of Mars bars and a bottle of water in her tote bag for good measure and bundled her out the back door with Harry, in a flurry of hugs and kisses and promises to come back again soon.

It was fully dark outside now and the snow lay deep on the roads – no more of that slushy stuff. It quickly became apparent that Alex had been right about the effect of the orange juice, in that her head was swimming and she felt both more stoned, but more awake at the same time. She was having an even harder time keeping herself upright and the dark water in the canals seemed to be calling to her.

Harry kept having to rescue her from lemming-it off the edge, his lips pressed flat. All Kay could think about was how they felt on her mouth, on her skin. She knew they needed to hurry, but her body was simply not co-operating.

'I'm so sorry,' she told him, leaning, almost doubled over, on a black bollard, snow squishing into her stomach. It felt like they had been walking for a century, and they'd only made it to the end of the second road.

'You don't need to be sorry, it was an accident,' he reassured her, then banded his duffel bag across his chest and got her to climb up onto his back so he could piggy-back her.

She knew she shouldn't be enjoying it quite so much, since it was obviously costing him a lot of effort, but having her body wrapped around his – even if they were bundled up in their coats – was pretty heavenly. Especially as they walked along with the snow falling and the lights of Amsterdam glittering in the canals. Kay rested her cheek against his head and breathed in the scent of his soft hair. This had to be a dream. And if it was, she wasn't sure she wanted to wake up from it.

Chapter Thirteen

Kay didn't exactly go to sleep. The car was small, the seat not particularly comfortable, and she wasn't feeling so stoned now that she could have slept draped over a wall. So, instead, she snuggled up into the corner as far as she could, while remaining beneath the seat belt, and closed her eyes.

Or, at least, she kept them *mostly* closed. She couldn't help opening them a crack, just enough to peer through her lashes and watch Harry. It was so dark out now, nothing much to see other than the lighting alongside the roads and the dusting of snow across the flat land, with the occasional hint of windmill – usually the modern kind.

The yellow lights flashed into his hair, making it look like it was kindling to flame every so often. He'd sucked his bottom lip in between his teeth and there was a furrow in his brow again. She wondered if this was his normal driving face. All tense concentration. So serious. He'd not had a licence when she knew him before, though he'd been taking lessons. She'd imagined him taking her out in his car when he eventually got one and them making out in the back seat up at the local viewpoint.

She knew what his kisses were like now. She could conjure the sensation of his tongue sliding along hers. His long fingers tightening in her hair, the sharp pleasurable tug on her scalp. She shivered at the memory.

Harry glanced over at her and she shut her eyes that extra millimetre, so he didn't catch her faking it. She heard him fiddling with some of the controls and then some awkward shuffling before a soft weight landed on her lap.

His coat. He'd just put his sorcerer's coat of many pockets over her because he thought she was cold.

She shifted with a murmur, to hide the sudden stiffness of her surprise, and he made a gentle hushing noise and proceeded to tuck her in one-handedly. Little incremental tugs to smooth the material out and raise it up her body, towards her shoulders.

Had she ever hated the sight of this coat?

Yes, she had. About twenty-four hours ago, she'd thought it was utterly ridiculous and pretentious and irritating. A bludgeon of negativity to hammer down all the positive feelings that bumping into him had brought about – excitement, desire. Perhaps he hadn't been so wrong, trying to get her to hate him so she didn't hurt so much.

But now . . .

Now she knew it suited him perfectly. Bright and warm, brimming with pockets full of sweet and creative things. And probably his mobile phone too.

She took in a deep breath, filling her lungs up with the scent of him, and it worked better than the weed she'd accidentally ingested. She dozed off.

A jolt and a bump made Kay's head knock against the door frame. Her head really was going through it that evening.

She twisted away, blinking as she realised there was a light flashing, and cold air coming into the car.

It took a moment for her eyes to adjust and take account of the fact the car was tilted at a strange angle. Through the windscreen, everything looked the same – dark sky and tiny floating flakes of snow. But through the passenger-side window, she could see a long barrier at a right angle to them and when she tried to move in her seat, gravity announced that the car was not in its usual four-wheels-on-the-ground position.

'H-Harry?' she called out croakily, looking over at the empty driver's seat. 'Harry?' she shouted louder, panic lacing her voice as she struggled to free her arms from underneath his big coat and find the button for her seat belt.

'I'm out here, Kay. Are you all right?' His muffled voice came to her from behind the car.

What the hell? Had he needed to stop and take a wee? Why would he park the car on a bank like this, though? She felt like she was in a fun house, and everything was the wrong way up.

She pressed the button on the window and leaned out, trying to see where he was. 'What's going on?'

Footsteps crunched in the snow and Harry appeared at the window, hanging onto the car. His cheeks and nose were pink, his face pinched.

'I hit a patch of ice and I couldn't get the car back under control. We spun and came off the road down this . . . lay-by? I think. It's like the hard shoulder, but it's got a barrier. I managed to shove it with magic so we missed hitting it, but I can't get the car back out now, so I'm trying to push it.'

She opened her mouth and then shut it again and rubbed her hand over her face. 'Wow. I really slept through that?'

'That'll be the drugs, I guess.' He gave her a chagrined smile.

'Or the head injury— I'm kidding, Harry,' she said at his sudden look of concern. 'Let's just get back on the road, yeah? Do you want me to get behind the wheel? I can give it some gas, while you push. I promise if we get unstuck, I won't drive off without you.' She made a cross over her chest and gave him a faux-solemn look.

His mouth lifted gratifyingly at the corner. 'Yeah, that's a good idea.'

She unclipped her seat belt and opened the door, misjudging where the actual ground was so she fell out, rather than stepped out.

'Easy does it,' he said, catching her, and she gripped his biceps hard to pull herself upright. She looked up at him; tiny snowflakes were catching on his pale eyelashes. One landed on his lower lip, and he swiped his tongue across it. 'There. You can stand?'

'I can.'

He dropped his hands and stepped back. 'If the police come by and catch you behind the wheel, you'll be in big trouble, though. Maybe you shouldn't drive.'

'Oh.' She wrapped her arms around herself. She was still wearing her own coat but missed the warmth of his. And she missed his arms. Missed him wanting to touch her. In the muddle of her memories from back at Leon and Alex's, she remembered him feeling bad that she'd been stoned while they were fooling around. That might have been why. Equally, it might be because they were currently stranded and had a ferry to catch. *Priorities, Kay.*

She shook her head and leaned in to the car to get his coat for him.

'What other option do we have? You drive and I push?'

He pulled his coat on, buttoning up, the relief on his face evident, and for a moment she wanted to shake him. Fancy coming out here in the snow without his coat, just so she could keep snoozing, cosy and oblivious.

'There's a good possibility you are the stronger of the two of us.' His smiled widened. 'You broke apart a sofa bed with your bare . . . feet.'

She snorted, and it was on the tip of her tongue to tell him that she had used magic. Albeit unintentionally. 'I appreciate that you're not a macho alphahole, Harry, you don't have to the labour the point. And we don't have to pretend that I, at five foot three, am going to pack more muscle than you.' She waved a hand to indicate his height.

'It's possible, but even if we were both built like Alex, I doubt it would work without magic.'

'Well, sure. You're still the best person to do the pushing then, aren't you?' She turned away and slid down the slope, only realising as she rounded the back of the car, how much pushing would actually be required to get it back onto the road again. 'Wow. Good work finding the only bit of hill in Holland.'

He laughed and followed her part of the way, stopping at the boot, while she continued on up the other side to get in the driver's seat. Her head was a little swimmy still now that the fresh air was hitting her, but it wasn't like she was going to do anything more than put her foot on the accelerator and guide the car back onto the road.

'OK, when I say go, just start gradually applying the gas. Take it easy so we can try to avoid it wheel-spinning,' he said, once she was in the driver's seat and had adjusted it so that she was close enough to reach the pedals and steering wheel.

'Got it.' She started the car up and kept it idling, waiting for his word.

'Go.' He grunted from behind and the car rocked slightly.

She glanced into the rear-view mirror as she pressed gently on the accelerator, building it. She could just see the top of his head as he pushed his shoulder against the back of the car. His grunts were getting louder, and the tyres were just spinning. Why wasn't he using his magic to help?

'Ugh. OK. Stop,' he called out breathlessly and she watched him straighten and step back, pressing the heels of his hands to his eyes as his chest worked.

She stopped and got out again, this time being a little more careful, so she didn't need rescuing. Harry looked like he needed someone to catch *him*.

'It's too heavy,' he groaned. 'And the ground's too slippery. The car can't find any traction.'

'Why don't you use your magic?' she asked.

To his credit, when he dropped his hands, he didn't look at her like the enormous hypocrite she was, having spent nearly a day avoiding or deflecting him whenever he asked *her* that exact question. He shook his head. 'I can't. Not on my own. I'm too tired.'

She looked at him properly then – not just with her crush goggles on – and realised he did look exhausted. And was it any wonder? He'd barely slept the night before. They'd been travelling nearly all day and he'd used his magic a number of times, most significantly doing the rune work for Leon, but also the umbrella, on the train with the little boy, and whatever surge he'd needed to avoid them crashing into the barrier. He'd piggybacked her across Amsterdam and then been the one to drive too because she was passed out. He must be really glad he let her tag along with him.

'What are we going to do then?' she asked. 'Call the road assistance people?'

'We'll miss the ferry if we have to wait. Do you think you can summon enough of a push? If we work together . . .?'

She was already shaking her head.

'Kay. Seriously? Why not? Is there a problem? Is that why you have that corn husk doll? Why you were outside Baba Yaga's on Friday?'

She should have known he'd be familiar with Madam Hedvika and her damn corn dolls. He was at the centre of the magical community, he seemed to know about everything.

'Regardless of whether there is a problem with my magic or not,' she began stiffly, 'it never would have been able to move a car. I'm just not that powerful. I haven't practised enough.' She let out a soft growl. 'Look, I don't want to get into this now.'

'Have you got something better to do?' he laughed incredulously. 'We have to figure a way out of this and if we can help each other, why wouldn't we? Isn't that the reason we teamed up in the first place?'

She crossed her arms over her chest. 'I'm aware you've been more helpful to me than I've been to you, all right?'

He gave a somewhat unhinged laugh and waved a hand at the car. 'Hardly. That's not what I was getting at. I just . . . If you're having a problem, you can tell me. I might be able to help.'

'You think you can help me more than Madam Hedvika could?'

'No. But I know what you're capable of when it comes to magic—'

'Harry, don't,' she started, a pain in her chest twinging like an elastic band.

'No, I know I haven't been around you since your gift came in, but even before that I saw you wield magic.

You were able to pick up spells I'd spent weeks practising, within a day or two. Whenever we mucked about with our magic — you were right there with me — utterly capable. So don't tell me you're not a powerful witch. Two years younger and still not tapped into your gift, you could do the same magic as me. I don't think . . .' He bit his lip as he looked at her, the expression in his eyes wary.

'What? Don't stop now. You're on a roll.'

'Whatever your problem is with magic, I don't think it's anything to do with the power you hold, Kay. I think it's to do with how you feel about your magic. You were so looking forward to it coming in. And when it arrived, obviously it wasn't . . . what you were expecting—'

'Wasn't what I was expecting? It tore my family apart,' she choked out.

'The magic didn't do that,' he said softly. 'Your gift didn't do that. It just exposed the problem that was already there. But you're so twisted up with guilt about it, that you treat your magic like it's a curse rather than a gift.'

Kay was breathing heavily, despite the fact he was the one who had just had an outburst. So much of that was true, but she didn't want to hear it. Especially not from him, when he'd not even been around for her during that time. It turned out that even if you knew you'd been unjustified in feeling such an intense level of anger at someone for so long, it wasn't so easy to put the habit of those feelings away. Especially when they were poking and prodding at a sore spot.

'What would you know about it, Harry? You've spent a grand total of twenty-four hours with me since I got my gift. You don't know anything about how I feel about it.'

He'd not seen her use her gift even once. Probably on purpose, now she thought about it. That was why he'd had to send the note. He'd been worried about breaking it to her in person, about having a conversation with her about needing to go to Edinburgh, because she would have been able to *see* how he felt about her, if she wanted to. And though she could understand now why he hadn't wanted to risk that – *if* the strength of his feelings for her back then were to be believed – it still hurt to think it was true. Her gift had kept him away.

'That's fair,' he replied. 'But I do know what it's like to be at odds with your magic. I know I'm so lucky to have a legacy like Biddi and the Ashworth line, but it took me a while to reconcile all that with also just being *me*. To get comfortable with it.'

Kay tightened her arms even further around her chest. There had been no time to 'get comfortable' with her gift or her magic, because as soon as it came in, it had blown up her life. It would have been like trying to get to know a terrorist. Everyone would have thought she was self-destructive and dangerous. Actively disregarding the damage she had done. That she *could* do.

'Sometimes I even wished I could just be "normal",' he continued. 'To not be a witch at all . . . and I've seen that you choose not to use your magic—'

'That's what Madam Hedvika said I *had* to do. OK? She told me to stop using it, to clamp down on every impulse.'

'Permanently?' His husky voice lowered to a barely audible murmur and her stomach lurched at the suggestion too.

Which was stupid. How was it possible to think she would miss something that had only ever caused her pain? That she'd never really experienced fully as part of her life.

'No. Not permanently. Until I've figured out . . . until I know what the problem is. Because it's gone totally screwy. It shoots off when it shouldn't. Causes mayhem.

Almost exposes me. It's a nightmare. It *is* a curse.' She pressed a hand to her stomach. If she pictured her magic as a well, then the water was poisoned. And leaking out into cracks. 'I can't use it. She told me not to, and I need it to be fixed, because what if I ruin Joe's wedding? What if I end up hurting someone?'

'You won't—'

'Harry. I think the sofa bed malfunctioning was me. You could have broken your foot or sliced open an artery or something. I'm a menace.'

He was quiet for a moment, his face so solemn it made the weight pressing down on her chest heavier. 'I get that you're scared. Of all those things. But the fact remains, if we don't even try right now, you *are* going to miss that ferry. And probably Joe's wedding. What have you got to lose by giving it a go?'

'Maybe our lives? The car could explode.'

Harry raised his eyebrows. 'I doubt it.'

'I set fire to that corn husk doll.'

'A small doll that is basically tinder, is not the same as—'

'A car full of highly flammable fuel?'

'Oh, for the love of the goddess, fine! Have it your way. Just stop arguing with me. I'll think of something.'

He turned away from her, linking his fingers at the back of his neck and staring off into the flat black night.

Kay rubbed the snow away from her eyelashes, angry at him and angry at herself too, because it turned out that saying sorry and kissing your teenage crush didn't automatically fix all your problems, personal or joint.

Even more annoyingly, a lot of what he'd said made sense. She had been so eager for her gift before, he was right about that, but him throwing that knowledge in her face just stirred up all her resentment about the years they'd lost because he hadn't trusted either of them to be able to deal with his problems.

He turned back without looking at her, and moved to the boot, fiddling with the catch. His hands trembling and practically blue from the cold. He popped it open and started rooting around inside.

'What are you doing?'

'Looking for something, *anything*, that might help,' he muttered.

He was shaking, and she couldn't entirely say it was the cold because she could feel the energy coming off him, whether she liked it or not. The desperation. Was that something she'd always been able to do? Something she had inherited from her mother without realising? Or was she just tuned into Harry and his moods, because this was so unlike him? Or unlike him to show it.

He clearly wanted to make that ferry.

And she *needed* to make it. She couldn't miss her brother getting married. Sure, she might have a magical accident at the wedding – but that was a risk whether she clamped down on her magic or not. Somehow, it had only been a day since she'd seen Madam Hedvika.

'OK, OK.' The words ripped out of her, but she touched Harry's shoulder gently, to stop him from crashing around in the boot, where he'd not found much except a tyre pump and an empty box. 'I'll try.'

Harry leaned on the rim of the boot for a second, before he straightened and looked at her again. 'I'm sorry, Kay. I'm sorry I'm asking it of you. Honestly.'

'You'll be even sorrier if I turn the car into a lump of smoking metal.' She said it as a joke because the shininess of his blue eyes was undoing her. He was looking at her with such a strange mix of gratitude and regret.

'You won't.'

She started to shake her head again, objections rising to her lips, but he stepped closer and put his hands on her shoulders.

'You can do this. I know you can.'

The cold air caught in her throat, the snowflakes whirling around them as a heat kindled in her stomach. And not the kind that was linked to how much her body responded to his proximity. No. It was like her magic was warming beneath the intensity of his belief in it. In her.

'How should we do this, then?' she whispered.

'Well, which do you think would be easier? I could help you do the lightening spell, like I did on your luggage and then I'll push – or we could try just putting as much force behind it as we can together?'

She chewed her lip. The lightening spell wasn't exactly easy and that would leave him having to use more physical energy when he was clearly shattered. The magical push might be riskier in terms of it going wrong, but then, even her magical mishaps tended towards the brute-force side of things, so it was probably best to lean into that.

'Let's push together.'

He nodded and looked back at the car. 'Right. If it starts slipping in the wrong direction or anything, you just get yourself out of the way, OK?'

'Right.' She imagined the car bursting into flames or exploding like something out of an action movie and then immediately pushed the thoughts out of her mind, shutting her eyes to centre herself.

'Kay. You can do this,' Harry said again, and then he placed a kiss on her forehead. His lips were freezing compared to earlier, but her heart still flipped over. 'Thank you.'

He let go of her and moved back, closing the boot, and putting his hands to one side of it, leaving a space for her on the other side. She mirrored his posture, the cold metal biting at her hands as she dug her boots in as much as she could to the icy ground.

It was the most elementary use of magic in all honesty. Something most witches had learned to do with control by the time they were eight or nine. The biggest challenge was getting kids *not* to use it when they were fighting or trying to get a cookie jar down from a shelf.

Harry looked at her, gave her an encouraging smile and then she felt it – he was pushing the little energy he had left into the car. Or rather, into a force to push the car. She felt the weight lifting off her shoulder somewhat and reflected for a moment that he had been bullshitting her a little bit. No matter what he said about how he believed her to be of equal power to him – he was still managing to shift an entire car, even if it was only a centimetre or two, when he was almost completely drained.

Although, maybe that was just his own physical strength doing it. Which was equally impressive.

'Kay?' he said with a slight grunt, and she realised she wasn't even trying yet.

She dipped down into her well of energy and imagined it funnelling up through her chest, through her arms, down to her palms against the car and pushing, a shove of kinetic energy drawing out from her. The car rocked forwards a little further.

'That's great. You're doing it,' he gasped and she felt his magic kick up a notch as though encouraged.

They made it a foot further up the slope, beads of sweat prickling at the edge of Kay's hair and a light-headedness making her feel odd. But then they hit a harder patch of ice and the wheels just kept spinning rather than moving forwards.

'C'mon, c'mon,' Harry muttered and when she looked at him, a stab of fear sliced through her. His freckles were stark against the pallor of his face, there were lines at the edge of his mouth and a bright red trickle of blood was just visible at the edge of his nose.

'Harry, we need to stop,' she managed to say. Her own heart was pounding in her ears.

'But we're so close, Kay,' his voice was little more than a wheeze.

'I know, but—' she broke off and forced more energy into her push. If only the ice would melt a little. They were exerting so much effort and the weight of the engine would probably put it onto the road if this ice just melted. Her muscles burned with the strain and she glared at the tyre to her right as it slipped and slipped, picturing it catching in her mind. They would have to stop in a minute if they couldn't get it that little bit further. Harry was going to pass out and then the weight of the car would roll back and run them both over because she couldn't hold it on her own, magic or no magic.

Then she noticed the water, the way the snow under her feet was softening, growing slick. Beneath the car too. It was melting.

But it was still snowing—

Before she could think of how or why that was happening, the car caught and all the energy they were pushing into it sent it forward in one big surge. It tipped forward and rolled onto the road. Both she and Harry lost their grip and went down on their knees in what was now puddles of icy mud, rather than snow.

They stayed there, side by side, for a moment, dragging in great lungfuls of air and staring at the car.

'I told you . . . you could . . . do it.'

She looked over at him slowly, catching him wiping his nose on the sleeve of his jumper. 'Are you OK?' she asked, shuffling on her knees towards him. He was swaying a little, and when she reached him, he sank back to sit on his feet.

'I'll be fine . . . it's just a little . . . overexertion. I'll be . . . all right in a minute.' He gulped some more air and then smiled at her. 'You did it, Kay.'

She nodded slowly back at him and tried to smile. She had done it. But she wasn't sure it was the way she'd intended. They were sitting in a puddle of melted snow when she'd been focused on wanting that ice beneath the tyre to disappear.

Did that mean . . .? Had she melted the ice without meaning to? Did she have some affinity to weather from her mum's side of the family that she'd never recognised before? She'd never learned the spell for melting things without conjuring a flame. It wasn't the kind of spell you could usually do without extra juice and lots of practice . . . unless you had an affinity to it.

And if she did, what if her magic had been throwing out other weather effects? Things that were hindering them more than helping?

Chapter Fourteen

9.26 P.M.: SATURDAY 30 OCTOBER

The Hook of Holland

258 miles and 17(+1) hours and 34 minutes until the wedding

They made it to the ferry port with four minutes to go before they closed boarding. Harry had taken the wheel again. Despite Kay being worried about how worn out he was, it was still the safer option than her driving while under the influence. It was hard to tell whether her level of distraction was from the drug still in her system or the way her mind was churning over each of the mishaps with her magic over the last few months, trying to see how many of them were of an elementary nature.

If she did have a partial affinity for weather – her mother and father's sides combining to give her an ability to influence it – that might explain why it was trying to erupt from her, since she'd never given it any attention. Never tried to use it, learn about it, or control it. It wouldn't be like the secondary affinity Harry thought she had, where she made people more aware of their feelings – that was just vibes really, a natural aura she was incapable of controlling. Weather affinities could be powerful if they were ones where you could affect it rather than just read it, like her Aunt Lucille.

Harry flopped back in his seat after driving onto the ship and parking in among the rows of other vehicles, like he'd barely taken a breath the whole way. She knew he'd been walking a line between trying to hurry so they made their boarding time, but also being ultra careful because of the snow and the fear that they might spin off the road again.

'We made it,' she told him, taking a sip from the massive water bottle Leon had insisted they take with them. She offered it to Harry. 'You got us here. Thank you.'

'Couldn't have done it without you.' He took the bottle and took a long drink himself. Kay tried not to ogle him too much as he swiped his tongue across his lips, screwing the cap back in place and tucking the bottle in the holder again. 'Shall we?' He tipped his head towards the car door.

'I guess so.' She half-laughed, half-groaned. 'The thought of moving, though . . .'

'I know, but there's food upstairs, and beds. It'll be worth the final effort.'

They climbed out of the car like a pair of octogenarians with arthritis and joined the queue to go up the narrow stairwell to the main deck. Harry left his bag in the back, even though Kay offered to carry it for him, saying he could always grab it later. He had other priorities, it seemed.

'Great Mabon, I'm starving,' Harry announced as they trooped up the stairs with everyone else.

'You know what – me too. I can't believe it. Leon's dinner was so good.'

They passed through the doors out into the hallway and Harry ducked his head down beside hers and whispered: 'You know, that might be a little something called the munchies.'

She shivered at the brush of his lips against the shell of her ear and laughed. 'What's your excuse?'

'I'm hollow inside,' he joked, but as she glanced at him, his eyes weren't lit in their usual way. Perhaps he was just tired, but it made her wonder how much of his self-deprecating humour was based on things he truly believed. He looked around him, hands in his pockets, frowning at the signs, the artificial lights showing how pasty he still was. 'What do you fancy?'

You. Even like this; wan and tired. It was like seeing the bones of him. The hardy pieces that kept going, kept trying, no matter how difficult it was. At some point, probably when he was literally bleeding to try to get the car back on the road, something inside her had accepted that she was lucky to have Harry in her corner. He would do everything he could to get her to Joe's wedding.

'I don't mind. You choose. Last time I made a decision about eating, it backfired spectacularly.'

After they'd both made use of the toilets, they went to the nearest restaurant and grabbed a toastie each. In actual fact, Harry grabbed two, plus a blueberry muffin, and they attacked their food in silence.

The moment their stomachs were full, the last of Harry's energy seemed to abandon him. He sat at the table, his chin on his fist, propping his head up and his eyes making longer and longer blinks.

'Come on, let's get you to bed,' Kay said, pushing her plate away.

Harry's eyes opened wide at that comment, and she heard it back to herself, her cheeks flushing, but she didn't exactly correct him.

When they stood up, she went to him and slipped her arm around his waist to help him stay upright. He'd done the same for her at least twice today. With his arm around her shoulders, he leaned his tired weight on her as they wandered the decks, looking for their cabin.

It was tiny and sterile but clean, with a set of bunk beds riveted to the wall on one side of a porthole and an armchair on the other side. Kay helped Harry over to the lower bunk and released him so he could collapse onto it with a groan.

She left her things on the armchair and debated climbing up onto the top bunk to sleep herself, but she didn't really want to. She wanted to sleep. But she didn't want to sleep up there, separate from him.

He'd kicked his shoes off and wrestling himself out of his coat off – or trying to – but his elbows were tangled in the arms, and he just flopped back with a sigh. She used it as an excuse to go over and help him out of it, sitting on the edge of the bed and holding onto the cuffs for him.

'Are we going to talk about it now?' he mumbled as he pulled his arms free and shifted onto his side, plumping the pillow up beneath his head, his eyes hardly open.

'Talk about what?'

'Whether you regret us kissing, now you're mostly sober and not under Leon's influence?'

She pressed her lips together. She didn't regret it.

Not yet.

But now the magical influence had eased and, as Harry said, she was mostly sober, she could acknowledge that this wasn't as easy as she'd imagined it to be when she was riding her high in Leon's bathroom. She was raised by an empath at the end of the day. She knew that feelings couldn't evaporate, like the water spilled over Madam Hedvika's table, no matter whether it was illogical to hold on to them. No matter how she felt like she was seeing him again properly for the first time in years – maybe even understanding him better than she ever had — it didn't mean her hurt and resentment were going to disappear.

And then there was the fact that he was an influencer with another affinity linked to the seer designation — and she was an empath, possibly with another affinity linked to influencing — and she'd spent many, many years strongly believing that was an absolute recipe for heartache and toxic relationships. What if one day he had inconvenient feelings for her again and instead of talking to her about it, he chose to avoid her, like she suspected had happened when he stood her up? That particular gift wasn't going anywhere, no matter how much she wished it would.

So, he might not regret the kissing. She might even want more kissing . . . OK, she *definitely* wanted more kissing. But if there wasn't any potential for more between them, maybe giving in to temptation wasn't for the best?

Instead of saying any of that, though, she just murmured: 'Sleep, Harry. You need to sleep. We've got all tomorrow morning with the drive back to talk.'

He nodded into the pillow, his eyes already closing. 'I guessso.'

She turned to drape his coat over the armchair with hers and when she looked back, he'd pressed himself up against the wall and had his hand outstretched to her.

Her heart gave a painful kick in her chest. Actions spoke louder than words sometimes and if she chose to lie down beside him, now that she was sober, without them even discussing the kiss or anything else about it, it would be saying something. At least partly. And she'd just reminded herself that it probably wasn't a good idea.

She hated the fact that he'd been right to warn her about this before they kissed. And she hated that his fingers curled in on themselves, forming a gentle fist as he pulled his arm back in towards his body as though he'd read her hesitation and was resigning himself to her rejection.

Only one day ago, she would have been rejecting him and thinking that it served him right. But now, she chewed her lip and took off her boots, going over to the bottom bunk, and leaning in to press a kiss to his forehead.

'We'll talk later,' she repeated, and his eyes opened wide for a moment, watching as she moved away again.

'I've missed you,' he said softly, his generous mouth barely moving around the words, but they landed like a sledgehammer blow. It was part solace and part pain because those were the words she'd sent him in the text when she'd asked him out at sixteen. What he'd said back to her when he suggested them meeting at the cave.

And it still hadn't stopped him from hurting her.

He dropped off, almost as soon as he'd spoken. Kay closed her eyes to stop herself from staring like a deranged stalker at his face. It wasn't like she couldn't picture it in her mind's eye anyway. The angle of his cheekbones and the hollow beneath, the creases at the corner of his eyes, the dip under his bottom lip . . .

She climbed up onto the top bunk, alone, and wrapped the blankets around herself.

Dreaming came faster than she would have expected. Maybe because she was sure it was a memory. She was out in the garden, lying on a blanket, reading a book about a hand-maiden of death; a mix of magic, myth, and history and romance that had her ignoring her coursework. The sun was hot on her back, the blanket cool and a little damp, the smell of freshly cut grass in the air. Her stomach flipped as Harry appeared, because Joe wanted to finish watching a football match before they started working.

The memory began to twist into dream then. Food laid out on colourful plastic plates between them that wasn't there a moment ago. Cookies, pastries, a Bakewell tart, a slice of wedding cake. She levitated the Bakewell tart away from him because they were her favourite and a game began. She could tell they were teasing each other and she knew Harry's husky voice was in her head, but she couldn't hear the words either of them were saying. It was more laughter than words anyway.

The plates were empty now and they were all up in the air, spinning like the art deco lampshade at Leon and Alex's. A bright yellow one lifted up and floated away. But she wasn't using the lightening spell. Or pushing it with a simple force of energy. She was using the spell Auntie L had taught her for harnessing the breeze, and it came so easily now.

'You see, I told you, you're powerful,' Harry said, standing up to watch the plate rise higher and higher.

A cool rush of wind whipped around her, billowing her summer dress up, so she laughed and pushed down with her hands.

But then she was lifting up too. And so was Harry. The tree at the end of the garden was swaying back and forth and Harry was floating away from her, higher now, up above the roofline of the house.

Her heart hammered in her chest. She needed to get back down to the ground, the buffeting wind was tipping her forwards and backwards, dropping suddenly so her stomach launched up into her mouth. And Harry, he was disappearing away from her. The more she tried to control it, the more it didn't work, and then she panicked and the wind grew stronger.

'Help,' she cried out. 'Harry. Help.' She reached her hands out to him, but he was vanishing from her sight and the ground was so far below her now. She had to get a grip on this or they were both going to die. All the air in her lungs was being stolen as she went higher and higher, the village tiny like something from a toy train set. 'Help,' she sobbed. 'Help—'

And then the force dropped and she was falling, falling, falling.

She woke up screaming, sitting up but narrowly missing hitting her head on the ceiling as she nearly tumbled out of the bed.

'Kay? What's wrong?' Harry was already halfway up the ladder and when she stared at him, gulping in air, trying to convince her panicked body that it had been a dream, he came the rest of the way, kneeling beside her. 'You were having a nightmare?'

She nodded, pushing her glasses back up her nose, feeling them mould back into their normal shape. Her fingers were shaking and she gasped as he suddenly wrapped his arm around her waist to stop her from falling against the wall . . . Because the ferry was rocking. Not the gentle, almost invisible swell of its buoyancy as it moved through the water. This was lurching and falling, her stomach going light, then plummeting down with it each time. The wind dashing rain and waves against the side of the boat.

'It's the storm, Harry,' she said in a strangled voice, grabbing onto his arms as he held her in the bed, trying to steady herself as their small cabin shifted on its axis, threatening to throw them out of the bunk.

'The water is rougher than earlier,' he commented, tightening his grip as he stretched out on his side, pulling her in closer.

'Bit of an understatement,' she yelped as her stomach rose up her throat again.

'We've caught up with the bad weather again.'

'Or I brought it to us.' She flinched when the window lit up with lightning. That wasn't good. Could lightning hit a ferry? What would happen to it? Her chest was tight, she couldn't get enough air in.

'What do you mean?'

It took Kay a moment to remember what she'd said. She looked up at Harry's face. He appeared better, thankfully – the pinched look and pallor having receded. She didn't know how long they'd been asleep, but it had done him good. She appreciated the way he was all but caging her in, like he was her own personal seat belt.

'What if it's me? With my faulty magic. What if I've got an elemental affinity to weather too and it's all gone crazy,' she babbled. 'I was angry at you on the plane and there was all that turbulence. With the car, I think I melted the ice and I've never done that before. And, just now, I was having a dream. Like the other night, when the sofa bed malfunctioned on you. Only it was all about the wind and we were floating away.' She broke off, trying to get air into her lungs. 'What if it's me? My dream made this happen.' Tears pooled in her eyes. 'I don't want to lose my magic, but what if it *should* be taken away from me? What if I've called the hurricane over here and . . . and the ferry capsizes and we die? What if everyone on here dies? Harry, I'm going to kill everyone.'

'Kay, no. No. That's not what's happening.' He leaned down on his elbows, sliding his fingers into her hair and holding her head gently so she'd look at him. 'I know I said you were powerful, but hurricanes can't be caused by one witch alone. Whether you've got issues with your magic or not. It would take a whole coven with a handful of dragon eye stones.'

'But . . . but it *is* happening—'

'It's more likely that you're exhausted from all the stress, and you felt the change in weather in your sleep and incorporated it into your dream. That happens all the time.'

She shook her head against his hands, her panic rising along with the ferry, and as it fell down into a trough again, a shriek climbed up her throat. 'No. It's me. I'm making it worse. I'm making it worse. When I get worked up, the magic escapes and gets more violent.'

'Kay, no—'

'Harry, I'm so sorry. I'm going to sink the ferry.' Her fingers grabbed at his shirt.

He shook his head but didn't say anything, this time, simply gathering her into his chest and holding her tightly as the ferry rocked. She started crying into his shoulder, her brain, her body, her magic, all crackling with fear.

'Shh . . . shh . . . it's OK. We're going to be OK,' he murmured, but when her sobs didn't ease, he pulled back a little, wiping at her cheeks. 'Listen. Say it's true. Say this is your magic and it's going crazy. The only thing that will help will be calming down, won't it? Let's concentrate on that. Breathe with me.' He took one of her hands and put it over his heart. 'Breathe in slowly.' He filled his chest with air, a steady count of four, then he held it and expelled it just as slowly. 'Now out,' he breathed.

She tried. She really did. Feeling his heartbeat beneath her palm, his solid sternum, the movement of his chest, it did help. But every time the ferry rolled, her heart galloped off again. She kept trying and more tears leaked out because she was failing. Failing this. Failing everyone. Always.

'Help me,' she whispered.

'I'm here, Kay. We can do it together. Just like the car. Teamwork.'

'Yes, like the car,' she panted. 'Magic. Do your magic on me, to get me to calm down. Influence me. You've got your . . . your energy back, haven't you? You can do it.'

He stilled over her. 'I have but . . . Kay, you hate my magic. You'd never want to be influenced by me.'

'This is different. I'm asking,' she said, because that was all she had the breath for. She didn't have enough time or brain capacity at that moment to explain that she didn't feel that way anymore. That she thought the way he wielded his magic was beautiful and that she trusted him to only use it in ways that were good — the best of intentions. And this was that.

'Are you sure?'

'Yes. I am. Please.'

He nodded and sat up further. When she grabbed at him, he squeezed her hands gently and detached them. 'I have to get my pen out of my coat.'

She nodded tightly and watched him go, wedging herself deeper into the corner by the wall. Having his presence gone from around her and seeing him swaying across the short space of the cabin to grab his coat made her chest tighten even more. Was she going to have a heart attack?

She squeezed her eyes shut until she felt him back beside her. He'd thrown his coat down the end of the bed, pen retrieved, and settled beside her again, moving in close, so his left hand was free to draw, and now when the ship rolled, she moved up against him.

'I don't have any more paper,' he explained as he took her hand and rolled up her sleeve to bare her forearm. 'I'll have to draw on your skin.'

'OK,' she squeezed out between breaths.

'It might take a little while too. Your body is full of adrenaline, and my magic can't make that disappear. But just watch me doing the drawing, try not to think about anything else.' He was using a soothing voice, like he was trying to lull her to sleep. 'Is there anything you ever wanted to get tattooed on yourself?'

'How do you know I haven't . . .' She swallowed and tried again to push out the teasing words. 'I haven't got tattoos already.'

His beautiful mouth curved up at the side and then he uncapped the nib with his teeth and, putting his pen to her arm, started to draw.

Chapter Fifteen

Kay watched the black lines appear on her skin, tickling but also tingling as Harry infused the lines with his magic. He paused every time the ferry moved to avoid ruining the image he was putting on her arm, but she focused on when he was going to start drawing again, what it was going to be, instead of thinking about the waves crashing and the big lump of metal they were on tipping over.

His concentration face was back. The tunnel vision as he created and allowed his magic to flow through him. She supposed she was getting a double whammy of it. Both being able to see it and feel it. If it worked like that.

He finished the first image and it made her smile, a spark of calm swirling beneath her skin and touching at the edges of her panic.

Straight away, he moved along to start drawing the next thing. And on and on he went until her arm was covered, and inside she was simmering with different feelings. He wasn't just concentrating on one emotion. It was a bundle of them, coaxing positivity against the fear swamping her. Like a school friend knocking at the door and asking if they could come out to play: serenity, happiness, humour, curiosity, bravery. Little delicious sips which lit her up from inside, some that hit a humming note more clearly than others. As she watched him draw, their village was slowly revealed. The walk up to her old front door.

'I've run out of arm,' he said as he finished putting the final touches to the rose bushes at her mum's house on the back of her hand. 'Do you think that's enough?'

She raised her arm to let her eyes run along the images as her head fell back on the pillow. Either the storm was calming or *her* calming down had made the weather ease back. Or perhaps the storm had never been as violent as she had at first thought it was.

She could have said to Harry that she was feeling a bit more in control of herself. Among other things. Her skin tingled, magic seeping down into her muscles and running through her bloodstream, as well as entering through her eyes and alighting on parts of her brain that conjured memories to match the emotions and the images. She could feel the languor of a summer's day as she walked down to the green in their village, the bumble bees droning lazy and slow at the honeysuckle bushes lining the lanes. She could smell the lavender in the garden outside the vicarage – that heavy scent that brought drowsiness along with it.

'Do you need to stop?' she asked. 'You've barely recovered.'

He studied her face. 'I've got more than enough energy for my gift. You know how little that takes up. If you need me to, I'll do this all night.'

She licked her lips and shifted further onto her back to push up the sleeve on her other arm, all the while thinking she could probably just take her jumper off entirely under the pretext of avoiding smudging. Rather than the truth, which was that she wanted to avoid melting from all this proximity and his hands on her skin.

Instead, though, she watched as he started drawing again, doing it upside down for her, this time creating a tableau of their journey together, with the clock from Prague, the pretty buildings in Dusseldorf.

'You must think I'm so stupid,' she blurted out.

'Never,' he replied without even looking up at her. 'Why would you even say that?'

'Because I hardly understand anything about magic. How easy it is to use your gift – how we can have a blend of affinities – I'm so clueless.'

'You know plenty, Kay.' He shook his head, his hair tickling her chin as he moved further up her arm. 'You just had a bad experience, so you chose a different path. I can understand that.' He paused as the ship rolled again.

'Nothing good ever comes of letting your fear stop you, though, does it?' she murmured.

'I respectfully disagree.' He flicked a stylised line across her arm, making a train suddenly appear in motion, a sense of steadiness rolling over her. 'Sometimes we have to listen to our fears, they help us remove ourselves from dangerous situations.'

'You're talking about actual harm, though. Not just . . . feelings, right?'

'Our feelings can do the biggest amount of damage to our lives, can't they?'

'Especially when you're a witch who can accidentally brew up a storm,' she said, drily.

He looked up at her for a moment with a half-smile, hearing the humour in her words. 'Do you still think that's what happened?'

'Things are calming down now, aren't they? Thank you.'

'My pleasure.' He let the tip of one of his fingers trace beneath a tree he'd drawn just above her elbow. Goosebumps broke out over her flesh. 'Did you ever think that maybe – if you *do* have another affinity for weather – you just helped? Like I said, it's really unlikely that you caused a whole weather system. But a little pocket of calm in a storm? That's doable for some witches. It never occurred to you to believe your magic was helpful rather than damaging?'

She was quiet as his words sank in. It was sort of what he'd been saying earlier about her seeing her gift as a curse. And she'd had good reason to believe that, because she couldn't see a single way it could help anyone . . . but she'd also assumed her ability to make people aware of their feelings had made things worse with her family. She hadn't stopped to consider how it could be a good thing. Maybe it was why her friendship with Ilina had clicked when they'd met in person at the conference?

And now she'd done the same thing, thinking about the possibility of her having a weather affinity, assuming it would only do something bad.

'No,' she said slowly, 'it didn't occur to me that it would bring anything good. My magic never has.'

'Have you ever really given it a chance to?' He tilted his head. 'Magic grows with us. I'm always learning more about the nuances of how my gift works. I didn't know this would work as well as it did.' His thumb pressed into the tender juncture of her elbow, stroking gently.

Her chest rose and fell heavily, tension easing. She didn't want to start feeling stressed again and talking about her magic generally did stress her out, so she fastened her eyes back on his artwork, letting his influence wash over her, inside and out.

It felt amazing. So much positivity bubbling through her, like a cool stream. The bedrock of fears and worries hadn't disappeared, but perhaps they were being eroded, the smaller pebbles dislodged and carried away.

And the heat of his body stretched out beside her, the sensation of him holding her, pressing, and guiding her limbs as he worked – that brought a whole other level of good feeling to her that had nothing to do with his magic.

'Do you think it would work if I couldn't see it?' she asked. 'Like, if you'd drawn on my back?'

'Hmm . . . I think so, if you can picture the image in your mind when you feel me drawing it, combined with it being on your skin . . . but not as strong maybe.'

'So . . . if it could work without me seeing it, does that mean it would work without the ink?'

'I can use any medium; paint, make-up—'

'What about something you couldn't see?

He frowned at her for a moment. 'How could I draw on you with something invisible?'

She took his wrist in her hand, turned it over and planted her lips against it. Then opened her mouth and lapped once against his skin.

His mouth went slack, his eyes heating as his gaze met hers.

'Would you like me to try doing that? On you?' His voice came out low, like a curl of smoke beneath a door.

She made a tiny shrug with one shoulder. 'It would save you ink.' She rolled her jumper up her midriff, folding it just over her bra. 'I used to want to get a sunflower tattoo. Around my belly button.'

He placed the cap on his pen with a decisive click and then threw it blindly over his shoulder, so it dropped down to the floor behind him, drawing a laugh from her even as her breathing began to speed up again.

Scooting a little further down the bed, he hitched her leg up to accommodate his bent knee beneath hers and let out a shaky laugh. 'Is there anything in particular you'd like me to try and infuse it with?'

She closed her eyes, thinking that at any other time she'd probably be dying of mortification at being so obvious, but she was just going to roll with it. In the space of the last hour, she'd gone from thinking she was going to die and send everyone to the bottom of the ocean, to peaceful, to having a simmering electricity beneath her skin.

Maybe this was going against the decision she'd made earlier, not to do anything else with him until they'd talked and she'd weighed up the sense of acting on their attraction, but the temptation was too much. She was tired of fighting it and it hadn't even been that long since she'd last made a move on him.

'You can use your imagination,' she said, resisting the desire to shift her hips.

He made a quiet hum and then his fingers curled around her hip, his thumb stroking the patch of sensitive skin just above her waistband. His lips landed next to her belly button, and she inhaled deeply at the heat of them. She could picture the press of them like a petal, his tongue lightly brushing between to draw a line. He shifted up to repeat the action, at an angle, another petal blossoming in her mind, and she felt the magic simmering – not as clear as before, but with that same way it heated and sank into her skin.

Another shift, another petal from his mouth directly onto her body. She couldn't tell what he was infusing it with yet. She couldn't have cared less, in fact. All she knew was that he had his lips and tongue on her skin and it felt amazing. Too good for her to keep still. She took a shaky breath and reached up to hold on tight to the corners of the pillow her head rested on.

A ragged noise escaped Harry's throat as her body flexed beneath him, his fingers tightening on her hip. He paused, his breath falling heavily on her skin as the moment stretched out. When he finally moved, he didn't plant another petal-kiss, he laved his tongue up from just above the button of her jeans, straight to her belly button, like a stem bursting from the earth, rising to find the sun. Heat rushed down between her legs, and she arched involuntarily.

'Oh Goddess, that feels amazing. What . . .? What, are you . . .? What influence . . .?' she stammered, trying to get out a coherent question and failing miserably.

'Fucked if I know,' he panted, and then he was lifting himself higher, his mouth mapping her whole stomach in random, lingering kisses. His teeth nipped at the small bow in the centre of her bra, peeking beneath her jumper, before he rose up further to find her lips. 'Is this—?'

She let go of the pillow and sank her fingers into his hair, gripping handfuls as she opened to him for a deep and desperate kiss.

It tasted like inevitability, his tongue caressing hers, his lips firm and frenzied as they slid over hers, drinking her in. The kiss earlier had been a scrabble to keep up with the rush of something she'd yearned for so long finally happening. Grabbing it by the scruff of its neck so it didn't get away from her. This was different. This felt like the sudden clearing of consciousness when a word you'd forgotten, that you knew would describe what you were talking about, came back to you. So obvious and perfect. So intrinsic to who she was, it was like arriving home earlier than expected. Falling into her own bed.

And she knew it wasn't his magic. Not the kind he controlled anyway. This was just them. This thing that had always been there between them and it was relief and anticipation and hunger all rolled into one.

More. She wanted more. All of him.

She unbuttoned his shirt, pushing it down his shoulders, marvelling at the curve of his bones under her hands, muscles cording as he held himself over her, shifting his weight to help free his arms. She dragged her nails lightly back up, from wrist to elbow, across his biceps, pressing her fingertips into the dip of his collarbone before smoothing down his back again. Goosebumps rose along his flesh at her touch, fine shivers as she pressed her palms to the sharp angles of his shoulder blades, traced the dents of his spine.

She was the one drawing on him and it was working a different kind of magic. But it reminded her of how she used to feel about it – full of wonder and anticipation, crackling with eagerness, knowing bursts of sheer joy were to be found.

His body was lean and hard, freckles dancing across his skin. She wanted to study every one. Her hand slid to his stomach, up higher and she faltered at his chest, lines of ink surprising her. 'You have a tattoo.' Right in the centre of his chest, deep blue lines overlapping in a complicated pattern.

'Yes.' He ran his nose along her jaw, pressed a kiss to the vulnerable underside. 'I'll tell you about it later.'

She made a hum of agreement and chased his mouth back to hers, bracketing his narrow waist with both hands and pulling him down to press his weight on top of her, making room for him between her thighs. They both rolled their hips as soon as they made contact and twin moans escaped around their kiss.

His chest was against hers, but she was still wearing her jumper, all rolled up and uncomfortable and he grabbed it at the neckline, like it had offended him simply by existing as a barrier between them. She started to lift her arms so he could drag it over her head, but instead, he pulled his mouth away from hers for a moment, gasping out a spell. She opened her eyes again and saw all the threads in the jumper unravel and wind themselves back up into a ball of wool beneath his hand.

She shivered and caught his eyes as he discarded the ball of wool onto the floor.

'That's a nifty trick,' she managed to say. She wrapped her hands around his neck, pulling herself up further from the bed, giving him access to her back. 'Just don't use it on my bra,' she warned and invited him at the same time, with a smile.

He nipped the smile off her lips, while he found the clasp on her bra, his long fingers unsnapping it with ease, pulling it free. Her stomach quivered as his hand cupped one of her breasts, gently kneading, seeing how she responded . . . how she couldn't help writhing and pressing up into him, soft, desperate noises falling from her lips.

His mouth found the other breast, tongue tracing a circle around her nipple, while he gently pinched and rolled the other, and she felt it tugging all the way down her body, right between her legs. He sucked hard and then soft, each change somehow making her squirm and yearn for more, ratcheting her higher and higher. He swapped his attentions, finding her damp nipple and twisting just right, mouth providing the intensity on the other that she was aching for. Magic fingers. Magic mouth.

She could feel her own magic flowing through her body, entwining with the energy of her arousal, but she didn't fear it – there was no room for fear alongside this maelstrom of pleasure and need.

'Please, Harry, please,' she groaned, fingers in his hair again, unsure where she wanted his attention most.

He lifted his head, eyes near black from his dilated pupils.

'What do you want?' he asked her, his naturally husky voice little more than a growling whisper, sending prickles of lust across her skin.

She groaned again. He'd picked the one question she was too overwhelmed to answer. 'Everything. You. Please.' She arched beneath him, brushing her sensitive nipples against his bare chest, causing delicious friction.

He took her mouth again, his tongue stroking deep, drinking her in with his beautiful lips, trailing his hands down her ribs and waist, tracing her curves as though she was a sculpture he was moulding from clay. He moved onto his side and popped the button open on her jeans and yanked them down with a few strong, alternating tugs, dragging her knickers and socks with them, so she was totally naked beneath him, clothes bunched up at the bottom of the bunk with his coat. Everything about him was a balance of delicacy and demand that was blowing her mind to bits.

His fingers dipped between her legs, spreading the evidence of her arousal over her in precise circles, making the muscles in her core clench so hard, it was almost painful. He slid down the bed, pressing her thighs wide, bending to inflict exquisite torture on her with his tongue. She twisted the rough blanket beneath her, then grabbed for the bars of the bunk bed as his fingers played at the entrance to her body.

'Oh Goddess, Harry, I need you, please,' she gasped as waves of ecstasy washed over her, stronger and stronger, but not breaking.

'Where? Here?' He pushed two fingers inside her, slowly, teasingly, and she cried out, bowing off the bed.

'Yes. Yes.'

He pressed a kiss against her, spoke the words into her hot flesh. 'Are you sure?'

'Yes.' Apparently, that was the only word in her vocabulary anymore.

He pressed his fingers inside her again, slow out, fast in, and then moved away, making her groan. He grabbed his big coat, opening it up to find the pocket on the silky inner lining which held his wallet, and the condom inside that.

He let everything else drop to the floor, including his own jeans, making short work of sheathing himself, seeming in a hurry, which she was ready to thank every deity for, until he moved back over her, kneeling between her legs to stare up at her. 'Beautiful. That's all I could think when I was trying to do the sunflower. You're beautiful.'

He bent his head down toward her navel, but she grabbed him, cupping his jaw, and lifting his face to hers. 'No. No more. I can't wait for you any longer.'

He met her eyes, nodding, and then settled himself in the cradle of her thighs. He notched against her, where she was soft and swollen and oh so ready, and she canted her hips to get to more of him. He swallowed, the crease forming between his eyebrows before he filled her, with one long, gradual thrust, until they couldn't get any closer and were both panting.

And then they were moving together, one of his hands at the base of her spine, supporting her as she tilted up to meet him, and every time he pushed into her, the friction inside and out was bliss. She dug her nails into his shoulders and bit his earlobe, trying to press how amazing she felt back into his skin. He gasped, burying his face in between her neck and shoulder, his own teeth grazing at her skin, and then he shifted angle again, bringing himself in deeper, rubbing over a spot inside her each time he moved and she broke into a million pieces, blown apart with the well of pleasure overflowing and sweeping across her nerve endings, soaring through her muscles. Even her teeth tingled.

He held still for her as she fell, pressing firm right where she needed him as she ground out the pleasure, her inner muscles clenching him tight until she went limp. When she threaded her fingers into his hair, damp from sweat, he began to move again, slowly, then building. She pulled his head up to hers so she could kiss him. Deep kisses that matched his rhythm and the pleasure began to rise in her again. She whimpered in surprise as the aftershocks of her orgasm tipped her over into a second. He groaned into her mouth as she clenched around him again, and then his pace was stuttering, his breathing ragged, as he thrust harder, faster, until he shuddered, and she felt him bucking and pulsing within her.

Kay wrapped her arms and legs around him as he collapsed down, their sweat-slicked skin touching everywhere, chests heaving as they both pulled in much-needed air.

He pressed kisses to her shoulder, her jaw, up along her cheekbone and hairline, languid and so tender, her heart ached. She stroked her fingers through his hair, down his neck and back. Then she started laughing.

He winced and leaned back.

'Sorry,' she said, trying to stop but giggling anyway.

'What?' he asked as he moved away, holding the condom in place, and looking down at her with a quizzical smile.

'I take it that pen wasn't permanent ink.' She lifted an arm to show his illustrations were completely smeared and unrecognisable. And then she pointed to his body, the long smudges of black along his chest and back and hips. He even had some on his cheekbone and she rubbed her thumb against it, making absolutely no difference to it.

He turned his head and kissed her palm before jumping down to dispose of the condom, using a brief pulse of magic to ease his descent – how did he have the strength? She was nothing but a puddle of sated nerve endings.

When he joined her again, she wiggled back to make room for him and he tugged the blanket up to their chins, heads close on the pillow, creating a little cocoon of their own on the rolling ferry. Pressure mounted in her chest, something light but powerful pushing against her diaphragm.

Don't think about anything now, she begged her brain. *Just enjoy this moment.*

She put her hand on his chest, framing his tattoo between her index finger and thumb. She knew he'd always recognised his centre of magic as being there, and he'd told her that was where he felt his itchy magic compass. Perhaps it was to do with that. 'Are these runes? When did you get it?'

'Have you been waiting the whole time to ask about that?' He pushed her hair back from her face, delicately untangling the strands stuck to her skin.

'Totally. All I could think about.' She smiled at him and coasted her hand lower, finally resting on his hip. 'I lost interest in the experiment we were conducting on your magic as soon as I saw it.'

'I think the experiment had long since ended at that point.' He raised an eyebrow at her and the hint of playful scolding made a tiny shiver of delight work its way down her back.

'All right, I'll be completely honest with you,' she stage-whispered. 'I was *never* interested in the experiment.'

He cupped the back of her neck and leaned in. 'Me neither,' he murmured against her lips, and pressed a long, soft kiss to them.

When they pulled away from each other, the pressure was squeezing up between her ribs, but she was still ignoring it. Or letting it be, more accurately, rather than trying to chase it away with worries about what was actually happening here between them.

'Is it to do with your gift?'

He laughed, pressing his hand over the top of hers, so she felt his heart beating beneath her palm. 'You're really persistent about this.'

'Just curious. I guess I—' She broke off, a blush touching her cheeks. Ridiculous considering the fact they were lying next to each other naked. But she'd almost admitted how often in the past she'd imagined getting his shirt off him, and never once had he been tattooed in her mind. It's not like he couldn't guess how much she'd always wanted him, but she didn't need to advertise the fact.

He saved her from her embarrassment, either not noticing or pretending not to notice. 'It's not for my gift.' He took a steady, slow breath, but even so, she felt his heart rate kicking up a little beneath her hand. 'It's part of the protective magic for Ashworth Hall and Biddicote.'

'Really? Why? What's it for?'

'It's . . .' He licked his lips, easing slightly back, and she could feel her glasses shifting as a frown pulled at her eyebrows. 'Whoever inherits Ashworth Hall also inherits the responsibility of anchoring the magic. Acting as a conduit of sorts. You know that, mostly, magic only resides in objects or places if it's been built with it by a witch with an alchemy affinity, or layered there from years and years of usage, or has the resonance from a rune. And that accounts for a lot of the framework, but the spells that get activated by a particularly big incident, they still need a focal point of live magic to draw from. The tattoo directs that.'

Kay lifted her hand, dislodging his, so she could examine the runes while she puzzled through what he was telling her. 'Like a call-back function,' she said.

She recognised a couple of the runes: the yew tree, for protection; the cross which was linked to gifts but also generosity and helping others. There were more there, though, joined and overlapping each other in a special way, surrounded by a runic pattern she'd never seen before. All, right there, over his centre of magic. She couldn't say why exactly, but she wasn't sure she liked the idea.

'On a phone?'

'A little bit, I guess, but I was thinking more of something that's used in coding.'

'Oh, then I have no idea.' He rolled onto his back, closing his eyes. 'There's a lot we have no idea about . . . just that it's always worked in the past.'

He was looking tired again, and it was the middle of the night, so she pressed her lips together on a lot of questions and comments she wanted to make. Like questioning the sense of allowing your body to be tattooed with powerful magic just because it had 'always worked' before. According to his family, no doubt. The same family who would influence his behaviour when he was a child to ensure he was upholding their legacy.

And why was this a secret from the rest of the community? Had no one wondered how it worked before, or was it as simple as them benefiting from it, and no one complaining, so no one bothered to ask? She certainly hadn't thought about it. But then she'd never really been aware of the extent to which Biddicote was protected until she went off to live outside of it.

'If you were to have tattooed those drawings on me, would the influence have worked permanently?' she wondered out loud. 'Is that how this works?'

'No. There's more to it than that. Spelled ink, some of the runes are unique and we have no definitive record of them and precisely what they mean. There's a ritual, with intention too. It's a whole big thing. I'm sure there are magical tattooists, but the tenets would apply – you can't stay in a state of one mood or emotion permanently, it's not physiologically good for us, is it?'

'But the witching tenets don't apply to the Ashworths and this tattoo?'

He was quiet for a moment. 'The Witches' Council don't know about it.'

'Why not?'

'They're not very keen on the set-up in Biddicote as it is, apparently.'

'What objection could they have to it?'

'None they can admit openly. Biddicote's community is rare and, because of its respect for my family, the Council feel threatened by the sway we could hold if we chose to use it. They're waiting for an excuse to take control from us, to get their hands on the magical artifacts, some of the grimoires we have, but they can't just bulldoze their way in because the Ashworths own it. Or at least that's the way my father has put it. He doesn't trust them.' He pinched the bridge of his nose, lines appearing in his forehead. 'I sometimes wonder if we'd be better off opening some access up to them, because if we shared information, maybe it would benefit all of us . . . but I *have* to respect my father's wishes on it.'

'Until you're the head of the family, I suppose.'

Now his hand covered his whole face. 'I don't want to even think about that.' He was pulling away from her mentally, the stress making his body tense in the way she'd noticed crept up on him regularly. Before, she'd assumed it was just about getting back to Biddicote, because what else could be wrong in Harry Ashworth's perfect life? It was amazing the lies you told yourself about someone when you were angry with them. Sure, there were a lot of benefits to being an influencer, and an Ashworth. But, also, a lot more complications than she'd ever guessed.

'It's too late to think about anything,' she groaned, trying to lighten the mood. 'I'm going to look like roadkill in the wedding photographs.'

'Not possible,' he said, dropping his hand and curling her in tighter to him, pressing a kiss on the top of her head. 'But it could be worse. We could have ended up as roadkill.'

'True.' She turned her head, brushing her lips over the curve of his shoulder. It could have been a lot worse than ending up here, in his arms.

Chapter Sixteen

Kay and Harry groaned simultaneously when his phone alarm went off a few hours later. Sadly, not because of shared pleasure this time.

'Nooo,' she mumbled, turning her face into Harry's shoulder. His stubble prickled lightly against her scalp and her glasses bent in that strangely fluid way they had. Even if they weren't going to break, they could still get dislodged, so she lifted her head and tried to push herself up onto one elbow, getting enough room to straighten them. Both she and Harry were in exactly the same positions they'd fallen asleep in. Or passed out in.

Harry looked even more edible than he had yesterday. Thoroughly messy bedhead and lips pink from kisses. He cracked one eye open, then blinked until the other was able to join in, bright blue spearing her, like she'd opened the curtains on a glorious summer morning.

'Hi.' His voice was all gravel, rasping over her nerve endings, sending goosebumps down her spine.

'Hi.'

The morning after. Why did this never get any easier?

It probably helped if you weren't still naked and entwined. She wrapped a bit of blanket around her and moved back as far as she could without stealing all the covers from him.

'We were going to talk,' he said.

But then they'd had sex instead. Very sensible decision there.

His phone alarm bleeped incessantly as background music, a stark reminder that she was still running against a clock to get to Joe's wedding. The sea seemed much calmer than the night before and, with any luck, the storm had passed from England and they wouldn't have any more trouble getting home. Provided she wasn't the bringer of all the bad weather.

Why did this all have to be happening at the same time? She felt like Leon's car last night, spinning her wheels, desperately trying to get traction.

'We still can,' she said, attempting to put her metaphorical big-girl panties on, because she had no clue where her *actual* underwear was. She squeezed her eyes shut hard enough to make starbursts bloom in her vision and took a deep breath. 'But the ferry will be docking soon, we need to get to the car.'

'I know.' She felt his stomach lift and fall, like he was taking a deep breath. 'I'll go grab my bag so we can get you something to wear. You just stay wrapped up warm. I'll be ten minutes.'

'Thanks,' she said weakly and shoved her head into the pillow so she didn't torture herself with the sight of him getting dressed. Not that it helped, she could still see flashbacks of his skin in her mind, freckles dipping into curves of muscle as they flexed over her. Her whole body flashed hot with the memory. Oh sweet, sweet, Goddess, it had been *good*. And she hadn't got her mouth on nearly enough of him . . .

When she heard the door click shut, she crawled out of her cave and sent stern words to all her exhausted – and horny – limbs that they needed to move. Wrapping the blanket around her like a toga, she climbed down from the bunk and found Harry had gathered her clothes on the chair next to her tote, folding them neatly, before leaving. Her heart gave a little kick before she had several more stern words with herself – these ones about setting the bar so low for men to impress.

She riffled in her bag for her toothbrush, making use of the sink in the corner of the room, and was just about to drop the blanket and get reluctantly back into her dirty clothes when the door opened again.

'That was quick.' She clutched at the blanket around her and Harry paused, his eyes roving from her head to her bare toes. She was nothing but a lumpy swath of fabric but his look made her flush.

He cleared his throat and closed the door behind him again, bringing his bag in. He placed it next to hers on the chair and stripped off his coat and shirt from last night, grabbing the maroon jumper from Friday to swap into. For dirty laundry, it smelt annoyingly fresh. That was the reason her mouth was watering. Definitely that. Not the sight of his stomach muscles tightening as he pulled the jumper on.

'You refreshed your clothes with magic already,' she thought out loud.

'It's a habit. I do it whenever I pack. Really saves on the washing when you get home. I can do the same to yours.' His eyes fell on the pile of clothes and Kay's cheeks flamed at the sight of her limp knickers.

'You are not cleaning my underwear.' She grabbed the offending pants with one hand, holding the blanket in place with the other, and stuffed them inside her bag. 'I'd rather die.'

'Touch dramatic.' He laughed and his mouth kicked up at the corner. 'You didn't mind me handling your knickers last night.'

'That was very, *very* different.' She bit her lip, trying not to grin quite so ridiculously at the flirtatious comment. She couldn't help that she liked having signs he was still interested in her. That possibly it wasn't just a one-night stand in his mind. Even though she didn't know whether she *needed* it to be for her.

Egos were delicate and dangerous things.

'I'd appreciate you doing the spell on the rest of my clothes though please . . . I'll go commando.'

His gaze travelled down her body again, before he swallowed and took the clothes over to the sink, sprinkling water and magical words over each item, before returning them to her, dry. He added the white shirt he'd worn under his jumper on Friday, too.

'Sorry I can't make it smaller for you or fix your jumper. It's not something I've ever bothered to learn.'

She took them and smiled. 'That's OK, it's actually reassuring to know you are not the perfect witch specimen.'

'Goddess, Kay, I'm so far from it,' he said, so grimly, her smile faltered.

'I was only teasing.'

'I know but . . . sometimes it feels like I'm always reading from the wrong grimoire, you know?'

She snorted. 'Yeah, funnily enough, I am familiar with that feeling.'

He raised a rueful eyebrow at her. 'But you don't go about putting lightening spells on luggage, or influencing salesmen, thinking you're doing the best without fully considering the consequences and it ends up causing more problems.'

No, she just set fire to things. But she didn't try to argue it with him. He was making a different point . . . and beating himself up again. They made quite a pair, with him always thinking he wielded his magic in the wrong way, and her, sure that her magic was cursed.

She reached out for his arm, involuntarily. 'Sounds like a Chaotic Good characteristic.'

'Chaotic Good?' he scoffed. 'I'm not exactly Robin Hood.'

'And I'm not exactly a Dungeons and Dragons expert.'

He smiled. 'Well, before you learn any better, I'll take it. We'd balance each other out quite well then.' Her heartbeat stuttered and a loaded silence settled between them, until Harry looked away. 'I'll just wash up while you get dressed, unless you'd like me to step out?'

She shook her head but waited until he was brushing his teeth over by the sink before donning the clothes at superhero-in-a-phone-box speed, sitting on the edge of the bottom bunk. When he turned back around, she was standing, tying the unbuttoned bottom half of his shirt in a knot at her waist to avoid it coming down to her knees. He bit his lip and she knew exactly how he was feeling. She didn't need to remove her glasses to know there was a bond of sexual tension snapping between them . . . but also a whole lot of baggage.

It would be too easy to give into what her body craved without thinking about the consequences. Everything had changed so quickly. She wasn't even supposed to *want* to get involved with an influencer. She knew that it made for messy relationships.

It wasn't as if she even knew if *he* wanted more than something physical.

And none of this weekend was supposed to be about her love life at all. Her brother was getting married. At some point today, she was supposed to put a bridesmaid dress on, get her hair and make-up done, and walk down an aisle before her soon-to-be sister-in-law. All eyes briefly on her as she tried not to cause an inadvertent magical mishap. Depending on what she chose to believe, either the last one she'd had was when she'd accidentally broken the sofa bed in Prague . . . or when she called a storm down upon them in the North Sea. In the calmer light of day, that did seem a lot less likely.

No time to think about that, though. She still had to *get* to the wedding before she started worrying about whether she was going to wreck it or not.

'Ready?' Harry asked, grabbing his duffel, and then holding out her coat for her.

Kay let him help her put it on, doing her best to ignore the way he smoothed his hands down from her shoulders to her arms, the heat of him behind her back, making her knees weak. 'As I'll ever be.'

England was a mess. That much Kay could tell as they drove out of the port in the weak grey light of the morning. There were fallen trees, debris, broken windows, and tiles missing from houses. The wind hadn't dropped fully yet and the rain continued to fall in a steady stream, neither heavy nor light, just the kind that made everything endlessly drenched.

It suited her state of mind. She'd left England last week with a clear purpose and a black and white conviction about the past. Now, it seemed she barely knew herself, let alone which way was up.

She'd offered to drive, but Harry had insisted he didn't mind. That he wasn't a great passenger. She wasn't sure why, but it didn't exactly ring true to her. She got the impression he needed to keep moving, like he had in Dusseldorf when he'd wanted to walk to the train station. His grip on the steering wheel was tight, his shoulders bunched, and despite what they'd said about talking about things, he was having to concentrate on the diversions that were cropping up and she was trying not worry about how it was impacting their ETA. Or what exactly she was going to say if they ever did talk about what was happening between them.

She turned on the radio, filling the silence with music, and then checked the messages on her phone.

The wedding WhatsApp group was full of photos from last night's wedding rehearsal dinner. It had taken place at the posh restaurant on the edge of the village, and from the photos and the joking comments, it looked like the bad weather had cut the power intermittently, leaving them using candles and flashlights on occasion. Kay was sure that wouldn't normally be permitted, but since her dad had helped the owners focus themselves to get the restaurant off the ground, she supposed they'd done their best to keep the party going for them. The result looked atmospheric and memorable. Her eyes stung for a moment at having missed it.

There were lots of pictures of Joe and Sandy looking adorable in the warm glow of candles and Sandy's other bridesmaids got a lot of attention too, which Kay didn't find surprising since it was Joe's best man who'd taken on the role of cameraman and he obviously fancied the pants off of at least one of them. Probably Chelsea, a knock-out blonde Kay had met at the hen do, who could flirt at gold-medal standard.

There were no pictures of her mother. She was sure she wouldn't have backed out of going, just because Kay wasn't there. Guilt needled at her, but no – she'd done everything she could to make it.

Shaking her head, she tapped out a message to tell them all she was back in the country and on her way. A couple of responses with cheering and confetti emojis came through. She was just about to put her phone away in her bag again when it started ringing.

Her eyebrows lifted as she saw Sandy's name on her display. They got along well – Sandy was a lovely person – but it was rare for her to call Kay. And given that this was her wedding day, it didn't bode well.

'Hey, bride-to-be,' Kay answered brightly, turning the radio down slightly and hoping that it wasn't completely the wrong thing to say. How likely was it that a bride would call the groom's sister if she was having second thoughts? Ordinarily, probably not – but Kay could read emotional bonds, exactly the kind of gift you might ask someone to use if you were worried about the strength of your potential husband's feelings.

'Hey,' Sandy's voice was so clearly waterlogged from tears, Kay found herself sending a look of panic towards Harry. He sensed it almost immediately, tilting his head towards her, his lips pressing together before he had to turn his concentration back to the road.

Despite obviously being on the verge of some kind of emotional breakdown, Sandy demonstrated her loveliness by first asking Kay if *she* was all right after all her travelling woes. Once Kay had confirmed she was, Sandy carried on.

'That's great. I'm sorry if you've been through so much stress getting back in time for the wedding, though . . . I'm not sure it's going to happen.'

'Why not? What's wrong?'

'It's the venue. A tree came down in the storm and caved in part of the roof and one of the windows.'

'In the rooms you'd be using?'

Kay knew the place. It was a big old building on pretty grounds about half an hour outside of the village. Typically, they hosted two weddings at a time there – one wing each – with the ceremonies taking place in one room and then a meal and the reception afterwards in one of the larger ballrooms.

'That's what I asked, but it doesn't matter – the building is unsafe. They can't have the electricity on, it's a mess.' Sandy broke off to start sniffling.

'Oh no.' Kay sat up further in her seat, as the desire to give Sandy a hug filled her. 'Is there another place you can go to?'

'Joe and your parents are ringing around all the venues closest to us to try to organise something, but, honestly, how likely is it at such short notice? And we can't really afford to pay for a whole other venue and the staff there, if they don't let us bring the catering firms we'd hired. It's taken months to plan this wedding – and we were keeping it fairly modest—' She sobbed again. 'The easiest thing would be to fix the problems at the venue, wouldn't it? Get it safe again?'

'I suppose so . . .' Kay said slowly, figuring they were getting to the crux of why she had been called, though she wasn't sure how she was meant to help with it. 'But I'm guessing builders and electricians are going to be just as difficult to get hold of today, with all the damage from the storm.'

'Do we need builders and electricians, though? What about . . . witches?'

'Ohh, I see.' Kay pushed her hair back from her face. 'That's . . . not as easy as it sounds, Sandy. I know it can seem like magic can fix everything, but first we'd have to *find* enough witches with the right affinities, and then how would we explain them coming in to do work on a property in a few hours that would ordinarily take days or even weeks?'

'Couldn't someone, you know, just hypnotise the people at the building to forget the damage even happened?'

'Wiping people's memories isn't as simple as that.'

'Isn't that what happens in the village when a non-magical person sees something they shouldn't?'

'Er . . . no. Not really. It's deflected. Influence is used to convince them they were mistaken in what they'd seen – not that it didn't happen altogether. People can be convinced to reconstruct a memory slightly . . . but it's not like plucking a photo from an album. Even if a witch could do something close to it, it's not easy or safe or . . . fair, Sandy,' Kay said softly.

Harry looked over at her again, his brow knitting together, and she blushed a little at explaining in front of him how the protective magic of Biddicote worked, when truly she'd only just learned the extent of it last night. Maybe she was getting it all wrong, but that was how the witches of Biddicote had always understood it.

'That's what your dad said.' Sandy took a shaky breath and Kay blinked at the surprise of her and her father being on the same page. 'I thought magic would be a bit more useful than it is, frankly. If it can't fix things like this, what good is it?'

'Oh Goddess, Sandy, I understand how you feel, believe me,' Kay admitted, even though she'd definitely seen more of the benefits over the last couple of days, and even missed using her own, on occasion. Strange to miss something that she'd always had the power to use, if she'd really wanted to, but had chosen not to. 'Sadly, magic isn't this superpower that can eradicate all the difficulties in life. Witches are still just people, with a slightly different skill set, that can bring as many problems as it fixes. We just have to try to do our best.'

'I know,' Sandy sighed. 'I'm sorry.'

'You don't have to be sorry. But we'll fix this for you. We will.'

'How? We've called nearly every wedding venue in the southeast and had no luck. Unless we're going to start knocking on doors, I don't see how we're going to make it happen.'

'We'll think of something. I'll be with you all by eleven o'clock, I should think, OK?'

Sandy thanked her, genuine but downhearted, and Kay hung up.

'What's wrong?' Harry asked, straight away.

She sighed, sliding back down in her seat, and explaining.

He listened and then went quiet for a moment, his eyes still scanning the road. The windscreen wipers worked back and forth against the sheets of rain, the repeated hush followed by a rubbery scrape pressing at her nerves. Then Harry spoke again. 'How many guests are there going to be?'

'About fifty at the service and just over a hundred at the reception, I think. Why? Have you got an idea for somewhere else they can have it?'

He nodded slowly, tapping his index finger at the top of the steering wheel. 'Maybe . . . I could ask my parents if they could use the Hall.'

'Aren't you having an event for Samhain?'

'No. We haven't done any of the festivals for years.' He straightened his arm, pushing his shoulders back against his seat. 'My dad's health isn't good. That's why I'm living back at home. Have been for a while.'

Kay's mouth opened. 'What's wrong with him?' She shook her head at her own bluntness. 'If you don't mind me asking.'

'We're not sure exactly.' He shifted again, this time gripping the gearstick. 'It seems to be respiratory, but none of the healers – or normal doctors – can make a difference.'

A weight pressed on her chest, like someone was doing compressions on her, as all of his stress to get home began to make sense to her. As well as Leon's comments about Harry not travelling far from Ashworth Hall for a long time because of his dad. 'I'm sorry. I didn't realise.'

'I know.' He glanced at her quickly, gave her a slight smile, and it skewered her straight in the heart.

She *should* have known. If she hadn't been nursing her own bruised feelings for so long, if her mum hadn't wrapped her up in cotton wool – she *would* have known. She would have known that he and Joe were still friends, that his dad was ill and Ashworth Hall had closed its doors. It might not have made her capable of being happy to see him when they had bumped into each other in Prague, because he had still owed her an apology for pushing her away so abruptly and trying to influence her, but maybe she wouldn't have been as hostile.

'I wish I'd known,' she admitted.

'I wish it wasn't happening,' he replied quietly, like he thought she was criticising him for not bringing up the painful subject. Sure, there had been opportunities, but there had also been a lot going on, and a lot of mercurial moods between the two of them.

'I'm sorry,' she said again.

'You're not a mind reader, Kay.' He raised his eyebrows and forced a bigger smile at her. 'Are you?'

'No. Thank Mother Nature.' She laughed weakly, appreciating he was trying to lighten the mood. 'It's really kind of you to offer the use of the Hall, but won't it disturb your dad?'

'I don't know. I don't think so. It's a big house and

he's bedridden these days.' He cleared his throat. 'We've even got a licence. My mum dabbled in hosting weddings when I moved back and we thought things might improve.'

Kay chewed on the edge of her thumbnail, still trying to picture Adrian Ashworth, the tall, commanding witch with a voice that could make puppets of people, unable to get out of bed. 'Are you sure, Harry? It sounds like too much to ask.'

'That house was made for witches and their non-magical friends and family to gather and celebrate together. And if my dad isn't up to it, my mum will say, I promise you. But I can at least ask the question, can't I? I want to.'

Well, that didn't really leave her with much room to argue, did it? And it wasn't really her place anyway. He knew his situation at home better than her, and the favour wouldn't be for her, it would be for Joe and Sandy.

'Thank you.' She reached over and put her hand over his on the gearstick. He twisted his wrist so he could lace his fingers through hers and lift it to his mouth to kiss the back of it. Her stomach flipped over, like a turtle on its back kicking its legs, desperate to get upright again. She inhaled sharply, trying to push the sensation away, and a violent squeaking filled the quiet of the car, as the wind-screen wipers started moving at double speed.

Harry let go of her to fiddle with the settings, but – of course – it made no difference.

'It's me.' She gave a small moan, pulling up the collar of the shirt he'd given her so she could hide her face.

'Doing *that* to the windscreen wipers?'

'Yes. It's my magic shooting off and doing stupid things again.'

'Well, that's . . . interesting,' he said, and she could hear the laughter in his voice.

'Is it?' She emerged slightly from the collar and raised an eyebrow at him.

'You told me the car would explode if you had an episode,' he deadpanned. 'Super dry windows is not exactly a hurricane, is it? Frankly, I was expecting something a bit more destructive. Where's my Galadriel experience?'

'Shut up, or I'll trap you in a bed again.'

He caught her in his gaze, eyes sparkling with laughter and heat. 'Kayla Hendrix, you can trap me in a bed anytime.'

She flushed, a livewire feeling shooting through her when he said her name like that. 'I meant by the ankle.'

'Well, you have more knowledge of that area, but I'm very open to exploring it with you.'

Her laugh erupted from her, and the wide smile on his face in response was everything, filling her with such a sweet lightness; she almost thought she would see it glowing from her skin if she looked in the mirror.

She watched the windscreen wipers, moving at a frenzied pace, and instead of trying to shut it down, she simply waited. Recognising the excess magic crackling from her, but not trying to bury it, feeling her magic flow . . . and then settle.

They made it to London without too much delay despite more diversions around flooding and fallen trees. The most frustrating part was trying to find a parking space near her flat, but that was to do with it being London, rather than the weather.

Kay took the umbrella, leaving Harry in the car to make the call to his mum, hurrying through streets that looked like the aftermath of a *Ghostbusters* movie, pumpkins capsized and decorations of ghouls and witches bedraggled, leaning haphazardly against gateposts, or crumpled into a wet heap on the lawns, amid bright yellow warning tape.

Taking the four flights of stairs up to her attic flat, she was breathing heavily by the time she got the door open and wondering how much time she should give Harry to talk to his mother. The clock was essentially on pause until they found a new wedding venue, but her sense of urgency hadn't disappeared.

She put her phone on charge and gathered together her two dress bags, and the multiple pairs of shoes she'd spent too much money on, sending out every good thought she could, that they would be needed. Unpacking her tote bag, she repacked the contents into a small leather holdall, then paused, debating whether to take her corn husk doll. She could just leave her at home, shoved under the bed to avoid the risk of her family spotting her and asking questions. But they'd been this far together and Kay was beginning to feel strangely attached to her. Maybe even like she'd been wrong to treat the doll as if she was the aggressor when, truly, she was the injured party, having been flambéed in an unprovoked attack.

Kay rubbed her eyes. Maybe the effects of the marijuana weren't entirely out of her system?

Twenty minutes later, loaded with bags she was trying to keep dry under the umbrella, she made it back to the car. Harry popped the boot open for her and she dumped everything inside. Before she could get back in, he climbed out of the driver's seat. 'You OK to drive the last leg?' he asked her, hunching against the rain.

'Sure.'

'Great,' he said with a smile. 'Because I need to get on the phone to your brother. He's got a wedding to relocate to Ashworth Hall.'

Chapter Seventeen

Even in the rain, there was something pretty about Biddicote. Leaves had been blown prematurely from the trees, yet, instead of looking stark, the colours mingled along the edges of the lane and turned the water of the duck pond into a beautiful marbled mirror.

Kay pulled up in front of her mum's cottage, the home she'd grown up in, and cut the engine. Harry had spent most of the time on and off the phone to Joe and the housekeeper at Ashworth Hall. He'd found a notepad and pen in the glovebox, so he could scribble down notes about things to prepare at Ashworth Hall, and questions he needed to call Joe back with answers to, once he was home again.

They were both going home. It was time to say goodbye.

'Joe said he'll be here in a minute.' Harry stretched over to the back seat to tuck the notepad and his phone in one of the pockets of his coat. The way his jumper lifted to reveal a tiny sliver of skin, his jeans low on his hips as they twisted in her direction, had Kay's breath shallowing.

'Great,' she managed.

He settled back into his seat, looking over at her. The rain was closer to a drizzle now and, with the wipers off, the sudden quiet was so obviously loaded.

'Thank—'

'Have you—'

They both spoke at the same time and then laughed, small and awkward.

'You go first,' she said, unclipping her seat belt and turning to face him too.

He rubbed his hands roughly through his hair. He'd rolled his sleeves up for the drive and she wanted to run her fingertips along his forearm, dancing her nerve endings along the light hair and freckles and lines of his muscles. 'I was wondering . . . have you got someone you're taking to the wedding?'

'Oh.' She opened her eyes wide. 'No. I don't. I decided to go stag. This is the twenty-first century after all.'

'So, no one would mind if I found you at the reception and . . . asked you to dance?' The way his eyes fastened on her mouth had her feeling that 'dance' might be a euphemism. But even if he did only mean dancing, the idea alone made her heart skitter. It had been palpitating so much over the last two days, she was beginning to think an ECG might be in order.

It felt like they were edging out over the ice towards each other again, but it wasn't their weight that might crack it – it was their heat melting a hole as they got closer. And she was no longer sure if falling through meant drowning . . . or learning to swim?

But she could commit to a dance, couldn't she? It wasn't like they were agreeing to go on a date. He wasn't asking *that*.

'No one would mind that. *I'd* like it.' Understatement of the century, but still, honest.

He smiled and leaned in closer to her. Her body immediately began getting very excited, as though all her cells recognised his and were vibrating at a higher frequency. 'You might change your mind when you see my dance moves,' he warned her in that low, husky voice, sending goosebumps racing across her skin.

'Do you just like to stand and sway?' Because she wasn't opposed to that, especially if their bodies were pressed together everywhere important.

'No. Quite the opposite. You ever seen the dance scene in *Airplane*?'

'Never even heard of it.'

'Whatever you do, don't look it up.'

She wrinkled her nose as she laughed and he suddenly reached out and stroked his finger down her scrunched-up nose.

'It feels like I'm turning inside out when you do that,' he whispered, and the laughter caught in her throat.

She took a shaky breath in and his hand moved to cup her cheek. She was just about to close her eyes when there was a sharp rap on the window behind Harry. They both froze.

'It's Joe, isn't it?'

Kay squinted over his shoulder, seeing the rain-blurred shape of a man with a hood pulled up, peering in. 'Yes.'

Harry lifted his eyes up to stare at the roof for a second, a rueful smile on his lips. He caressed his thumb once down her cheek and dropped his hand. 'Just like old times.'

Kay didn't have time to process what that meant before he grabbed his coat and turned to open the car door. As he climbed out to greet her brother, she gave herself a moment to adjust. The thud of the door closing behind him was like her ears popping after being underwater, everything rushing back in at full volume. She could hear her brother thanking Harry, and Harry typically demurring, as he headed for the boot.

Joe was here. The wedding was happening.

She grabbed her coat too, shivering in the rain as she got out, but finding Harry had already fetched the umbrella for her and was coming to meet her with it open, like she was some kind of celebrity. 'Thank you,' she said, taking it from him.

Joe was waiting at the open boot.

'We've been so worried,' he said, giving her a big hug, despite the umbrella, the waterproof material of his coat squeaking. 'Thank the Goddess you made it back OK.' She patted his shoulder and was about to say something about how sweet he was, when he pulled back and lifted his dark eyebrows up so they nearly hit his hairline. 'What in the name of Samhain did you do to your hair?'

Kay laughed, putting her hand up to it. 'Don't you like it?'

'Depends. Did you do it as a wedding present for me? Because it's my football team's colour?'

'Er, yeah, sure, we can say that.'

'You are such a bullshitter.' He tousled her hair like she was seven and turned to Harry again. 'Seriously, thanks so much for getting Kay home to us. It was so lucky you were there.'

Harry pushed his hands into his pockets. 'I was just as lucky. She got me home too.'

'Yeah, but not with magic.' Joe pointed to the boot. 'These all yours, Kay?' When she pointed out her bags, he gathered them from the boot and started moving towards the house. 'I'll see you soon, Harry.' He clapped him on the shoulder as he went past and turned to walk backwards as he got on the pavement. 'If you can make it to the ceremony, that would be great, but we understand if you've got to be with your dad.'

'I'll do my best.' Harry lifted his hand to wave goodbye to Joe and looked back at Kay. She took a step towards him—

'C'mon, Kay, there's so much to do.'

Harry laughed. 'Good luck.'

'You too.' She didn't trust herself to kiss his cheek, so she caught his hand as she walked by, the brief brush of their skin like a sip of expensive wine. The temptation of warmth spreading from her stomach. The worry that she could never afford to buy the bottle.

When she reached the gate of her mum's house, she looked up at it, with its pretty whitewash and thatched roof, remembering the image Harry had drawn on her skin, infused with a sense of peace. There *was* a part of her that naturally felt centred here, but it was tangled up with other emotions too. Perhaps that peace had been more to do with what *he'd* felt when he visited, able to escape the pressure of his parents for a short while.

She walked up to the open door and when she glanced back, Harry was in the driver's seat, waiting to see her safely inside. Just in case she'd been swept off by the left-over winds on the way up the garden path? For the first time in over twenty-four hours, she was going to be separated from him and she shouldn't feel quite so forlorn about the prospect.

She waved once more from the doorstep and he waved back and drove off.

Shaking the rain off the umbrella, she stepped into the warmth of the house, struggling to pull her emotions back in order. It was a ritual for crossing the threshold of that door, something to both help her mother not become overwhelmed and also maintain a sliver of privacy. But she was too exhausted, everything raw and bright within her.

Kay hung her coat up and went down the short hallway to the kitchen. She was surprised to find only Joe in there, bustling about making coffee. 'Where's Mum?'

'Finishing up a phone call. She's ringing around all the guests to get them to Ashworth Hall instead. We've had to move it to 4 p.m. instead of 3 p.m. now, did Harry say?'

She nodded, leaning forwards on the counter. She didn't want to sit after spending so many hours in the car already today, her butt was numb.

He poured a coffee into her favourite mug, which still lived in the cupboard over the kettle, and slid it across the island towards her. 'So, everything good between you two now, is it?'

'Yeah,' she said, briefly.

Joe nodded, his eyes dipping down briefly, seemingly to her folded arms on the island, before raising to her face with a smirk. She glanced down, belatedly realising she was still wearing Harry's shirt.

'I didn't have anything clean . . .' she started, but he just laughed and shook his head.

'Squirt, I haven't got time to tease you. There's too much to do.' He lifted his mug and took a big mouthful despite it still being hot. 'That place is going to blow Sandy's mind. She's already so happy and she's not even seen it yet.' He shook his head, like he'd got distracted. 'I've already called Dad and got him dealing with the people at the old venue and the catering company and a removals firm, convincing them to help us move the extra furniture we need to the Hall. Don't pull that face,' he scolded her gently. 'This is my wedding, Kay. We've paid for their services and he'll only use his gift if he absolutely has to.'

She nodded and held up her hands, pushing away her reflex to find it icky when her father went around 'motivating' people to do stuff. She remembered how Sandy had said her dad had responded to the suggestion to use magic to get their first venue fixed and accepted he wouldn't be doing it if it was any harm to anyone. 'What can I help with?'

'It would be great if . . .' he paused and flicked his fingers to indicate his throat. 'May I?'

'Go for it.'

When he spoke again, Kay felt the faint wash of her brother's magic so that the logistics made sense to her easily. 'Could you go over to the Hall and help when people start arriving? Actually, Sandy and the other bridesmaids are at the hotel she stayed at with her parents and Harry said he'd sort out rooms for the wedding party to get ready in, so swing by the hotel on the way and take them all over. I'll text you the address. You can use my car. No. Mum's car – she can go with Auntie L because they're going to be getting ready here. Sandy said the hair and make-up person and the photographer need to be there in an hour or so.' He checked his watch. 'If you're there you can meet the minister too and show him where the ceremony will take place and basically help Dad with anything that crops up.' He paused, and even though he'd been rambling and jumping from subject to subject, Kay understood precisely what he wanted of her.

'OK, done.'

'Thank you.' Joe paused with his coffee cup halfway to his mouth and clicked the fingers of his free hand. 'Oh, the flowers too. Did you know Jaz is doing them?'

'I didn't.' Kay smiled at the thought of seeing her old school friend. They had kept in touch, but after going to different universities and Jaz starting her own business up in Biddicote, while Kay moved to London, visits, phone calls and even texts had become more sporadic. 'You need me to meet her?'

'I think Michelle, Sandy's mum, said she'd help out there. I'll call you if she can't for any reason.'

'Right, I'll keep it on my radar.'

'Great.' He checked his watch again. 'Shit. I have to go.' He put his half-drunk coffee down and moved around the island to head out of the kitchen, holding his hand up for a high-five. 'Seriously good to have you back, Kay.'

She gave his palm the slap he was requesting. 'Good to be back.' Part of her felt like she didn't just mean in the village or the country. She was a mess, and she was exhausted, but there was also something which felt lighter inside her too. A weight easing back, or that she'd grown stronger from carrying.

The letter box rattled as Joe slammed the door behind him and there was the distant murmur of her mum's voice from upstairs, where she was still on the phone. Other than that, the house was quiet, and it felt like the first time in days when Kay could take a deep breath. It turned into an enormous yawn. She tipped the coffee down her neck and wandered into the pantry, which doubled up as a still room, seeing if there was anything in there that might help her recoup some energy. She was going to need it.

She examined the jars and herbal plants growing on the shelves, not knowing quite what she was looking for. It had been a while since she'd turned to healer remedies to help her with a physical ailment.

'Sweetheart, there you are.' Her mum stepped inside the small room, wearing her old pink fleece pyjamas. Her greying chestnut hair was back in a messy bun, fastened with her black tourmaline hairpins. All signs that she was seeking some inner peace. She held her arms out to Kay and when they hugged, she felt her mum's sharp intake of breath, no doubt getting the full brunt of the emotions Kay couldn't temper. 'Goodness, has it been stressful, my darling?'

'You have no idea.'

'Well, I might. It's not been an easy ride here either.' She patted Kay's cheek gently as she eased back.

'How did it go last night?'

'I survived.' She gave a weak smile.

Kay shifted, looking back at the shelves. That seemed like an odd response to have to what looked from the photographs to be a lovely evening. It was on the tip of her tongue to ask about whether her parents had spoken, but she didn't really want to get into a session demonising her dad's behaviour when there was so much to do and she had so little energy.

'So much conflict within you, Kay. Something playing on your mind?'

'Just whether to take something as a pick-me-up. I'm running on fumes.'

'Ah.' Her mum held up one finger and opened a cupboard, pulling out a box of tea. 'Here we are. *Rhodiola rosea* and ginseng with our healer's extra-special boost, to help with fatigue. Let's make you a cup.'

Kay followed her mother back into the kitchen and watched as she placed an old-fashioned kettle on the hob, clicking her fingers to light the gas. She could have boiled the water in the normal kettle, or with a spell too, but healing teas needed intention and that meant putting effort into the ritual of it. Maybe Kay should have just stuck with another coffee?

'Don't be impatient,' her mother scolded, without Kay saying a word.

Kay tried to picture a calm, happy place in her mind, so her emotions stopped firing off at her mother every second. Birdsong. The sun on her face. The memory of reading in the garden with Harry came can-can dancing into her mind. And that led to the bad dream she'd had on the ferry, which led to what happened *after* the bad dream, and she definitely didn't want to be thinking about that when her mother could sense her moods.

'Are you sure the conflict is just about beverages? I heard about you travelling with Harry Ashworth. That couldn't have been easy.'

'No. It wasn't.' She could at least admit that. But as soon as she said the words, they tasted like a lie. Some of it had felt very easy, when she'd let it. Laughter, kissing . . . other things . . . *they'd* felt easy. Too easy.

'Oh, sweetheart.' Her mum was coming at her with the hugs again. Bollocks.

She accepted it, of course. It wasn't that she minded her mother giving her a hug obviously, but sometimes she just wanted some time to sit in an emotion without a forensic investigator coming over to pick it apart and dig up the bones of it, like it was a crime scene.

'This is what I was worried about when I found out. Harry hurt you so much. I'd hate that to happen again. I couldn't bear feeling you go through something like that again.'

Kay shifted and pulled herself up onto the kitchen stool to get a little space. Guilt pressed at her. She remembered how hard her mother had found it. 'I'm sorry. My feelings may have been a bit exaggerated by teenage hormones.'

'You never have to be sorry for what you're feeling. And just because you were a teenager doesn't mean your feelings weren't valid. Emotions forge associations in our minds. The things we feel when we are young are particularly strong and leave impressions that can shape us for years to come – that's why we have the rules about influencing minors.' Her mother's lips pressed together and Kay knew she hadn't forgotten what Harry had done.

'It was a mistake. He's apologised.'

'Yes, that's all well and good, but it takes more than "sorry" to fix it. A couple of days travelling together doesn't cut it, either.'

Kay looked over at the kettle, watching steam escape the spout. When her mother put it like that, her brain could totally acknowledge that two days was no time at all, but it had been the longest weekend of her life – and she wasn't sure her heart agreed.

Hearts didn't think, though. That was the problem. They just felt.

'I would hate for you to go through the pain I did with your father,' her mother added, like a pestle grinding her point into the mortar of Kay's psyche. It looked like there was going to be no avoiding this topic, after all.

'Did something happen with Dad last night?'

'No, we steered well clear of each other and I took one of my pills, so that kept it manageable. I'll have to take another soon, especially with all this.' She ran her hand over her forehead, like Kay's very presence was giving her a headache.

Maybe it was. If Kay made people more aware of what they were feeling, and her mother was feeling everything

Kay was . . . well, poor woman. The best thing she could think of doing was getting out of the house and getting her emotional state under control before she spent unmedicated time with her mother again.

'D'you mind if I just go sort my things out while the tea's brewing? Joe wants me to pick up Sandy and the other bridesmaids in your car, if that's OK? He said you are going with Aunt Lucille.'

'Oh, yes. Of course, no problem. Once I've made this tea for you, I need to get back to making those phone calls. Almost done. Just ones I couldn't get through to the first time.'

'That's good.' Kay jumped down from the stool and pushed her hair off her face, making it into a ponytail for a second.

'Oh, Kay. You'll make sure you're sitting in between me and your dad for the ceremony, won't you?'

Kay paused. 'I'll be the last of us to sit down though, won't I? It would be easier if you just sit next to each other and leave a space for me at the end. So I don't disrupt things, squeezing through.'

'It won't cause that much disruption. I'll save the space for you.'

'Why don't you ask Joe? It's his day. Wasn't this the kind of thing you talked about at the rehearsal last night?'

'We did. But I'm sure he won't notice. He'll only have eyes for Sandy.' Tallulah smiled wistfully. 'They're so happy together.'

'They are.' She didn't need her mother's gift – or her own – to know that.

Leaving her mum in the kitchen, Kay took her bag from the hall and headed up the narrow staircase. Her mangled feelings all came rushing back as she shut the door to her old bedroom behind her. She couldn't seem to keep the stopper in the bottle today. The small room with its white furniture and the pale wallpaper with little pink sprigs had witnessed it all. The nights she'd fallen asleep dreaming of Harry's kiss. All the tears she'd cried when he'd stood her up and given her that note.

If being with him all weekend had clouded her judgement, maybe she needed to reset it. Remind herself what he'd done. Or rather – because she now knew why he'd done it – remind herself what he *could* do to her, if he felt so inclined.

Going to her wardrobe and pulling out a box at the back with her old diaries in, it was easy to find the one with the napkin in the back. She took it out and forced herself to open it. There it was – the smiley face.

Despite all the years, magic still pushed itself upon her. It must have been so strong at the time. He'd put so much into it. She knew he said how strong it had been was purely accidental, but wow.

She crumpled it in her hand, tears pricking her eyes as the fabricated feelings sloughed away. All she'd done was prove to herself how little she hated him, despite what he'd put her through. Despite how it would probably all go wrong because of their complicated designations.

'Shit.' She drew her hand back as heat bit at her fingers, dropping the napkin which was now aflame. 'Shit.' She stomped on top of it, to put out the fire. When she removed her foot, there was nothing but ashes left.

Chapter Eighteen

Ashworth Hall

o miles and 3 hours and 30 minutes until the wedding

Joe hadn't been wrong about Sandy's reaction to Ashworth Hall if her squeal as Kay drove beneath the archway at the bottom of the driveway was any indication. A shiver of magic started at Kay's head and passed all the way down her spine, similar to when she'd crossed into Leon's witches-only restaurant. Glancing in the rear-view mirror, she saw some very old runes carved around the plaster images decorating the wide brick arch. Was that the protective magic that was linked to Harry's tattoo? Part of her wanted to go and do a tour of the house, grounds and Biddicote as a whole so she could see exactly how much there was that she, and everyone else, appeared to take for granted.

It couldn't have been designed to deter non-magical people though, because none of the others in the car even blinked or looked mildly uncomfortable. In fact, as Kay followed the gravel driveway, flanked by Scots pines, up to the front of the house where it wrapped around a circle of grass with a large rowan tree at its centre, it was clear from the bridesmaids' faces that – despite not having any clue the house had been home to witches for over three hundred years – they thought the place was pretty magical.

Kay parked over to one side and they all stepped out of the car, faces tipped up regardless of the slanting rain, to stare at the imposing manor house. Mansion? Kay wasn't sure at what point it tipped over. She'd always just thought of it as 'the Hall'.

Somehow, the rain had made it even more attractive, dampening the orange brick to a warm ruddy colour, the stone lintels around the doors and windows bright in contrast and the tiles on the dormer roofs glistening.

Sandy covered her mouth, tears coming to her eyes. 'I can't believe it,' she mumbled behind her hands. 'I thought we weren't going to be able to get married at all, and now we have this place . . .' she broke off with a little hiccup of a sob.

'Right, get those tears out now,' Sandy's cousin, Erin, instructed her firmly, while placing an arm around her shoulders. 'Because no crying is allowed once your make-up is done.'

'But we *should* go inside before you start crying,' Chelsea, Sandy's friend, said, hurrying up the steps to the double doors. 'Don't want to waste those tears out here, if the inside is a wreck.'

'It's definitely not a wreck,' Kay assured her with a rueful smile. It had been a long time since she'd been in there, but she remembered the big rooms, tall ceilings, massive fireplaces, richly varnished wood. The way she didn't want to breathe on anything in case she broke it. The way she *couldn't* breathe whenever she'd spotted Harry, dressed up in dark trousers and a white shirt, but his freckles, wild hair, and wide smile always there, stopping him from looking formal and imposing. Like a flame in the darkness.

Her chest ached at the memory – that brand from his smiley face was back to burning a hole over her heart, an old injury she'd aggravated so it gave her phantom pain.

The door opened, but instead of it being Harry, her dad was standing there. Marvin was slightly taller than average, his short, curly dark hair going to salt and pepper, but still looking younger than his years. Witches did tend to age well and live long lives, between whatever different chemistry there was in their bodies and their ability to make use of healer magic. But it wasn't always a guarantee – Harry's dad was proof of that.

'Marvin.' Sandy pulled away from her cousin to throw her arms around Kay's dad in a familiar, comfortable hug. 'You're here already?'

He embraced his future daughter-in-law back with the same ease and pulled away to smile down at her. 'Yeah, been here for about half an hour. No time to waste. Harry's already shown me the rooms for you ladies. Let's get you out of the rain.'

Kay hung back, letting the others grab their bags from the boot before she locked the car up and followed them inside. As she dried her feet off on the enormous doormat inside the entrance hall, the bridesmaids were doing their meerkat routine, looking around them like their necks were adjustable periscopes.

On the centre table in the vestibule was a cornucopia display with an array of pinecones, mini squash and pumpkins spilling out, russet and gold and cream colours bringing an immediate sense of warmth and welcome to the home. A touch of magic wafted off it to create that hospitable atmosphere. It curled around her like sitting by a fireplace and made her feel a much-needed sense of serenity.

She wondered if that was Harry or his mum's doing. With his dad being so ill, his magic would be drained . . .

What did that mean for the magical tattoo? She couldn't remember exactly how Harry had explained it, they'd both been so tired, but surely it didn't use them like a battery? If it did and Adrian Ashworth was ill, the tattoo couldn't be helping. Maybe he'd had it removed and all of that burden was falling to Harry now?

Thinking about the logistics of it unsettled her. When it came to the magic for the wards and deflective spells, how was Harry to know when his magic would be called upon? They were reactive to things outside of his control. If someone – like her – was having an off day on the edge of the village, risking a non-magical person spotting something they couldn't explain, did that mean he would suddenly find himself wiped out? Like he'd been when they needed to move the car? Would the magic even have communicated with him when he was that far away? Or was there some other charm that avoided that?

Her curiosity over how it worked was interrupted as her dad left the rest of the bridal party to join her, opening his arms, a little hesitantly. 'Kay. Hey there, sweetheart. Can I have a hug?'

A wave of guilt added to her niggling concerns. How awful was she for making her own dad unsure about whether she'd welcome his hug? She didn't insult him by saying *of course*, because it wasn't a given with them. Instead, she just stepped forward and hugged him. 'Hi, Dad,' she said.

'I was so worried about you.' He gave her an extra squeeze.

It was on the tip of her tongue to question that because it wasn't like he'd tried to contact her to see if she was OK at any point over the weekend. But then, they'd grown used to mainly communicating through Joe until they met up in person.

She'd spent so much time in the lead-up to the wedding thinking about how to help her mum get through all the forced-proximity with her dad – dreading it, if she was honest – but those weren't the thoughts coming to her mind now. Perhaps it was because of finding out how ill Harry's dad was, or perhaps it was because she'd had a wake-up call about how prejudiced she'd been about influencers in general, but part of her was wondering if she'd let her bad feelings towards her dad go on for long enough.

So, she didn't give a barbed retort, she just squeezed him back and said, with all honesty: 'It was quite an adventure.'

'You'll have to tell me all about it later. You always did want to do a road trip. Just like life to give you what you want and disguise it as a problem.' Her dad stepped back and nodded at her hair. 'Did you do that for your brother?'

Kay laughed. 'Joe said that, too. Football on the brain, the pair of you.' And so alike. It was part of the reason she and Joe had fallen out so badly when the divorce had happened and she was full of rage and disappointment in her dad. They were so close; Joe had probably felt like she disapproved of him as much as she did of their dad. She'd put the blame entirely on their dad for the divorce. For stringing her mother along for so long when he didn't love her. She'd picked a side, she realised now. Whereas Joe had refused to.

But she and Joe had still been able to mend things. Eventually. All the bridge-building between them had taken place away from home because there had been no room near their mother for the messy, honest feelings they needed to unpick to make it better . . . which, now Kay thought about it, hadn't been overly helpful of Tallulah.

Shaking off the thoughts, she gave her dad a smile. 'How is it all going?'

'Like a military operation. I got the manager at the old venue on board with letting us use the plates and cutlery and tables and chairs as planned. And I got some of my team on it.'

'You got your football team here? That's like having an army at your disposal.'

'Sure. We needed it. We can't use the furniture here – a lot of them are antiques – and I needed a crew for some heavy lifting. They were happy to help.'

She raised her eyebrows.

'They genuinely were! It's a little-known fact that footballers are romantics. No additional persuasion was required.' He made a cross over his heart and she shook her head with a soft laugh.

'Someone thinks he's the Ted Lasso of Surrey,' she joked.

He gave a sharp blast of a laugh, his eyes wide with a little bit of shock. 'Please, I was motivating footballers when he was still growing his moustache. Come on. I'll show you the rooms and then I'll get back to mobilising the troops.'

Marvin picked up as many of their bags as he could manage and led the way up the wide staircase, which curved around the entrance to a gallery. There were paintings hanging on the walls, a mix of landscapes and portraits, some very old, some modern. Her legs were sluggish as they went up yet more stairs, a buzz starting in her chest in a way that worried her – like static on a broken TV.

If she lost her grip on her magic at the wedding . . . Set fire to something in this old house full of people . . .

But maybe the sensation wasn't anything to do with her magic at all and she was just jumping to negative conclusions like she always did. Coming back into the Hall as an adult, no longer used to the constant magical atmosphere of Biddicote, it was even more obvious how the house was infused with it. Partly by design and partly just because of the long-standing history of the witches who'd lived there.

Her dad took them into a large suite decorated in pale green and cream pinstriped wallpaper, with a soft patterned carpet, a four-poster bed and a view overlooking the lawns out the back. There was a family-sized adjoining bathroom with double sinks, two dressing tables, a wardrobe with full-length mirrors on the doors and a sofa and armchairs. Other than some faded patches on the wall as though pictures had been removed, like it had belonged to someone who'd left, rather than meant just for guests; it was the perfect bridal suite. Sandy restrained herself from squealing and crying this time, but she did hop up and down on her toes a little bit, making them all laugh and tease her.

Marvin dropped off their bags and went over to assure Sandy that he and Joe had it all under control and she was to relax, pamper and enjoy herself. And if Kay thought he might have used a little bit of his influence to motivate his soon-to-be daughter-in-law to leave the stress behind and enjoy this part of her wedding day, she couldn't really hold it against him.

In a frenzy of excited chatter, they all began hanging up their outfits and organising the space, ready for the hair and make-up artist to arrive. Chelsea pulled out two magnums of champagne and a set of half a dozen plastic glasses from her case. Remembering the atomic-level hangover Kay had experienced after the hen do, she wasn't entirely surprised. Chelsea had been the one leading the group challenge for most shots consumed and yet still looked to be the soberest of them all at the end of the night. Erin had brought along a bunch of silky dressing gowns too, and they all took turns showering, donning the dressing gowns and making up ridiculous toasts to Sandy and Joe.

Something loosened momentarily inside Kay as she settled into the fun and anticipation of the day. She needed to get her mind off things, particularly her magic. Focusing on it, even clamping it down, never seemed to work. Distraction definitely seemed a better tactic, or concentrating on positive feelings, like Harry had helped her with on the ferry—

There was a knock at the suite door and Sandy jumped up with a whoop, opening it to let in the hair and make-up artist.

'Kay, wow, what are you doing here?'

She slid off the end of the bed in surprise as she looked over and saw Tina parking a large wheelie case over by the dressing table. Luckily, her feet found the floor before her butt and she only splashed a little champagne onto her robe. 'Tina.' She hadn't seen her old friend in anything but passing in the village since the summer they'd fallen out. Over Joe. She went to join Tina and Sandy at the dressing table, glancing between them. 'I'm one of Sandy's bridesmaids.'

'You two know each other?' Sandy smiled, like it was the best surprise in the world. She leaned in closer to them and lowered her voice. 'I should have known, with you both being witches from Biddicote.' She winked and practically skipped back over to the bed. If Kay's dad had used magic on her, it was working in tandem with champagne now.

'We went to school together,' Tina said, unzipping her case and starting to get out smaller bags and packages. Her eyes caught Kay's and she gave a chagrined smile. 'I had the biggest crush on her brother.'

'No way! You didn't date, did you?' Chelsea roared with laughter. 'How did you not know this, Sandy?'

'It's not like Joe helped me pick my make-up artist.' Sandy had flushed as red as her dressing gown.

Tina's eyes were rivalling the size of the powder puffs she held in her hands. 'You're . . . you're marrying Kay's brother, Joe?'

Sandy nodded silently.

'I think we need more champagne,' Erin announced, grabbing the bottle to top everyone up, and bringing Tina a glass too.

Kay put her hand over her mouth, her own awkwardness paling as she watched Tina shove her hands inside the deep pockets of her chunky cardigan. Her eyes met Tina's again and her old friend suddenly laughed.

'Don't worry, Sandy, I have a partner and it was just a crush when I was, like, seventeen. Well over it now. I swear I won't ruin your make-up or hair.' She made an X sign over her chest and help up three fingers. 'Brownie's honour.'

Sandy laughed, but still looked a bit weirded out.

'How about I go first?' Kay offered. 'So Tina and I can catch up.'

Sandy nodded her head vigorously and Kay perched on the edge of the vanity.

'Well, shit,' Tina said in a soft voice as the other brides-maids put on some music from the playlist they'd had at the hen do. 'I think this is what you call karma.'

Kay tilted her head. 'And why would that be?'

'Oh come on. I only brought up the crush as a reason to apologise to you. I was out of line with how I reacted when you told me Joe didn't like me back.'

Kay took a sip from her drink and shrugged. 'That's OK.'

She wondered if she'd have found it as easy to forgive Harry if he had approached her with such a direct apology as soon as they'd bumped into each other in Prague. She wasn't sure she would have. Tina's behaviour had hurt her, but it hadn't been entirely out of character. They'd been close friends and Kay had missed her, but it hadn't felt like a betrayal, just something inevitable brought about by her gift. A lesson learned about keeping it to herself.

'I blame all the books and TV. They're always telling us when boys are rude to you it means they like you. Sexual tension, blah-blah. No. Turns out they really just think you're their little sister's annoying friend.'

Kay burst out laughing. 'Fiction has a lot to answer for.'

'Older brother's best friend trope, huh?' Tina smirked and Kay forced a smile as her laughter faded. There was the Tina she remembered; tongue as sharp as a sewing needle. The pricks might be small, but they could still draw blood. 'Shall we get started?'

Tina set to work with a mixture of make-up and magic. Nothing permanent, but as she applied minimal blush, Kay's cheeks naturally pinked, as did her lips under the application of the lipstick. She took her glasses off and kept her eyes shut as Tina worked on the puffiness and bags from lack of sleep, feeling the skin tingle and rejuvenate beneath the smoky eyeshadow.

Opening her eyes briefly for the mascara application didn't compromise anyone's privacy; she was sitting so close to Tina the bonds between them were just a glimmer in her periphery as Kay fastened her gaze on a high point. When that was finished, she slipped her glasses back on and smiled at her reflection. Roadkill she wasn't, thank the Goddess. And – even better – Tina's magic wouldn't fade until the following morning.

As she worked Kay's hair into an updo that involved a thick plait across the top of her head, pushing her hair forward and allowing tendrils to escape artfully around her face, there was another knock at the door.

This time, Chelsea flung it open, causing a shriek from Erin, who was being helped into her second layer of Spanx by Sandy. Both women hit the deck behind the bed like a gun had gone off, and everyone else broke out with laughter. Kay still had it on her lips when she looked over to the door and saw Harry stood there with a familiar-looking dark-haired young woman – his cousin, Becca. She was the photographer, it turned out. Was there a witch in Biddicote not working on this wedding?

Harry had changed, into a pair of light blue jeans and a beige cable-knit sweater, and looked like he should be posing for an aftershave commercial, broad shoulders hunched, hair windblown, in the middle of a forest. His blue eyes met hers in the mirror, lips parting, and she felt like she was the one who had taken the bullet to the chest, heart stuttering and heat blooming.

'So, you're the hero of the hour?'

He dragged his gaze away as Chelsea spoke to him. She was looking him up and down with a slow smile.

'This is your place?'

'My parents. They're the heroes. I'm just . . . helping.'

Sandy came out from behind the bed, tightening the belt on her dressing gown. 'We're so grateful.'

'Yeah, if there's any way we can thank you,' Chelsea flicked her hair over her shoulder and Harry winced and took a step back towards the door.

'No need. You're busy and I should get going.'

'You're coming to the service and the reception?' Sandy checked.

'I'll do my best.' He stuffed his hands in his pockets and backed out the room, with a final, darting glance at Kay. 'Give me a shout if you need anything. Becs knows where to find me.'

'Oh, we will,' Chelsea hung out of the door into the hallway, calling after him as he presumably escaped. She closed the door and scanned the rest of the women with a devilish grin. 'I call dibs if he's at the reception.'

'Before you say anything more,' Becca said, unhooking the camera bag from her shoulder. 'I feel I should point out; Harry is my cousin.' She glanced at Kay for a long moment and Kay wondered if she'd recognised her too from the festivals at the Hall when they were kids. Back before Kay had had the courage to talk to Harry and just had to be content with watching him from across the function room.

'That is bad luck for you,' Chelsea retorted. 'Tall *and* cute *and* loaded *and*—'

'*And* terrified of you, judging by the way he ran from the room.' Sandy laughed.

'It's like watching a velociraptor ambush someone when you spot an attractive man,' Erin said drily, fully ensconced in her Spanx now.

Chelsea shrugged. 'You snooze you lose.'

Kay forced a laugh, conscious of Tina's eyes on her, and tried to push away the desire to run after Harry and confirm that he'd come and find *her* at the reception. Not the blonde, leggy force of nature that was Chelsea. Kay could tell him that she wanted to do more than dance. Because it wasn't a lie. She did want more.

But that didn't mean she should have it. It was sensible for her to try to slow this snowball of attraction she had towards him, wasn't it? Even if the thought of coming across him wrapped up in the other bridesmaid's toned arms made her jaw ache from clenching her teeth. Thankfully, her lipstick was all done.

As soon as her hair was finished, Kay shimmied carefully into the golden chiffon bridesmaid's dress and sleek heels in the bathroom, so she could go and meet the minister who would be arriving soon.

She paused at the top of the stairs and took a selfie to send to Ilina, as she'd promised she would once she was all dressed up. Out of the tall windows behind her, a vibrant sun set fire to the sky valiantly behind the heavy clouds, the rain having finally stopped.

Ilina: Stunning. Give your brother and his bride my best wishes. It'll be weird, because they don't know me, but still do it.

Kay laughed as she typed out a reply.

Kay: Thank you. I will. And thank you for the help over the weekend.

Ilina: Which you ignored to take the train with your hot 'acquaintance'.

Kay: I never said he was hot.

Ilina: You never said he wasn't either. I'm not an idiot. Did anything happen?

Kay: I'll call you tomorrow and tell you everything. Unless you have plans?

Ilina: You had sex! I do have a date myself tomorrow after work. Tuesday?

Kay: Done. Xxx

Ilina: Enjoy the wedding. xxx

Goddess, Kay was really going to try. Picking up her skirt so she wouldn't trip over the long hem, she hurried down the stairs.

They were using the 'second parlour' for the ceremony and she didn't have a clue where it was. Every corner she turned on the ground floor, there were witches and non-magical people side by side. In the ballroom, tables were being set out. Sandy's mother was decorating chairs, while Jaz set the flower arrangements in the centre of each table, and Sandy's dad looked like he was trying to make sense of the seating plan and place cards. Behind them, a group Kay didn't recognise were laying the head table. She winced as someone knocked a vase on a sideboard, but a witch was there to reach out with their magic and stop it falling the whole way to the floor and smashing.

She inhaled sharply, but no one batted an eyelid, so either they were all witches – other than Sandy's parents – in that room, or the protective magic was working to gloss over the magical act.

Jaz waved like she was trying to flag down a rescue helicopter when she spotted Kay, but all she could do was blow her a kiss and continue her search. She dodged the stream of catering staff who were trooping through the side door towards the kitchens, her heart lifting and crashing each time she thought she saw a glimpse of Harry's coppery hair.

She pressed a hand to her chest and willed the vital organ to get a handle on itself. Walking around this house was like going back in time. The witching community all around her. Her body chemistry making her into a walking bag of hormones. She'd only been there once after Harry had left for university and the memory of how heartsick she'd been smashed into her like a bowling ball in the middle of sponge cake.

There was a reason she was freaking out about these feelings for him. Harry had even said it himself on the ferry, fears were there to protect you from dangerous situations. Letting herself care this way about Harry Ashworth again was a dangerous situation.

Finally, she found the door that had to be the 'second parlour'.

'Holy grimoire,' she gasped as she walked in on a scene that was like something out of a Disney movie, with chairs floating through the air and swaths of fabric wrapping themselves around the chairs that were stationary and orders of service floating down to rest on the seat cushions.

Her dad and two other witches swung around to stare at her, everything pausing in mid-air.

'There must be at a dozen NMs in this house at the moment,' Kay hissed. 'At *least*.'

'It's fine. We're almost done,' Marvin told her. 'The protective magic would have barred the door. Someone was trying to get in earlier. It only let you in because you're a witch.'

'Oh, OK.' She took a deep breath.

Marvin laughed and came over to her. 'You look lovely, honey. Don't get yourself flustered. This house is designed for this kind of event. No need to worry. Have you got time to help us?'

Suddenly all the champagne Kay had drunk was leaching the moisture from her mouth. She couldn't use her magic. Not unless they wanted a chair to smash through one of the Grade listed windows. But she hadn't told anyone about her magical problems – except Ilina and Harry – and now wasn't the time to bring it up.

She shook her head and backed away, relieved she had an excuse. 'I've got to meet the minister. He'll be here any minute and we'll be coming in here, so be prepared.'

'We will be.'

She didn't have time to help them. She hadn't even had time to help herself.

Chapter Nineteen

Ashworth Hall

The Wedding

The final hour before the wedding disappeared in a blur. Kay's dad and the other two witches finished decorating the parlour (manually) around the minister being shown in. All the chairs had been placed facing the rear of the room, where there was a long table beneath a wide mirror, reflecting the windows with their view of the trees and hill down to the woods. The ushers arrived and, not long behind them, the guests.

Kay hurried upstairs to join Sandy and the other bridesmaids and discovered they'd already gone and had to rush back downstairs to find them.

Jaz was carrying a box across the lobby and spotted her. 'This way,' she called, leading Kay into what turned out to be a dining room. All the bridesmaids were in there, now in their gowns, along with Sandy's dad. Sandy was luminous in her lush green dress, covered in embroidered flowers that wound from the deep V neckline, around one side of the bodice, to spread out across the long skirt. Her caramel hair was down, adorned with a simple tiara, and shining, but not as much as her eyes.

'There you are, Kay,' she exclaimed and Kay hurried forward to kiss her cheek.

'You look so beautiful, Sandy.'

'It's almost time. We'll be sisters soon.'

They could hear the chatter in the room beyond a door, which must have led into the parlour where the ceremony would take place.

Jaz was busy unboxing the bouquets at the end of the long glass table and handed them out as they got in line. Kay stood behind Chelsea, in front of Erin, breathless, even though it wasn't her getting married.

'How are we old enough for this to be happening?' Jaz said, as she gave Kay hers, refreshing the petals with a brush of her fingers that was either too subtle for any non-magical person to notice or deflected by the spell work in the house. Kay had noticed runes over the door of nearly every room.

'It's crazy, isn't it?' She looked down at the flowers in her hands, a mix of amaryllis, eryngium and sunflowers, nestled within orange oak-leaf foliage. The sunflower made a blush come to Kay's cheeks, but she smiled up at Jaz. 'These are gorgeous.'

'Thank you.' Jaz squeezed Kay's arm. 'Hopefully I'll catch you at the reception.'

'We might be old, but at least it means we don't have to steal the dandelion wine now.'

'And try to figure out how to open it.'

Kay laughed, and a few moments later, the door cracked open and the music started. The empty room from earlier was full of guests now. Her eyes darted over the people gathered, and it felt like there was a hum of magic in the air, but she wasn't sure whether it was from the high concentration of witches, or simple excitement.

Either way, as she followed Chelsea's slow walk, a few paces behind, it was like it was building beneath her skin, her diaphragm heavy with a pressure she thought she recognised as the need to dispel her magic. She concentrated on the tender stems of the flowers in her hands and taking even steps and then, as Chelsea moved off to sit on the left, on her brother, the smartest he'd ever looked, standing in front of the minister with his best man beside him.

Kay matched his huge grin with one of her own and then came to the end of the aisle and looked to the right. There was her seat, next to her mother, and in the row behind, Harry.

Her heart leapt dangerously as he looked up at her, and his smile was so warm and inviting, she almost decided to sit on his lap. It was stupid and extremely vain that it felt like he was there for her, when both Joe and Sandy had asked him to come. And it was his house. Still, his presence made her feel like all her harassed and nervous energy was easing a little.

Her mother looked up and Kay remembered herself. Tallulah patted her hand as she settled down, latching onto her wrist, her smile trembling. There was a handkerchief already in her other hand. They weren't going to make it through this without tears – thank the Goddess for Tina's magical mascara.

Kay's own smile faltered as she looked down the row of chairs and saw that her mum had placed Auntie L and her husband between her and Kay's dad. He was the father of the groom and he had been shoved almost into the corner. She stiffened and was tempted to pull her arm away from her mother, but it wasn't like they could discuss it right then and she didn't want to taint the ceremony in any way.

Joe's face when Sandy appeared at the back of the room started the avalanche of emotion again within her. The wedding march began and when Sandy had been given away and they started to say their vows, everything was bubbling up inside Kay. It was the equivalent of knowing you had a sneeze building while you had a mouthful of food, a tension developing in her chest as she tried to suppress it rather than metaphorically spray the congregation with crumbs.

Resting her flowers on her lap, she reached back with her left hand, slipping it behind the gauzy tail of the bow decorating the top of the chair, not quite sure what had possessed her, but Harry's fingers were there a fraction of a second later. Top digits hooked over hers, which should have seemed tenuous, but instead just focused all her nerve endings on the warmth and strength of his hand.

She took a couple of deep breaths, still jangling inside, and he shifted, the spicy scent of his aftershave wafting over her as he inched close enough for his hand to cover hers, fingers around her wrist and his thumb tracing a shape in the centre of her palm. He repeated it slowly.

A heart.

He was tracing a heart on her palm. There was no medium for the magic, despite the tingling. He was just there, holding her hand and distracting her because he knew she needed it.

It was possible it was backfiring though, because now inside she was full to bursting. And when Joe and Sandy were declared husband and wife, and they leaned over the beautiful autumn bouquet for a kiss, there was a crackle overhead and a shower of light like the falling sparkles from a firework erupted around the room.

A collective gasp sounded and heads tipped back, watching the gold and silver as it fluttered down towards the crowd and then dissolved away. Everyone clapped and began standing up to see the happy couple walk back down the aisle.

Harry's hand withdrew so they could stand too and Kay's eyes skittered over the guests when her brother and new sister-in-law made it out of the room, going back into the dining room. Luckily, there were only knowing smiles on some faces and curiosity on the non-magical ones. The protective magic had worked. The non-magical guests thought it had been a clever special effect, planned for the moment.

'That was very pretty,' Harry leaned forward to murmur in her ear, sending a shiver down her neck as his breath brushed her skin.

'As far as mistakes go, I guess.' She bit her lip, a flush on her cheeks as she turned to look at him. Now they were standing, Kay could see he was wearing a dark charcoal suit with a bright blue tie . . . and that her family were watching them with interest.

They fell into step as they followed everyone out to line the wide hallway and throw confetti. Her shoulder brushed his arm as though her body couldn't stop itself from seeking his, and she caught a small glimpse of his lopsided smile. There were shadows back under his eyes and the hollows of his cheeks seemed more pronounced than they had earlier, but she supposed he didn't have Tina's magic make-up to repair the damage of their jaunt across Europe. At least, she hoped it was that.

'How is your dad doing?' she asked.

'No change that I can tell. He's been pretty stable for the last week, according to my mum.' He rubbed a hand on his chest, beneath his tie. 'I was so convinced when I was away that I had to get back to him, I should feel relieved now, but . . .' He shrugged.

'Has the itchy–magic–compass feeling not gone?' She leaned closer, lowering her voice. Honestly, she'd be sneaking inside his suit jacket in a moment.

'The what?' His smile was slow. And dazzling.

'Oh,' she wrinkled her nose. 'That's what I call it.'

His eyes scanned her face, before he seemed to remember himself. 'Right. I like it. But no. I'm home but it's still . . . coming and going.'

'That must be driving you to distraction.'

He laughed. 'You could say that.'

'You won't try to figure it out?'

'I already gave that my best shot when I went out to Prague in the first place. I thought I was moving in the right direction, but nothing has actually changed, so maybe . . .' His eyelashes lowered as he glanced down at her mouth. 'I just have to be patient.'

He wasn't talking about *her*, was he? There was no way Leon had been right when he said he thought Harry's magic had sent him to Prague for her? He was talking about his dad and somehow helping him with this mystery illness. That would be the thing his magic would be focused on.

'Kay.' Her mother appeared with some of the small boxes of confetti Jaz had prepared. 'You need to come and stand with the rest of the wedding party.'

Kay took a box by its little cardboard handle, juggling it with her flowers, and flicked a glance at Harry. She wanted to invite him along. She knew that Joe and Sandy wouldn't mind. Their big day wouldn't be happening at all if it hadn't been for him.

Maybe *that* was why he'd had to find her? To be with her for when Joe and Sandy needed the use of Ashworth Hall – his magical link to protect the witching community of Biddicote teaming up with his itchy magic compass. But

. . . Joe was married now. Harry had saved the day. The feeling would be gone, wouldn't it?

Before Kay could invite him, her mum offered Harry a box of confetti too, accompanied by a politely dismissive smile, and then hooked her arm firmly through Kay's to pull her away.

Joe and Sandy emerged and the hallway was full of cheers and a shower of pastel petals – which might have lifted up higher and swirled in perfectly aesthetic eddies – while Becca stood at the end, taking photographs of their beaming faces.

The wedding party followed, heading for the first of many staged photographs that would be taken during the break between the ceremony and the reception, and when Kay looked back down the hallway, Harry was already gone.

Half an hour later, Kay's cheek muscles were spasming from smiling so much, she was desperate for a wee and sure the effects of the energising tea had stopped working. Joe and Sandy had disappeared to have a break before the reception started and the rest of the wedding party were finishing up with family and couple photographs.

'Where are you going?' Her mum noticed her breaking away from the group and followed her to the door.

'Just for a comfort break.' *Please don't say you'll come with me,* she thought. She needed a breather.

'OK, sweetheart, hurry back, won't you.'

Kay forced a smile. She'd been hurrying since 6.30 a.m.

After finding a downstairs bathroom far away from the reception room, she came out into the hallway and let the quiet wrap around her. Small sconces lit the way, making pools of golden light at intervals on the deep carpet. She sighed and checked her watch. She could afford ten more minutes of solitude. One of these rooms must have a sofa.

She moved further down the corridor. She recognised this part of the house. It was where Adrian Ashworth's study was, and the door which led out to the path down to Biddi's cave. It sounded very unlikely he'd been using it recently, so maybe it would be a good place to go undetected for a while.

Pushing the thick door open, it resisted a little against the pile of the carpet before swinging smoothly back. She closed it behind her and a couple of lamps automatically began to glow.

It was bigger than she'd imagined it would be. The huge windows were set deep into the walls and gave away the fact she was in the oldest part of the house. A big desk, with stately armchairs facing it, was loaded with books. To its left was a wide fireplace, a clock and some photographs along the mantel. Above was an old family portrait, at least half a dozen people at a variety of ages, in a picnic scene. They all had ruffs around their necks, a woman – likely the mother – sitting at the centre, a tendril of fiery red hair visible beneath the fashionable grey wig. Kay drew closer, wondering if she was actually looking at Biddi and if there were any further clues about the witching family hidden in the scene.

A sudden snap and flare of light made her jump. The fire had kindled to life. Magic worked like an Alexa in this house, switching everything on as soon as it thought you might need it.

Much as she wanted to keep examining the portrait on the wall, she wanted to sit down too. She sank into the armchair closest to the fire and eased her shoes off her feet. The books on the table were a strange mix. Some old and delicate, frayed spines and yellowed pages, alongside newer, leather-bound tomes. Were some of these the grimoires the Witches Council wanted to get their hands on? She was reaching out to touch one of the newer ones – too in awe to touch the old ones without permission – when the door swung open, making both her and the person coming through the door shriek.

Becca used a spell similar to an invisible yo-yo to yank the camera she'd dropped back into her hand before it hit the floor.

'Kay, what on earth are you doing in here?' She fumbled her folded tripod to rest against the wall and shut the heavy door with a brief flick of her fingers.

'Sorry. I was just looking for a bit of peace and quiet.' Kay began to get up. 'I'll go.'

'Wait.' Becca paused, a frown pulling her dark eyebrows down. 'It's fine. You stay. You must be welcome.' She took her camera equipment over to the table at the other end of the room and said, almost to herself, 'You wouldn't have been able to open the door to get in here otherwise.'

'Oh.' Kay wasn't quite sure what to make of that. Who decided who was welcome in the house? The family or the magic? She glanced around, looking for the runic symbols she was used to seeing everywhere, but instead her eyes fell upon a photo on the desk. Harry in his black graduation gown and cap, lined with white fur. She would have looked away again, but something about his eyes caught her and she couldn't resist leaning forward and picking it up for a closer look. 'Becca? What colour are Harry's eyes to you?'

'Ah.' Becca smiled and came over, settling down in the other armchair. 'So you know about the influencing thing.'

'He told me. But he didn't tell me what colour his eyes actually are.' She blushed a little, but her curiosity was pressing her too hard for her to drop the conversation. His eyes had always had such an effect on her, suddenly the thought that it was just magic, trying to seduce her – and working – made a lump appear in her throat.

'Well, since he's my cousin and I do *not* want to find him attractive, I can see the true colour of his eyes. They're blue.' Becca nodded towards the photo in Kay's hands and started to redo her ponytail. 'You can see it in any photo of him – the magic doesn't work through a lens.'

Inexplicably, the lump in Kay's throat grew, making it hard for her to breathe. His eyes *were* the exact colour she'd always thought they were. A deep, vibrant blue, near purple in some lights.

'He said they *weren't* the shade of bluebells,' she whispered.

Becca cringed a little bit. 'You compared his eyes to bluebells?'

The blush deepened on her cheeks and she tried to defend her sappiness: 'We were young.'

Becca laughed and leaned over to look at the photo, tilting her head as she considered it. 'I guess they are a similar shade. Depending on the type of bluebell.'

She sat back, but Kay could still sense her scrutiny. She fumbled the photo frame back onto the desk, turning it a little so that he wasn't looking at her. She hadn't been fooled by his magic. She saw him for exactly who he was.

'Harry can never take a compliment, though. He's painfully determined not to see the best in himself.' Becca sighed.

'I've noticed he has that tendency.'

They were quiet for a minute and then Becca got up and went to a cabinet by the window. She pulled out a decanter and a couple of glasses. 'Fancy a drink?'

'I think I will fall to sleep if I have any alcohol.'

'Fair enough.' Becca poured herself a drink and took a few long swallows, wincing and gasping. 'Goddess, that tastes like arse.'

Kay burst out laughing.

'Listen, Kay, I'm going to talk to you about something, and there's a possibility Harry might get mad at me, but I'm going to do it anyway.'

Kay straightened up in the armchair, as Becca leaned back against the windowsill. 'All these books,' Becca waved towards the table. 'They're because we're trying to figure out why the tattoo isn't working. You know about the tattoo?' A dimple showed in her cheek as the blush reappeared on Kay's face. 'Oh, yeah, you know about the tattoo,' she answered herself, slyly.

'I've seen it.' Kay cleared her throat. 'What do you mean, it's not working?'

'Harry's one hasn't anchored. We've been trying to figure it out for months.' Becca waved her hand to the books on the table. 'See if there's something we've missed. We did it all according to what his mum and dad could remember, but . . . there should be a period where the current anchor and the next share the responsibility. Before it's permanently passed on. And it's not happening. I thought maybe his dad was just too weak to put the magic needed into the ritual but . . . I don't know. I have no proof for that and Harry has a different idea.'

'If it's not working, does that mean . . . every time the protective magic is invoked it's draining him? While he's ill? The wedding—'

'No. Well, it would have, of course. But Harry's activating all the runes and spells in the village, and here when needed, directly at the moment. So that they don't need to seek the anchor for energy, if something happens. Manually bypassing it, as it were.'

Kay thought of all the instances where magic had been used in front of non-magical guests that day. It was no wonder Harry looked so tired. 'That's . . . a lot. Too much. He should have said. We shouldn't have come here.' Which was exactly why he didn't say, she realised about a half a second after she said it. He knew she'd object.

Becca sighed. 'I'm sorry, Kay, I know it's your brother's wedding, but I agree. It's not sustainable. It's like a game of whack-a-mole, but instead of the anchor just responding when the mole pops up, Harry's literally hitting every single hole all the time to try to shield his dad.'

'Can't someone help him? Spread the load?'

'It's rune magic. There aren't a lot of witches who can do that and . . . there are other complications.' Becca took another swig of whatever alcohol it was she was subjecting herself to. 'The problem is, Harry's got this idea in his head about why the transfer isn't working. He's convinced it comes down to this particular rune, which is unique to the tattoo. It's about inheritance, but Nanny and Granddad Ashworth – or whatever witches they had working on this with them – adapted it. So, it's not based on blood, like usual, which is nice. I mean, they were probably thinking of the fact that mortality rates were so high, but from a modern-day perspective, it's nice to know that the Ashworth family doesn't actually have to produce blood heirs. One day someone might not want, or be able, to have kids.'

'True. So how does it recognise the heir, then? If not based on blood or simply whoever the tattoo is on?'

'It's this ambiguous symbol, which we think means something like a trusted family member. And Harry has convinced himself that the problem is, he *isn't* a trusted family member.'

Kay pulled her knees up under the cool chiffon of her dress, hugging them to her chest. 'Why would he think his dad doesn't trust him? Surely Mr Ashworth wouldn't have bothered to expend the energy going through the ritual if he felt that way. Wouldn't he have just said who he *did* trust?'

'I've tried to say this to Harry. But he feels guilty about moving so far away, against their wishes. There's no denying his parents were disappointed that he left. But then Uncle Adrian got sick and Harry came home and . . .' she shrugged. 'It doesn't matter what we say to him, he's sure that's the reason. Even his dad has tried to reassure him, as much as he can when he can't speak. But, instead, Harry's running himself ragged, expending all this energy to protect the village and shield his father.'

'Have you tried it on another family member?'

'Not yet.' Becca shifted and looked up at the ceiling. 'Harry says he doesn't want to put the burden on anyone else. He's desperate to prove himself, I think. If he's still not become the anchor when . . . it's time . . . I'll get the tattoo as well, but I dread to think how that will affect him. I mean, maybe it won't work and it'll prove the point that something else is going wrong with the magic, but what if it *does* work, for some other reason we have no knowledge of, and Harry takes that as confirmation his dad thought he wasn't worthy? It's hard enough losing a parent without that on top.'

The crackle of the fire was conspicuous as they went quiet. Kay played with one of the pleats in the skirt of her dress, smoothing it out and refolding it as she tried to wrestle the ache in her chest into submission. 'Why did you decide to tell me all this?'

Becca put the glass down and pulled out the chair behind the desk. When she sat down, the lights picked out the red in her hair, showing it had a touch of auburn within the brown.

'Kay, he went to Prague because his magic called him there. The pull was so strong, he couldn't *not* go. He found *you* there. Then this room let you in, when we put wards on it. Maybe you have some magic that can fix this or figure something new out that we haven't thought of?'

She shook her head. 'I wish I could, but I don't have any healing magic . . . I don't know much at all about runes. I like history, so maybe I could help with that, but I wouldn't think Harry needed to get me from Prague so urgently to help you do research. I'm really not a powerful or knowledgeable witch at all.'

'Well, Harry disagrees.'

'He thinks that's why he needed to find me? To help with this?'

'No. Or at least, if he does, he hasn't mentioned it to me. It's just the way he talks about you. He thinks you're brilliant.'

Kay took a shaky breath. Becca might have just been flattering her ego, but to what end? It truly wasn't like she could do anything to help. She *hated* the way Harry seemed to have this capacity to think the worst about himself. She wished she could magic away his guilt. Her heart cracked at the thought that Harry might live the rest of his life never truly believing that his dad forgave him or thought him worthy. She would do anything . . .

Her stomach tumbled slowly, like the huge wheel at a mill, churning the water up and over.

She *could* do something. She could use her gift. It should have occurred to her immediately, but she'd spent so long thinking of it as useless, as a curse, it had taken her until now to realise it . . .

'The only thing I might be able to do, is tell him how his dad truly feels for him.'

'You think he would listen to you?' Becca's eyebrows pinched together. 'He trusts your opinion that much?'

'It wouldn't be opinion. It's fact. That's what my gift does. When I take these off,' Kay touched the edge of her glasses, 'I can see the emotional make-up of the bonds between people.'

Becca's eyes widened. 'That sounds like it might be it then.'

'Maybe.' Kay scrunched her toes. A pain burned beneath her breastbone. The giddy minute she'd experienced earlier when she thought he might have come to Prague to help *her* was over, wasn't it? This made a whole lot more sense.

She didn't doubt there was attraction between them. She didn't even suspect Harry of using her. She knew better than that now. But the romantic, childish idea that he'd been somehow *fated* to find her just wasn't true. His magic was just desperate to stop him from beating himself up constantly. To help his family. She couldn't begrudge it, but she could feel like an idiot for hoping. 'That's literally it, though, I can't do anything about Mr Ashworth's illness or the anchor tattoo working.'

'No.' The sadness was clear in Becca's brown eyes. 'But it might give Harry some peace before his dad leaves us. I don't think it's going to be long.'

Kay hugged herself, a shiver going through her even though the fire was warm and steady beside her. She didn't want to think badly of a man who was obviously critically ill, but what she'd seen and heard of Mr Ashworth didn't leave her feeling confident he loved his son unconditionally. 'What if Harry's not wrong?' she asked quietly. 'What if I look at their bond and see that his dad *doesn't* trust him? That won't bring him any kind of peace, will it?'

'I appreciate you don't know really him, but he's my uncle and I know there's no way he isn't proud of Harry. How could he not be? Harry gives and gives . . . it just comes naturally to him. He may have chafed at the other elements of being the Ashworth heir. But looking after everyone,' she shrugged. 'It's just what he does.'

Kay chewed on her fingernail, turning over the risk in her mind. The thought of breaking Harry's heart, the way she broke her mother's . . .

Becca rolled her fingers back and forth idly, making the book in front of her fan its pages slowly. 'And there would always the option to just . . . not tell him, wouldn't there. If that's what you see. I don't for a minute believe that you will, but you wouldn't *have* to tell him, would you?'

'I can't lie. And he'll know I've seen it. I need them both to be in the same room, and he'll know I'm seeing it as soon as I take my glasses off.'

'I could figure out a way to make it work, I'm sure.'

'So, I invade his privacy?'

Becca dropped her hand, the book thudding shut. Then she took a deep breath and linked her fingers together. 'Please, Kay. I honestly wouldn't ask this if I didn't think it was going to help. People are never mad when you give them good news. You will be giving him good news. I'm so sure, I'd bet my . . . my cat on it. And I love Michael Kitten like he's my actual child.'

Kay blinked her way past Becca's offer and searched inside herself, trying to ignore her automatic rejection that her gift might actually be good for something for once, to whether or not she should use it without Harry's permission. Could she do this? *Should* she do this? Would she be able to live with herself if she saw something that she could never tell him about? Not without breaking his heart, anyway.

As difficult as that idea was to bear, the thought of turning her back and not helping him when she might have the ability to remove his pain was harder to swallow.

'OK,' she said. 'OK, I'll do it.'

Chapter Twenty

The West Wing, Ashworth Hall

Becca didn't seem to want to risk Kay changing her mind. As soon as she'd agreed, she was bustled out of the study and up the nearest staircase.

'There's not long until the reception starts,' Kay objected, despite still hurrying after Becca, her shoes in one hand and her skirt lifted in the other.

'I know. This won't take long will it. In and out. Uncle Adrian won't be up to a visitor any longer than that.'

A fuzzy edge of panic surrounded her like a migraine halo by the time they reached the second floor. Becca whispered that her uncle's room was at the end and Kay stopped in her tracks. Was she *really* doing this?

Becca knocked on the door, beckoning sharply for Kay to join her. Before she could lift a foot to move in either direction, Harry opened the door. He rested his shoulder on the frame like it was easier to prop himself up than use his own strength to stand up straight.

Why? Why had he pushed himself so hard to make Joe's wedding happen, when he'd already been exhausted from their troublesome journey home? Was he that kind, or desperate to show he was the right person to safeguard Biddicote's witching community?

She suspected it was a bit of both, but even if it was just the latter, it was even more important that Kay helped him see he didn't have anything to prove. Kay wanted to do this for him. And that meant she had to be brave.

She dropped her shoes and slipped her feet back into them, giving herself an excuse for having lingered down the end of the hallway.

'Everything OK, Becs?' He'd taken his jacket and tie off, his top button undone, sleeves rolled up to his elbows.

'Yeah, I brought Kay up because she wanted to say a quick thank you to your mum and dad. Would you take her in?'

'Kay?' He pushed himself off the door frame, digging one hand into his hair, as his eyes, their true, bright blue, found her. He glanced back over his shoulder to his dad's room.

If he said no, this was going to be a short-lived plan.

'It might give him a boost, eh? Remind him that this place is still the heart of the witching community.' Becca turned towards her and raised her eyebrows, so only Kay could see.

Kay pressed her sweaty palms together and gave in to the urge to move closer, which she always felt when Harry was near. 'I'll be really quick,' she said, her voice coming out like a bad Marilyn Monroe impression; her lungs appeared to have been steamrollered flat.

His soft mouth compressed for a second, paling under the pressure and showing up those freckles that crept onto the edges of his lips. Then he spoke again. 'Erm . . . sure, I think that should be OK, but I'll check.'

Becca nudged Kay closer to the gap in the doorway as he went back inside. It was dim in there, but Kay could just about make out the bed, and Harry's mum sitting on a chair beside it. With trembling fingers, she reached up to pull her glasses down, but Harry was already turning back before she even got them unhooked from her ears. She fumbled them back into place and tried to step back, but Becca was right there.

Goddess, what was she doing? Using her gift on him without his permission. How to become a massive hypocrite in three short days? All her doubts came rushing back in.

She turned her eyes to Becca, shaking her head. 'This was a stupid idea,' she whispered.

Becca's eyebrows pulled up in the middle, her brown eyes rounding plaintively. She touched Kay's elbow as though she thought to prevent an escape attempt.

'Mum thinks it should be fine as long as it's only for a couple of minutes,' Harry said in a hushed voice as he picked up another chair and moved it closer to the bed. 'Come in.'

Well, she couldn't run now, could she?

'I'll see you downstairs,' Becca said.

'What?' How was she supposed to get a sneaky peek without Harry noticing she wasn't wearing her glasses, if Becca wasn't even coming into the room with her? She thought she'd at least be coming in to help distract him.

Becca reached up with her two index fingers, whispered a spell and tapped the lenses in Kay's glasses. They promptly fell out into Becca's hands as Kay gasped.

'I'll catch you downstairs,' Becca said and then she was making a swift exit with half of Kay's glasses in her hands.

'Kay?'

Fuck. She blinked and stepped into the room, as shimmering ropes of colour unfurled before her. What kind of idiot was she to forget that she'd see her own emotional bonds too. She only had one stretching out before her, leading to where Harry waited for her. The golden glow she'd seen a touch of when she'd removed her glasses in the bathroom of the apartment in Prague.

Her hands clenched as she resisted the impulse to press her hands over the point on her stomach it emanated from, as though she could tuck it back inside, like a soldier who'd been disembowelled on the battlefield. It wouldn't work, she knew that. It would just shine straight through her fingers anyway.

Love.

She'd fallen in love with Harry Ashworth over a decade ago and despite the other feelings that were there, it still glimmered like long-lost treasure.

It *wasn't* the only thread of colour, though. There was a lot of red there – desire – no big surprise about that, and a vivid dark purple like a bruise, which also, sadly, made a lot of sense. Hurt. Pain. Some grey of guilt winding through. She remembered that from her dad's bond with her mother, and the memory snagged like a hangnail on a jumper. She'd always interpreted that as her dad feeling bad for using her mum, because that was how her mother had felt. Used. But the emotions didn't tell you their origins. Maybe her dad felt bad for *hurting* her mother. Or for not being able to love her back.

Maybe Kay should have stopped to ask him at some point.

She blinked and lifted her gaze up, trying to evade her bond and the storm of painful associations it brought with it. It wasn't what she was there for and her feelings for Harry were only what she'd already known, even if she hadn't been able to admit it to herself. It would get easier not to look at it when she was closer to Harry.

She hurried over to him and he indicated to the chair for her to sit in.

As she took a seat, Harry's mum, Elenor, smiled at her. She was a tall, thin woman, her white hair pulled over one shoulder, somehow looking elegant despite the obvious strain and the simple lounge wear she had on. 'It's lovely to see you again, Kay. It's been a very long time.'

'It has.' Kay's throat was trying to close up and suffocate her, she was sure. Maybe it was her magic, finally fully turning against her. She immediately caught that idea in its fledgling state – her magic was doing what it was supposed to. And she was scared. That was what was happening. 'My family is so grateful to you for opening your home to us and saving the wedding.'

Elenor nodded at her but her attention was drawn to Harry as he moved around to the other side of his dad. Adrian Ashworth was propped up by pillows, a plastic mask attached to his face as oxygen rattled in and out of his labouring chest. It hurt Kay to look at. She had no particular feelings for him – and the innate respect she'd been raised with had certainly been dented by the way he'd heaped pressure onto Harry – but seeing anyone struggling that hard just to draw breath was harrowing. How Harry and his mother felt with it being a man they loved, she couldn't fathom.

And they did love him. She could *see* it. Bonds that were strong, golden vines rooted deep between their bodies. There was more there. Other feelings interwove, and she had a woozy moment, surrounded by so many bonds, all intersecting. It was a criss-crossing pattern, like the back of one of those elaborate rugs in the hallways leading up here, the hidden tangle which created the intentional picture on the other side.

'Dad, did you hear that? Joe's sister Kay is here.'

Dark eyes, rimmed in red, blinked and looked up. Adrian Ashworth tilted his head to the side.

Kay leaned forward. 'I wanted to come and say thank you on behalf of my family. I think them being able to have the wedding here was even better than what they'd had planned. Ashworth Hall is such a haven for us.'

His fingers moved, a slight lift and drum, before he dropped them back down, like even that was too much effort, but his eyes crinkled at the edges, similar to the way his son's did when he started to smile. He turned his head on the pillow to look at Harry.

Kay took the moment to examine how he truly felt for his son. She blinked, but the colours were swimming in front of her eyes. She couldn't do it. It was too much, all the overlapping twists, she didn't have the ability to separate it all out. So many bonds, it was a blur—

No.

No, she wasn't going to fail at this. She wasn't going to fail Harry.

She focused on his dad's chest and instructed her magic to listen, rather than project. Her stomach fluttered as her own bond faded away, until she could just see the ones between Harry and his parents. That was a start. It was more than she'd ever managed before.

The ties between the Ashworth family were equally thick and strong, just as much love from his dad as there was from his mum, and the relief made Kay's throat tight. But there was more to unpick – she pushed the bond with his mother into the background to concentrate on his dad and make sense of the hurt and regret, a feeling of . . . difference in some way, like they'd always been on different wavelengths – but still love, so much love. And trust, a pure light blue, unwavering and quietly radiant.

She found she was able to separate them out, the longer she looked, find more colours inside, like opening up the black casing of a cable to find the different wires within. There was even a translucent one, joining the three Ashworths, coming into a knot that had been cut off at the other side. It made Kay think of loss. Maybe that was what happened when someone you loved died. But who had they lost? And why would it connect the three of them that way?

Her head ached and she forced herself to stop trying to figure it out. The point was, Becca had been right. Adrian Ashworth loved and trusted his son.

Thank the Goddess.

Harry's mum moved to take her husband's hand, and then looked up at Harry in a way that he seemed to translate as a dismissal.

He came around to Kay's chair and held out his hand to her. She wrapped her fingers around his. Those long, magical, creative fingers that had changed since they were teenagers. They still had the same tapering length, the agile way of moving, but his knuckles were bigger now, his nails kept square, neat and clean instead of bitten down. The leap in her heart when he touched her was just the same, though.

She thanked them again and allowed Harry to lead her out of the room. She'd controlled her gift. She hadn't thought that was possible. Just that small amount of concentration had wiped her out, though. She pulled away from him to lean back against the wall between two doors.

'Are you feeling OK?' he asked, even though the tightness in his face, the lines at the corner of his mouth and pallor of his skin made him look like the one who was ill.

The hallway was uncomfortably bright after the sick room, and the colours of the bonds between them sparkled at the edges of her vision. But she wouldn't look. Would try not to, anyway. This wasn't about them, and with him this close to her, maybe she could avoid seeing what was between them altogether. She told herself it was because it was one thing to pry into his relationship with his father in the hopes of helping him, and another to take advantage of that moment to see how he truly felt about her.

That was what she told herself.

'I'm fine.' She put her hand on his chest, above the point where his feelings were visible, covering most of it with her arm. Best to just focus on his face. Even if he looked worn out, he was still the most beautiful man she'd ever seen. She wished she could send something soothing into his skin, the way he'd done for her, but she did the next best thing: 'He loves you, Harry. There's no anger towards you. No disappointment. He has regrets, but he's proud of you. He trusts you.'

'What?'

'Becca told me about the tattoo. The reason you think you've not become an anchor. And you're wrong. Whatever the problem is, it isn't about your dad not trusting you.'

'What? How do you know that?' His husky voice broke for a moment.

'Becca told me,' she repeated, curling her fingers on his chest, not wanting to drop her arm but also not as comfortable with the way his expression had sharpened.

'No, about how my dad feels.'

She reached up and pushed her fingers through the holes in her glasses where her lenses should be.

He stumbled back, and Kay's heart gave a hard kick of fear. Here was the anger. Here was the censure for using her gift on him without asking.

'Have you . . . Have there *never* been any lenses in those?' he asked.

She threw her arm up to cover her eyes, letting the frames bend under the weight. 'No, it was Becca just now. She magicked them out before I went in.'

And she'd better be able to magic them back in or she'd be getting the bill for a new pair.

'So, you're using your gift right now? I mean, if your arm wasn't over your face.'

'I'm sorry. I just wanted to help.'

'You don't have to be sorry.' His fingers touched her wrist, the heat of his body giving away that he'd moved closer again. 'I'm just trying to process what's going on. Will you come out? You're going to have a hard job navigating the reception with your arm over your face,' he teased her, softly.

'You don't mind if I see . . .?'

'It's part of you, Kay, you never have to stifle that against your will.'

Her chest hitched and she took a second to just stay in the dark with that feeling of acceptance. More acceptance than she'd ever given herself.

When she finally lowered her arm, he was close enough she could see the stubble dotting the underside of his jaw.

'So, you used your gift and you saw . . .' he licked his lips, 'you saw the bond between me and my dad.'

She nodded, keeping her eyes fastened tightly on his. 'He loves you. He trusts you, Harry.'

He took a ragged breath and tipped his head back, letting out a sound that was half laugh and half sob. She could almost taste his relief on her tongue. Either that or she was having a stroke.

'Holy grimoire. You're sure? You wouldn't lie to me?' He looked back down at her.

'I promise you. I swear it.'

His chest rose and fell and then he gathered her into a hug, wrapping his arms around her tightly. 'Thank you. Thank you, so much.'

She squeezed him back, his body in her arms, warm and right, sinking into her. A little too much actually. His weight was suddenly too heavy for her to hold up. And she *was* holding him up. 'Harry?'

'I feel a bit weird,' he slurred and put his hands to the wall either side of her shoulders to prop himself up. All the blood had leached from his skin.

'Harry?'

He pressed his hand to his chest, wincing, and she looked down automatically. Her eyes filling with the tangle of colours between them. They were too close to decipher and it wasn't anywhere near her priority.

'Harry?' She touched his cheek, the hand he was pressing over his heart. This time when she said it, she thought she heard an echo of it coming from his dad's room. 'What is it?'

'I think . . .' he panted and started to unbutton his shirt further. Beneath the bright colours of the bonds, the ink of the magical tattoo was so stark, it was like liquid, his skin raising like an old scar around the edges.

Elenor came to the bedroom door. It said something for how preoccupied she was that she didn't even react to seeing him virtually pinning Kay to the wall and baring his chest to her. 'Harry, your dad just called for you.'

Harry pushed himself upright, swaying a second later, like he had a head rush. Kay grabbed his arm to steady him. His eyes were wide as he looked between her and his mum. 'He hasn't been able to speak in months.'

'I know.' His mum's voice was thick. 'Come now.'

'I will. Just. A second.' He tried to straighten again. Kay

was reluctant to let go of his arm in case he face-planted, but he lifted his hand to wipe it down his face.

'Are you OK? What is it?' Elenor's voice rose.

'I think it's the anchor, Mum, I think it's finally happened. It's finally working.'

She gasped. 'Oh my love, that must be why.' She hurried out to him, putting her arm around his waist and staring at the exposed tattoo. 'You'll need to sit down and rest for a little while. It's normal to feel weak.'

'Kay?' Despite his mum being right there, ready to drag him to a chair it seemed, Harry's hand caught at hers.

She squeezed it and forced herself to let go. 'It's OK. You need to go. Go speak to your dad and rest. I've got to get back to the wedding, too.'

'I'll find you later,' he promised as his mother started walking him away.

'Only if you're feeling up to it.'

As the distance between them widened, it became impossible to ignore the bond stretching out across that space between them. The gold of her feelings looked like it continued all the way to his, but then she realised at around halfway the proportions changed. They became his. There was more grey, red, blue . . . and purple, too.

She'd hurt him? At first, her mind automatically jumped on the defensive, wondering how *she'd* hurt *him*. But she knew how. Because she was holding back. Had she ever actually said that she'd forgiven him after he apologised? And she had judged him and his magic so harshly when they first met back up. Whether he had instigated that bad feeling between them or not, she'd pushed him away, said harsh words to him. There was guilt in her bond for a reason.

But . . . that was all entwined with the *gold*. Travelling from him to her. Reciprocal. Gold.

Harry loved her back.

It was . . . utterly overwhelming. Everything she'd once dreamed of and yet nowhere near the simple joy she'd thought it would be.

Chapter Twenty-One

Ashworth Hall

The Wedding Reception

On the way down to the massive function room, Kay did her best to stuff her discovery about Harry's feelings for her away. It reminded her of trying to get one of those pop-up snakes back into its can, but she was determined. There was nothing she could do about it at the moment. Nothing necessarily to be done about it *ever*, unless he wanted to ask her for more than a dance.

What if he never did? What if he was content to draw a line under them because it was all such a mess? Loving someone didn't always mean it would work.

Stop thinking about it.

Until the speeches and first dance were done, she wasn't going to have an opportunity to get hold of Becca. And that meant she was going to have to brave the reception without functional glasses. That was enough to try to cope with for the moment.

She'd have taken the empty frames off her face, but then it would have been obvious to all her family that she was using her gift, and she had no idea how they'd take that.

Harry's reassurance that he never expected her to stifle her gift if she didn't want to rushed like a sweet spring breeze through the brittle limbs of a winter-stripped tree. He knew that she knew now.

Stop.

The room was full and immediately the overlapping threads of colour made it appear like the guests were all swimming in a rainbow fog. To think she was supposed to not be using her magic at all and here she was in a room full of more people than she'd ever been around while using her gift. Twenty-five times the number. She wasn't just tearing up the rulebook, she was dousing it in gasoline and setting it alight with an eternal flame spell.

She made her way to the head table, smiling despite the distraction and waving to family and friends as they spotted her, and then taking her seat next to her mother.

Tallulah pressed her hand to her chest. 'Oh thank the Goddess, Kay. I thought we were going to have to send out a search party. I was worried about you.'

Kay hoisted a smile onto her face, grateful beyond words that her mother couldn't pick up on her reeling emotions at that moment. There was a flute of champagne on the table in front of her. 'No need to worry. Is this for me?'

'Yes. For toasting the speeches.'

'Great.' She took a big gulp and directed her gaze out onto the room. For the moment, letting the colours flood in seemed easier than trying to suppress them, as she allowed the burble of conversation to wash over her the same way the swirling bonds surrounding her were. She could do this. One thing at a time.

Applause began as the bride and groom came in and took their seats at the centre of the table. She clapped with everyone else and tears threatened when she saw the strength of their love for each other. The relief was like tipping her face up into the rain of a summer thunderstorm. No secrets or hearts for her to break if either of them asked her.

It was impossible not to turn and look at them as the speeches took place, so she did her best to block out their bonds, the way she'd done upstairs. Because even though this day was all about them sharing and celebrating their love for each other, they deserved their privacy.

And she really deserved not to see how horny her brother was for Sandy.

With all the guests facing Joe and Sandy, there was an overlap of so many threads leading up to them that her eyes began to ache and – maybe it was the champagne – but she felt like her brain was expanding at the edges. There was a loosening sensation in her chest, the feeling of pressure she'd been troubled by recently easing. Her magic was flowing and she was communicating with it. She was asking things of it and directing it, instead of just rejecting it . . .

Was that it? It wasn't the glasses that had caused the block, because lots of witches had to throttle their gifts depending on their circumstances but they still had control of it. So maybe it wasn't about choosing not to use her magic, so much as the *reason* she was not using it. She'd suppressed it out of fear. Treated it like an unwanted roommate she was forced to live with. Never bothered to get to know it.

But why this year? Had it just reached a tipping point? Or had it been something to do with the wedding? Had her magic started misbehaving before or after Joe and Sandy had announced their engagement? Now she thought about it, the two things had happened coincidentally close together.

Why would that have triggered it though? It wasn't like she wasn't happy for them.

Had it been the concern that Sandy – ever curious and eager to see how magic could be useful to her – would ask for reassurance about Joe's feelings for her? As well as the stress of helping her mum cope with being around her dad for the first time in years. It had pressed on every sore spot Kay had about her gift. The damage it had done in the past. The damage it might do in the future.

But she was realising it wasn't her fault now. The relationship between her mum and dad had been complicated. The bonds of relationships were built over time, like individual fibres twisted into thicker and thicker rope – they were not easily cut through, without severing the bond entirely.

And she'd just used her gift to do something good. It was the application, not the tool. You could use a sewing needle to fix a tear or embroider a pillow . . . or you could stab it into someone's eye. Intention was important when it came to magic. She had to take responsibility for her gift and set boundaries about how and when she was going to use it, but she didn't need to cut it off from her life entirely. Part of her had never truly wanted to. How could she? Her magic *was* her.

The realisation made her light-headed. Or maybe that was the buzz of energy she was releasing by giving her gift freedom. Sitting upright was becoming an act of sheer willpower in the face of her exhaustion. Between the wedding, the hurricane, Harry and her fritzing magic, she was about ready to crawl into bed for a week. Everything in her life looked different and not just because of the strands of magical bonds weaving through the room. Things she had believed were true for so long, things she'd been anxious or angry about, were falling away. It was freeing, but those beliefs had been like armour too, and now she felt exposed.

She straightened in her seat and tried to put those thoughts to rest and concentrate on the speeches again.

'I'm so happy to be here today, watching my daughter marry a good man. A man who loves her and whom she loves. It makes me all the more happy because she came to me a year ago, upset after she had found something out about Joe that she hadn't expected to.' Kay tensed, as she was sure almost every witch in the crowd did. 'It wasn't the thing she found out that had upset her really. It was the fact that she hadn't known it. That she had been dating him for a year, they were about to move in together, and she hadn't any clue. And I told her not to worry about it. She asked me why.

'People are fathoms deep, I said to her. Trying to get to the bottom of someone, to think you should be able to see clear through to the bottom of them, is asking to drown yourself. You don't need to know everything about each other at once. Where would the fun in that be? Besides – most people don't really even know themselves. I've been married to my beautiful wife for thirty-five years, and she still surprises me.

'So, to my daughter, the light of my life, I say, enjoy the journey as Joe shows you his hidden depths, as you reveal yours to him, and you both grow together. To the beginning of a long, joyous marriage, full of the thrill of discovery.'

Everyone clapped and Kay blinked, resisting the temptation to rub at her eyes. Everything was starting to get blurry. Becca was still floating around taking photos of the wedding party and guests. Kay would have to keep it together a bit longer before she could approach her to retrieve her lenses. Kay might be learning to accept her gift, but it would take time to get used to using it again for any significant period of time.

She made it through the other speeches, and Joe and Sandy sharing their first dance. The buffet opened and even though she was both starving and desperate to grab Becca, she caught sight of her dad watching other couples joining the bride and groom on the dance floor. She pinched the bridge of her nose, trying not to pick up on his bonds, but she was finding the strain too much. Rose gold and purple ran from his chest towards her, meeting the same colours from her side. He wasn't just the spectre threatening her mother's happiness, he was her dad and he loved her.

She wished she knew more about him. By pushing him away for so long, he was virtually a stranger these days. Thinking of Harry and his dad's time running out, how close he'd come to losing him without knowing if they'd truly mended the breach between them, she realised she could avoid that if she wanted to. There was time. Not endless amounts of time, because no one really knew how long they would have – but they were here now and, regardless of how awkward it would be, she could try, safe in the knowledge that her dad loved her and she loved him.

Another thing her gift could be thanked for.

She stood up, but her mum caught her hand before she could move away. 'What's going on with you, Kay? You're acting strange. Is there something I need to know?' Her eyes darted between Kay and her dad for a moment.

Kay almost said 'no'. But that wasn't strictly true. She realised it had never even occurred to her to talk to her mother about the problems she was having with her magic. It had become her – and Joe's – habit to try to shield their mum from any additional emotional trauma. Her gift to sense what others were feeling was overwhelming. Just seeing the bonds between people had been an onslaught for Kay; she couldn't imagine feeling their emotions too.

But that meant they didn't lean on their mother for any emotional support. Not since they'd been adults.

Her mother hadn't been angry with her when Kay's gift had come in and revealed that her husband didn't love her anymore. She'd never blamed Kay, but she'd never tried to address it or help them deal with it and move on either. Just because Kay was now ready to try to didn't mean Tallulah would be and they'd have to talk about it if they wanted to avoid further upset.

'We'll talk soon, Mum. Hopefully tomorrow.' She kissed her on the cheek and shuffled around the guests to reach her dad, doing her best to ignore the spot between her shoulder blades her mum was probably boring a hole into. 'Dad, would you like to dance?'

He looked at her with that same joy and shock that had infused his expression earlier. 'I'd love to.'

He finished the last of his drink and led her out onto the dance floor, where he took her hand, putting the other on her waist to hold her in a formal dance pose.

'So, was this a pity dance for your old man, because I didn't bring a date?' he asked, humour in his voice but also an undercurrent of curiosity, as though he wasn't quite sure what to make of her change of heart.

'I didn't bring a date either, remember?' she pointed out, but before he opened his mouth to possibly ask her anything about her love life, she carried on. 'Have you been seeing anyone recently?'

'Oh. No. Not for a while. I guess I'm getting to the point where it feels like a bit too much effort.' The coloured lights from the DJ's lighting rig caught at the white hairs at his temples.

'Too much effort? Sounds a little unmotivated of you,' she teased.

'If the right person comes along, I'll be motivated. Finding the person shouldn't be the bit where you expend all your effort. That's just the fates. It's the relationship once you've found them that you need to work on.'

Maybe her dad had a secondary affinity she'd not found out about and he was reading her mind a little. Because her problem hadn't been finding the person. In fact, he'd flown out to Prague and found her.

'Surely it shouldn't all be hard work, though. How do you know when you need to stop trying? When you're trying to make a square peg fit into a round hole? Figuring out if you're fundamentally different in ways that will always cause problems.' Like being an influencer with a secondary seer designation and an empath.

He scrunched his nose and gave a small shrug. 'That is the million-dollar question, isn't it? I would say when the salt water is mostly tears of sadness rather than tears of joy. When it's turned to brine. That's probably when to stop. It's hard for most people to realise, I think . . . especially when there are kids involved.'

She nodded and they grew quiet, a heavy weight between them. Kay reminded herself that it was not all going to be fixed with one dance. They'd been talking about romantic relationships, but the same was true with all of them really. They took work and time.

'D'you remember when you used to do this, putting your feet on top of mine?' he asked after a moment.

She smiled. 'Yeah, I do. Kind of wish I could do that now, to be honest, I'm not much of a dancer.' Her mind leapt to Harry's joking with her about his dancing skills. Would he be able to make it downstairs? Or was he still too wiped out from the anchor being activated?

'Please don't. Those shoes look like they would do GBH to my toes.'

She laughed and caught her dad looking at her, a tell-tale sheen in his eyes. The bond between them pulsed. Something she'd not seen before. Like the moment had infused it somehow.

The dark and the closeness of all the couples made the colours blur, like she was swimming in marbled ink. It was kind of beautiful really.

The alcohol must be going to her head.

When the song finished, Joe and Sandy came over to them. Her brother's eyes were lit up, like seeing Kay and their dad together, voluntarily, was the best wedding gift he'd received. But he didn't say anything. He just caught them up in a hug, and when the next song started up, Kay danced with him, while her dad and Sandy took a turn around the floor.

That dance turned into another with Sandy's dad, then the best man and all the women from the hen do when a song came on from that alcohol-soaked evening. Kay kept dancing despite her fatigue until hunger drove her to the buffet and she was caught up talking to relatives and Jaz and family friends from Biddicote whom she hadn't seen in years. She tried not to keep looking for Harry, just like she could almost ignore the shimmering bonds all around her, treating them like they were just an extension of the flashing lights for the disco.

Becca caught up with her eventually, motioning for her to follow her and they headed back down to Mr Ashworth's study. Kay's ears rang in the sudden quiet. Someone had put a noise-muffling spell on the function room. Subtle but enough so that anyone not drunk might wonder about it – if the protective magic wasn't working.

But it was. Because of Harry. And because of her.

'I'm sorry,' Becca said as she fiddled in the zipped side patch of one of her camera bags. 'I didn't mean to corner you.'

Kay raised her eyebrows. 'Didn't you?'

'Well, OK, maybe I did.' She grimaced. 'But you don't regret it, do you?'

'No,' Kay conceded, pulling the glasses frames off her face and holding them out. 'Do you know what happened?'

Becca grinned. 'Harry messaged me. Thank you. It totally makes sense why it worked now. It was Harry blocking the anchor taking hold. He had to believe in himself.'

Kay laughed tiredly. 'There's a lot of that going around. How is he?'

'Normal enough that he tore a strip off me for doing this.' Becca indicated to the glasses, and then she fitted the lenses back into the frames and whispered an incantation as she blew around the edges, then smoothed her thumb over it. 'My mum used to craft objects with magic – I picked up a few tricks.'

'Thank you.' Kay put the glasses back on and the slim bond, which was barely there between her and Becca, fell away entirely. 'Can you do anything for these heels?'

'Not without ruining them. I do have a pair of ballet flats I keep here though – round the corner in the vestibule. If they'll fit you, you're welcome to borrow them. The very least I can do.' Becca hesitated for a moment and then wrapped her arms right around Kay, pinning her own arms to her side, in a tight hug. 'Thank you. Oh, and Harry mentioned about your luggage. If you have trouble, let him know and we'll meet up to try to track it down.'

Becca hurried back towards the reception, while Kay stepped down into the cool vestibule that she'd once run through with Jaz and Tina. She found the shoes Becca was talking about and swapped into them, thankful for the good luck that they were the same size.

She was about to head back to the party, when a light outside the small leaded window caught her attention. A tiny blue wisp. You'd have thought she'd have had enough of magical lights, but she couldn't help opening the door to get a better look. And then following it down into the moonlit woods.

Chapter Twenty-Two

9 P.M.: SUNDAY 31 OCTOBER

The Cave of Lost Things

The night air was refreshing on Kay's cheeks, flushed from dancing and champagne, but the temperature was surprisingly mild considering there had been a storm. Perhaps it was just in comparison to the snow and ice in Holland.

Folklore said never to follow a wisp, but that was because they often led somewhere magical, and witches had been sure to keep stories of mischief and danger circulating. She was sure this one was just a leftover from the lights the Ashworths charmed to lead the way to and from the cave. A lone wisp tending its watch. Perhaps it was being in touch with her magic again, resurrecting her curiosity, or a desire to find some calm in the quiet woods, after the overload of the reception . . . or maybe even a need to confront the last ghosts of the past . . . but she wanted to see if she was right.

Nothing much had changed in the clearing. Shadows and moonlight created a textured darkness, the trees having lost their leaves completely to the storm, but the entrance of the cave had nearly disappeared under ivy. Only a glimmer of silver gave a hint there might be stone beneath.

The log she'd sat on as she waited for Harry was still there, in the same spot. She stopped and stared at it the way someone might when finding an old photograph they had no recollection of being taken. Uncomfortable but familiar.

She sat down and took a deep lungful of the damp air, tinged with magic. The moss was saturated, her dress and bottom getting soggy. She couldn't bring herself to care at that moment as the dragging pain of her past disappointment pressed upon her chest.

Wiping a hand under her eye, she forced a laugh. So many people had come and waited here, desperate for Biddi to return things to them. She'd just wanted Harry to meet her, like he'd said he would.

But even if he had, it didn't necessarily mean there wouldn't have been more heartbreak for her. She'd be naive to think that even if she and Harry had met that day, dated, and then tried to have a long-distance relationship – whether it was London or Edinburgh – they wouldn't have struggled. Between them missing each other and their family problems, would two teenagers really have been equipped to make it work?

It didn't stop her from feeling loss as she sat there. But maybe it wasn't the loss of what she and Harry could have had, so much as the loss of who she'd been. Starry-eyed and optimistic. Eager and hopeful.

'Hey Biddi, could you help me find my faith? I can offer payment in pretty shoes that I've bought even though they pinch my toes.'

The blue light flared within the entrance to the cave, a wink of colour among the mass of slick ivy. A small flutter of adrenaline pushed into Kay's stomach.

Just a coincidence? It had to be.

Still, Kay couldn't help approaching the entrance to the cave. She pushed the curtain of ivy to the side, drips of rain landing on the back of her neck, sending goosebumps cascading over her skin. Inside was the same inky dark she remembered. She fumbled for the piece of chalk, wondering if it would still be there on the little ledge, closing her hand around a lump that was dry but powdery around the edges.

Running her hand along the wall, she tried to remember the position of the rune Harry had invoked. She had to be crazy to think she'd be able to make it work, but what was the alternative? Staying in the dark? Turning around and going back when possibly the magic was calling her onwards to something important?

Her finger dipped into a groove and she traced the arrow shape, a tingle of energy reaching out to her like a fish hook, trying to connect with her.

OK, here went nothing. She placed the chalk against the stone and scraped it along the line, while calling her magic to flow through her.

The first time didn't work. She took a breath against the initial flutter of disappointment, reminding herself that she'd known it would be unlikely to work so easily. She had a lot still to learn. But she *wanted* to.

She didn't remember Harry reciting any spell when he'd done it, but maybe it would help direct the intention. She repeated it one more time, whispering the name of the rune, calling her magic to meet that which was buzzing over the skin of her hand now and imagining it catching, like the strike of a match.

There was a gentle magical tug on her abdomen and she hadn't realised she'd closed her eyes until warm light came through her eyelids. Gasping, she opened them, dropping the chalk and standing up. The passageway was lit with glowing golden light from the torch further down. It was like the warmth of coming home.

'Kay.'

She screamed and jumped back a few paces into the cave, heart hammering, before she saw that Harry was there. She'd not heard him come in. 'By all the elements, what are you doing here?' she wheezed, hand to her chest.

'Itchy magic compass,' he explained with a lopsided smile. The flickering light was playing over the edges of his messy hair, flame meeting flame, while keeping his blue eyes in shadow. It gave him a slightly dangerous look, like a fire barely contained, capable of warming you or giving you third-degree burns.

It didn't help her heart particularly.

She glanced behind her and walked through to the chamber at the back like it would help her get some distance from the way her whole being was screaming to her, *you love each other.*

And, of course, Harry followed, as though their bond had them physically tethered.

The seating area around the fire looked even smaller than it had years ago. To think Biddi had gone from actually living in here to founding Ashworth Hall and the whole village that had been established. But she hadn't done it all by herself. It was a long legacy, and one to be proud of, but Kay had a lot of questions about it, now she'd been given the inside knowledge about how it worked. It sounded like even the Ashworth family had questions about it. That was all for another time though.

'How is your dad?' She paced around to the other side of the fire, unable to help herself from glancing back at him and trying to assess his welfare in the shifting light. 'How are you?'

'I'm feeling fine. Tired, but that could be from any number of things. And Dad,' his voice caught and he swallowed, 'we can tell the strain on him has eased already. I mean, he's not jumped out of bed like Charlie Bucket's Grandpa Joe, but he's spoken . . . I haven't heard his voice in so long. Didn't think I would again, to be honest.' He scrubbed the heel of his hand over each of his eyes roughly.

Kay couldn't help herself. She went to him, pulled his head down to her shoulder and kissed the spot behind his ear.

'I don't think I can ever thank you enough,' he murmured into her skin. She shivered and he straightened, pulling off his huge blue coat and bundling it around her.

'You don't have to,' she said. Trying to breathe around the feeling of being wrapped up in the silky lining of his coat, his scent fogging up her mind. 'It was down to you accepting the anchor, wasn't it? You needed to accept that he trusts you before the magic could work.'

He nodded and when she looked up at him, he framed her face with his hands. His thumbs smoothed beneath the lowest edge of her glasses to her cheekbones. Touching her in that careful, reverential way he'd examined the tree painting in Leon's café. 'But no one else could make me believe it—'

'Because of my gift—'

'Because I know what it took for you to do that for me. It was brave.'

'I don't feel brave, Harry. I'm scared of . . . this.' She pressed her hands to his shirt. She couldn't even bring herself to say the words.

'Kay, you know how I feel about you.' His blue eyes shone at her, reaching down to that part which belonged only to him. 'You've seen it. I love you.'

Kay's breath caught in her throat. She *had* seen how he felt, she would be able to see it again now if she wanted to . . . but hearing him saying it was different. That was him making a conscious choice to act on those feelings. She might be able to read how someone felt, but that didn't mean she could predict how they would act. What they wanted to do about it. That was all down to the person.

And those were the things which built the threads of emotion in the first place. The choices. How to treat people, whether that was with magic or without.

She could choose to let the hurt build, allow the purple bruise to spread and smoother out the gold, or she could try to heal it. Just like she was doing with her dad. Biddi wasn't going to gift her the faith she needed to do that, though, she needed to find it on her own.

Or maybe, not quite on her own.

'I understand if that's overwhelming. Too much,' Harry continued, quietly, his gaze downcast, eyelashes spiky from the tears he'd recently shed. 'Especially with how I treated you—'

'Stop,' she interrupted. 'Stop punishing yourself, Harry. I don't want you to do that anymore. I understand why you did it and I forgive you. I do. And . . .' She swallowed hard, gathering her strength. In her mind's eye she could picture their bond like a tightrope across a chasm. She wanted to believe he wouldn't immediately let go of his end the moment she took a tentative step out towards him. She licked her lips and his gaze dropped to them briefly before going back up to her eyes. 'I love you, too,' she whispered.

His hands trembled as he tightened their grip at the sides of her neck. He lowered his forehead to press against hers but didn't do anything more, as though sensing she wasn't done. 'Are we going to give this a shot? Us? Do you want to try?'

She gave a short, little laugh that bordered on hysterical. 'I *want* to. But . . . I know you didn't mind me using my gift today. What about going forwards? You said you would never ask me to stifle it, but how do I avoid letting it control how I react to things? What if I find myself trying to make you love me if I see your feelings waning? I'll end up in an even worse situation. It's all so messy.'

Harry straightened slightly, moving his hands to rub her back beneath his coat, firm and soothing. 'Relationships *are* messy. But we can figure it out together. We might make mistakes, but we've already done that anyway and yet here we are.'

Here they were. Back where their paths had split off from each other so long ago . . . but perhaps it had just been a necessary detour?

None of the relationships she'd seen back at the wedding had been one colour on their own. How had they started out? Pure lust? Affection? Misguided dislike? And then they'd discovered more about each other over time. Made themselves vulnerable with the deepest parts of themselves and sometimes it brought people closer together, and sometimes it didn't. Harry was willing to do that with her. To see what else lurked beneath her surface. Possibly to end up trapped in a sofa bed. It wasn't risk-free for him either.

Their magic wasn't the issue. Trust was. It lay at the heart of every relationship. This wedding would never have happened if Sandy hadn't decided to trust Joe when he'd revealed he was a witch. She had no magic, she couldn't see how Joe genuinely felt for her – all she had was his word, but it had been enough.

'OK.' Kay nodded. 'OK.'

'OK?' His throat rippled as he swallowed. 'You're sure? Because I'll wait if you need me to—'

She shook her head, lifting her hands to run her fingers into his hair, along his scalp. 'No. We've spent enough time apart. Maybe it was necessary. Maybe it wasn't. There's nothing we can do about that anyway. But we don't have to waste any more.'

He took a deep breath in and banded his arms around her waist to pull her in close. Her whole body lit up as it aligned with his. She tugged on his fiery hair, tiptoed up and Harry's mouth pressed gently against hers. A soft kiss, sealing the emotions between them. They stayed still, lips touching but not moving, chaste by all standards, except the steady pressure of it heated something up inside of her, unwinding knots of uncertainty. This kiss said they were both there, in the same space, no rushing required to ensure they didn't miss out. No ending in sight.

Her dad's words came back to her about how the fates determined when you found the person that you'd decide was worth the work of a relationship. And maybe it was.

But, as the fire bloomed beside them, crackling up with heat and light like more fuel had been added, Kay thought that maybe it was also a little bit of magic.

Epilogue

4.30 P.M.: 7 DECEMBER

Baba Yaga's, Old Town Square, Prague

Outside, flakes of snow swirled in front of the astronomical clock, making the picturesque medieval city even more like something out of a snow globe. They'd checked the forecast with Aunt Lucille before they began the trip to return Leon's car and then flew over to Prague to take some time to enjoy being tourists and visit the Christmas markets together. Next it would be a quick stop-off in Berlin to see Ilina.

Kay had finished her last day with the IT company she'd worked at since uni just before they'd left for the holiday. She'd given her notice when her boss had tried to demand she pay for all the missing marketing materials that were in her lost luggage. Becca may have been able to tell her that the suitcase had ended up in Italy, but Kay physically getting her hands on it had still been an issue, and totally not *her* fault. She wasn't prepared to put up with working in a job she didn't care about with an unreasonable boss anymore.

While she'd worked her notice, her dad had helped her get a foot on the ladder of a career she wanted and after

Christmas she'd be starting work in the heritage department of the Witches Council. She'd worried that Harry would be concerned about her working for the Council, given their tense relationship with the Ashworths, but he'd supported her. He trusted her to keep his family's confidences, but also to challenge him if she could understand more about the Council's perspective.

Kay was already helping Harry, Elenor, and Becca as they continued to piece together the make-up of the magic woven through Biddicote and Ashworth Hall, too. For her own selfish part, she wanted to make sure Harry wouldn't wind up exhausted too, and see if there was some way the spells could be reworked so that it didn't all fall upon the Ashworth heir.

Adrian's health was improving little by little, as the burden of the anchor being alleviated gave his body a chance to heal, but they still weren't sure of the origin of his illness. He was well enough for them to plan a family Christmas at the Hall though. All the Ashworths and Hendrixes together celebrating, as well as Sandy's parents.

So, as much as the idea of spending a week trapped in a hotel room, snuggled in bed with Harry was appealing, they had to get back for that, and understandably Harry still wasn't comfortable being away from his dad for too long. Kay had her fingers crossed that the weather would keep being kind. And since she was ninety-nine-point-nine per cent sure that she didn't have any weather affinities now, crossing fingers was about all she could manage.

'Tell me,' Madam Hedvika began, winding thread onto a spool rapidly, her eyes staying trained on Kay across the craft table the whole time. 'Did you work out what the blockage was and attempt to channel your magic into your corn husk doll again?'

'Yes and no.' Kay put her tea to the side and leaned down to pull her corn husk doll out from her handbag.

Kay caught the wrinkle of Madam Hedvika's nose, even though when she glanced up the older witch was quick to smooth out her expression into something neutral again. Admittedly, though the doll hadn't befallen any more accidents – magical or otherwise – it looked a tad battered. She had been on an epic journey, all the while stuffed in Kay's tote as she'd crossed Europe through a hurricane, so it was to be expected.

'I have a confession,' she said as she attempted to smooth the large piece of husk which was still just about pinned in place like a skirt around the doll. 'I'm afraid I didn't exactly follow your instructions. I didn't clamp down on my magic. I tried to, but I only lasted a couple of days.'

And after the wedding, she'd started to use her magic again. Slowly but purposefully – including her gift. Practising to see if she could suppress it or focus it at will. She'd still worn her glasses all day at work, to stop herself from being distracted and from invading the privacy of the people around her, but with her family and Harry, she was figuring it out and stretching her muscles with her everyday magic too. She was a little like a toddler learning to walk. Sometimes she used too much energy, sometimes not enough, but she had people to help her, who weren't judging her.

And she was enjoying it. For the first time as an adult, she could see a glimpse of her potential as a witch and knew she would get there one day.

'I see,' Madam Hedvika replied, poker-faced. 'Shall we try to project the image of you, using your magic, onto the doll again then?'

'Yes. I'm ready.'

Madam Hedvika raised one finger, got up from her chair, went into her kitchen and came back with a small fire extinguisher. Kay would have been insulted but . . . fair play.

Once Madam Hedvika was settled again, Kay unpinned the husk at the bottom of the doll, stood it up before her on the table and accessed her magic as she thought of herself using it. Instead of dipping into a well like she had before, she felt it come awake all throughout her body, centred in her abdomen where the relationship bonds she could see with her gift came from. She pictured herself with Harry and his mum and dad, using her gift to bring comfort to the man she loved.

Her chest grew warm and when she blinked, she saw the doll was glowing. Golden light flowing out from her centre. It was beautiful, the light suffused by the corn husk. She glanced up at Madam Hedvika who was smiling at her.

'You were always meant to ignore my advice, Kay. Your magic is yours. It is you and you are it and you needed to embrace it wholly again. It was not for me or anyone else to tell you when or how you should wield it. You needed to take ownership of it again, and I'm so pleased to see you have.'

Kay thanked the older witch and finished her tea as the glow from the doll eased away. When she left, she found Harry in the shop downstairs, standing by a rack of incense sticks, occasionally picking up the little bundles tied with ribbon and giving them a sniff, eyebrows rising as though the scent surprised him, freckles dancing across his forehead.

He looked over before she reached him, like he sensed her there, and she never grew tired of seeing the way his blue eyes lit up.

'How did it go?' he asked, sliding an arm around her waist, and pressing a kiss to her temple, just above her glasses.

She stayed close but leaned back a little to show him the doll, nestled in her bag again. 'Well. She glowed this time.'

He looked down at the misshapen, lumpy creation, with its scorch marks from the fire and smiled. 'Of course she did. No Cinderella transformation, though?'

'No. Sadly, not.' She closed her bag and hooked the strap back over her shoulder, so she could wrap both arms around him, inside his open coat-of-many-pockets.

'That's not sad. Perfect is boring and she has character. She's been through things and still she's capable of glowing. That's so much better.'

'I think so, too,' Kay said, studying his lopsided smile and meaning it with every human fibre and magical thread in her being.

She didn't want perfect. She wanted *them*.

2 years until the Next Wedding
0 miles from Where They Were Supposed To Be

Acknowledgements

An absolutely enormous thank you to Sanah, whose ideas and enthusiasm for Kay and Harry's story made working on this book even more of a joy than I anticipated (and I anticipated quite a lot when I planned a witchy romance with only one bed). To Rhea, for being open to my pitch, to Jade and Emily Courdelle, who created a cover that totally captures the vibes I was hoping for. (Don't tell anyone but I can't stop looking at it.)

The fantastic 'Bar Babes'; Emma, Kate, Katie, Sandra, Julie, and Jenny. You are all amazing, and your support is making me a braver writer, both in a creative and business sense. All the other wonderful writers who make up the community I couldn't be without, including Lucy Keeling, Leonie Mack, Jaime Admans, Anita Faulkner, Katie Ginger, and Kate Smith, as well as so many others. To Sue, Suzanne, Deirdre, Margaret, Maureen, Liz and Wendy who I haven't been able to see nearly as much as I would have liked to over the last couple of years, but are still always there with advice and support.

I can't forget all the bloggers and social media friends I've made over this writing journey too. You can always be counted on to spread the joy of romance novels and add to my endless TBR.

Jessica, who this book is dedicated to. The SFFRomCast sums up our silliness, book love, nostalgia, and friendship (I'm counting the outtakes too). If we hadn't met and joined romantasy forces, I'm not sure

I would have followed this particular path so far. I'm so pleased we did.

To all my friends and family.

Dan, who is mostly getting used to the ups and downs of having a writer as a partner – thank you so much for supporting me, and for putting up with it. And to my two girls, you make me so proud, always.

Credits

Emma Jackson and Orion Fiction would like to thank everyone at Orion who worked on the publication of *Witch You Weren't Here* in the UK.

Editorial
Sanah Ahmed

Copyeditor
Jade Craddock

Proofreader
Sally Partington

Audio
Paul Stark
Jake Alderson

Contracts
Dan Herron
Ellie Bowker
Alyx Hurst

Design
Emily Courdelle
Joanna Ridley
Nick Shah

Editorial Management
Charlie Panayiotou
Rachael Hum
Anna Egelstaff
Sinead White
Georgina Cutler

Operations
Jo Jacobs
Sharon Willis
Jane Hughes
Bartley Shaw
Tamara Morriss

Finance
Jasdip Nandra
Nick Gibson
Sue Baker

Production
Ruth Sharvell

Sales
Jen Wilson
Esther Waters
Victoria Laws
Toluwalope Ayo-Ajala